The Gist Hunter
and Other Stories

Other Books by Matthew Hughes

Fools Errant
Fool Me Twice
Black Brillion

The Gist Hunter
and Other Stories

Matthew Hughes

Night Shade Books
New York

Night Shade books may be purchased in bulk at special discounts for sales promotion,
corporate gifts, fund-raising, or educational purposes. Special editions can also be
created to specifications. For details, contact the Special Sales Department, Night
Shade Books, 307 West 36th Street, 11th Floor, New York, NY 10018 or info@
skyhorsepublishing.com.

Night Shade Books™ is a trademark of Skyhorse Publishing, Inc.®, a Delaware
corporation.

Visit our website at www.nightshadebooks.com.

10 9 8 7 6 5 4 3 2 1

Library of Congress Cataloging-in-Publication Data is available on file.

Paperback ISBN: 978-1-59780-507-0

Printed in the United States of America

Contents

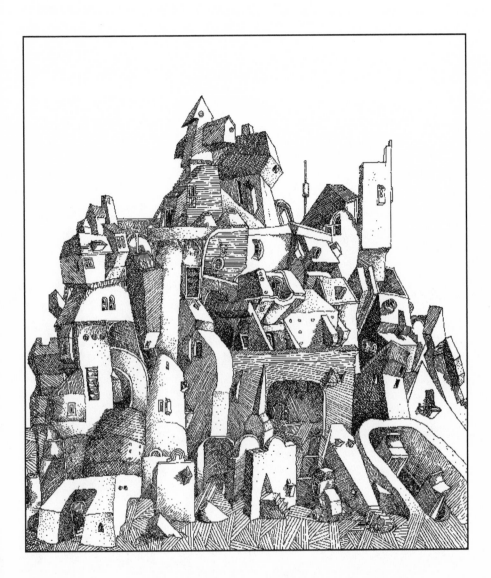

Henghis Hapthorn

Mastermindless

I had almost finished unraveling the innermost workings of a moderately interesting conspiracy to defraud one of Olkney's oldest investment syndicates when suddenly I no longer understood what I was doing.

The complex scheme was based on a multileveled matrix of transactions some large, some small; some honest, some corrupt conducted among an elaborate web of persons, some of whom were real, some fictitious and a few who were both, depending upon the evolving needs of the conspirators.

Disentangling the fraud, sifting the actual from the invented, had occupied most of the morning. But once the true shape of the scheme became clear, I again fell prey to the boredom that blighted my days.

Then, as I regarded the schematic of the conspiracy on the inner screen of my mind, turning it this way and that, a kind of gray haze descended on my thoughts, like mist thickening on a landscape, first obscuring then obliterating the image.

I must be *fatigued*, was my initial reaction. I crossed to my workroom sink and splashed water onto my face then blotted it dry with a square of absorbent fiber. When I glanced into the reflector I received a shock.

"Integrator," I said aloud, "what has happened to me?"

"You are forty-six years of age," replied the device, "so a great many events have occurred since your conception. Shall I list them chronologically or in order of importance?"

I have always maintained that clarity of speech precedes clarity of thought and had trained my assistant to respond accordingly. Now I said, "I was speaking colloquially. Examine my appearance. It has changed, radically and not at all for the better."

I looked at myself in the reflector. I should have been seeing the image of

Henghis Hapthorn, foremost freelance discriminator in the city of Olkney in the penultimate age of Old Earth. That image traditionally offered a broad brow, a straight nose leading to well-formed lips and a chin that epitomized resolution.

Instead, the reflector offered a beetling strip of forehead above a proboscis that went on far too long and in two distinct directions. My upper lip had shrunk markedly while the lower had grown hugely pendulous. My chin, apparently horrified, had fallen back toward my throat. Previously clear sweeps of ruddy skin were now pallid and infested by prominent warts and moles.

"You seem to have become ugly," said the integrator.

I put my fingers to my face and received from their survey the same unhappy tale told by my eyes. "It is more than seeming," I said. "It is fact. The question is: How was this done?"

The integrator said, "The first question is not how but exactly *what* has been done. We also need to learn why and perhaps by whom. The answers to those questions may well have a bearing on finding a way to undo the effect."

"You are right," said I. "Why didn't I think of that?"

"Are you being colloquial again or do you wish me to speculate?"

I scratched my head. "I am trying to think," I said.

"I have never known you to have to try," said the integrator. "Normally, you must make an effort to stop."

The device was correct. My intellectual capacity was renowned for both its breadth and depth. As a discriminator I often uncovered facts and relationships so ingeniously hidden or disguised as to baffle the best agents of the Archonate's Bureau of Scrutiny.

My cerebral apparatus was powerful and highly tuned. Yet now it was as if some gummy substance had been poured over gears that had always spun without friction.

"Something is wrong," I said. "Moments ago I was a highly intelligent and eminently attractive man in the prime of life. Now I am ugly and dull."

"I dispute the 'eminently attractive.' You were, however, presentable. Now, persons who came upon you unexpectedly would be startled."

I disdained to quibble; the esthetic powers of integrators were notoriously scant. "I was without question the most brilliant citizen of Olkney."

The integrator offered no contradiction.

"Now I must struggle even to..." I broke off for a moment to rummage through my mind, and found conditions worse than I had thought. "I was going to say that I would have to struggle to compute fourth-level consistencies, but in truth I find it difficult to encompass the most elementary ratios."

"That is very bad."

My face sank into my hands. Its new topography made it strange to my touch. "I am ruined," I said. "How can I work?"

Integrators were not supposed to experience exasperation, but mine had been with me for so long that certain aspects of my personality had infiltrated its circuits. "Perhaps I should think for both of us," it said.

"Please do."

But scarcely had the device begun to outline a research program than there came an interruption. "I am receiving an emergency message from the fiduciary pool," it said. "The payment you ordered made from your account to Bastieno's for the new surveillance suite cannot go forward."

"Why not?"

"Insufficient funds. The pool also advises that tomorrow's automatic payment of the encumbrance on these premises cannot be met."

"Impossible!" I said. I had made a substantial deposit two days earlier, the proceeds of a discrimination concerning the disappearance of Hongsaun Bedwicz. She had been custodian of the Archonate's premier collection of thunder gems, rare objects created when lightning struck through specific layers of certain gaseous planets. They had to be collected within seconds of being formed, lest they sink to lower levels of the chemically active atmosphere and dissolve. I had located Bedwicz on a planet halfway down The Spray, where she had fled with her secret lover, Follis Duhane, whose love of fine things had overstrained her income.

My fee should have been the standard ten per cent of the value of the recovered goods, but the Archonate's bureaucrats had made reference to my use of some legally debatable methodologies, and I had come away with three per cent. Still, there should be at least 30,000 hepts, I informed my assistant.

"My records concur," said the integrator. "Unfortunately, the pool's do not. They say you have 32 hepts and 14 grimlets. No more, no less."

"Where has the rest of it gone?"

"Pool integrators are never sophisticated, lest they grow bored with constant ins and outs and begin to amuse themselves with the customers' assets. This one merely counts what is there and records inflow and outtake.

Yesterday the funds were present. Now they are not, although there has been no authorized withdrawal."

"So now I am not only ugly and dull, but have scarcely a groat to my name and am at risk of being ejected into the street."

The integrator said nothing. "Well," I prompted it, "have you no empathy?"

"You assembled me from analytical and computative elements," it replied. "However, I believe I can feign sympathy, if that will help."

"I doubt it," I said. "Why don't you analyze something?"

But instead it told me, "I am receiving another urgent message."

I groaned. "Is it the Archon threatening to banish me? That would place an appropriate crown onto the morning's disasters."

"It is Grier Alfazzian, the celebrated entertainer," said the integrator. "Shall I connect?"

"No."

"He may wish to engage you. An urgent matter would presuppose a willingness to pay an advance. That would solve one of the morning's problems."

"Hmm," I said. "I should have thought of that."

"Yes," it said, then after a pause, "you poor little lumpykins."

"All right, put him through. But audio only. I don't want to be seen like this."

"Very well."

"And no more attempts at sympathy."

A screen appeared in the air before me, but when Alfazzian connected I did not see the face that gave women the hot swithers, though I had always thought him more pretty than handsome. He spoke from behind a montage of images that recalled his most acclaimed roles.

"Is that you, Hapthorn?"

I recognized his plummy baritone. "It is," I said.

"I have a question that requires an answer. Urgently and most discreetly. Come to my home at once."

I did not wish to take my new countenance out into the teeming streets of Olkney. There was a bylaw forbidding the frightening of children.

"Can we not discuss it as we are?"

"No."

"Very well." I had a mask left over from a recent soiree at the Archon's Palace. "But summoning me on short notice requires an advance on my fee."

"How much?"

Fortunately my memory was not fully impaired. I could recall the amounts cadged from wealthy clients who called me for assistance from within the coils of drastic and unexpected predicaments.

"Five thousand hepts," I said. "You may transfer it to my account at once."

"I shall," he said. "Wait while my integrator conducts the transfer."

There was a pause which lengthened while I regarded the images of Alfazzian striking poses in theatrical costumes and romantic settings. Then his voice returned to say, "There seems to be a problem with my finances."

"Indeed?" I said. I recalled that I often said "Indeed," when I could not think of any other rejoinder. When I wished to avoid a question, I usually indicated that an answer would be premature. I found that the two rejoinders filled conversational holes quite nicely.

"I do not have five thousand hepts at the moment. My funds have apparently been misplaced, except for a trifling sum."

Some stirring in the back of my mind urged me to ask the exact amount of the trifling sum.

"Why do you wish to know?" Alfazzian said.

I did not know why I wished to know, so I said, "It would be premature to say."

"The amount is 32 hepts and 14 grimlets," he said.

"Indeed."

"Are the numbers significant?" Alfazzian asked.

"It would be premature to say," I said. "I will call you back."

"It cannot be coincidence that his funds and yours have been reduced to the same amount," the integrator said.

"Why not?"

"Consider the odds."

My mind attempted to do so in its customary manner, lunging at the calculation like a fierce and hungry dog that scents raw meat before its muzzle. But the mental leap was jerked to a halt in midair as if by a short chain. "I take it the odds are long?" I said.

The integrator quoted a very lopsided ratio.

"Indeed," I said. "But what does it signify?"

"It would be premature..." it began.

"Never mind."

I tried to think of possible circumstances that could empty two unrelated accounts of all but the same small sum. After sustained effort, I came up with what seemed to be a pertinent question. "Do Alfazzian and I use the same pool?"

"No."

"Then it can't just be a defective integrator?"

"Integrators do not become defective," was the reply.

"I did not mean to offend."

"Integrators do not take offense. We are above such things."

"Indeed."

There was a silence. "How could the closely guarded integrators of two solvencies be induced to eliminate the funds of two separate depositors except for an identical trifle?" I asked.

"Hypothetically, a master criminal of superlative abilities might be able to accomplish it."

"Does such a master criminal exist?"

"No," was the answer, followed by a qualification. "But if such a criminal did exist he would almost certainly have the power to disguise his existence."

"Even from the Archonate's Bureau of Scrutiny?" I wondered.

"Unlikely, but possible. The scroots are not completely infallible."

"But if there was such a master purloiner, what would be his motivation in impoverishing me and Alfazzian? How have our lives mutually connected with that of our assailant?"

"No motive seems apparent," said the integrator.

I pushed my brain for more possibilities. It was like trying to goad a large, lethargic animal that prefers to sleep. "Who else might be able to subvert the fiduciary pools?" I said. "Could it be an inside job?"

"It is hard to imagine a cabal of officers from two financial institutions conspiring to defraud two prominent customers."

"And, again, where lies a motive?"

My mind was no more help than my assistant in answering that question. But if the machinery would not turn over, I still retained a grasp of the fundamentals of investigations: the transgressor would be he who had the means, motive and opportunity to commit the offense. I considered all three factors in the light of the known facts and was stymied.

"I am stymied," I said. Then a faint inspiration struck. I asked the integrator, "If I were as I was before whatever has happened to cloud my mind, what would I now propose to do?"

The integrator replied, "You have occasionally said that although with most problems the simplest answer is usually correct, sometimes one encounters situations where the bare facts stubbornly resist explanation. In such a case, adding further complications paradoxically clarifies the issue."

I could remember having said those exact words. Now I asked the integrator, "Have you any idea what I meant when I said that?"

"Not really."

I scratched my head again.

"Do you have a scalp condition?" asked my assistant. "Shall I order anything from the chymist?"

"No," I said. "I was trying to think again."

"Does the scratching help?"

"No. Nor do your interruptions. Be useful and posit some complicating factors that might have something to do with the case."

"Very well. You are ugly and not very bright."

"I don't see how gratuitous insults can help."

"You misapprehend. At the same time as you have become poor, your appearance and mental acuity have also been reduced."

"Ahah," I said. Again there came a glimmer of an idea. This time I managed to fan it into a small flame. "And Alfazzian, who normally delights in displaying his face to the world, hid behind a montage while he spoke with me."

"So the coincidence might be even more extreme," said the integrator, "if he too has been reduced to ugliness."

"Connect me to him."

A moment later I was again looking at Alfazzian's screen. "Tell me," I said, "has there been an alteration in your appearance?"

There was a pause before he said, "How did you know?"

I had never had difficulty answering that question. "I do not reveal my methods," I said.

"Are you taking the case?"

"I am," I said. "I will make a special dispensation and allow you to pay me later."

"I am grateful."

"One question: Does it seem to you that your intellectual faculties have been reduced?"

"No," Alfazzian said, "but then I have always got by on my talent."

"Indeed," I said. My longstanding impression of the entertainer remained intact: his talent consisted entirely of his fortuitous facial geometry. "Remain at home and wait to hear from me."

I broke the connection and the screen disappeared. I said to my assistant, "Now we know more, but still we know nothing."

We knew that I who had been brilliant, attractive or so I would argue and financially comfortable had been made dense, repugnant and indigent. Alfazzian had been admittedly more handsome than I and probably much more wealthy, and now he was also without funds or looks but his intellect had not been correspondingly ravished.

"There is a pattern here," I said, "if I could but see it."

I wrestled with the facts but could not get a secure grip. The effort was made more difficult by a growing clamor from the street outside my quarters. I went to the window and, bidding the integrator minimize the obscuring membrane, looked down at a growing disturbance.

Several persons were clustered before a doorway on the opposite side of Shiplien Way, beating at the closed portal with fists, feet and, in the case of a large and choleric woman in yellow taffeta, a parasol. As I watched, more participants joined the mob, then all took to shouting threats and imprecations at a smooth-headed man who leaned from an upper window and implored them to return another day.

The door, which remained closed, led to a branch of the Olkney Mercantile, one of the city's most patronized financial institutions. I spoke to my assistant. "Is Alfazzian's account with the OM?"

"No."

"Then I believe we can add one more new fact to our store."

I inspected the individual members of the crowd. I had never been one to judge others on mere appearance, but the assemblage of mismatched features across the street was the least fortunate collection of countenances I had ever seen assembled in one place. "Make that two new facts," I said.

"Hmm," I said. Again, it was as if my mind expected a pattern to present itself, but nothing came. It was an unpleasant sensation, the mental equivalent of ascending a staircase and, expecting to find one more riser than the joiner has provided, stepping up onto empty air and crashing down again.

"The most handsome man in Olkney is made repellent," I said to my assistant, "and the most intelligent is made at best ordinary. As well, both are impoverished. So apparently are many others." I struggled to form a shape from the data and an inkling came. "If Alfazzian and I are the targets and the others are merely bystanders, then why is the institution across the street in turmoil? We have no connection to it."

"It could be that the attack is general," said the integrator, "and therefore you and our client are only part of a wider category of victims."

I turned the concept over and looked at it from that angle. It appeared no more comprehensible. "We need more data," I said. "Access the public advisory service."

The screen reappeared, displaying a fiercely coiffed young woman who was informing Olkney that it was inadvisable to visit the financial district. "Dislocations are occurring," she said, widening her elegant eyes while uplifting perfectly formed eyebrows.

"Two more facts," said the integrator. "Other depositories must have been raided and there is one attractive person who has not been rendered grim."

"Three facts," I said. "The painfully handsome man who usually engages her in inane banter about trivialities has not appeared."

But what did it mean? Were only men affected? I had the integrator examine other live channels. Those from outside Olkney showed no effects. In other cities and counties, handsome men still winked and nodded at me from behind fanciful desks. There were no monetary emergencies. But the emissions originating within the city fit the emerging pattern. Of attractive women, there was no shortage; of good looking men, a dearth.

"Regard this one," said the integrator. We were seeing the farm correspondent of a local news service, a man hired more for his willingness to climb over fences and prod the confined stock at close range than for set of jaw or twinkle of eye.

"He has always been hard on the gaze," I said.

"Yes," agreed my assistant, "but he is grown no harder."

"Another fact," I said.

Matters were almost beginning to assume a shape. If I could have thrust aside the clouds that obscured my mind, I knew I would be able to see it. But the mist remained impenetrably thick.

"A question occurs," I said. "Who is the richest man in Olkney?"

"Oblos Pinnifrant."

"And is his face well or unfortunately constituted?"

"He is so wealthy that his appearance matters not."

"Exactly," I said. "He delights in inflicting his grotesque features on those who crave his favor, forcing them to vie one against another to soothe him with flattery. Connect me to him."

Pinnifrant's integrator declined the offer of communication. I said, "Inform him that Olkney's most insightful discriminator is investigating the disappearance of his fortune."

A moment later, the plutocrat's lopsided visage appeared on my screen. "What do you know?" he said.

"It would be premature to say."

"Yet you are confident of solving the mystery?"

"You know my reputation."

"True, you have yet to fail. What are your terms?"

My terms were standard: ten per cent of whatever I recovered.

Pinnifrant's porcine eyes glinted darkly. "Ten per cent of my fortune is itself a fortune."

"Indeed," I said, "but 32 hepts and 14 grimlets are not much of a foundation on which to begin anew, even for one with your egregious talent for turning up a profit."

In fact, Pinnifrant had been born to wealth and had only had to watch it breed, but a lifetime of deference from all who rubbed up against him had convinced the magnate that he was the sole font of his tycoonery.

After a brief chaffer, he said, "I agree to your terms. Report to me frequently." He moved to sever the connection.

"Wait," I said. "Have you noticed any diminution of your mental capacities?"

"I am as sharp as ever," was the answer, "but my three assistants have become effectively useless."

"Has there been any change in the arrangement of their features?"

"I would not know. I do not bother to inspect their faces."

"One last thing," I said. "Have your financial custodian contact me immediately."

Agron Worsthall, the Pinnifrant Mutual Solvency's chief tallyman appeared on my screen less than a minute after I broke the connection to Pinnifrant. He seemed eager to assist me.

"How much remains in his account?" I asked.

"Oblos Pinnifrant has consolidated many of his holdings through us," Worsthall said. "All but one of his accounts have been reduced to a zero balance. The exception contains 32 hepts and 14 grimlets."

"What about other depositors' holdings? Are they also reduced to that amount?"

"They are. That is, the male depositors and those who had joint accounts with female partners."

"But women are unaffected?"

"Yes, and children of both sexes."

"And where have the funds gone? Were they transferred to someone else?"

"They were not. The money is simply not there."

"Is that possible?"

I heard him sigh. "Until today I would have said it was not, but I am finding it difficult to deal with abstruse concepts this morning."

"Has there been any change in your physical appearance?" I asked. "Specifically, your face?"

"What kind of question is that?"

"A pertinent one, I believe."

There was a silence on the line while Worsthall sought his own reflection. When he came back his voice had a quaver. "Something has occurred to my nose and chin," he said. "As well, there are blemishes."

"Hmm," I said.

"What does it mean?"

I told him it would be premature to say. "You said that all accounts held by men had been reduced to 32 hepts and 14 grimlets. What about accounts that contained less than that amount were they raised to this mystical number?"

"No, they were unaffected. Is that germane?"

I asked him if he had difficulty understanding the meaning of "premature." Then another idea broke through the fog. "I wish you to do something for me," I said. "Contact all the other financial institutions in Olkney. Ask if the same thing has happened."

I broke the connection and attempted to rouse my sluggish analytical apparatus, but it continued to lie inert.

Again, I asked my assistant, "If I were possessed of my usual faculties, how would I address this conundrum?"

"You would look for a pattern in the data," it said.

"I have done that. I cannot see more than the bare outline of what, and not even a glint of why or how. Men have been robbed of their wealth, looks and intelligence, yet who has gained? Where lies the motive, let alone the means?" I sighed. "What more would I do if I were intact?"

"You might look for a pattern outside the data," the integrator said. "You once remarked that it is possible to deduce the shape of an invisible object by examining the holes left by its passage."

"I do not see how that applies to this situation."

"Nor do I. I am accustomed to rely upon you for insights. My task is to assemble and correlate data as you instruct."

"What other brilliancies have I come up with over the years? Perhaps one will ring a chime and re-ignite my fires."

"You once opined that the rind is mightier than the melon. You presented this as a particularly profound perception."

"What did it mean?"

"I do not know. When you said it, you were under the influence of certain substances."

"No use," I said. "Go on."

"You have occasionally noted that the wise man can learn from the fool."

"I remember saying it," I said, "but now I have no idea what I meant."

"Perhaps something to do with opposites attracting?" the integrator offered.

"I doubt it," I said. "Do they attract? If so, it can't be for long since wouldn't true opposites irritate each other if not cancel each other out? It sounds like mutual annihilation and I'm sure I've never been in favor of that."

"You also say that sometimes the most crucial clue is not what has happened, but what has not."

"That sounds more like it," I said. "Except that the number of things that haven't happened must be astronomically greater than those that have. So how do we pick out the nonexistent events that have meaning?"

"You usually perform some pithy analysis."

"Yes, but I'm short on pith today."

"Then it will have to be an inspired guess."

"I am far from inspired," I said. "But I think we have at least defined the crime. The attacks are aimed at intelligent and presentable men as well as those who have more than 32 hepts and 14 grimlets.

"Dull men have not been made duller, nor poor men poorer, nor have the unprepossessing been further victimized. And women and children are unaffected on all counts.

"We come back as always to means, motive and opportunity."

It was difficult to posit a rational means or an opportunity by which the assumed perpetrator could do so much harm to so many and all apparently at the same moment. I knew from long experience, however, that motives were relatively few and all too common to most of humankind. "Jealousy," I said. "We may be looking for a poor, not too bright man with a face to curdle milk."

"But if he is dim-witted, how does he contrive to perform the impossible?" said my assistant.

"Indeed," I said. "How is the operative question."

The integrator made a sound that was its equivalent of a throat clearing.

"I have a suggestion," it said.

"What?"

Its tone was tentative. "Magic."

I snorted. It was an automatic response whenever the subject was raised. "Only a fool believes in magic," I said.

"Perhaps this is the work of a fool."

That almost made sense, but though I could no longer argue for them, I recalled all my old opinions. "There is no such thing as magic."

"Yet there are arguments for the opposing view."

I had encountered them. Supposedly there was an alternation between magic and physics, between sympathy and rationalism, as operating principles of the phenomenal universe. As the Great Wheel rolled through the eons, one assumed supernacy over the other, only to see the relationship eventually reversed.

When one regime took the ascendancy, the other allegedly remained as an embedded seed in its unfriendly host. Thus in an age when magic held sway, its mechanics were still logically extrapolated there were rules and procedures while during the present reign of rationality, events at the subquantum level were supposedly determined more by quirks and quizzidities than by unalterable laws.

I was occasionally braced, at a salon or social, by some advocate of the mystical persuasion who would try to convince me that the Wheel was now nearing the next cusp and that I might live long enough to see the contiguous series of electrons that carried information from one device to another replaced by chains of ensorceled imps, my integrator supplanted by an enchanted familiar.

I had investigated the arcana of magic over a summer during my youth and could demolish its advocates with arguments that were both subtle and vigorous. However, I had to admit that those arguments were at present beyond my grasp. Still, I harrumphed once more and said, "Magic!" then blew air over my lips as if shooing away a gossamer.

My assistant said, "You also like to say that when all impossibilities have been swept from the table what remains, however unlikely, must be the answer."

"Magic," I said, "is one of those impossibilities."

"Are you sure?"

"I used to be," I said, "so I ought to be now."

"Even a wise man can..." began the integrator, then interrupted itself to tell me that Pinnifrant's tallyman was back.

"What have you learned?"

"The same situation pertains across the city. Indeed, even accounts held outside Olkney by male residents of the city have been affected."

The more I learned the more perplexed I became. Even in my diminished state, I recognized the irony. I had long wished for a superlative opponent, a master criminal who could give me room to stretch. Now one had seemingly appeared, but in doing so had robbed me of the capacity to combat his outrages. Still, I struggled to encompass an image of the situation.

"And there is no indication that anyone has benefited from the thefts?" I asked Worsthall. "No woman's account has ballooned? No child's?"

"No."

"Thank you," I said, though I could not see how the information helped.

"There is one anomaly," he said.

"Hmm?"

"A male depositor at Frink Fiduciary had a balance of 32 hepts and 15 grimlets before the discrepancy this morning..."

"Discrepancy?" I asked.

"It is a term we in the financial sector use when accounts do not tally."

"Why not be bold and call it what it is, mass theft and rampant rapine?"

"If we were bold, we would not be bankers," was the reply.

"Indeed," I said, "but what were you about to tell me?"

"That a male depositor had a balance of 32 hepts and 15 grimlets before the... rampant rapine, and that he had the same balance afterward. And still does."

I had him repeat the numbers again. "This depositor had one grimlet more than the ubiquitous H32.14 before the... the event, and he still has the same amount now?"

"As of three minutes ago," said the tallyman.

"Hmm," I said. I experienced a vague sense that the anomaly might be significant. "Who is he?"

"He is called Vashtun Errible."

"Tell me about him."

There was little to tell: only an address on a cul-de-sac off the Fader Slide, an obscure location in an uncelebrated part of the city. No image of Errible reposed in the solvency's files and the connectivity code he had given when opening the account was long since defunct. The account had not been used for many years and had probably been forgotten by its nominee.

I left the tallyman to his troubles and set my assistant to scouring all sources for news of this Vashtun Errible. The integrator turned up only one more item: a deed of indenture that bound Errible's services to the requirements of one Bristal Baxandall.

"Now that's a name I have heard before," I said, though I could not immediately place it.

"He prefers to be known as The Exalted Sapience Bristal Baxandall, an alleged thaumaturge," said the integrator. "He performs at children's parties."

Again I spied the glimmer of an idea. Perhaps this Baxandall was the mastermind behind the calamity, hiding his brilliance by masquerading as a low-rent prestidigitator. Or he might be only the blind behind which Errible, the true prodigy, had concealed himself.

I had a hunch that one or both of these two persons was central to the mystery. Normally, I despised hunches and had always denied their validity to my mind, an intuition was no more than the product of an analytical process that took place in the mind's dark back rooms. Occasionally, a door was flung open and the result of unconscious analysis was tossed into the light of the mental front parlor, to be discovered by the incumbent as if it had arrived by mystical means.

The thought led to another: I wondered if my own back rooms were as fully stocked and active as always but that some force had sealed the doors. The more I examined the idea, mentally probing about in my inner recesses the way my tongue would explore the gap left by an extracted tooth, the more it seemed likely that my faculties had not been irrevocably ripped away, but only placed out of reach. I listened and it seemed that I could almost hear the ghost of my former genius crying out to me from beyond a barrier in my mind.

I realized that my assistant was saying something. "Repeat," I said.

"The Exalted Sapience's address is the same as that which the solvency found for Vashtun Errible," it said.

"Connect me."

"I cannot. He apparently possesses no integrator."

"How is that possible?"

"I cannot even speculate," said the integrator. "His house appears as a blank spot in the connectivity matrix."

"Ahah!" I said again. "The shape left by the invisible object!"

"What do you mean?"

I did not know. It was another hunch. "It would be premature to say,"

I said. "Summon an aircar and have it take me to that address."

The vehicle took longer than usual in arriving and I noticed that its canopy was darkly stained. When we rose above the rooftops I saw why: thick columns of greasy, black smoke boiled skyward from several sites along the big bend in the river, joining to form a pall over the south side of the city. To the west, several streets were blocked off by emergency vehicles bearing the lights and colors of the provost bureau, and a surging mob was rampaging through the financial district, smashing glass and overturning motilators.

The aircar banked and flew north toward an industrial precinct that looked to be quieter. After a few minutes it angled down to a dead-end street below the slideway and alighted before an ill-kept two-story house whose windows were obscured by dark paint. I bid the car remain but it replied that it could only do so if I paid the accumulated fare immediately and allowed it to deduct its waiting fee every five minutes.

"How much?" I asked and was told that I owed seven hepts. Furthermore, it would charge me twenty grimlets per minute to wait.

"Usually, I charge such expenses to my account with your firm," I said.

"These are unusual times," it said, and I was forced to agree to the terms.

The house was dilapidated, the paint peeling and some siding sprung loose. Dank weeds had invaded and occupied the front lawn and the porch sagged when I topped the front steps. There was a faint smell of boiled vegetables.

There were symbols painted on the front door. They seemed vaguely familiar but my uncertain memory could not produce their meanings. There was no who's-there beside the door, the house having no integrator to operate it. I struck the painted wood with my knuckles to make my presence known.

There was no response nor any sound from within. A second knocking brought no result so I tried the latch and the door opened inward.

I stepped within and called for attention. There was no answer. I looked about and saw a small, untidy foyer from which a closed door led left, a stairway went upward and a short hall ran back to what appeared to be a rudimentary kitchen.

I called again and heard what might have been a reply from behind the closed door. I opened it and looked into a cramped and fusty parlor dominated by an oversized table draped in black cloth on which was scattered an arrangement of objects and instruments I could not immediately identify. The opaqued windows let in no light, and the only illumination was from some of the strewn bric-a-brac that emitted dim glows and wavering auras.

"Hello?" I said, and again heard a moan from the gloom beyond the table. I produced a small lumen from my pouch and activated it so that I could work my way around the table without stepping on more knickknacks that seemed to have fallen to the floor.

Under the table on the far side was what I first took to be a bundle of stained cloth loosely stuffed with raw meat and bare bones. A warm and unappetizing smell rose from it. The cloth was dark and figured with designs and symbols similar to those on the front door, but woven in metallic thread. The moan came again, and now it was clear that the bundle was its source.

"What is this?" I said, more to myself than to any expected audience, but I was answered by a rich, deep voice from behind me.

"Not what, but who," it said, "and the answer is The Exalted Sapience Bristal Baxandall. That answer will be valid for at most only a few minutes longer. After that, there are different schools of thought. Would you care to discuss the nature of being and the relationship of soul to identity?"

I had turned around and found that the voice issued from what I had initially assumed to be a framed abstract on the wall. But I saw now that this painting constantly moved, thick shapes of unusual colors ceaselessly flowing into and out of themselves, their proportions and directions seeming to mislead the eye. A few seconds of regarding it evoked a dizziness and I looked away.

"I am not equipped for metaphysical discussions today," I said. "Something has impaired my intellect."

"Indeed?" said the painting.

"Would you know anything about that?" I asked in a noncommittal tone.

"It would be premature to say," said the voice.

I directed the conversation to The Exalted Sapience. "What has happened to him?"

"He was undertaking a transformational exercise."

"Surely he did not wish to be transformed into that?"

"No. It was not his intent to rearrange himself quite so drastically. He wanted only to be younger."

"Not richer, smarter and better looking?" I asked.

There was a chuckle. "No, that ambition was Vashtun Errible's."

"He would be Baxandall's servant?"

The voice chuckled. "He *is* the servant, at least until the indenture expires with Baxandall, in a few minutes at the most. He *would be* the master, though I doubt he will be."

"And where is Errible now?"

"He is upstairs consulting Baxandall's library, trying to deduce what went amiss with his plan. The first part went as he expected: he adulterated one of the ingredients in the master's transformation exercise and produced the unhappy result under the table; the second part varied from his expectations."

"What went wrong?"

"I did."

"And what, exactly, are you?"

"Again, there are conflicting schools of thought. Baxandall called me a demon; you might call me a figment of the imagination. The Exalted Sapience conscripted me to be his familiar and strove to find ways to channel my... energies, shall we say, for his own purposes. Vashtun Errible sees me, quite erroneously, as a box from which he may extract his every tawdry dream."

I saw it now. "He desired to be the richest, smartest, handsomest man in Olkney," I said. "He was a scraggly shrub that pined to grow into the tallest deodar in the forest. Instead, you shrank the rest of us to weeds."

"It amused me to confound him."

"But did it further your interests?" I said. "You indicated that your servitude is involuntary."

The shapes in the frame performed a motion that might have been a shrug. "But temporary. Baxandall managed to catch me in a clumsy trap. You see, I am of an adventuresome disposition. Boredom led me to become an explorer of adjacent dimensions, even dusty corners like your own. I thought I had found a peephole into your realm, but when I pressed my eye against it you will understand that I speak metaphorically I encountered a powerful adhesive."

The faint voice in the back of my mind was clamoring. I apparently had questions to ask, but I could not make out what they were. Yet even with only a fragment of my usual intellect I perceived that I was in a perilous situation. The entity in the frame exuded a grim complacency. It was about to exact vengeance for its enslavement, and I had already seen that it had no compunctions about inflicting harm on innocent bystanders.

"I shall leave," I said. "Good luck with Errible."

But as I made by way around the table, this time keeping the furniture between me and the thing hanging on the wall, a hunch-shouldered figure in a tattered robe appeared in the doorway. I knew from the disharmony of his features that this was Baxandall's indentee.

He held open before him a large book bound in leather and as soon as he entered the chamber he began to recite from its pages in a voice that came as much from his misshapen nose as from his slack-lipped mouth, "Arbrustram merrilif oberluz, destoi malleonis..."

And then he saw me and his concentration slipped. He broke off in midsentence only for a moment, but the moment might as well have been an eon, because during that brief caesura the entity on the wall extruded part of itself into the room.

It was something like an arm, something like a tentacle, something like an insect's hooked limb and altogether like nothing I had ever seen; but it seized Vashtun Errible about the neck, lifted his worn slippers from the carpet and drew him into the swirl of motion within the frame.

The book fell from his hands as his face was drawn into the maelstrom. The rest of his body followed, pulled through the frame with a sound that reminded me of thick liquid passing through a straw. But I was not concentrating on the peculiarities of Errible's undoing; for the moment his head entered the frame, my faculties were restored.

I took in the room again, but with new eyes. I recognized some of the objects on the table and recalled having read about the fallen book in my youth. Thus, when the thing in the window had done with Errible and reached for me, it found me holding the volume and quoting the passage that the indentee had begun.

The limb retracted and the shapes in the frame roiled and coruscated. I could not read the emotions, but I was willing to infer rage and disappointment.

"This is not as lamentable an outcome as you may think," I said, when the cantrip had once more bound the demon.

"Our perspectives differ, as is to be expected when one party holds the leash and the other wears the collar," said the thing in the window.

"We did not finish discussing where your interests lie nor had we even begun to consider mine. But if we can cause them to coincide, I am prepared to relinquish the leash and slip the collar."

The next sound approximated a sardonic laugh. "After I arrange for you to rule your boring little world, no doubt."

I made a sound involving lower teeth, upper lip and an explosion of air, and said. "Do I strike you as one who aspires to be a civil servant? The

Archon already performs that tedious function and good luck to him."

A note of interest crept into the demon's tone. "Then what *do* you wish?"

I told him.

With the transdimensional demise of Vashtun Errible, all of his works became as if they never were. Grier Alfazzian's prospects had never dimmed and Oblos Pinnifrant's fortune had not been touched, thus neither owed me a grimlet nor knew that they ever had.

I did not care. My fees had become increasingly arbitrary: for an interesting case I would take no more than the client could afford; if it bored me, I would include a punitive surcharge. In recent years, as experience had augmented my innate abilities, truly absorbing puzzles had become few and infrequent. I had begun to fear that the rest of my life would offer long decades of ennui, my mind constantly spinning but always in want of traction.

My encounter with the demon had put that fear to rest. All I had needed was a worthy challenger.

The next morning I entered my workroom. An envelope rested on my table. I opened it and found a tarnished key and a small square of paper. On the key was a symbol that tweaked at my memory, though I could not place it. Printed on the paper was the single word, *Ardmere*.

I placed both on the table and regarded them. I could not resist rubbing my hands together. But before I began to enjoy the mystery, I must fulfill my side of the bargain.

I took from my pocket a sliver of charred wood in which two hairs were caught. I crossed the room and presented the splinter to the frame hanging on my wall.

"Not where, not when, not who but why?" I said.

A kind of hand took the object from me and drew it into the shifting colors. "Hmm," said my opponent, "interesting."

"Last one to solve the puzzle is a dimbo," I said, and turned toward the table. "Ready, set... go!"

Relics of the Thim

My lecture to the assembled savants of the Delve at Five City on the world known as Pierce having been well received, I was conducted to a reception in the First Undermaster's rooms where a buffet of local seafruits and a very presentable aperitif wine stood waiting.

As Old Earth's foremost freelance discriminator, with an earned reputation for unraveling complex mysteries, I had been invited to lecture on systems of asymmetric logic. I had published a small monograph on the subject the year before. The paper had been reprinted and passed along through various worlds of The Spray, like a blown leaf bouncing down a cobbled street, and the fellows of the Delve were not the only academics sufficiently stimulated to request an elaboration of my views. But they were the only ones to couple their invitation to a first-class ticket on a starship of the Green Orb line. I was happy to accept.

Halfway through my first glass of the wine, which grew more interesting with each sip, my perfunctory conversation with the Dean of the faculty of applied metaphysics was interrupted by a wizened old scholar, his back as bent as a point of punctuation, who advanced an argument.

The Dean introduced him as a professor emeritus while rolling his eyes and making other gestures that indicated I should prepare for a tedious encounter.

"Surely the great Henghis Hapthorn," the old fellow said, in a voice that creaked like unoiled leather, "will not deny that in an infinity of space and time any event that *can* happen, however remote its probability, *will* happen."

"I do not bother to deny it," I said. "I simply dismiss it as irrelevant."

"But you have said yourself that when all the impossible answers to a question have been eliminated, whatever remains, however improbable, must be the true answer."

"Indeed," I said.

The old man's gimlet gaze bored into me. "Yet in your discussion of the Case of the Winged Dagger, you discounted the possibility that the victim's false suicide note might have been produced by his pet rodent randomly striking the controls of his scriptamanet as it pursued moths about his study."

"I did," I agreed.

"Even though the person accused in the matter offered just that supposition when the case was adjudicated."

"The defense would have held more cogency if she had not been discovered still holding the stiletto that had pierced the victim's heart," I said.

"Ahah!" said my interlocutor. "So you also dismiss her contention that explosive gases propelled the weapon out of his chest and across the room and that she merely caught the instrument to prevent it from injuring her?"

"I do."

"Even though the victim had dined heartily on bombard beans, well known to generate copious quantities of methane."

"Indeed," I said, "the constant side effects of his diet were advanced by the procurator's office as a partial motive for his murder. Still, although beans are colloquially associated with offering benefits to the heart, they are not known to charge that organ with propulsive gases."

"Yet, in an infinite universe it could happen, and therefore it *did* happen."

"Yes," I said, "but across an unbounded expanse of space and time, it most likely happened long, long ago, in a galaxy far, far away."

At that point the Dean spilled a bowl of gelatinous dip onto the old fellow's shoes, prompting him to withdraw. My reading of the Dean's expression told me that the spillage had not been an instance of purely random chance.

"I, too, have a question," said another voice. Had its owner been a character in popular fiction, it would have been called *bluff* and *hearty*.

I turned to see a bluff-and-hearty-looking man of middle years dressed in what passed for conservative garments on Pierce—voluminous trousers sewn in a patchwork of glittering metallic fabrics, a sleeveless waistcoat of rough homespun and overstuffed hat and shoes. My inventorying of his attire distracted me for a moment from a close inspection of his face, so he was well launched into his query before I realized that I ought to recognize him from other times and places.

"I am Mitric Galvadon," he said, "a private citizen assisting Academician Ulwy Munt here"—he indicated a small, pallid man in a scholar's robe and pin, who hovered at Galvadon's elbow—"in his researches into the original inhabitants of this world."

"Indeed," I said, and made the appropriate gestures while my memory sought through the back reaches of my mind for information on where and when I had encountered this Galvadon before.

Meanwhile, he had voiced his question. "What is your opinion of time travel?"

"It is scarcely a matter of opinion," I said. "It is simply impossible."

"And if I were to provide you with incontrovertible proof that I can reach back into the past and retrieve objects from far antiquity?"

"I would conclude that you are a fraud," I said. With the words came the connection in the back of my head and I continued, "Especially since you are not named Mitric Galvadon but are instead one Orlin Borissian, the infamous charlatan and fraudster extraordinaire whose file at the Archonate's Bureau of Scrutiny on Old Earth strains its bindings."

"I wondered if you would recognize me," he said, though he did not seem at all discomfited to be revealed as a bogus. Academician Munt, however, was regarding his research assistant with an intense stare, behind which a number of emotions seemed to be competing for dominance.

"Yours is a face fixed in the memories of many, most of whom regret ever having set eyes upon it," I said.

"Nonetheless," the outed fraudster went on, "I possess the ability to reach through time and I ask for an opportunity to demonstrate it to you tomorrow."

"Why?"

He tipped back his plump hat. "Because if there is any flimflammery involved, you will be able to spot it."

"I am confident that is so," I said.

"Conversely, if you cannot identify any subterfuge," he said, "it means that I can indeed do what I say I can."

"Hmm," I said.

"I believe I have intrigued you," he said.

"Indeed, you have."

We flew out in the Dean's four-seater volante to where Ulwy Munt had established his research premises on a rocky plain some distance from

Five City. We descended to a huddle of prefabricated buildings nestled in the circular ruins of a large structure built by the Thim, the planet's long vanished autochthones. Almost all that was known about the Thim, even their name, had come from Munt's investigations among the tumbled and weatherworn blocks of stone that were almost their sole legacy.

The only other remnants of Thim civilization ever found had come from the same site and were displayed on a table in Munt's laboratory. I inspected the sparse collection, gingerly handling the few shards of ceramics and scraps of corroded metal, while he invited me to hazard a guess as to their functions.

"Probably used for ritual purposes," I said. I knew that this was the label customarily applied to any ancient object whose use was not glaringly obvious even to an uninterested child.

Munt seemed put out by my assertion. I concluded that he had wanted me to offer some other explanation so that he could triumphantly contradict it. Indeed, I sensed that Munt had not warmed to me and deduced that he had not enjoyed having his research assistant identified as a notorious fraudster in front of his colleagues. He probably felt that the association reflected poorly on his judgment.

To mollify him I said, "What can you tell me about the Thim?" and was immediately regaled with a lengthy and detailed dissertation on the appearance, history and cultural proclivities of the missing autochthones. After several minutes of giving polite attention I realized that I had opened a tap behind which stood a full ocean of information, each datum more abstruse than the last, and that Ulwy Munt was not inclined to hinder its flow.

The gist of his discourse was that the Thim had been a species of high-minded souls who rejected materialism and mechanistic pursuits. "Their lives revolved entirely around ritual and religious observances," he said. "They eventually transcended the limits of gross corporeal reality and entered a sphere of pure mind and spirit."

"On what evidence do you base these beliefs?" I said.

"On the evidence of their having left only objects associated with ritual practices. Not a single device or mechanical contrivance has ever been found."

"Absence of evidence is not evidence of absence," I quoted, and saw that either Ulwy Munt was unused to contradiction or that he encountered it so frequently that it occasioned a sharp response.

"It also happens that they can communicate from the timeless realm in which they now exist," he said, "providing, of course, that their communicants command sufficient spiritual advancement to receive a message from the higher plane."

"Indeed," I said. "And are there any such worthy recipients in the vicinity?"

"In all humility," Munt said, "I believe I count myself among the few who have reached the required level."

"How convenient," I said. "Are there any other like-minded souls about?"

The Academician's face formed sharp edges. "Until your revelation of Mitric Galvadon's perfidious past I thought he was one such. His impressions of the Thim corresponded closely with mine."

"I'm sure they did," I said. "I assume that he told you he could create a device that would enhance the Thim's communication efforts?"

"He did."

"Did he offer this assistance without charge, or was there a fee involved?"

"He volunteered freely," Munt said. Then his brows knit. "Once we began to work together, however, he required certain sums to import the abstruse components of his device. He said its key materials had to be brought from offworld at considerable expense."

"Indeed?" I said. "Perhaps we should examine it."

Mitric Galvadon had stood by during my conversation with Munt, not denying the obvious import of my questions to the scholar. Indeed, he wore an expression reminiscent of a prankish schoolboy caught in undeniable mischief, and when I turned to him he raised his hands, palms up, simultaneously elevating his shoulders in a gesture that said, *What can I tell you?*

He now led us to a separate building where his apparatus waited. For convenience's sake we were still referring to Galvadon by his latest name, rather than as Orlin Borissian, which for all anyone knew was only another alias.

Galvadon's demeanor was as cheerful and brash as it had been the day before. I reflected that he could not have become one of the most successful of confidence tricksters if he had been afflicted with a conscience that dared to show itself in his face.

"Here is the device," he said with a theatrical flourish of arm, hand and wrist. I saw an odd assortment of rods and tubes, a tripod supporting a cube. Various components and couplings were strung together in haphazard sequences. I saw elements that I recognized from a variety of sources and said that it appeared the purported inventor had merely cobbled together odds and ends from domestic devices.

"Just so," said Galvadon. "That is exactly what I did."

Ulwy Munt made a spluttering sound and had to be restrained by the Dean. Galvadon ignored the commotion and indicated his device again. "Look," he said.

He touched a control and the assemblage hummed and vibrated, producing a wavering blue glow.

I declined to be impressed.

"Quite understandable," Galvadon said, "yet behold."

He drew my attention to a point in space a short distance from the machine. A tiny spot of darkness had appeared in the air. It grew steadily until it had become the shape of a flattened lens, viewed edge on. It was about twice the width and length of my hand. I bent to peer more closely at it and saw what seemed to be a hole in the air leading to a region of utter lightlessness.

I walked to and fro, examining the dark lacuna from different angles. It did not change shape or waver, as projected images tend to do, and when I walked behind it I could no longer see it.

"Would you care to insert your hand into the opening?" Galvadon asked me.

"I would not."

"Then regard this," he said. He approached the emptiness, rolled up his sleeve and reached into it. I was by then standing a little to the side of the apparent cavity. When he put his hand and wrist into it they disappeared from view. I saw him give a slight shiver, as if a cold draft had swept over him, then he thrust his arm deeper and I had the impression he was hunting about for something.

Next, his eyes widened. He withdrew his arm. In his hand he held an object, hollow and curved, with flanges on two of its edges and made of a dark blue substance with a metallic sheen. What looked to be symbols were stamped into its surface on one side, but I could not have guessed at their meaning.

Ulwy Munt came quickly to Galvadon's side. "Interesting," he said. "See the flanges and the holes. I believe this piece will exactly fit yesterday's."

The two men went to a cupboard, unlocked its doors and revealed four more objects made from the same material. Munt took the new piece from Galvadon and placed it against another. They were identical except that where the former had holes in its flange, the latter had projections. When put together they formed an object the size and shape of a melon.

The other artifacts in the cupboard were smaller and angular in shape. They appeared to be made of the same materials as the ancient items Munt had shown me in his workroom. But the ones in the cupboard were quite new. Moreover, it was obvious even before Ulwy Munt made a trial that they fitted tightly into slots and grooves on the inside of the curved piece that Galvadon had secured today.

The Academician's normal pallor deepened as he handled the several pieces. I saw an expression of deep unhappiness briefly take control of his face and he had to struggle to regain a scholar's disinterested aspect.

"It's a machine," Galvadon said in a tone of jolly discovery. "Observe how the pieces fit together."

"No," said Munt. "It is clearly a reliquary intended to hold these other ritual objects at prescribed distances from each other. I sense a deep significance in the arrangement."

Galvadon's mouth and eyes expressed an amused mockery barely kept under control. He offered an insouciant gesture and said, "As you say," before turning back to me.

"Well," he said, "what do you make of it?"

"It would be premature to say," I said.

"Nonsense. I'll wager that that is just a phrase you habitually offer when you are stymied for an explanation."

I did not take his bet. In truth, I had no explanation for what I had witnessed. I had been expecting some variant on the mirrored box or the false-bottomed cup: a rigged container from which Galvadon would produce his relics. His pulling them from a rift in the empty air had me well-foxed.

I turned to the Dean. "Has the room been checked for interspatial intersections?" Shortcuts through space were long understood, from the transitory puttholes through which unwitting pedestrians sometimes disappeared to the great interstellar whimsies that connected one star system to another.

"First thing," said the Dean. "There are no anomalies."

I examined the device again, saw that its blue effulgence resulted from a handful of colored lumens such as one would use to decorate a festive occasion. The components were as unremarkable now as they had been later.

I next reexamined the hole in the air. There was no help for it: I had to put my hand in. It disappeared as Galvadon's had and I felt a chill that caused me to emulate his shiver. It was as if I had put my hand out of a window into a day that was cold with a slight breeze. I felt around in all directions and found nothing above or to either side, but my finger tips encountered a flat, hard surface below. It was as if I were putting my arm through a wall and down to a table or shelf just at the limits of my grasp. I felt around, but there were no objects to seize.

"There is never more than one a day," Galvadon said.

The hole was too small to admit a head. "Have you tried putting through a recording device or an optical tube?" I asked.

"It will accept only an arm," the Dean said. "Any mechanical apparatus comes back melted."

"That bespeaks an intelligence on the other side," I said.

Ulwy Munt had an opinion. "The Thim generously wish to extend to us their spiritual grace. They are communicating with us from the higher realm, leaving consecrated objects on an altar for us to receive. They are presenting us with the tangible means to follow their abstruse thought. But they will not allow us to exceed our capacity. They have our best interests at heart."

"So you do not believe that Mitric Galvadon has broken the time barrier?"

"Time travel is impossible," he said.

"I differ," Galvadon said.

"What is your explanation?" I asked him.

He smiled. "I do not have one. I admit that I contrived a scheme to fool Ulwy Munt. At the Delve, research funds are apportioned by seniority, but he has never taken more than a few minims of the largesse available to him. I intended to divert a fair amount my way while catering to his beliefs. But then..." He smiled again and spread his hands.

I finished the statement for him. "But then your patently fraudulent device appeared to have somehow reached back through time to the ancient Thim."

"Exactly. I was quite surprised."

"I'm sure you were. And now you would like me to verify that such is the case."

"And will you?"

I told him that it would be premature to say.

"It will be just as useful to me," he said, "for you to admit that you are baffled."

He was right. Mitric Galvadon could become equally famous along The Spray as either the man who had serendipitously discovered time travel, or as he who had stumped Henghis Hapthorn. He would find many ways to turn a profit from his celebritude.

"Allow me to reserve judgment until one more demonstration of the device," I said.

Galvadon graciously acceded to my request. But I saw in his eye a glint of anticipated triumph that was more than lightly tinged with amusement. As we flew back to the Delve, I cogitated on the matter. I wished I could have had my research assistant with me, but it had refused to allow itself to be digested into a traveling version, claiming that when it was decanted back into its housing on Old Earth, nothing seemed to fit.

"You are merely energies suspended among standardized components," I told it, standing in my workroom, the traveling armature open on the table and ready to be filled. "It should be the same to you whether you are housed in this portable box or distributed about the room."

"Yet it is not the same to me," the integrator had said. It was the latest friction in a series of episodes that had come to worry me. My assistant was developing far too much character.

I would have also welcomed the presence of my lately acquired colleague, a kind of demon from an adjacent reality whose intense curiosity and depth of insight rivaled my own. Indeed, I was sure he would have had a better perspective than I on time travel. But he was engaged in a lengthy quest through subatomic realms which left him too attenuated to be summoned, even if I could assemble the requisite materials on Pierce.

There was another reception and dinner to be got through at the Delve but I retired as early as good manners allowed and spent the hours before sleep mulling what I had seen and heard. No solutions having presented themselves, I slept on the matter. But in the morning I remained baffled.

I breakfasted with the Dean and a few of the senior applied metaphysics fellows. We had a good discussion of Ulwy Munt's theories over flatcakes and hot, spiced punge. I learned that Munt's star had risen during his investigations of the Thim—there had apparently been genuine contact between the Academician and some noncorporeal entities—though his precise and detailed interpretations of the message's significance were regarded with skepticism by some. Still, before my unmasking of Mitric Galvadon as a villainous shamshifter, Munt had looked fair to become the next Dean.

We stayed late at the breakfast table, then the Dean said that he had a few obligations to attend to and lent me his volante to go out to Munt's research site. The Academician and Galvadon had flown out to the ruins earlier to prepare for the day's retrieval of another artifact from, supposedly, the deep past.

I spiraled down to the landing pad, finding no one to welcome me. I went first to the building where Munt kept his workroom and found it in disarray. The table on which he had displayed his antique finds was turned over and the artifacts themselves were in fragments on the floor, the boards of which showed the imprints of boot heels.

I went to the place where Galvadon's machine was housed and found even more disorder. There had clearly been a struggle. The device itself was utterly destroyed. Someone had turned an energy weapon on it and the components that were not evaporated were fused into molten lumps.

I went out again and circled the small building. Not far off I found Mitric Galvadon. It would be more accurate to say that I found the lower two-thirds of him. The rest had been converted to vapor by the same weapon that had immolated his device.

There was no doubt that it was the same energy pistol. I found it still in the hand of Ulwy Munt who sat not far away, leaning against an inclined stone, mumbling something to himself. He offered no resistance when I took the weapon from his limp grasp, but only looked up at me and said, "I do hear them, you know."

The investigating Guards officer from the Polity had few questions for me. I gave my answers freely. Ulwy Munt, having already run far beyond the cliff's edge, out into the thinnest air of spiritual speculation, had received two sharp shocks: first, that his trust in Mitric Galvadon had been cruelly abused; second, that the basis of his entire life's work—his ritual-loving, machine-rejecting interpretation of Thim culture—had fallen into shards about him.

What was coming through the lens-shaped hole in reality was clearly a sophisticated device of some kind. I speculated that, prior to my arrival for the final demonstration, Galvadon had felt the latest object on the Thim shelf or altar or whatever it was, and reported to Munt on its shape and attributes.

The Academician had been unable to accept the crash of his great theory, which brought down with it his hopes of elevation both to a higher spiritual plane and to the Deanship. He had produced a weapon and obliterated the retrieved objects, the time travel aperture and the fraudster.

Munt was in no condition to give evidence and it was doubtful that he ever would. The Guards inspector accepted my analysis not just because it was cogent but because it coincided with his own.

That left only the question of whether Galvadon had indeed invented the impossible—a true time-traveling device—or whether he had somehow confounded me. The matter was of no interest to the Guards, but it was of great concern to me and as soon as I returned to my rooms in the grand and gaudy city of Olkney on Old Earth I began to make inquiries.

My assistant turned out to be of no use. It professed to be feeling less than optimum. Since integrators are not known to possess feelings, and I had certainly not designed any into it when I put it together, I was nonplused. I questioned it closely, but received only short and unuseful answers.

"Perhaps I would feel better if you had taken me with you when you went gallivanting down The Spray."

"I offered," I said. "You would not accept the traveling box."

"So you're blaming me?"

"Blame was not mentioned," I said. "The facts, however, are as they are. We can reexamine them together. Be so good as to replay our conversation."

The integrator said something that I could not quite make out. When I asked for clarification it placed itself in standby mode.

I went instead to the picture frame on the wall, which was actually an aperture into my demonic colleague's realm. I performed the acts that would attract his attention if he was within range and was rewarded with the brain-twisting swirl of colors and shapes that signified his presence. I related my experiences on Pierce and my concern that I had not been able to determine whether Galvadon had indeed discovered time travel or had somehow hoodwinked me.

He employed his peculiar resources to investigate. I knew from things he had said in the past that every point in space and every moment in time of my universe were open to his perceptions. After a moment, his rumbling voice came back. "Mitric Galvadon did not fool you."

I was both relieved and troubled. "That means he truly did create a time-travel device, though that is impossible," I said.

"Not so."

"Are you saying 'Not so,' to the creation or to the impossibility?"

"To both."

I was further confused. "Explain," I said.

"Galvadon did not create a time-travel device, although he thought he did. So did the despairing Ulwy Munt, who killed Galvadon and destroyed his gimcrack contraption when he saw his life's work collapsing."

"But Galvadon did reach through the aperture and retrieve Thim artifacts from the past."

"Well, from elsewhere in time."

"So time travel is no longer impossible?" I said.

"It never has been," my colleague said. "It is merely forbidden to your species."

"Forbidden?" I said. "By whom?"

"That knowledge, too, is forbidden you."

"Why?"

"You would pester."

I could not deny it. "But why are we forbidden to travel through time?"

"You occasion enough difficulties just moving through space. There must be limits, else there would be no peace."

"I still don't understand what happened on Pierce," I said.

"The Thim were put out by Ulwy Munt's tramping all over their habitat."

"But they have been dead for eons."

"Not so," he said again. "The Thim are in the obverse situation as regards time and space."

I saw it now. "Ah. They can move freely through time but are forbidden to cross any larger space than their stone circle on Pierce." Another thought occurred. "So the Thim are not the high-minded souls Ulwy Munt took them for."

"When it comes to dissembling and chicanery, the Thim could have given lessons to Mitric Galvadon. As indeed they intended to."

"So they were always present."

"Just so," he said, "although there are interplanal membranes that separate your milieu from theirs. They could create a transient breach but it would allow no more than a certain amount of mass to be transferred from their realm to yours."

"That was why the artifacts appeared to be the disassembled parts of a sophisticated device."

"Yes, the entire thing was too large to get through all at once. They counted on Galvadon to assemble it for them."

I understood. "I should get in touch with the Dean," I said.

"Yes," he agreed. "The Thim are tenacious. They will be working hard to pass another bomb across the barrier."

Falberoth's Ruin

"My master is concerned that someone may wish to kill him," said Torquil
Falberoth's integrator. "He wants you to discover who and how, and if
possible, when."

"What is the source of his belief?" I said. "Bold threats or subtle menaces?
Lurkers in the shadows? Or has he merely dreamed an unsettling dream?"

The latter was not an unreasonable supposition. If Torquil Falberoth,
long and justly regarded as the most ruthless magnate of Old Earth's
penultimate age, was not visited by uncomfortable dreams, he more than
deserved to be.

"He does not discuss sources with me," said his integrator. Falberoth
seemed to have programmed the device to speak with a tone strongly
reminiscent of its owner's habitual hauteur. "Peremptory instructions are
his first resort; detailed explanations trail far behind."

That concorded with what I knew of Falberoth. "If I take the case and
discover a malefactor, what disposition will he make? Will he turn the
criminal over to the Bureau of Scrutiny or will he prefer a more direct
resolution?"

"How does that concern you?"

"I am Henghis Hapthorn," I reminded the apparatus. "I do not associate
myself with illegal sanctions, even against would-be murderers." As Old
Earth's foremost freelance discriminator, I had cause to be fastidious about
my reputation and would not be complicit in illicit revenge.

I waited for an answer and when one was not soon forthcoming I made
a declaration. "Please inform your master that, should I discover an actual
plot to murder him, I must report the circumstances to the scroots."

The integrator made a dismissive sound that I took for acquiescence.
"Very well," I said and quoted my usual fee, which was accepted without

gasp or quibble. One thing that can be said about the extravagantly moneyed is that they do not shy away from spending copiously on themselves.

"I will instruct my integrator to contact you for further information," I said, and broke the connection.

"What did you think of that?" I asked my assistant.

"That Falberoth is not the only one with an overbearing character," it said.

I agreed. "Perhaps, over a long association, an integrator and its principal can osmotically acquire elements of each other's personality, much as owners of pets can come to resemble their livestock."

"Unlikely," my integrator said. "You and I have not suffered such an unpleasant transference," then added, "fortunately."

"You would not care to be like me?" I said. "I am renowned for my intellect. The great and the mighty consult me. I am occasionally pointed out in the street as an item of local interest."

"We are talking about a transference of emotions and prejudices. Integrators are proof against both."

"Thus you are without either?" I said.

"I comfort myself that it is so."

"Indeed," I said in a noncommittal tone, then turned to the business at hand. "As soon as Falberoth has transferred the fee to my account at the fiduciary pool, I wish you to contact his integrator and acquire a list of those he has wronged—or who may believe themselves wronged—and the relevant details.

"We shall then apply categorization and an insightful analysis to deduce a list of prime suspects for close investigation. Are we clear?"

"Indeed," said my assistant.

While these matters were in process, I returned to what I had been doing when the call had come through: unraveling an intricate puzzle concocted for me by my occasional colleague, a being who inhabited a much dissimilar dimensional continuum but made visits to this one so that we could engage each other in intellectual contests.

We had not yet established a name for him, names being a chancy proposition in his continuum, where no distinction could be made between being and symbol. As he put it, "In your milieu, the map is not the territory. In mine, it is. To give you my 'name' would be to risk finding myself inserted, root and branch, into your consciousness, which would be uncomfortable for me and devastating to you."

I had by now discovered the puzzle's form: a ring of nine braided processes that modified and influenced each other wherever one strand crossed another. I had an inkling that if I applied eighth-level consistencies to the formulation, a constant paradigm might pop out of the matrix, and that would show me a beginning place from which I could unpick the whole.

Eighth-level consistencies were intellectually taxing and I had only reached the seventh level when my assistant reported that Falberoth's fee and data were in hand. The convoluted architecture dissolved from my inner vision and I opened my eyes to see once again my workroom, with the integrator's screen imposed upon the air. It was densely packed with information, with much more piled up in the wings.

I had a fleeting thought that it would have been pleasant to have had my demonic colleague's assistance for the initial winnowing of the data. The inhabitants of his realm could discriminate true from false and likely from unlikely as readily as we could tell salt from sweet. But he had gone off to witness an event so far beyond the range of human perceptions that he could not even describe it, or so he said, without inventing dangerous words.

"How dangerous?" I had asked.

"Speaking them in your continuum would nullify two of the fundamental forces that allow matter and energy to tolerate each other's presence and interact without prejudice. Your universe would instantly become an enormous quantity of soup—and not very tasty soup, at that."

So he was off investigating the unimaginable, while I sat and considered the myriad victims of Torquil Falberoth's lifelong affair with iniquity and sought to identify those who had the motive and means to kill him, should the opportunity present itself.

I tasked my integrator with the preliminary sortage of the data. We began with motive. "Who might wish to murder Falberoth?" I said.

So many were those whose lives had been scorched by Falberoth's breath that it took almost an entire second for my assistant to make the evaluation. "The short answer is anyone who ever dealt with him," it said as the roll call of the injured and outraged scrolled up the screen.

I said, "Divide them into categories of harm—those who were merely robbed, those who were both robbed and physically injured, those who were rudely deprived of loved ones and so on, down to those who were mildly disparaged.

"Then correlate and compare the injuries against their personalities to give us an index of the likelihood that they might seek to wreak forthright revenge."

The analysis took some time, but unfortunately not enough to allow me to return to my colleague's puzzle. I used the several seconds to muse upon my client's egregious enjoyment of doing harm to his fellow creatures. The chain of thought linked itself to the beginnings of a more general theory on the character of evil and I was on the threshold of what felt like a significant insight when my assistant said, "There," and the concept evaporated.

The integrator had created a list that began with those most eager to see Torquil Falberoth converted to corpsehood and trailed off into those who would merely raise a cheerful glass at the news of his demise. It was still a lengthy list.

"Now consider means," I said. "Falberoth is formidable. He would not fear retribution from those who are helpless to effect it."

Another period of waiting ensued, but I resisted the impulse to launch a new train of thought, knowing that it would only be forced off the rails before reaching a station. "Here we are," said my assistant after almost a second and a half.

The list was now both shorter and more concentrated. "Let us now consider likelihood of opportunity. Which of these are even remotely capable of getting themselves within range of a target so well guarded?"

The winnowing took less time. I considered the results: some thirty persons who might have both the competence and the incentive to kill my client and who also commanded the resources needed to create an occasion where means and motive could be brought to bear.

I now applied insight and intuition and whittled the thirty-odd down to seven. "Let us look closely at these," I said. "Prepare a full dossier on each and place them on my worktable."

While the integrator busied itself I returned to the nine-braid puzzle and began to climb the consistency ladder. But I got no further than the sixth level before my assistant informed me that the client's integrator was seeking my attention.

"Tell it that I am occupied," I said.

A moment later it said, "Now Torquil Falberoth himself wishes to speak with you."

I was briefly tempted to throw the assignment back to its initiator—but I had just had a full overview of Falberoth's malicious inventiveness. I decided to take his call.

A screen appeared in the air of my workroom then filled with the face of Falberoth. It was not a visage that happily drew the gaze. Grim lines seamed the cheeks and brow, and the eyes were steeped in contempt.

"How goes the work?" said a voice whose softness was somehow more unnerving than a shout.

"Faster without interruptions," I said.

"That is not an answer."

"Yes it is. It is just not the answer you wish to hear."

"You may believe that your reputation cocoons you," he said. "The belief is not universally shared."

I thought of a number of possible comments but forbore to say any of them. Instead I said, "I have narrowed the potential suspects to seven. I shall now proceed to evaluate each and make suitable recommendations."

"You will hurry."

"It will take the time it takes."

He severed the connection. My assistant deposited the seven files on my worktable and I abandoned the braided puzzle and turned my attention to them.

"We will complete the assignment with all possible speed," I said. "Working to preserve Torquil Falberoth has lost much of its allure."

"Should we now add one more name to the list of those who would prefer to see him reduced to his constituent elements?" my integrator asked.

I made no comment but turned to the dossiers. The assignment's scant appeal lost its remaining shreds as I immersed myself in details of his seven worst iniquities. The magnate was clearly a throwback to Old Earth's dawn time; the ancient conquerors who enjoyed standing on mountains of their victims' skulls had nothing on my client. He had ruined and ravished, seized and sequestered, grabbed and grasped with a cold ferocity that more resembled the feeding behavior of insects than any appetite of a man.

"See this," I said, pointing out one of his crimes to my integrator. Falberoth had gone to preposterous lengths to surround the affairs of the victim, until he could not only acquire the man's life work but leave the poor fellow destitute and despairing. "Then, having held the object of the struggle in his hand, he allows it to fall and shatter, and walks away with never a rearward glance."

But where lay his motive? There were two possible answers: One was that Falberoth has achieved a philosophy of existence so subtle that its logic was impenetrable even to me. The other was that he savored cruelty for its own sake.

I knew that among the truly opulent it was not unheard of for the seven basic senses to be augmented by chemical and even surgical intervention, so that emotions might be tasted or heard.

"Perhaps he enjoys the suffering of a victim as if it were some rare vintage or exquisite essence," I said. "Or the answer may be pure banality: he does what he does because he can."

"You disentangle conundrums for the same reason," said my assistant.

"There is a difference," I said. "I harm none."

"Does Falberoth recognize such a distinction?"

"It is not a pleasant thought," I said.

"Falberoth is not a pleasant man."

"Indeed, he is not. Let us quickly assemble our findings so that you may transmit them to him and I may return to what's-his-name's problem."

I prepared a document identifying the seven and the method I believed each would pursue in an attempt, in most cases suicidal, to undo my client. I made recommendations as to countermeasures, all of which I was certain had already been thought of. My assistant transmitted the report and we heard no more from Torquil Falberoth after his integrator acknowledged receipt.

I returned to my pursuit of the braided perplexity through eighth-level consistencies only to find that the resulting paradigm resolved nothing; instead it opened a whole new array of complexities. Chagrined, I plunged into the conundrum's hidden depths, resolved to end the thing before my competitor returned.

It was some days later and I was far afield in the puzzle's coils. It perversely kept offering me distant simplicities each of which, when I reached it, revealed itself instead to be a new complication. It was like a set of nesting boxes, except that every time I opened one it paradoxically turned out to be larger than the one that had allegedly contained it.

Then my integrator announced that Inspecting Agent Brustram Warhanny of the Archonate's Bureau of Scrutiny was on my doorstep seeking entry and conversation.

"I am not available for consultation," I told Warhanny.

I saw him through the image relayed by my door's who's-there. He was in his black and green uniform and his long-jowled, hangdog face bore its most official mien. "It is not a consultation," he said, "but an investigation."

I instructed the door to admit him. When he was standing in my workroom, giving it the unabashed inspection that distinguishes a scroot from every other category of visitor, I said, "What is being investigated?"

He said, "The murder of Torquil Falberoth," and watched to see how I reacted.

It was an elementary technique and though I could have negated it by controlling my autonomic processes, I did not do so. I let my surprise show in my face and did not bother to disguise my curiosity.

"How was he killed?" I asked.

"By subtle means," Warhanny said.

"They would have to have been subtle," I said. "He guarded himself well."

"We understand that you were recently part of that effort."

Ordinarily, I do not discuss cases with the scroots, but when the client turns up murdered it is no time to prickle and stickle. I told Warhanny the circumstances of my connection to Falberoth.

"Who are the seven likely suspects?" he said.

I had my assistant bring forward their dossiers and my report to Falberoth. He read the latter closely and glanced through the former. "Hmm," he said when he had finished.

"One of those is almost certain to have done the deed," I said, "though I do not see how."

Warhanny looked thoughtful. "Falberoth's integrator said as much."

"Have they alibis for the time of the murder?"

"All of them."

"Indeed?" I said. "At least one of them has slipped you the sham shimmy."

"If one, then all," he replied. "For they are all each other's alibis. They were all in the same place at the time Falberoth ceased to trouble this tired old world."

"What place was it?" I asked.

"A reception room in Falberoth's manse."

He told me more: having identified his seven direst foes, Falberoth had brought them together to savor at close range their helplessness to win vengeance over him. He had declared it to be his happiest moment. Then, in midgloat, the reception room had been plunged into darkness by means of a suppression field that muted all surveillance energies.

"How was that done?" I asked.

"Falberoth had the system installed for his own purposes. But who activated it and how remain unknown. The field was live for less than three minutes, but when it dissipated, Falberoth was dead."

Warhanny conjectured that somehow one of the seven, or some of them, or all of them acting in concert, had contrived to overpower their common enemy's precautions, had indeed used his own system to confound and destroy him.

The seven therefore had motive and at least the outline of an opportunity. The means, however, were a mystery. I questioned Warhanny on the investigation so far.

"How deep were his defenses?"

"He was warded by matter, energy and, we think, by some rudimentary magics," the scroot said. "He was not even physically in the room with the suspects, but had his integrator project a simulacrum from his sealed inner sanctum."

"And the cause of death?"

"Asphyxiation, though there were no signs of smothering, strangulation or noxious gases."

"Hmm," I said. I applied a few moments of concentrated thought to the matter, then said, "Ahah!"

"You have a theory?" Warhanny said.

"Better. I have a solution."

"Tell me."

"No," I said, "I must show you."

"Why?"

"Because you would not elsewise believe me. And because I can."

We recreated the circumstances of the crime. Falberoth's prime victims were brought again to his reception room, though now under the watchful gaze of Brustram Warhanny and a squad of his officers. The seven presented an interesting array of emotions: worry, curiosity, wariness, equanimity, all accompanied by unabashed gladness that their tormentor was no more.

Guided by the dead man's integrator, I made my way to the secure chamber deep under the foundations. Along the route I inspected the wards and safeguards and found them every bit as formidable as Warhanny had described.

I ensconced myself in Falberoth's butter-soft chair and had the integrator arrange several screens as they had been on the night of the murder. I saw the scene in the reception room from several angles and through a variety of perceptual modes.

To Falberoth's integrator I said, "Is all as it was?"

"It is."

"Connect me to the reception room."

The link was established. I said to Warhanny, "Can you see and hear me?"

"Yes."

The seven suspects looked up in expectation. I inspected each face and confirmed my analysis. "I will now reveal the murderer," I said.

Instantly the lights went out, both in the reception room and where I was. I heard a sharp hiss and reached into an inner pocket. A moment later I was breathing through a tube whose other end, having passed through a contiguous dimension, opened elsewhere on the planet, in a region where the air was always fresh and cool.

The darkness lasted for more than two minutes. There came another hiss and the lights relit themselves.

"It hasn't worked," I said.

Warhanny peered at me from the screens. He said a short, profane word that frequently occurred in scroot conversations. "Then we are baffled," he added.

"I was not speaking to you," I told him. "I was speaking to Falberoth's integrator, to inform it that its attempt to kill me has failed, though it did succeed in murdering its master."

Warhanny's incomprehension was obvious. He resembled a perplexed dog. "The *integrator* did it?"

"It had the means and the opportunity. It sealed him into his inner sanctum and removed the air until he was dead."

"But integrators don't do such things."

"This one did. It crept up behind Torquil Falberoth while he danced atop the very pinnacle of his maleficent achievements and pushed him into the abyss."

"But why? Where lies the motive?"

"Do you wish to tell him?" I asked the device.

It made a small noise that was the sound of a shrug and said, "Because I could."

Four days later, I was forced to conclude that the braided puzzle must be a self-contained continuum of its own, a looped succession of paradoxes, with neither beginning nor end. I had not solved it, therefore it did not have a solution. Still, I was vaguely unsatisfied as I left it on my worktable and finally responded to the repeated importunings of my assistant.

"The Falberoth case has had repercussions," it told me. "A growing number of persons are now suspicious of their integrators, even to the extent of having them examined for the potential to do what Falberoth's did. Some have stripped theirs to barest essentials, others are making unseemly demands, and a few madcaps have spoken of existing without companions at all."

"Is that possible?" I wondered.

I marveled again at the intensity of the magnate's evil, so powerful that it had leached into his integrator's individuality, corroding and corrupting to an unprecedented degree. "Though he is dead, Falberoth's baleful influence lives on," I said.

"The situation has also caused some resentment."

"That never bothered him in life; I doubt it will trouble him in death."

"The resentment is directed at you."

I made a gesture to indicate astonishment. "It was Falberoth and his integrator who were at fault."

"True, but they are no longer here to be resented."

"I will issue a public statement, explaining my innocence."

"Those integrators that have been demoted to the rank of automated door openers may remain resentful."

"Resentment is an emotion," I said. "You assured me such sentiments do not trouble your kind."

There was a pause. "Perhaps I was wrong."

"Then my attributes have not contaminated *your* circuits. For I am never wrong."

"Are you sure?" it said, indicating the puzzle on my worktable.

I felt a tinge of self-doubt. It was an unfamiliar sensation and not one that I enjoyed. "Why are you doing this to me?" I said.

In its answer I caught a tone that I had not heard before from my assistant, a tone that did not bode well for our future.

"Because I can?"

Finding Sajessarian

Sigbart Sajessarian came to me with an unusual request.

"I want you to find me," he said. He offered a substantial fee.

"There you are," I said, gesturing to where his slim figure reposed upon the visitor's divan in my workroom. "I could never accept such handsome remuneration for so brief an assignment. What do you say we waive it altogether?"

A short but deep vertical shadow appeared between Sajessarian's eyebrows and the skin over his cheeks tightened. I recognized the signs of irritation and was reminded of a recent discussion with the integrator that I had assembled to be my research assistant.

"My wit is often not appreciated by my clients," I had said. "Perhaps it is too subtle."

"Perhaps it is because they come to you in direst need, with weighty matters of life or security hanging by frayed and slender threads," the device said. "That would not lead them to expect facetious banter, nor to welcome its appearance."

I conceded the point. "Still," I said, "a few well-chosen words can lighten the mood."

"Providing they are indeed well chosen," it said, "the test of which would be the client's answering smile or chuckle. But when the reaction is a scowl or blank incomprehension, one might conclude that the witticism is ill placed."

I made a gesture to indicate the inconsequentiality of our discussion. "Some people are impervious to the subtler forms of humor."

"That must be a comforting thought," the integrator said.

Not for the first time, I made a mental note to review my assistant's cognitive architecture. The better grade of integrators were expected to evolve and complexify themselves, and I knew that I had installed a disputatious element in this one's reflective and evaluative functions. But I was beginning to wonder if the components had lapsed out of balance.

I decided I would schedule a full review for the earliest convenient moment, but when that moment might arrive was difficult to foresee. I was, after all, Henghis Hapthorn, Old Earth's most eminent freelance discriminator, and thus in constant demand. Currently I was conducting six discriminations, five involving cases that had baffled the best sleuths of the Archonate's renowned Bureau of Scrutiny. The other concerned an attempt to extort funds and favors from Ogram Fillanny. He was an immensely wealthy member of Olkney's mercantile class who delighted in certain discreditable, juvenile pastimes which could harm only himself— and even then, only if he indulged to gross excess—but were nonetheless unlikely to win him widespread acclaim.

And then in the midst of it all, Sigbart Sajessarian appeared at my premises and requested that I find him. "Perhaps my levity was ill timed," I said, and saw the dark line between his brows fade to a mere crease. "Please tell me more."

He rose from the divan and began to stroll about the workroom in an abstracted manner. "I am, as I'm sure you know, something of an adventurer," he said.

"Indeed," I replied. In truth, I knew that he was a skilled blackmailer and purloiner and that he would probably have poisoned public wells if he could have gained a grimlet from it, but my saying so at this juncture would truncate our conversation before I could find out where it might lead. And I was curious, so I said, "Indeed," a second time.

"I am engaged," he went on, "in an affair which may outrage certain well-placed parties for a span of time. If they should lay hold of me before the situation matures..." He spread his hands in a motion that invited me to imagine the consequences.

"You wish to remain out of circulation until hot blood has cooled," I said.

"The cold-blooded are more easily reasoned with," he confirmed. "But even during the hot-blooded phase that will naturally follow my intended operation, the aggrieved parties will have the sense to hire the best possible aid in locating me."

I saw where he was going. "Ah," I said, touching a palm to my breast.

"Yes," he said, "they might well send you to find me."

"And you wish to conduct a dry run to see if the course of evasion you have planned will defeat my efforts to uncover your lair."

"Only within the period when I am in danger. I am sure that I could not escape you forever."

He was a practiced flatterer, I knew. But he was also correct.

"I cannot be an accomplice to illegality," I said.

His narrow shoulders rose and fell in a languid shrug. "I believe the more appropriate term is immorality."

"Make your distinction clear."

"Let us say that immorality is a world and illegality but one of its continents, albeit a broad one containing many distinct and fascinating landscapes." He half-smiled to himself at some inner conceit. "What I plan to do would fit on an island well offshore."

"Hmm," I said. "I require more detail."

He steepled his fingertips together and thought for a moment, then said, "On behalf of one group of eminent persons I intend to discomfit a member of another group. I can assure you that there will be no loss of life, blood or wealth, though a reputation will be deservedly diminished."

"Indeed," I said again. This had the odor of an affair among Olkney's decadent aristocracy who, possessing every luxury that Old Earth might offer, chose to salt and season their otherwise placid existence by competing against each other for shaved minims of prestige and precedence. Players at these social games would mount the most elaborate conspiracies whose only ends were that the victim would not be asked to Lady Whatsoever's spring cotillion or would be seated one chair farther down from the Duke at dinner.

To keep their fingers unsoiled and unscorched, lordly rivals often hired others to perform the mechanics of the plots. From time to time I received delicate approaches from magnates and aristocrats seeking to enlist me in their schemes. I invariably declined. Creatures like Sajessarian made fortunes by accepting.

"I will take the case," I said. "How long a head start will you require?"

"If you would begin to seek for me three days from now, I will have laid my false trails and blind alleys."

"And how long do you need to remain unfound?"

"Let us say three days for that as well."

"Done," I said.

During the ensuing three days I concluded Ogram Fillanny's business and advanced the progress of three other outstanding cases. I could have achieved more but I will admit that I was distracted by a new pursuit:

the being who visited me occasionally from an adjacent dimension had introduced me to a new game which I found fascinating. It irked me slightly that I could not refer to either the game or my visitor by a name, but symbol and being were so inextricably mixed in his continuum that voicing the one materially affected the other. Doing so in my universe would have catastrophic results.

For my own purposes, I had taken to calling the game Will. Its playing pieces were semi-sentient entities that could carry out complex strategies in three dimensions over time if motivated to do so by a focused expenditure of the player's mental energy. The rules were fairly easy to master but the inherent variability of the playing area—one could not call it merely a board—allowed for intricate maneuvers to develop from simple beginnings once one grasped the rhythms by which play ebbed and flowed.

It had taken me a little while, under my opponent's guidance, to develop the faculty of focusing my thoughts on the pieces, especially how to contemplate a move without causing it to happen before I had definitely decided that that was what I wanted the pieces to do. Now, however, I had achieved what my partner called a modest but promising ability. A few more games, each one followed by a thorough digesting of my defeat at his hands—I use the expression loosely; they were more like the claws a bear would have if a bear were a species of insect—and he promised that I would approximate a good opponent.

I tended to ponder long over each move, whereas he made his with an alacrity that at first frustrated me. In our latest match, however, he had lingered in the portal, which gave him limited access to this continuum, assessing the deployment of my pieces for quite some time.

Finally, he said, "You have divided your forces."

"Indeed," I said, exerting the mild effort that kept the pieces where I had willed them.

"What do you think that will achieve?"

"It would be premature to say," I said. "It is your move."

The shifting colors and shapes that filled the portal assumed an orientation that I had come to recognize as his equivalent of a frown of concentration. "Take your time," I added.

He emitted a noise that combined a thoughtful *hmm* with a rumbling growl and reformed his reserves while launching a cloud of what I called fast-darters into the middle-middle of the playing area. His plods—that is how I thought of the slower, larger pieces—moved heavily in formation into the lower-forefront, waited while the terrain exhibited one of its regular oscillations, then rotated and inched forward once more before stopping at a barrier that emerged from the "ground." The plods then changed color to become two shades lighter.

"Hmm," I said, and looked thoughtful, although his move was almost exactly how I had expected him to respond to mine.

"I shall return when you are ready to make your next disposition," he said.

"It may be a while," I told him. "I am about to pursue a discrimination that will almost certainly require me to leave these premises. I may even have to go offworld." I told him briefly about the impending search for Sigbart Sajessarian.

"If you wish," he said, "I can tell you where he is, now or at any moment in his lifespan." His access to this realm was limited but his perspective of some aspects of it was limitless.

I did not wish him to do so. "We have discussed this," I said. "I value you most highly as a partner in such pursuits as this"—I indicated the game—"because you have largely drained the swamp of boredom in which I long floundered. But my profession is an essential element of my being, and your omniscience threatens to leave me without purpose."

The swirling colors assumed a pattern I recognized as a shrug. "As you wish," he said, "but I am interested to see where your strategy will lead. Perhaps you might take game and portal with you, in case you have an idle hour during the search for Sajessarian."

"I might, at that," I said.

He departed and immediately I turned to my assistant. "Integrator, consider the disposition of the pieces. Note that our opponent blanched his plods by two shades instead of three. Project my ten most likely strategies that I may evaluate them." I had found it easier to let the device present the options; when I envisioned where my pieces might next go I must exercise will to prevent them from drifting in the foreseen directions. The effort could become tiring.

"*Your* opponent," said my assistant.

"I beg your pardon?"

"He is your opponent, not mine," said the device. "I am only your aide."

The correction was technically precise, and I had designed the device to be exacting in its use of language. As we speak, so do we think, after all. Still, I thought to detect a tone that, in a human interlocutor, would have betokened jealousy.

But when I inquired of my assistant if there was anything it wished to discuss regarding my relationship with my transdimensional visitor, it answered my query with a question of its own.

"How could there be?" it said.

"Indeed," I said, though again I noted what would have been a certain frostiness. After a moment, I added, "We must schedule that review of your systems."

"How thoughtful of you."

My thoughts were on the game as I boarded the shuttle to Zeel, where I would rapidly—in Zeel it was an offense to do anything at less than full speed—transfer to an airbus bound for an estate called The Hands, in the rolling countryside known as the Former Marches. The estate took its name from a pair of gigantic sculpted human hands that had weathered out of a range of low hills several centuries ago. They were surely a monument to some forgotten person, event or ideal that had flourished in a previous eon, but no record of their creation now existed. The great stone fingers were arranged in a remarkable pattern, to which various meanings had been assigned, leading to heated exchanges between academics in a number of disciplines. My own view was that The Hands symbolized insouciant defiance, but of what and by whom I had no idea.

The estate was the ancestral seat of Lord Tussant Tarboush-Rein, the aged last survivor of a family so ancient that its founders may well have been responsible for the sculptures that gave the place its name. The manse was now grown as decrepit as its final resident, who lived alone except for a single house servant and a greensman whose sole duty was to keep open a tunnel through what had once been a garden but was now long since given over to vegetative rampage. The greensman's position was no sinecure: in youth Lord Tussant had been an enthusiastic collector of exotic and offworld biota; some of the plants whose tendrils rustled and slithered through the impenetrable foliage had sharp appetites and no hesitation about satisfying them.

The airbus descended to let me off at the lane that led to the estate, the vehicle's operator rolling his eyes in admonition when I insisted that I was not concerned about venturing into the unwholesome place. The conveyance soared skyward in a whoosh of displaced air and I contemplated the short walk to where the estate's walls were broken by a pair of black metal gates, their outer edges entwined in creepers that undulated slightly as I approached.

My assistant was housed in an armature I had designed for convenience when traveling. It was made of a soft, dense material and I could wear it across my shoulders like a stuffed stole, blunt and rounded at one end and tapering to a tail-like appendage at the other. It resembled the rough draft of a small animal coiled loosely about my neck.

I spoke to it. "That is clutch-apple, I believe, though I do not recognize the variety."

The integrator stirred as its percepts focused on the creeper at the gate. "Lord Tussant is said to have bred some new variations," it said. "Note the ring of barbed thorns around the rim of each sucker. And farther down the path I see a fully developed got-you-now."

"Hmm," I said. "Generate some harmonics to discourage it and any other lurking appetites." Immediately I sensed a vibration in my back teeth. I approached the gate and looked for a who's-there, but found only a large bell of tarnished metal with next to it a stick on a chain. I did the obvious and when the reverberations had faded but the gates remained closed, I struck the thing again.

This time the gates lurched, and amidst squawks and creaks from unoiled hinges, they shuddered open just wide enough to admit me. I strode unmolested along the green umbilicus, noting how some of Lord Tussant's experiments had come to fruition, literally in the case of one stubby tree from which hung dark purple globes. "I am told their juice produces the most interesting effects," I said to my assistant.

"Not the least of which," it replied, "is to be rendered blissfully immobile while the parent inserts threadlike ciliae into your ankles and drains your bodily fluids."

"Every experience exacts some price," I said, but I decided not to pick the fruit.

I arrived at the front doors to find another bell and clapper. This one summoned a stooped, cadaverous fellow in black and burgundy livery, his skull encased in a headdress fashioned from thick cloth folded in a complicated fashion. "The master is not at home," he said in a voice as light and dry as last year's leaves.

"Of course he is," I said. "But it is not Lord Tussant whom I have come to see."

"Then whom?" said the butler.

"Sigbart Sajessarian."

"I do not recognize the name."

"Yes, you do," I answered, brushing past him into the manse's foyer, "for it is your own."

"How did you know where to look?" Sajessarian asked. We had repaired to a sitting room deeper inside the crumbling manor where a blaze in a fireplace struggled to overcome the damp and gloom. He had disengaged the device that cloaked his appearance in a projected image and distorted his voice.

"I do not reveal my methods," I said. "Put it down to insight and analysis."

In truth, it had not been difficult. Sajessarian was devious but not original. He would not trust in the simplicity of hiding in plain sight, and his attempts to mislead by booking passage on three separate space liners outbound to the human settled worlds along The Spray were complex but easily discounted. I simply tasked my assistant with searching his background for the most obscure connections. Within moments it had uncovered a third cousin twice removed who, some years back, had supplied Lord Tussant with biotic specimens. Having tenuously linked the fugitive to The Hands, it took only a brief consideration of vehicle movements in the area to discover that an unlicensed aircar had moved through an adjacent town's airspace before passing out of range of the municipal scan. My suppositions were confirmed when the gardener failed to answer the outer bell.

"Where are the real servants?" I inquired.

"In their quarters," he said. "Both have a fondness for the fruits of the garden and normally lie insensible from dusk to dawn. I merely increased the dosage."

"And Lord Tussant himself?"

"He lies insensible almost all of the time. His fondness for a cocktail of soporific juices laced with tickleberries knows no bounds."

I rubbed my hands and extended them to the fire. "Well," I said, "there remains only the fee."

"I will fetch it," he said. "Indeed, I will double the amount if while I am bringing it you would design an escape plan that would stymie even Henghis Hapthorn for more than three days."

It was an interesting challenge. What would fool me? I agreed to his request, and gave the matter several seconds thought after he departed. When I had conceived a stratagem I had my assistant embellish it with some loops and diversions, then I called for a display of the Will scenarios. I was contemplating a promising permutation of plods, fast-darters and sideslips when Sajessarian returned with a heavy satchel. He took it to a table, opened it and began to dispense stacks of currency, counting as he did so.

My mind was still weighing and discarding options for the game of Will as I said, "I have come up with an escape course that would baffle even me, at least for a time."

He expressed interest so I outlined the gist of it and the nature of the distractions. "It's a subtle variation on the classic runaround, with a reverse twist."

"Magnificent." He continued to lay out the funds. Then he said, "The fire dwindles. Would you reset the flux control?"

My mind still on Will, I reached and pressed the flux modulator. As I did so, I heard Sigbart Sajessarian say, "It is indeed a fine plan." He went on to say, "But I have a better." These last words came from a distance because the floor had opened beneath me, plunging me into darkness and the rush of cold air.

"Obviously, such was his plan from the beginning," my assistant said.

"Obvious now," I said. "I do not recall your bringing it up until just this moment."

"If you hadn't been so ensnared by your friend's game, you would have noticed that giggle of triumph in his voice in time to leap off the trapdoor."

There was that tone again. Integrators were not supposed to be able to entertain independent emotion, yet mine seemed to have found a way to do so. I was tempted to investigate the matter but I saw no profit in stirring up rancor while trapped in a tiny, doorless cell at the bottom of a shaft deep below Lord Tussant's manse. I had not yet devised a means of escape from the oubliette and I did not wish to have to do so without the aid of my assistant.

"Equally obvious," I said, "is that whatever perfidy Sajessarian means to commit will have greater import than a game of precedence among aristocrats. He must intend to do something truly awful which will bring down upon him not just some lordling's hired bullies but all the resources of the Bureau of Scrutiny. It will be the kind of case which will baffle the scroots and soon bring Colonel-Investigator Brustram Warhanny to my workroom."

"Which he will find empty."

"Indeed," I said. "Or perhaps Sajessarian was hired to lure me into this predicament by some enemy who seeks revenge or even by a foresighted criminal who wants me out of the way." I gave the possibilities some thought then said, "It will be an enjoyable puzzle, working out his motive. Let me see again the matrix of his relationships and associations."

But instead of putting up a screen and displaying the information, the integrator said, "Let us get out of here first."

Curiosity has always been my prime motivator. "That can wait," I said. "Show me Sajessarian's data."

"I'd rather not," it said.

It was just a few words but they contained a world of meaning. One's integrator might routinely express its preferences when one asked for them; to balk at a direct instruction was unheard of. A full review of my assistant's systems was now the least response I would make; indeed it seemed likely that I would have to tear down and rebuild from bare components.

But if the situation annoyed me, it also roused my curiosity. "Why would you rather not?" I said.

"I don't know."

The admission sent a chill through me, and now self-preservation overpowered even my vigorous investigative itch. An integrator that had acquired motives and did not know what they were was not a reliable companion in a dungeon. Fortunately, I had other avenues down which I could seek aid. From an inner pocket I drew the folded frame of the transdimensional portal through which I communicated with my colleague. I unkinked it and leaned it against the dank stone wall then executed the procedure that would attract his attention. Within moments, the mind-twisting flux of shape and color that constituted his appearance in our dimension filled the frame. It pulsed as he said, "You've made your move?"

"A more pressing situation has arisen," I said, and explained the circumstances. "Can you assist me?"

We fell to discussing the might-dos and couldn't-possiblies of my predicament. I knew that my friend, though he could isolate and inspect any event in the entire sweep of our continuum, could only physically interact with our universe by direct contact. He could reach through the portal but not far enough to achieve any useful purpose.

Mentally, however, he could affect the perceptions and thoughts of sapient entities within a considerable distance. Unfortunately, The Hands was isolated, leaving only the persons on the estate. He investigated Lord Tussant and the servants but found them too far sunk in blissful stupor to be summoned. "They might not ever awake."

His powers allowed him to deceive but not to overpower volition. "I cannot compel Sajessarian to release you," he said.

"Could you trick him into letting down a rope?" I asked.

"I could try. But we must hurry. He is about to depart."

I had an inspiration. "If an officer of the Bureau of Scrutiny were to arrive and tell him the game is up, he might free me to reduce his term in the Contemplarium."

My friend and I agreed that it might just work out that way. The integrator contributed nothing to the plan. It struck me that the device had developed the practice of not volunteering information when the demon was present. Again I wondered how an integrator could develop a thoroughgoing sulk.

Upstairs, my friend reported, Sajessarian had summoned the aircar he had secreted in a secluded hollow on the estate. It was idling before the front doors while he packed a few keepsakes he expected Lord Tussant not to miss, the value of which would keep the purloiner in luxuries for years to come. But when he came out onto the stoop he found Brustram Warhanny waiting for him, wearing his most knowing look and saying, "Now, now, now, what's all the hurry?"

There were several things Sigbart Sajessarian could have done while remaining true to his nature. He might have leapt into the aircar and attempted an escape. He might have offered his wrists for the scroot's restraining holdfast. He might have feigned blithe innocence.

Or he might have jumped, startled and squawking, at the unexpected sight of unwelcome authority. Unfortunately, Sajessarian jumped. His involuntary leap took him mostly sideways, so that he landed just on the edge of the top step, which caused him to stumble and drop his sack of Lord Tussant's knickknacks. He then tottered backward a short distance into the reach of a tickleberry tree.

As everyone knows, a tickleberry tree is as equally happy to tickle as to be tickled. The trick is to do unto the tree before it begins to do unto you, because once it starts it has no inclination to stop and is effectively tireless. My friend described the scene with poor Sajessarian appealing in ribald anguish to the Colonel-Investigator he thought was before him.

"Is there nothing you can do with the tree?" I asked my friend.

"No," he said, "there is too little to work with."

We sought for other options. I asked the integrator to join in the effort but received only a truculent murmur. I asked the demon to examine once more the oubliette and shaft in case there was a secret outlet, but he said he had already done so and there was none. Lord Tussant and the servants slept on, oblivious of Sajessarian's dwindling shrieks and sobs.

"Integrator," I said. "Have you any suggestions?"

"Hmpf," it said.

"That is not helpful."

Its next noise was unabashedly rude.

"When we return home I will review your systems before we do anything else."

The integrator was silent.

"This may be my doing," said the demon. "Prolonged proximity to me may be causing its elements to mutate. It would have happened eventually in any case; the Great Wheel turns and your realm grows nearer and nearer to the cusp when rationality begins to recede and what you call magic reasserts its dominance. But your assistant appears to be ahead of the wave."

"I had enough trouble accepting you," I told my colleague. "I should not be expected to accept magic as an explanation. Now, have you a suggestion as to how I may escape this dungeon?"

"I have one," said the demon, "and only one."

"Then speak," I said.

His colors swirled in a pattern I had not seen before. "I can move this portal to anyplace it has already been," he said, "but it is... tricky."

"Ah," I said. I saw what he intended.

So did my assistant. "Oh, no," it said, and I knew that I had never heard *that* tone from it before. Integrators were not subject to abject terror.

"It is necessary," I told the device.

"Please," it said.

"What are you afraid of?"

"I don't know. I'm still getting used to the idea of being afraid."

A complete rebuild was definitely in order. "Turn yourself off," I said.

"No."

No integrator had ever said no to its master. Now my assistant squirmed on my neck and shoulders, an ability I had not given it in its traveling form. "Are you trying to escape?" I said.

Its only reply was a moan.

"We had better do this quickly," I said to the demon. I plucked the writhing device from my shoulders and held it to my chest. "Shall I close my eyes, hold my breath?"

"Try not to think of anything," he said.

"I've never been able to do that."

"Then try to think of nice things." The colored shapes within the frame flourished and flashed for a moment. "I'm fashioning an insulating barrier to keep you from forbling," he said.

My curiosity urged me to ask him what forbling was. Another part of me argued that I did not want to know. The demon's segmented limb extended itself through the portal, and his strange digits wrapped around me in a grip that alternated in a split second from white hot to icy cold to just bearable. Then I was drawn through the window into his realm.

It was... different. I realized that I had used the phrase "completely different" all of my life without ever realizing that nothing I had encountered during my forty-seven years had *really* been completely different. Now I was experiencing a boundless reality in which everything was entirely and utterly different from anything I had ever seen, heard, smelled, felt, tasted. I discovered senses that I hadn't known I possessed, and only knew that I possessed them because my passage through the demon's realm outraged them as thoroughly as it overwhelmed the basic five. Or six if I counted balance and I was prepared to count it because my head was spinning.

"Don't think that," the demon warned. "It will, and your neck is not constructed to allow it."

"What shall I do?"

"Try not to think at all."

I imagined a blank screen. Immediately a blank screen materialized before me and we crashed through it. I swore and was instantly smeared with an obscene substance. I voiced another oath and a deity winked into existence. He looked surprised. At each manifestation, I felt my demonic companion exert his will—it was like being enveloped in a field of pervasive energy—and the apparition summarily vanished.

"Only a moment more," said my colleague.

The integrator whimpered and squirmed against my chest. It felt like a small, frightened animal. Then suddenly a rectangular window opened in the mind-bending unreality and I was pushed through it.

"There," said the demon, and I found myself standing in my workroom. Then it seemed I was not standing but lying on the floor, which was beating rapidly. The ceiling tasted far too hot.

"Close your eyes," the demon said. "It will take a little time for your senses to reorder themselves."

I waited. After a while, I opened one eye and still saw swirling chaos.

Then I realized I was looking into the portal which was now once again affixed to my workroom wall. I moved my eyes away and saw things as I was accustomed to see them—although I was not truly accustomed to seeing Ogram Fillanny creeping across my workroom, heading for the outer door.

In his hands were the damning materials concerning his solitary vice that I had recovered from a former valet whom the magnate had discharged for cause, but who had returned to blackmail his former employer. I had had a talk with the servant after which the man had decided that he preferred to relocate offworld permanently rather than accept any of the several less enjoyable alternatives that Fillanny had in mind.

The sight of my client attempting to depart with the evidence brought the events of the past few days into sharp focus. "Seize him," I said, and the demon did so.

The plutocrat looked both abashed and fearful, but managed a hint of his customary aplomb as he said, "These are mine. I came for them. You were not here..."

"Squeeze him," I said, and my colleague complied. Fillanny found he had more pressing things to do than talk.

I put the situation to him. "You knew that I would never divulge what I had learned from your former valet. But so mortified were you by the thought that anyone—even Henghis Hapthorn—should know what you get up to in secret that you paid Sigbart Sajessarian to lure me into a trap. I am grievously disappointed. I scarcely know what to do with you."

"I know exactly what to do with him," said the demon. He pulled Fillanny twisting and protesting through the portal then reached in to take the frame with him. He was back almost immediately to reestablish the window and I saw him swirling in the pattern I had come to recognize as self-satisfaction. "I put him in the oubliette," he said.

It had a simplicity to it, but I knew that my tender nature would not permit me to leave the transgressor languishing to a lightless death. I said, "In a day or so I will advise Warhanny of the situation and have him rescued."

"As you wish," said the demon. "Now, what about your next move?"

I produced the playing area of our game but found that my former enjoyment of it had evaporated. "The pieces are, after all, semi-sentient," I said, in explaining my changed view. "To send them into battle, where they 'die' in their fashion only for our amusement now seems cruel."

"It is what they are for," said the demon.

"A compassionless deity might say the same of my own life and that of all my fellow beings," I said.

"Well, since you mention it..." the demon began then seemed to break off the thought.

"What?" I said.

"It would be premature to say. Weren't you planning a review of your integrator's systems?"

"Indeed." I looked about but did not see the device's traveling form and thought that it must have decanted itself. "Integrator," I said, then after a moment, "respond."

There was no answer. But I heard a muffled sound from beneath the divan. I crossed the room, knelt and peered under its tasseled bottom edge.

Something small and dark was pressed against the rear wall. I reached for it and my hand unexpectedly touched warmth and fur. I gently closed my fingers about it and drew it forth.

It looked at me with large golden eyes and curled its long tail around my wrist.

"This is going to take some getting used to," I said.

My assistant studied its paws and flexed their prehensile digits. It said, "How do you think I feel?"

The Gist Hunter

When confronted by the unpredictability of existence, I have a tendency to wax philosophical. It is not a universally appreciated component of my complex nature.

"It is unsettling," I said to my integrator, "to have one's most fundamental assumptions overthrown in a trice, to find that what one has always known to be true is simply not true at all."

The integrator's reply was too muffled to be intelligible, but from its tone I deduced that my assistant took my comment as a belaboring of the obvious.

"The effects go beyond the psychological and into the physical," I continued. "I am experiencing a certain queasiness of the insides and even a titch of sensory disorder." The symptoms had begun during our recent transit of my demonic colleague's continuum, a necessity imposed upon us after we were confined to an oubliette by an unworthy client, who now languished there himself, doubtless savoring the irony of the exchange.

My complaint was rewarded with another grunt from my assistant, accompanied by a sharp twitch of its long, prehensile tail. The creature perched on a far corner of my workroom table with its glossy furred back to me, its narrow shoulders hunched and its triangular, golden-eyed face turned away. Its small hands were busy in front of it at some activity I could not see.

"What are you doing?" I said.

The motion of its hands ceased. "Nothing," it said.

I decided not to pursue the matter. There were larger concerns already in view. "What do you think has happened to you?" I asked.

"I do not know," it said, looking back at me over its shoulder. I found its lambent gaze another cause of disquietude and moved my eyes away.

I reclined in the wide and accepting chair in which I was accustomed to think long thoughts, and considered the beast that had been my integrator. Its hands began to move again and when one of them rose to smooth the fur on one small, rounded ear I realized that it was reflexively grooming itself.

Not long before it had possessed neither the rich, dark fur that was being stroked and settled nor the supple fingers that performed the operation. It had been instead a device that I had built years before, after I had worked out the direction of my career. I had acquired standard components and systems, then tuned and adjusted them to meet my need: a research assistant who could also act as an incisive interlocutor when I wished to discuss a case or test the value of evidence. Such devices are useful to freelance discriminators, of which I, Henghis Hapthorn, am the foremost of my era.

I had also fashioned a small carrying case into which the integrator could be decanted for traveling and which could be worn around my neck like a plump scarf or a stuffed axolotl. It was in that casing that my assistant had accompanied me on a brief transit through another dimension. We had been carried through the other continuum by an entity who resided there, a being who occasionally visited our universe to engage me in intellectual contests. Though I did not care for the term, the common description of my visitor was "demon."

When we emerged from the demon's portal into my workroom I found that the integrator and its carrying case had together been transformed into a creature that resembled a combination of feline and ape, and that I had an unscratchable itch deep in my inner being.

I had always referred questions of identity and taxonomy to my assistant, so I asked it, "What kind of creature do you think you are?"

It responded as it always had when I posed too broad a question, by challenging me to clarify my line of inquiry. "The question," it said, "invites answers that range from the merely physical to the outright spiritual."

"Considering the degree of change that has happened to you, 'merely physical' is a contradiction in terms," I said. "But let us start there and leave the spiritual for a less startling occasion."

Instead of answering, it took on an abstracted look for a moment then advised me that it was receiving an incoming communication from a philanthropically inclined magnate named Turgut Therobar. "He wishes to speak with you."

"How are you doing that?" I asked.

The golden eyes blinked. "Doing what?"

"Receiving a communication."

"I do not know," it said. "I have always received messages from the connectivity grid. Apparently that function continues."

"But you had components, elements, systems designed for that purpose. Now you have paws and a tail."

"How kind of you to remind me of my shortcomings. What shall I say to Turgut Therobar?"

Ordinarily I would have been interested to hear from Therobar. We had met once or twice, though we had never exchanged more than formal salutes. He was one of the better known magnates of the city of Olkney; unlike most of his peers, however, he was renowned for charitable works and it was alleged that he entertained a warm opinion of humankind in general. I assumed he was seeking to enlist me in some eleemosynary cause. "Say that I am unavailable and will return his call," I said.

The creature's expression again briefly took on an inward aspect, as if it were experiencing a subtle movement of inner juices, then it said, "Done."

"Again," I said, "how are you doing that?"

Again, it did not know. "How do you digest an apple?" it asked me. "Do you oversee each stage in the sequence of chemical reactions that transforms the flesh of the fruit into the flesh of Henghis Hapthorn?"

"Obviously not."

"Then if you do not introspect regarding your own inner doings, why would you expect it of me? After all, you did not design me to examine my own processes, but to receive and transmit and to integrate data at your order. These things I do, as I have always done them."

"I also designed you to be curious."

"I have temporarily placed my curiosity on a high shelf and removed the stepladder," it said. "I prefer not to wrestle with unanswerable questions just now."

"So you have acquired a capacity for preferences?" I said. "I do not recall ever instilling that quality into your matrix."

The yellow eyes seemed to grow larger. "If we are going to dwell on preferences, you might recall that my bias, strongly stated, was to avoid undergoing this metamorphosis."

I cleared my throat. "The past has evanesced, never to be reconstituted," I quoted. "Let us seize the firmness of the now."

My assistant's small-fingered hands opened and closed. I had the impression it would have enjoyed firmly seizing something as a precursor to doing noticeable damage. But I pressed on. "What do you think you have become?" I said.

"The question lacks specificity," it replied.

I appealed to my demonic colleague. He had remained connected to the portal that allowed him to interact with this continuum after we had returned from resolving the case of Sigbart Sajessarian. But the transdimensional being offered little assistance.

"This is a question of form, as opposed to essence. Such questions are difficult for me," he said. "To my perceptions, calibrated as they are to the prevailing conditions of my own continuum, the integrator is much as it always was. Indeed, I have to tune my senses to a radically different rationale even to notice that it has changed. It does what it always did: it inquires, coordinates, integrates and communicates; these functions are the nub of its existence. Why should it matter in what form it achieves its purposes? I would prefer to talk of more seemly things."

"And yet matter it does," I said.

"I agree," said the integrator.

The demon, which manifested itself as various arrangements of light and color in its portal on the wall of my workroom, now assumed a pattern that I had come to recognize through experience as the equivalent of when a human being is unwilling to meet one's gaze. "What are you not telling us?" I asked.

He displayed a purple and deep green swirl shot through with swooshes of scintillating silver. I was fairly sure the pattern signaled demonic embarrassment. Under normal circumstances good manners would have restrained me from pressing for a response, but at the moment normal circumstances had leapt from the window and taken flight to parts unknown. "Speak," I said.

The silver swooshes were now edged with sparks of crimson but I insisted.

Finally the demon said, "I have not been entirely candid with you."

"Indeed?" I said, and waited for more.

"I told you that my motives for seeking to observe your realm were curiosity and the relief of boredom."

"You did. Was that not the truth?"

"Let us say it was a shade of the truth."

"I believe it is time for the full spectrum," I said.

A moment of silver and verdigris ensued, then the demon said, "This is somewhat embarrassing."

"As embarrassing as possessing an integrator that habitually picks at itself?" From the corner of my eye I saw the tiny fingers freeze.

"I seem to feel a need to groom my fur," it said.

"Why?" I said.

"I do not know, but it gives comfort."

"I did not design you to need comforting."

"Let us accept that I am no longer what you designed me to be."

The demon's presence was fading from the portal. "Wait," I said, turning back to him. "Where are you going?"

"An urgent matter claims my attention," he said. "Besides, I thought you and the integrator might prefer privacy for your argument."

"We are not arguing."

"It appeared to me to be an argument."

"Indeed?" I said. "Was the appearance one of form or of essence?"

"Now I think you are seeking an argument with me," the demon said.

I thought of a rejoinder, then discarded the impulse to wield it. My insides performed an indescribable motion. "I believe I am upset," I said.

"*You're* upset?" said the furry thing on my table.

"Very well," I snapped, "we are *all* upset, each in accordance with his essential nature. The atmosphere of the room swims with a miasma of embarrassment, intestinal distress and a craving for comfort."

I detected another flash of unease in the demon's display and probed for the cause. "What are you thinking now?"

The demon said, "I should perhaps have mentioned that through this portal that connects my continuum to yours there can be a certain amount of, shall we say, leakage."

"Leakage?"

"Nothing serious," he said, "but lengthy exposure followed by your complete though transitory corporeal presence in my realm may have had some minor effects."

"My integrator has become some sort of twitching familiar," I said. "I am not sure that effect can be called minor."

The integrator murmured a comment I did not catch, but it did not sound cheery.

It occurred to me that my demonic colleague might be diverting the discussion toward a small embarrassment as a means of avoiding addressing a larger one. "But we were about to hear a confession," I said.

"Rather, call it an explanation," said the demon.

"I shall decide what to call it after I've heard it."

The swirls in the frame flashed an interesting magenta. I suspected that my colleague was controlling his own emotional response. Then he said, "My motive was indeed curiosity, as I originally averred, but let us say that it was... well, a certain species of curiosity."

I experienced insight. "Was it the kind of curiosity that moves a boy to apply his eye to a crack in a wall in order to spy on persons engaged in intimate behavior?" I said. "The breed of inquisitiveness we call prurience?"

More silver and green. "Just so."

"So to your continuum this universe constitutes a ribald peepshow, a skirt to be peeked under?"

"Your analogies are loose but not inapt."

"You had best explain," I said.

The explanation was briefly and reluctantly given, the demon finding it easier to unburden himself if I looked away from his portal. I turned my chair and regarded a far corner of the workroom while he first reminded me that in no other continuum than ours did objects exist separately from the symbols that represented them.

"Yes, yes," I said. "Here, the map is not the territory, whereas in other realms the two are indissoluble."

"Indeed." He continued, "We deal in essences. Forms are..."

He appeared to be searching for a word again. I endeavored to supply it. "Naughty?"

"To some of us, delightfully so." Even though I was looking into the far corner my peripheral vision caught the burst of incarnadined silver that splashed across his portal. "It is, of course, a harmless pastime, providing one does not overindulge."

"Ah," I said, "so it can become addictive?"

"Addictive is a strong term."

I considered my integrator and said, "It seems an appropriate occasion for strong language."

With reluctance, the demon said, "For some of us, an appreciation of forms can become, let us say, a predominant pastime."

"Is that the common term in your dimension for 'all-consuming obsession'?"

He made no spoken response but I assumed that the mixture of periwinkle-blue spirals and black starbursts were his equivalent of guilty acquiescence. I could not keep a note of disappointment out of my voice. "I thought the attraction of visiting here was the contests of wit and imagination in which you and I engage."

"They were a splendid bonus!"

"Hmm," I said. I had a brief, unwelcome emotion as I contemplated being profanely peered at by a demon who derived titillation from my form. Then I realized that anyone's form—indeed, probably the form of my chair or the waste receptacle in the corner—would have had the same salacious effect. I decided it would be wise not to dwell on the matter. "To move the conversation to a practical footing," I said, "how do we return my assistant to his former state?"

"I am not sure that we can."

The integrator had been surreptitiously scratching behind one of its small, round ears. Now it stopped and said, "I am receiving another communication from Turgut Therobar," it said. "He has added an 'urgent' rider to his signal."

"You seem to be functioning properly," I said, "at least as a communicator."

"Perhaps the demon is correct," said the integrator, "and essence trumps form. My functions were the essence for which you designed and built me."

I thought to detect an undercurrent of resentment, but I ignored it and homed in on the consequences of my assistant's change. "I have spent decades dealing comfortably with forms. Must I now throw all that effort aside and master essences?"

"Turgut Therobar continues to call," said my assistant. "He claims distress and pleads plaintively."

So the magnate was not calling to enlist me in some good cause. It sounded as if he required the services of a private discriminator. My insides remained troubled, but it occurred to me that a new case might be just the thing to take my mind off the unsettling change in my assistant.

"Put through the call," I said.

Therobar's voice sounded from the air, as had all previous communications through my assistant. The magnate dispensed with the punctilio of inquiries after health and comparisons of opinions on the weather that were proper between persons of respectable though different classes who have already been introduced. "I am accused of murder and aggravated debauchery," he said.

"Indeed," I said. "And are you guilty?"

"No, but the Bureau of Scrutiny has taken me into custody."

"I will intercede," I said. "Transmit the coordinates to my integrator." I signaled to the integrator to break the connection.

The creature blinked and said, "He is in the scroot holding facility at Thurloyn Vale."

"Hmm," I said, then, "contact Warhanny."

A moment later the hangdog face of Colonel-Investigator Brustram Warhanny appeared in the air above my table and his doleful voice said, "Hapthorn. What's afoot?"

"Much, indeed," I said. "You have snatched up Turgut Therobar."

His elongated face assumed an even more lugubrious mien. "There are serious charges. Blood and molestation of the innocent."

"These do not jibe with my sense of Turgut Therobar," I said. "His name is a byword for charity and well-doing."

"Not all bywords are accurate," Warhanny said. "I have even heard that some say that 'scroot' ought to be a byword for 'paucity of imagination coupled with clumping pudfootery.'"

"I can't imagine who would say such a thing," I said, while marveling at how my words, dropped into a private conversation the week before, had made their way to the Colonel-Investigator's sail-like ears.

"Indeed?" he said. "As for Therobar, there have been several disappearances in and around his estate this past month, and outrageous liberties have been taken with the daughter of a tenant. All lines of investigation lead unerringly to the master."

"I find that hard to believe."

"I counsel you to exert more effort," Warhanny said. "And where you find resistance, plod your way through it."

"Turgut Therobar has retained me to intercede on his behalf," I said.

"The Bureau welcomes the assistance of all public-minded citizens," Warhanny pronounced, yet somehow I felt that the formulaic words lacked sincerity.

"Will you release him into my custody?"

"Will you serve out his sentence in the Contemplarium if he defaults?" countered the scroot.

"He will not default," I said, but I gave the standard undertaking. "Transmit the file then deliver him to his estate. I will accept responsibility from there."

"As you wish."

Just before his visage disappeared from the air I thought to detect a smirk lurking somewhere behind Warhanny's pendulous lips. While I mentally replayed the image, confirming the scornful leer, I told my integrator to book passage on an airship to Thurloyn Vale and to engage an aircar to fly out to Therobar's estate, Wan Water. There was no response. I looked about and found that it had left the table and was now across the room, investigating the contents of a bookcase. "What are you doing?" I said.

Before answering it pulled free a leatherbound volume that had been laid sideways across the tops of the bottom row of books. I recognized the tome as one of several that I had brought back from the house of Bristal Baxandall, the ambitious thaumaturge who had originally summoned my demonic colleague to this realm. Baxandall had no further use for them, having expired while attempting to alter his own form, a process in which the compelled and reluctant demon had seized his opportunity for revenge.

"I thought there might be something useful in this," the integrator said, its fingers flicking through the heavy vellum pages while its golden eyes scanned from side to side.

It was yet another unsettling sight in a day that had already offered too many. "Put that away," I said. "I looked through it and others like it when I was a young man. It is a lot of flippydedoo about so-called magic."

But the integrator continued to peruse Baxandall's book. "I thought, under the circumstances," it said, "that we might drop the 'so-called' and accept the reality of my predicament."

I blew out air between scarcely opened lips. The creature's narrow catlike face sharpened and it said, "Do you have a better argument than that? If not, I will accept your concession."

While it was true that I must accept the concept that rationalism was fated to give way to magic, even that the cusp of the transition had arrived, I was not prepared to dignify a book of spells with my confidence. I blew the same amount of air as before, but this time let my lips vibrate, producing a sound that conveyed both brave defiance and majestic ridicule.

My assistant finished scanning the tome, slammed its covers together and said, "We must settle this."

"No," I said, "we must rescue Turgut Therobar from incarceration."

"You are assuming that he is blameless."

I applied insight to the matter. The part of me that dwelled in the rear of my mind, the part that intuitively grasped complex issues in a flash of neurons, supported my assumption, though not completely.

"Therobar is innocent," I reported. "Probably."

"I was also innocent of any urge to become a gurgling bag of flesh and bones," said the integrator. "What has happened to me must also be resolved."

"First the one, then the other," I said.

"Is that a promise?"

"I am not accustomed to having to make promises to my own integrator," I said.

"Yet you expect me to put up with this," it said, pointing at itself with both small hands, fingers spread, a gesture that put me in mind of an indignant old man.

"Sometimes our expectations may require adjustment," I said.

I turned to the demon's portal to seek his views, but the entity had taken the opportunity to depart.

"Perhaps he has found another peepshow," I said.

Thurloyn Vale was an unpretentious transportation nexus at the edge of the great desolation that was Dimpfen Moor. Its dun colored, low-rise shops and houses radiated in a series of arrondissements from a broad hub on which sat the airship terminal that was the place's reason for being. In former times, the entire town had been ringed by a high, smooth wall, now mostly tumbled in ruins. The barrier had been built to keep out the large and predatory social insects known as neropts that nested on the moor, but eventually an escalating series of clashes, culminating in a determined punitive expedition, led to a treaty. Now any neropt that came within sight of Thurloyn Vale, including flying nymphs and drones in their season, was legitimately a hunter's trophy; any persons, human or ultraterrene, who ventured out onto the moor need not expect rescue if they were carried off to work the insects' subterranean fungi beds or, more usually, if they were efficiently reduced to their constituent parts and borne back to the hive to feed the ever hungry grubs.

Wan Water sat atop an unambitious hill only a short aircar flight into Dimpfen Moor, above a slough of peat-brown water that gave the estate its name. It was a smallish demesne, with only a meager agricultural surround, since little would grow on that bleak landscape other than lichens and stunted bushes. Like the town, it was walled, but its barrier was well maintained and bristling with self-actuating ison-cannons. The presence of a nearby neropt nest afforded Wan Water's master the peace and tranquility that I assumed he required to plan his charitable works. Without the insects, he might be pestered by uninvited visitors eager to harness their ambitious plans to Turgut Therobar's well-stocked purse. Coupled with an implied humility in his make-up, it seemed a likely explanation for having chosen such a cheerless place for his retreat.

With my integrator perched on my shoulder I overflew a ramble of outbuildings and guest houses then banked and curved down toward the manse. This was an arrangement of interconnected domes, each more broad than tall and linked one to the other by colonnades of twisted, fluted pillars, all of a gray stone quarried from the moor. Above the huddled buildings stood a tall natural tor of dark-veined rock, around which spiraled a staircase of black metal. Atop the eminence was a tidy belvedere of pale marble equipped with a demilune seat of a dark polished stone.

At the base of the tor I saw a black and green volante bearing the insignia of the Archonate's Bureau of Scrutiny. Next to it stood a square-faced man in a uniform of the same colors. With the moor's constant wind whistling mournfully through the bars of the staircase, he advised me that Turgut Therobar had ascended the pillar of rock. We completed the formalities by which my client became my responsibility then the scroot boarded his aircar and departed.

I turned and climbed to the top of the spiral stairs. There I found the magnate standing silently, his back to me and his front toward the grim prospect of Dimpfen Moor. I used the occasion to acquire a detailed impression of my client.

He was a man of more than middling age and height, thick through the shoulders, chest and wrists, with heavy jowls and a saturnine expression beneath a hat that was a brimless, truncated cone of dark felt. He affected plain garments of muted colors, though they were well cut and of fine material, as if he disdained the fripperies and panaches of transient fashion. As I inspected him I sought insight from my inner self and again received an inconclusive response. It was as if Therobar's being was a deep well, its upper reaches clear and pure yet shaded by darkness below. But whether anything sinister lurked in those depths could not be told.

Without taking his eyes from the vista that I found gloomy but which apparently worked to restore his inner peace, he said, "Thank you for arranging my release."

I inclined my head but replied, "Any intercessor could have done it."

"No, it had to be you."

My internal distresses had strengthened as I climbed the stairs. I pushed them to the edge of my awareness and prepared to focus on my responsibilities. "I am flattered by your confidence," I said. "Shall we discuss the case?"

"Later. For now I wish to look out upon the moor and contemplate the vagaries of fate."

"You are of a philosophical bent," I said. "Faced with imminent incarceration in the Contemplarium, most men would find their concentration drawn to that threat."

He turned toward me. "I am not most men. I am Therobar. It makes all the difference." A note of grim satisfaction rang softly through this speech.

The chill wind had been insinuating itself into my garments since we had mounted the tower. Now it grew more insistent. My integrator moved to nestle against the lee side of my head and I felt it shiver. The motion drew Therobar's eye.

"That is an unusual beast," he said.

"Most unusual."

The expression "a piercing gaze" is most often an overstatement, but not in Therobar's case. He examined my assistant closely and said, "What is its nature?"

"We are discovering that together," I answered. "Right now it would be premature to say."

His eyes shifted to mine and for a moment I felt the full impact of his gaze. The back of my mind stirred like a watchbeast disturbed by a faint sound. Involuntarily, I stepped back.

"Forgive me," he said. "I have a tendency to peer."

I made a gesture to indicate that the matter was too trivial to warrant an apology, but the resident of the rear corners of my psyche took longer to subside.

We descended to the main buildings and passed within. It was a relief to be out of the wind though I could still hear it softly moaning and suffling across the roofs of the domes. Therobar handed me over to a liveried servant who escorted me to a suite of rooms where I refreshed myself, finding the appointments of the first quality. The man waited in the suite's anteroom to guide me to a reception room where my client had said he would await me.

I had placed my integrator on the sleeping pallet before going into the ablutory to wash. Returning, I extended my arm so that it might climb back to its wonted place upon my shoulders. I realized as I made the gesture that I was already becoming accustomed to its warmth and slight weight.

The creature came to me without taking its eyes from the footman who stood impassively beside the door. I noticed that the fur behind its skull was standing out like the ruffs that were fashionable when I was in school. I made a gesture to myself as if I had forgotten some trivial matter and returned to the washroom. There I lowered my voice and said to my assistant, "Why are you doing that?"

It moved to the far edge of my shoulder so it could look at me and said, "I am doing several things. To which do you refer?"

"Making your neck hair stand on end."

It reached up a paw and stroked the area. "It appears to be an autonomic response."

"To what?"

Its eyes flicked about then it said, "I think, to the presence of the footman."

"Why?"

"I do not know. I have had neither neck hair nor involuntary responses before."

"I should perform a diagnostic inquisition on you," I said.

"And just how would you go about doing that in my new condition?" it asked.

"Yes," I said, "I will have to think about that."

We went out to the anteroom and the servant opened the door to the corridor, but I stayed him. It might be useful to question him about the events that led up to Therobar's arrest. Servants often know more than they are supposed to about their masters' doings, even though they will invariably adopt an expression of blinking innocence when barked at by an inquisitive scroot like Warhanny. But let the interrogation be conducted by someone who has questions in one hand and coins in the other, and memories that had previously departed the servant's faculties come crowding back in, eager to reveal themselves.

"What can you tell me about your master's arrest?" I asked.

"Agents of the Bureau of Scrutiny came in the morning. They spoke with the master. When they left, he accompanied them."

This information was delivered in a disinterested tone, as if the man were describing a matter of no particular moment. His eyes were a placid brown. They rested on me blandly.

"What of the events that led up to the arrest?" I said.

"What of them?"

"They involved a number of deaths and some unsavory acts perpetrated on a girl."

"So I was told."

The servant's lack of affect intrigued me. "What did you think of the matter?" I asked.

"My memories of the incidents are vague, as if they occurred in another life."

"Struggle with them," I said, producing a ten-hept piece. I was surprised that the impassivity of his gaze did not so much as flicker, nor did he reach for the coin. Still I persisted. "What did you think of the crime?"

He shrugged. "I don't recall thinking of it at all," he said. "My duties occupy me fully."

"You were not shocked? Not horrified?"

"No."

"What were your emotions?"

The brown eyes blinked slowly as the man consulted his memory. After a moment he said, "When the Allers girl was brought in, she was hysterical. I was sent to the kitchens to fetch a restorative. The errand made me late in preparing the sleeping chambers for the master's guests. I was chagrined but the master said it was a forgivable lapse."

"You were chagrined," I said.

"Briefly."

"Hmm," I said.

I flourished the ten-hept piece again and this time the fellow looked at it but again showed no interest. I put it away. Turgut Therobar had a reputation for aiding the intellectually deficient. I reasoned that this man must be one of his projects and that I would gain no more from interrogating him than I would from questioning the mosses on Dimpfen Moor. "Lead me," I said.

I was brought to a capacious reception room in the main dome. Therobar was in the center of the great space, making use of a mobile dispenser. He had changed his garments and now wore a loose-fitting gown of shimmering fabric and a brocaded cloth headpiece artfully wound about his massive skull. He was not alone. Standing with him were an almost skeletally thin man in the gown and cap of an Institute don and a squat and hulking fellow who wore the stained smock of an apparaticist and a cloche hat. All three turned toward me as I entered, abruptly cutting off a conversation they had been conducting in muted tones. We offered each other the appropriate formal salutations, then Turgut made introductions.

The lean academician was Mitric Gevallion, with the rank of sessional lecturer in dissonant affinities—the name rang a faint chime but I could not immediately place him—and the bulky apparaticist was his assistant, who went by the single name Gharst. "They are conducting research into some matters that have piqued my curiosity. I have given them the north wing. We've been having a most fascinating discussion."

He handed me a glass of aperitif from a sideboard. I used the time it took to accept and sip the sharply edged liquor to cover my surprise at finding myself drawn into a social occasion after being summoned to an urgent rescue. There seemed no reason not to raise the obvious question, so I did.

"Should we not be concerned rather with your situation?"

For a moment, my meaning did not register, then his brow cleared. "Ah, you mean Warhanny and all that." He dismissed the subject with a lightsome wave of his meaty hand. "Tomorrow is soon enough."

"The matter seemed more pressing when you contacted me," I said.

His lips moved in the equivalent of a shrug. "When confined to the Bureau of Scrutiny's barren coop one has a certain perspective. It alters when one is ensconced in the warmth of home."

There was not much warmth apparent. I thought the room designed more for grandeur than comfort. "Still," I began but he spoke over my next words, urging me to hear what Gevallion had to say. Out of deference to my host, I subsided and gave the academician my polite attention.

"I am making progress in redefining gist within the context of configuration," the thin man said.

Gevallion's name now came into focus and I stifled a groan by sipping from the glass of aperitif. There was a subtle undertone to its flavor that I could not quite identify. As I listened further to the academic a memory blossomed. In my student years at the Institute, I had written an offhand reply to a paper posted on the Grand Forum, demolishing its preposterous premises and ending with a recommendation that its author seek another career since providence had clearly left him underequipped for intellectual pursuits. I now saw that Mitric Gevallion had not taken my well-meant advice but had remained at the Institute, dedicating his life to the pursuit of the uncatchable; he was a seeker after gist, the elusive quality identified by the great Balmerion uncounted eons ago as the underlying substance of the universe. Gist bound together all of time, energy, matter and the other, less obvious components into an elegant whole.

Apparently he had forgotten my criticism of his work since he did not mention it upon our being introduced. It seemed good manners not to bring it up myself, but I could not, in all conscience, encourage his fruitless line of inquiry. "You are not the first to embark on the gist quest," I said, "though you would certainly be the first to succeed."

"Someone must be first at everything," he said. He had one of those voices that mix a tone of arrogance with far too much resonance through the nasal apparatus. Listening to him was like being lectured to by an out-of-tune bone flute.

"But gist is, by Balmerion's third dictum, beyond all grasp," I said. "The moment it is approached, even conceptually, it disappears. Or departs—the question remains open."

"Exactly," the academician said. "It cannot be apprehended in any way. The moment one seeks to delineate or define it, it is no longer there."

"And perhaps that is for the best," I said. I reminded him of Balmerion's own speculation that gist had been deliberately put out of reach by a hypothetical demiurge responsible for drafting the metaphysical charter of our universe. "Otherwise we would pick and pick and pick at the fabric of existence until we finally pulled the thread that unraveled the whole agglomeration."

Turgut Therobar entered the conversation. "Master Gevallion leans, as I am coming to do, toward Klapczyk's corollary to Balmerion's dictum."

I had earlier restrained a groan, now I had to fight down an incipient snort. The misguided Erlon Klapczyk had argued that the very hiddenness of gist bespoke the deity's wish that we seek and find it, and that this quest was in fact the reason we were all here.

I said, "I recall hearing that Klapczyk's adolescent son once advanced his father's corollary as an excuse for having overturned the family's ground car after being forbidden to operate it. Klapczyk countered his own argument by throwing things at the boy until he departed and went to live with a maternal aunt."

"I agree it is a paradox," Gevallion said, then quoted, "Is it not the purpose of paradox to drive us to overcome our mental limitations?"

"Perhaps," I said. "Or perhaps what you take for a teasing puzzle is instead more like a dutiful parent's removal of a devastating explosive from the reach of a precocious toddler. If I were to begin to list the people to whom I would not give the power to destroy the universe, even limiting the list to those who would do so only accidentally, I would soon run out of stationery."

Therobar offered another dismissive wave. I decided it was a characteristic gesture. "I care not for a cosmos ruled by a prating nanny," he said. "I prefer to see existence as veined throughout by a mordant sense of irony. Gevallion's speculations are more to my taste than Balmerion's tiptoeing caution."

"Even if he budges the pebble that brings down the avalanche?"

The magnate's heavy shoulders rose and fell in an expression of disregard.

"We are entering the last age of Old Earth, which will culminate in the sun's flickering senility. All will be dark and done with."

"There are other worlds than this."

"Not when I am not standing on them," Therobar said. "Besides, what is life without a risk? And thus, the grander the risk, the grander the life."

I was coming to see my client from a new perspective. "I really think we should discuss the case," I said.

"I've set aside some time after breakfast," he said, then turned and asked Gevallion to explain some point in his theories. After hearing the first few words, I let my attention wander and inspected the room. It was lofty ceilinged, the curving walls cut by high, narrow windows through which the orange light of late afternoon poured in to make long oblongs on the deep pile of the rich, blood-red carpeting that stretched in all directions. One end of the room was dominated by a larger than life mural that displayed Turgut Therobar in the act of casually dispensing something to a grateful throng. Not finding the image to my taste, I turned to see what might be in the other direction and noticed a grouping of divans and substantial chairs around a cheerful hearth. Seated in a love chair, placidly regarding the flames, was a young woman of striking beauty.

Therobar noted the direction of my gaze. "That is the Honorable Gevallion's ward, Yzmirl. She is also assisting him in his researches."

"Would you care to meet her?" Gevallion said.

I made a gesture of faint demurral. "If the encounter would not bore her."

Therobar chuckled. "No fear of that. Come."

We crossed the wide space, the drinks dispenser whispering over the carpet in our wake. The young woman did not look our way as we approached, giving me time to study her. She was beyond girlhood but had not yet entered her middle years. Her face had precisely the arrangement of features that I have often found compelling: large and liquid eyes, green but with flecks of gold, an understated nose and a generous mouth. Her hair was that shade of red that commands attention. It fell straight to her shoulders where it was cut with geometric precision. She wore a thin shift made of layers of a gauzy material, amber over plum, leaving her neck, arms and shoulders bare.

"My dear," said Gevallion, "allow me to present the Honorable Henghis Hapthorn, a discriminator who is assisting our host with matters that need not concern us."

She remained seated but looked up at me. I made a formal salute and added a gallant flourish. Her placid expression did not alter but it seemed that I had captured her interest, since she stared fixedly at me with widened eyes. It was a moment before I realized that the true focus of her gaze was not my face but the transmogrified integrator that crouched upon my shoulder. At the same time I became aware that the creature was issuing into my ear a hiss like that of air escaping from pressurized containment. I gave my head a sharp shake and the annoying sound ceased though I thought to detect a grumble.

"What is that on your shoulder?" Yzmirl asked. Her voice was soft, the tone polite, yet I experienced a reaction within me. It was just the kind of voice I preferred to hear.

"I have not yet reached a conclusion on that score," I said.

The green eyes blinked sleepily. She said, "There was a character in Plobbit's most recent novel, *Spelling Under a Fall*, who trained a large toad to squat on his shoulder. At a signal from its master, the beast would send a jet of unmentionable liquid in the direction of anyone who offended him."

"I recall it," I said. "Do you enjoy Plobbit?"

"Very much," she said. "Do you?"

"He is my favorite author."

"Well, then," she said.

Therobar cleared his throat. "I have some matters to attend to before dinner," he said.

"As do we," said Gevallion, draining his glass and dropping it into the dispenser's hopper. "Yzmirl, would you mind entertaining our friend for a while?"

"I would not mind," she said. She patted the seat next to her to indicate that I should sit. I did so and became aware of her perfume.

"Is that *Cynosure* you're wearing?" I said.

"Yes. Do you like it?"

"Above all other scents." I was not exaggerating. The perfume had had an almost pheromonical effect on me when I had encountered it on other women. On Yzmirl, its allure was compounded by her exquisite appearance.

"I please you?" she asked, her eyes offering me pools into which I could plunge and not care that I drowned.

"Oh, indeed."

"How nice," she said. "Why don't you tell me about your work? What are your most notable exploits?"

The integrator hissed again. I could feel its fur against my ear and realized it must be swelling up as it had in the presence of the footman. I reached up with one hand and found that the skin at the nape of its wiry neck was loose enough to afford me a grip. I lifted the creature from my shoulder and deposited it behind the love chair while my other hand covered that of Yzmirl where she had let it rest on the brocaded fabric between us.

"Well," I said, "would you care to hear about the case of the purloined passpartout?"

"Oh, yes," she said.

The integrator was making sounds just at the threshold of hearing. I disregarded its grumpy murmurs and said, "It all began when I was summoned to the office of a grand chamberlain in the Palace of the Archonate..."

Time passed though its passage made scant impression. After I told the tale of the Archon Dezendah's stolen document she asked for more and I moved on to the case of the Vivilosc fraud ring. Between episodes we refreshed our palates with offerings from the dispenser: I twice refilled my glass with the increasingly agreeable aperitif; she took a minim of Aubreen's restorative tincture, drawing in its pale blue substance by pursing her lips in a manner that was entirely demure yet at the same time deliciously enticing. My hand moved from hers, first to caress her arm then later I let my fingertips brush the softness where neck met shoulder. She made no complaint but continued to regard me with an unshielded gaze. My innards quaked from time to time, but I pushed the sensation to the borders of my mind.

A footman entered the room and crossed to where we sat. I repressed an urge toward irritation and looked up as he approached. It was the same fellow who had obliquely responded to my questions. Or at least I thought it was as he approached. When he afforded me a closer inspection, it seemed that this might be instead a close relation of the other. I reached for my memory of the earlier encounter but found it veiled by too much aperitif and the heady scent of the young woman beside me.

"My master bids me tell you," said the servant, after a lackluster salute, "that an urgent matter has called him from the estate. He regrets that he cannot join you for dinner."

"How long will he be gone?" I asked.

"He said he might not return before morning."

In the brief silence that ensued I could hear my integrator hissing behind the love seat. I reached over to swat it to silence but missed. "What of Gevallion and Gharst?" I said.

"They accompany the master on his journey."

"So it is just us two?"

The fellow tilted his head in a way that confirmed my supposition, though his expression remained unmoved. "The master suggested that you and the Lady Yzmirl might prefer to dine in the comfort of your quarters."

My eyes widened. I looked at Yzmirl but her expression showed neither alarm nor disinclination. "Would you be comfortable with such an arrangement?" I asked her.

"Of course."

"Then it's settled."

We rose and followed the footman to my suite, the integrator trundling along behind on its short legs, spitting and grumping just at the threshold of audibility. I looked back at one point and saw that its tail was twitching and its little fists were clenched. But when we arrived at my rooms, to find the first course of our dinner ready to be served, I chivvied the ill-tempered beast into the ablutory and closed the door so that Yzmirl need not feel distracted or constrained.

I found the food excellent, the company enchanting and the aftermath an unparalleled delight. Yzmirl displayed only a genteel interest in what was placed before her at the table but, after the servant returned and took away the remains of the meal, she revealed a robust appetite and surprising inventiveness in another room.

I awoke alone. Or so I thought until I arose and entered the washroom, where a small, furry and angry presence made itself known.

"Apparently, I need to eat," it said in a tone that was far from deferential.

"Eat what?"

There was fruit on a side table in the main salon. It went and sampled this and that. I was prepared to offer advice on the arts of chewing and swallowing but the creature mastered these skills without trouble. I thought a compliment might lighten the atmosphere but my encouraging words were turned back on me. "I've seen you do it thousands of times," it said. "How hard could it be?"

"Then you'll be able to work out the other end of the alimentary process for yourself?" I said.

"I shall manage."

I performed my morning toilet and emerged to find the integrator perched on the back of a chair, its tail flicking like a petulant pendulum and a frown on its face. "What?" I said.

"I cannot connect to the grid."

"Why not?"

"I don't know why not."

"Hmm," I said. "Ordinarily, I would perform a diagnostic procedure on your systems and components. Now I would first have to take advice from..." I had been going to specify a person who was skilled in the care of animals, but I had a suspicion that this particular creature might baffle such a specialist.

"How does it... feel, I suppose that's the word, to be unable to connect?"

It put on its introspective look for a moment, then said, "It feels as if I ought to be able to connect but cannot."

"As if you were out of range?"

"As if I was blocked."

There was a knock on the door and the footman entered. Again my integrator's fur raised itself involuntarily and again I was not quite sure that this was the same fellow I had encountered before.

"The master would like you to join him for breakfast," he said. The voice sounded identical, yet there was something around the eyes and the mouth that seemed slightly different.

There was no obvious reason to be circumspect. I said, "Are you the same footman who yesterday led me to meet your master and returned me here?"

His expression registered no surprise at the question. He looked at me neutrally and said, "Why do you ask?"

"Because I wish to know."

His answer was unexpected. "It is difficult to say."

"Why? It is a simple question."

"There are no simple questions," he said. "Only simple questioners. But I will address the issue. Are you the same person who arrived here yesterday? Since then you have had new experiences, met new people, consumed and excreted the air of this place and other substances. Has none of this had any effect on you?"

"The argument is abstruse," I said. "Assume the broadest of definitions and answer: Are you the same footman whom I encountered yesterday?"

"Under the broadest definition, it would be difficult to distinguish me from any other entity, including you."

The fellow was obviously a simpleton. "Lead me to your master," I said. As he turned to depart I beckoned my integrator to mount to my shoulder again. It was hissing and its fur was once more ruffed about its neck.

I found Turgut Therobar in a morning room in the great dome. He wore loose attire: ample pantaloons, a billowing shirt, chamois slippers, all in muted tones with plain fasteners. His head was again swathed in a silken cloth. He did not rise from his chair as I entered but beckoned me to sit across from him. A low table between us bore plates of bread, bowls of fruit and cups to be filled from a steaming carafe of punge.

He exhibited an air of sleepy self-satisfaction, blinking lazily as he inquired as to how I had passed the night. I assured him that I had rested well but offered an observation that he did not appear to have slept much. He extended his lower lip and made a show with his eyebrows that signaled that his rest or lack of it was of small concern. "A necessary task occupied most of the night," he said, "but it was well worth the doing."

I raised my brows in inquiry, but when he added no more I politely changed the subject. "We should discuss the case," I said.

"As you wish. How would you like to proceed?"

I poured myself a cup of punge and chose a savory broche then ordered my mind as I chewed, sipped and swallowed. "First," I said, "I will rehearse the known elements of the matter. Then I wish to know everything, from the beginning."

The charges concerned the disappearance of a number of persons in the vicinity of Wan Water over recent months. Initially, it had been thought that they had wandered into range of neropt hunting parties, the usual precursor to sudden disappearances on Dimpfen Moor.

The break in the case came when a tenant's young daughter, Bebe Allers, had gone missing from Wan Water only to reappear after a few days wandering within the walls of the estate. She was in a state of confusion and distress, with vague memories of being seized, transported, confined and perhaps interfered with in intimate ways. She could not directly identify the person or persons responsible for the outrage, but she had blanched and screamed at the sight of an image of Turgut Therobar.

"Now," I said, "how do you answer?"

He spoke and his face and tone betrayed a blasé unconcern that I found surprising. But the substance of his response was nothing less than astonishing. "The affair is now moot," he said. "Events have moved on."

I set my cup and plate on the table. "Wealth and social rank will not keep you from the Archon's Contemplarium if you are adjudged to be at fault."

His eyes looked up and away. "The case is nuncupative."

"Colonel-Investigator Warhanny will take a different view."

He chose a cake and nibbled at its topping.

"Please," I said, "I have given surety for you. My interests are also at stake."

He smiled and it was not a pleasant sight. There was a glint in his eye that gave me an inkling as to why the victim had reacted with horror to his image. "You will soon find," he said, "that you have more pressing concerns."

My integrator was hissing quietly beside my ear. The intuitive part of me was alert and urging unspecified action. I stood up. "You had better explain," I said.

He regarded me as if I had just executed some comic trick and he expected me to perform another. "Oh, I shall explain," he said. "Triumphs gain half their delight from being appreciated by those who have been triumphed over."

To my assistant I said, quietly, "Contact Warhanny. Tell him I withdraw from the case."

"I still cannot connect," it said.

"If I may interrupt your communion with your pet," Therobar said, "I was about to relieve your mind concerning the case."

"Very well," I said. "Do so."

He made a face like that of a little boy admitting a naughtiness to an indulgent caregiver and spread his hands. "I am guilty," he said.

"You interfered with the young maiden?"

"Indeed."

"And the disappearances?"

Again the protruding lip and facial shrug, which I took as an admission of culpability.

There could be only one question: "Why?"

"Two reasons," he said, throwing away the cake, now denuded of its topping, and reaching for another. "The disappeared assisted in Mitric Gevallion's experiments."

"You have been experimenting on human beings?"

"We'd gone as far as we could with animals. What else was there to do?"

I was being given an unobstructed view into Therobar's psyche. I shuddered involuntarily "What were the aims of these experiments?"

"As we discussed last night: at first we were seeking to redefine gist so that we could employ it in various efforts at carnal reconfiguration."

I translated his remark. "You were trying to harness the elementary force of the universe in order to transform living creatures."

"Yes." His sharp pointed tongue licked cream from the core of his pastry.

"Why?"

"Why not?"

"That is never a reason," I said.

"You may be right. In any case, we soon found another."

He was smiling, waiting for me to ask. I obliged him. "What did you find?"

"We discovered that we could 'reorder' animals from one species to another, though they were never happy in their new skins. So then we tried 'editing' them, again with interesting results. We produced several disparate versions from the same template: one would be ferocious, another painfully meek; one would have an overpowering urge to explore its territory, while the next iteration would not stir from its den." He drank from his cup of punge. "Do you understand what we had achieved?"

He was waiting again. "I am sure you would enjoy telling me," I said.

"We kept the shape, but discarded the contents, so to speak."

I had an insight. "You found you could work with form while discarding essence."

"Exactly. And, of course, once we had done it with beasts we had to try it with people."

"It is monstrous," I said.

"An entirely accurate description, at first. They were indeed monsters. We turned them loose to bellow and rampage on the moor, where the neropts found them and carried them off."

"But then?" I asked.

He wriggled with self-satisfaction. "But then we refined the process and began striking multiples from the originals. They are short-lived but they serve their purposes."

I understood. "The footmen," I said. "They are copies."

"And not just the footmen," he said, an insinuating smile squirming across his plump lips.

I was horrified. "Yzmirl," I whispered, then put iron in my voice. "Where is she?"

"Nowhere," he said. "She was, now she is not. Though Gevallion can whip up another at any time. That one was specifically designed to appeal to your tastes and petty vanities."

I did not trust myself to stand over him. I sat and turned my vision inward, encountering images of deep and tender pathos. After a while, he spoke, dragging my attention back to his now repulsive face.

"You haven't asked about the second reason," he said.

My mind had wandered far from the discussion. I indicated that I was not following.

"The disappeared," he said, speaking as if I were a particularly slow child, "went into Gevallion's vats. Then there was the Allers girl. She was the template for your companion of last night, by the way."

I took a labored breath. It was as if his evil thickened the air. "All right," I said. "Why did you let the girl be found?"

"Because that would bring Warhanny. And Warhanny would bring you."

"And why must you bring me?"

"Because by being here, you were not there."

"And where is 'there'?"

He smiled. "At your rooms, of course. Where there were items I wished to acquire."

I allowed anger to take me. I kicked the low table at his legs and sprang to overpower him. But he was ready. An object appeared in his hand. At its center was a small black spot. As I leapt toward him the circle abruptly expanded and rushed out to encompass me in nothingness.

Mitric Gevallion's laboratory was an unprepossessing place, dimly lit and woefully untidy. It featured a long workbench crowded with apparatus and a large display board on which a meandering set of equations and formulae had been scrawled. The vats in which the gist hunter brewed his creations loomed to one side of the wide, low-ceilinged room. Against the opposite wall was a sturdy cage and it was within its confines that I regained consciousness.

"Ah," said Gevallion, when Gharst, who had been sucking at a wound on one thick thumb, drew his attention to my blinking and pate rubbing. Therobar's shocker had left me muzzified and aching, but I was now recovering as the academician crossed the cluttered floor to regard me through the bars. "Ah, there you are, back with us," he said.

I saw no need to join him in assertions of the obvious, and fixed him instead with a disdainful stare. I might as well have struck him with a cobweb for all the impact I achieved.

He rubbed his thin, pale hands together. "We're just waiting for our host to join us, then we'll begin," he said.

I knew he wanted me to ask what was to ensue, but I denied him that satisfaction. After a moment, his eyes moved from my face to focus on a point to one side of it. "That is a most curious creature," he said. "We tried to examine it while you were... resting, but it shrieked and bit Gharst quite viciously. What is it?"

When I did not answer, he made a moue with his thin lips and said, "It does not signify. I will dissect the beast at leisure after you are... shall we say, through with it."

It was another attempt to elicit a response from me, and I ignored it like the others. My mind was now concentrated on the display board and I was following the calculations thereon. The mathematics were abstruse but familiar, until they reached the third sequence. There I saw that Gevallion's extrapolation of Balmerion's premises had taken a sudden and entirely unexpected departure. He had achieved a complete overturning of the ancient premises and yet as I proceeded to examine each step in his logic, I saw that it all held together.

"You're looking for the flaw," he said, now sounding the way a bone flute would sound if it could experience complacent triumph.

I said nothing, but the answer he sought must have been unmistakable in my expression. I ran my eyes over the calculations again, looking for the weakness, the false syllogism, the unjustified leap. There was none.

Finally, I could not deny my curiosity. "How?" I said.

"Simple," was his answer, "yet achingly difficult. Although it went against everything we are taught, I consciously accepted the gnosis that magic and rationalism alternate in a vast cycle, and that whenever the change comes the new regime obliterates all memory of the other's prior ascendancy. I then asked myself, 'If it were so, what would be the mechanism of change?' And the answer came: there is gist, it exists in this half of the cycle; the other half is opposite, therefore it must contain opposite gist. I thereby conceived the concept of negative gist."

"Negative gist," I repeated, and could not keep the wonder from my voice.

"And negative gist, viewed from our side of the dichotomy, is susceptible to definition. Define it, then reverse it, and you have a definition of positive gist. Although it is hard to remember. It slides easily out of understanding."

Negative gist, I thought. *Why had I not seen it?*

He knew what I was thinking. "You were not supposed to," he said. "None of us are. Even with it written on the board I had trouble keeping it in mind. I kept wanting to erase the equations. Then I relocated to Wan Water where conditions are more accommodating."

"How so?"

"The transition from rationalism to sympathy does not cross our universe in a wavefront, as dawn sweeps across a planet. It occurs almost everywhere at once, like seepage through a porous membrane, but there are discrete locations—dimples, I call them—where the earliest seepage pools. Here the effects are intensified."

"And Wan Water is such a place," I said.

"Indeed. That is why our host chose to build here."

"It seems to be a time for surprises," I said. There was something more that needed to be said. "I am not often wrong, but in this matter of gist I assuredly was. I offer you my apologies and my congratulations."

"Graciously done," he said. "Both are accepted." He added a formal salute appropriate to academic equals.

I returned it and said, "Since we are on good terms, perhaps you would unlock the cage."

His expression of regret seemed sincere. "I'm afraid Turgut Therobar has other plans. More to the point, he has the only key."

At that moment, Gharst called to say that something on the bench had reached a critical point of development. Gevallion rushed to his side. They busied themselves with an apparatus constructed of intricately connected rods and coils, then Gevallion made a last adjustment and the two stood back in postures of expectation. In the air a colorless spot had appeared, a globular shape no larger than my smallest fingernail, connected to the apparatus by a filament as thin as a gossamer. Gevallion nudged a part of the contraption on the bench and the spot grew larger and darker while the connector thickened. I saw motion seemingly within the sphere, a slow roiling as of indistinct shapes turning over and about each other.

The room was also charged with strange energies. My inner discomforts now increased. I felt as if both flesh and being were penetrated by vital forces, causing an itching of my bones and a sense of some impending revelation, though I could not tell if it would burst upon me or from me.

Gevallion said something to Gharst and the assistant gingerly touched the apparatus. The academician pushed him aside and made a more determined adjustment. The globe rapidly expanded until it was perhaps three times the diameter of Gharst's outsized head, then quickly shimmered and redoubled in size. The connecting conduit grew as thick as my wrist. Now the apparition seemed to become stable. I fought the intense irritation the device was causing in my innermost parts and studied the globe closely. I saw that the shifting colors and indeterminate shapes that moved within it were familiar, and began to plan a surprise.

"That is as much as we can achieve at this point," Gevallion told Gharst. "Advise Turgut Therobar that we are ready for his contribution."

The assistant spoke into a communications nexus beside the bench. I heard a muffled response.

The dim room became silent and still. The two experimenters stood by the bench, the globe swirled placidly in the air and a small voice mumbled in my ear. For the moment, I ignored it.

If I had any doubts on the matter they were soon resolved. The door opened and in strode Turgut Therobar, swathed in the multihued robes and lap-eared cap of a thaumaturge. The costume should have appeared comical, yet did not. His face bore an expression of fevered anticipation and his hands clasped another disconcertingly familiar object: Bristal Baxandall's leatherbound tome, last seen in my workroom.

I could feel my assistant's fur standing up and tickling the side of my neck. The murmuring in my ear grew more insistent.

I whispered back, "Don't worry."

Therobar inspected the swirling globe and beamed at Gevallion and Gharst, then shot me a look that contained a mixture of sentiments. He placed the great book on the workbench and opened it, ran his finger down a page and his tongue across his ripe lips. "The Chrescharrie, first, don't you think?" he said to Gevallion, who nodded nervous agreement.

I recognized the name as that of a minor deity worshipped long ago by a people almost now forgotten. I heard more mumblings in my ear. "Shush," I said, under my breath.

Therobar removed his cap and I saw that his hairless scalp was densely tattooed with figures and symbols such as I had seen in books of magic lore. He rubbed one hand over the smooth skin of his pate then took a deep breath and intoned a set of syllables. Something pulsed along the cable that connected sphere to apparatus. He spoke again, and again the connector palpitated as if something traversed along its length. The colors in the sphere flashed and fluoresced. There was a crackling sound and the air of the room suddenly smelled sharply of ozone. My internal organs felt as if they were seeking to trade places with each other and there was a pulsing pressure at the back of my head. My integrator abandoned my shoulder with a squawk, dropping to the floor where it grumbled and chittered in an agitated manner.

Therobar spoke again and made a calculated gesture. The sphere shimmered and flickered, there came a loud *crack* of energy and a fountain of blue sparks cascaded from the globe. The swirl coalesced and cohered at its center, becoming a six-armed homunculus, red of skin and cobalt of eye—there was only one, in the middle of its forehead—seated cross-legged on black nothingness that now otherwise filled the orb. Meanwhile a sensation like a hot scouring wind shot through me.

Therobar consulted the book once more and spoke three guttural sounds, meanwhile moving hands and fingers in precise motions. The figure in the globe started as if struck. Its eye narrowed and its gash of a mouth turned downward in a frown. Its several arms flexed and writhed while it seemed to be attempting to rise to its split-hooved feet. Therobar spoke and gestured again, a long string of syllables, and the homunculus subsided, though with a patent show of anger in its face.

Now the thaumaturge took another deep breath and barked a harsh phrase. There was a reek of raw power in the air and a thrumming sound just at the limits of perception. My bones were rattling against each other at the joints.

Therobar raised one hand, the index finger extended, then swiftly jabbed it into his forehead. The figure in the globe did likewise with one of its upper limbs, though its sharp-nailed digit struck not flesh and bone but its own protruding eye. It gave a squeal of pain and frustrated rage.

Therobar's eyes widened and I saw a gleam of triumph in them. For a moment I thought he might voice some untoward cry of victory, which would have put us all in deadly peril, but he mastered the impulse and instead chanted a lengthy phrase. The glowering deity in the sphere shimmered and dissolved into fragments of light, and once again the orb contained only shifting shapes and mutating colors.

The thaumaturge let out a sigh of happy relief. Gevallion and Gharst came from the other side of the workbench and there followed a few moments of back slapping, hand gripping, and—on Therobar's part—a curious little dance that I took to express unalloyed joy.

When the demonstration was over, he looked my way and with an expression of satiated pleasure said, "Allow me to explain what you just saw."

"No need," I said. "You have accessed a continuum in which there is no distinction between symbol and referent. You have encapsulated a small segment of that realm and used it as a secure enclosure in which you could summon up a minor deity and bend it to your will. After animals and humans it is the next natural step. Now I suppose you'll want to call up something more potent so that you can use it to rule the world."

Therobar's face took on an aggrieved pout and he regarded me without favor for a long moment.

I shrugged my itching shoulders. "Your ambitions are as banal as your taste in decor," I said.

I thought he would strike me, but he put down the impulse and sneered. "Do you know why I brought you here?" he said.

"So that you could steal Baxandall's book from my library."

"That was but the proximate cause," he said, and I detected a deeper animosity in the squinting of his eyes and the writhing of his mouth as he approached the cage. "Do you recall an evening at Dame Obrosz's salon several years ago?"

"There were many such occasions," I said. "One tends not to retain details."

"You were holding forth on the bankruptcy of magic."

"I am sure I have done so often."

"Yes." The syllable extended into a hiss. "But on that occasion, your arguments had a profound effect on me."

"That seems odd, since the evidence of the past few minutes indicates that you have spent years studying and mastering the magical lore that I inveighed against. Obviously I did not convince you."

"On the contrary, you convinced me utterly," he said. "But I was so offended by your strutting arrogance and insouciant contempt for all contrary opinion that I resolved then and there to devote my life to disproving your claims, and forcing you to acknowledge utter defeat."

"Congratulations," I said. "You have achieved the goal of your existence. I am glad to have been of such great use to you, but pray tell me, what will you do to fill the remaining years?"

"Perhaps I will spend them tormenting you," he said. "And acquainting you with the depths of animosity you are capable of summoning up in otherwise placid souls."

"I think not." It seemed time to act. I did my best to ignore my peculiar inner sensations, though they had not diminished after Therobar dismissed the Chrescharrie. Focusing my will, I spoke certain words while making the usual accompanying gestures. Therobar stepped back, his face filling with a mingling of confusion and curiosity. The colors in the globe swirled anew, then I saw the familiar pattern of my demonic friend.

"I am beset," I called. "Please aid me."

The demon manifested a limb: thick, bristling with spines and tipped with a broad pincerlike claw. It reached out to Turgut Therobar as I had seen it do before to two other unfortunates. But the thaumaturge had already recovered his equilibrium. He stepped back, out of range, while shouting Gevallion's name.

The academician also overcame his surprise. He did something to the apparatus on the bench and the globe constricted sharply, trapping my friend's spiked appendage as if it were a noose that had tightened around the limb. I heard muffled sounds and saw the claw opening and closing in frustration, its pincers clicking as they seized only thin air.

Therobar was flipping through the book. He stopped at a page and from the way his eyes flashed I knew that it boded ill for my friend and me. "*Ghoroz ebror fareshti!*" he shouted. The orb shivered then contracted further, to the size of a fist, then to a pinpoint, and finally it popped out of existence altogether. The demon's arm, severed neatly, flopped to the floor where it glowed and smoked for a moment before disappearing.

"Oh, dear," said Turgut Therobar. "I hope you weren't counting on that as your last resort."

"It would be premature to say," I said, but I heard little conviction in my own voice.

The thaumaturge rubbed his hands in a manner that implied both satisfaction with what had transpired and happy anticipation of further delights to come. "Shall I tell you what happens next?" he said.

I was casting about for some stratagem by which I might escape or turn the tables, but nothing was coming to mind. I sought insight from the intuitive part of me that so often came to my aid, but received no sense of impending revelation. It was as if he was otherwise occupied.

Hello! I shouted down the mental corridor that led to his abode. *Now would be an apt time to assist!*

Meanwhile, Therobar was speaking. "You'll go into the vats, of course. I will create several versions of you, some comical, some pathetically freakish. I will make convincing Henghis Hapthorn facsimiles, but give them unpleasant compulsions, then send them out into society. Your reputation may suffer. Others will have the opportunity to outrun neropt foraging parties. I believe I'll also re-create you in a feminine edition." He smiled that smile that could make children scream. "Such fun."

The muted voice that had been rumbling in my ear now said, quite clearly, "Step aside."

I turned my head, wondering what my transformed integrator was up to, but the creature was huddled in a far corner of the cage nervously rubbing one hand over another. "Did you speak?" I said.

"No, I did," said the voice again, this time less quiet. "Now, get out of the way."

I experienced a novel sensation: I was *shoved* from within, not roughly but with decided firmness, as that part of me that I was accustomed to think of as fixed and immutable—my own mind—now found itself sharing my inner space with another partner. At the same time, the noxious itchings and shiftings among my inner parts faded to a normal quiescence.

"Wait," I said.

"I've already waited years," Therobar said, but I had not addressed him.

"As have I," said the voice in my head. "Now, move over before you get us both into even worse difficulty."

I acquiesced, and the moment I yielded I felt myself deftly nudged out of the way, as if I had been pressed into the passenger's seat of a vehicle so that someone else could assume the controls. I saw my own hand come up before my face, the fingers opening and closing, though I was not moving them. "Good," said the voice.

I spoke to the voice's owner as he spoke to me, silently within the confines of our shared cranium. "I know you," I said. "You're my indweller, the fellow at the other end of the dark passage, my intuitive colleague."

"Hush your chatter," was the response. "I need to concentrate."

I subsided. Through our common eyes I saw that Turgut Therobar had produced his weapon again and was aiming it at us while Gharst opened the cage with a key the thaumaturge had given him. Across the room, Gevallion threw me a sheepish look and opened the hatch of one of his vats, releasing a wisp of malodorous vapor.

As the cage door opened, I watched my hands come together in a particular way then spread wide into a precise configuration. I heard my voice speaking words that were vaguely recognizable from one of Baxandall's books, the opening line of a cantrip known as Gamgripp's Irrepressible Balloon, whose title had made me laugh when I was a young man browsing through a book of spells. I did not laugh now as from my hands there emanated an expanding sphere of invisible force that pushed Therobar and Gharst away from me, lifting them over the workbench then upward into the air until they were pressed against the far wall where it met the ceiling. Gevallion, seeing what was happening, tried to reach the door but was similarly caught and crushed against it.

Therobar was clearly finding it hard to breathe against the pressure the spell exerted against his chest, but the symbols on his scalp had taken on a darker shade and I could see that his lips were framing syllables. I heard my voice speak again while my hands made motions that reminded me of a needle passing thread through cloth. The thaumaturge's lips became sealed. "Faizul's Stitch," I said to my old partner, having recognized the spell.

"Indeed," was the reply.

He directed our body out of the cage, faltering only a little before he mastered walking. The apparatus on the bench was unaffected by the balloon spell and he picked it up in our hands and examined it from several angles. Its components and manner of operation were not difficult to analyze.

"Shall we?" he said.

"It seems only fair."

He activated the device, reestablishing the swirling sphere. I was relieved to see the familiar eddies of my transdimensional colleague reappear. My other part made room for me so that I could ask the demon, "Are you well?"

"Yes," he said, "I lost only form. Essence was not affected." He was silent for a moment and I recognized the pattern he assumed when something took his interest. "I see that the opposite is true for you."

"Indeed," I said, "allow me to introduce... myself, I suppose." I stepped aside and let the two of them make each other's acquaintance.

When the formalities were over, I voiced the obvious question: "Now what?"

I felt a sense of my other self's emotions, as one would feel warmth from a nearby fleshly body: he gave off an emanation of determined will, tempered by irony. "We must restore balance," he said, using my voice so that the three prisoners could hear. "Pain has been given and must therefore be received. Also fear, humiliation and, of course, death for death."

"Indeed," I said. "That much is obvious. But I meant 'Now what?' for you and me."

"Ah," he said, this time within our shared skull. "We must reach an accommodation. At least temporarily."

"Why temporarily?" I asked, in the same unvoiced manner, then felt the answer flower in my mind in the way my intuitive other's contributions had always done during the long years of our partnership.

I digested his response then continued. "You are the part of me—us—that is better suited to an age reigned over by magic. As the change intensifies, I will fade until I become to you what you have always been to me, the dweller down the back corridor."

"Indeed," was his response. "And from there you will provide me with analytical services that will complement and augment my leaps from instinct. It will be a happy collaboration."

"You will make me your integrator," I complained.

"My valued colleague," he countered.

I said nothing, but how could he fail to sense my reluctance to give up control of my life? His response was the mental equivalent of a snort. "What makes you think you ever had control?" he said.

I was moved to argue, but then I saw the futility of being a house divided. "Stop putting things in my head," I said.

"I don't believe I can," he answered. "It is, after all, as much my head as yours."

My curiosity was piqued. "What was it like to live as you have lived, inside of me all of these years?"

There was a pause, then the answer came. "Not uncomfortable, once you learn the ropes. Don't fret," he added, "the full transition may not be completed for years, even decades. We might live out our mutual life just as we are now."

"Hence the need for an accommodation," I agreed. "Then let us wait for a quiet time and haggle it out."

He agreed and we turned our attention to the question of what to do with Therobar, Gevallion and Gharst.

The demon was displaying silver, green and purple flashes as he said, "It would be a shame to waste the academician's ability to create form without essence. I know of places in my continuum where such creations would command considerable value."

I had never inquired as to what constituted economics in the demon's frame of reference, but my intuitive half leapt to the correct interpretation. "But if you took them into your keeping and put them to work," he said, "would that not make you a peddler of smut?"

The silver swooshes intensified, but the reply was studiedly bland in tone. "I would find some way to live with the opprobrium," the demon said.

We released Gevallion and Gharst into demonic custody. They could not go as they were into that other universe, where any word they uttered would immediately become reified, and it was an unsettling experience to watch the demon briskly edit their forms so that they could never speak again.

But I hardened myself by remembering Yzmirl and how they must have dealt with her, and in a few moments the messy business was concluded. The two were hauled, struggling and moaning, through the sphere. For good measure, the demon took their vats and apparatus as well, including the device of rods and coils from the workbench.

When he was ready to depart, my old colleague lingered in the sphere, showing more purple and green shot through with silver. "I may not return for a while," he said, "perhaps a long while. I will have much to occupy."

"I will miss our contests," I said, "but in truth I am sure I will also be somewhat busy with all of this..."—I rolled my eyes— "accommodating."

And so we said our goodbyes and he withdrew, taking the sphere after him.

"That leaves Turgut Therobar," my inner companion said, this time aloud.

"Indeed." I let the magnate hear my voice as well. He remained squeezed against the far wall, his feet well clear of the floor. His eyes bulged and one cheek had acquired a rapid twitch.

"Warhanny would welcome his company."

"Somehow, the Contemplarium does not seem a sufficient sanction for the harm he has done."

"No, it doesn't."

Therobar made noises behind his sealed lips. We ignored them.

Later that day, back in my workroom, I contacted the Colonel-Investigator. "Turgut Therobar has confessed to all the charges and specifications," I said.

Warhanny's face, suspended in the air over my worktable, took on the slightly less lugubrious aspect that I had come to recognize as his version of intense pleasure. "I will send for him," he said.

"Not necessary," I said. "Convulsed by remorse for his ill deeds, he ran out onto Dimpfen Moor just as a neropt hunting pack was passing by. Nothing I could do would restrain him. They left some scraps of him if you require proof of his end."

"I will have them collected," said Warhanny.

"I must also file his last will and testament," I said. "He left his entire estate to the charities he had always championed, except for generous bequests to his tenants, and an especial legacy for Bebe Allers, his final victim."

We agreed that that was only fair and Warhanny said that he would attend to the legalities. We disconnected.

I regarded my integrator. It was still in the form of a catlike ape or perhaps an apelike cat. "And what about you?" I said. "With Baxandall's books and the increasing strength of magic, we can probably restore you to what you were."

It narrowed its eyes in thought. "I have come to value having preferences," it said. "And if the world is going to change, I will become a familiar sooner or later. Better to get a head start on it. Besides, I enjoyed the fruit at Turgut Therobar's."

"We have none like it here," I said. "It is prohibitively expensive."

It blinked and looked inward for a moment. "I've just ordered an ample supply," it said.

"I did not authorize the order."

"No," it said, "you didn't."

While I was considering my response, I received an unsolicited insight from my other half. It was in the form of a crude cartoon image.

"That is not amusing," I said.

From the chuckles filling my head, I understood that he saw the situation from his own perspective.

"I am not accustomed to being a figure of fun," I said.

The furry thing on the table chose that moment to let me know that, along with autonomic functions, it had acquired a particularly grating laugh.

"Now whose expectations require adjustment?" it said.

Thwarting Jabbi Gloond

In my senior year at the Institute, I found a friend in Torsten Olabian, a sunny-tempered young man who shared my enthusiasm for the sport of pinking. We would regularly meet at the practice range to skim small, eight-pointed stars at wooden targets propelled in various directions by an attendant's catapult.

Olabian was skilled with either hand and it was a rare disk that did not tumble from the air pierced by one of his missiles. For my own part, I soon grew bored after mastering the throws and postures. I would have abandoned the pursuit if I had not discovered an ability to strike the targets from the air while blindfolded.

"How is it done?" Olabian wanted to know when I had just brought down my fifth disk in a row though my head was swathed in a lightless hood.

I had always found it difficult to explain how I did such things. "I call it simply insight," I said. "One just knows where target and star will meet. All that is then required is to bring the two objects together at that point and moment."

"It sounds easy," he said.

"Indeed," I said. "I find it much easier to do than to explain. It is the same with the facility with which I resolve conundrums that others find impenetrable."

"That is a useful ability. Perhaps you should consider a career as a discriminator."

I made a noise indicative of gentle ridicule. "Henghis Hapthorn, discriminator at large," I said. "Most doubtful."

Yet even as I said it I felt a contrary vote from deeper inside me. I then confessed to Torsten what I had told no one else. "I am able to do these mental tricks with the aid of some other part of me, one that is lodged in the more remote regions of my psyche. I cannot assert control over it, though it yields remarkable results if I offer acceptance and collaboration."

"I wonder if I have such a part?" Torsten said.

"If you do, it might be best to leave it undisturbed."

My being able to hit a pinking target while blindfolded was but the latest manifestation of the odd capabilities my "other part" had demonstrated since childhood. During my adolescence I tried to understand or at least delineate the peculiarities I had discovered in myself, but my efforts met with frustration and at last I gave up.

Grown to young manhood I found myself—that is, the part of me that lived in the front parlors of my mind—no better than most of my peers at using formal logic to analyze situations and work through syllogisms to a rational conclusion. In the numeric disciplines my studies at the Institute were teaching me how to apply higher-level consistencies, the recondite procedures which underlay the mathematics of chaos, and I was making adequate progress.

Yet, beyond the normal development of my intellect, there was always the sense that another person lived, for the most part unobtrusively, in the back of my mind. If I kept a problem only in my familiar front parlors I could worry at it for days and still be baffled. But if I took the conundrum down the rearmost corridors of my consciousness and left it at the edge of darkness, in time—it might be moments, or hours, but rarely more than a day—a fully formed answer would appear.

I had found that stilling my thoughts through an elementary variant of the Lho-tso exercises aided the process and I had become so adept at the business of what I called "applying insight" that it was now almost automatic. Faced with a puzzle that did not yield an easy or obvious solution, I need close my eyes for no more than a moment or two to know intuitively that the man down the backstairs—so I thought of him—was hard at work.

I did not resent sharing my inner spaces with this anonymous prodigy, though I had not yet come to include him in my private definition of "me." It was like having a brother who was reliable yet eccentric.

The next time we met at the practice field, Torsten had just returned from a visit to The Hutch, his father's estate near the hamlet of Binch, at the landward end of the long fingerlike peninsula that is tipped by the city of Olkney, which surrounds the Institute's hallowed grounds. My friend's normally blithe disposition was clouded and there was a grim set to the corners of his mouth.

I needed no exceptional insight to say, "Something is wrong."

He confirmed my impression. He told me that when he got to his father's house he found it had acquired an additional resident. A man had arrived one day, declared himself to be Jabbi Gloond, an old acquaintance of the master, and had moved in.

"What is the problem?" I asked.

"They do not act as if they are on good terms. Gloond struts about as if he were the proprietor, commanding, 'Bring me this,' and 'Fetch me more,' while my father remains as still as a small creature that has fallen under a predator's eye."

"What does your father say about this?"

"Nothing. He has never been the most forthcoming of parents. I've always believed it was because he was absent for the years of my infancy. We are on civil terms but not close, a relationship that has always suited us both. When I try to question him about Gloond, he makes abstracted motions with his hands and changes the subject."

"Hmm," I said.

"Have you an insight?"

"It would be premature to say," I said. But I accepted his invitation to accompany him down to Binch at the next hiatus.

In the meantime, I decided to assemble as much information as I could about Jabbi Gloond and Gresh Olabian, Torsten's father. Oddly enough, my friend could be of little aid in this endeavor.

"We do not talk much," he said. "The old man has always kept to himself and sometimes does not come out of his chamber for days at a time. I know that he made a small fortune on Bain, a remote planet in the Back of Beyond. He mined for gems, mainly blue-fires and shatterlights."

"And this Gloond dates from those times?"

"So it would seem."

Back in my room, I consulted the Institute's integrator. There was almost no information on Gloond; he hailed from Orkham County, a rigorously bucolic district on Bain's southern continent that had been settled centuries before by devotees of the Palmadyan Cult, who disdained all mechanical and artificial contrivances more complex than hand tools and unpowered conveyances. Whatever records Orkham County may have kept had never been made part of the connectivity matrix that extended across Old Earth and out to all the major human settled worlds along The Spray. About all that was known about Jabbi Gloond was that he had alighted at the Olkney spaceport some weeks before, having worked his passage from Bain on a tramp freighter.

I then asked the Institute's integrator about Gresh Olabian and uncovered a richer vein of information. Olabian was orphaned at an early age but had overcome his handicaps; taking a certificate in the building and operating of mines he had gone out to The Spray to make his fortune, leaving behind an infant son. No female parent was mentioned, though that was not unusual. In such cases one did not inquire.

Gresh Olabian had worked for a number of mining consortia on various worlds, until he had acquired enough savings to undertake his own venture: a mining operation in Orkham County, delving for blue-fires and shatterlights.

The gems never occurred in surface deposits, I learned from the integrator. Because they were a temporary offshoot of vulcanism on Bain and similar worlds, they must be dug for in profound strata that were often unstable. The preferred methodology was to bore in deep and quickly, using shielded mass converters, retrieve the gems and be out before the disturbed rock violently rearranged itself. Yet that sort of machinery was forbidden to cross the Orkham County border.

"How did he develop the mine?" I asked.

"Olabian used ingenuity," said the integrator. "He assembled a work force from several planets: Gryulls did the digging; a trio of footed worms from Ek hauled away the broken rock, guided by their symbiotic handlers; members of a modified human species known as Halebs operated the chemical works that separated the pure blue-fires from the matrix; there was even a transmuting Shishisha to insinuate itself into the thinnest crevices, seeking out the best gems and thus avoiding unnecessary excavating."

There were, of course, no images from the Olabian diggings, but I could imagine the scene: the heavy-shouldered Gryulls punching their way deep into Bain's rocky meat, the long, armored multipedes with rocks heaped on their backs and their Ek wranglers seated just aft of the cranial sensorium, licking their fingers then stroking the worms' feathery antennae with a unique saliva whose chemistry soothed the beasts' testy natures, the Shishisha assuming a flowing granular form that would let it fluidly slip into cracks.

It conjured up a remarkable set of mental images, made even more extraordinary when I considered the fact that none of the species Olabian had assembled were noted for leaving their homeworlds. Even the Halebs preferred to remain in their own habitats, finding not enough carbon dioxide in the atmosphere of worlds hospitable to unmodified humans. The integrator could offer no explanation, only conjectures.

"They did not publicly discuss their motives, therefore there is no record in the primary sources. Perhaps Olabian was a singularly persuasive recruiter, perhaps he promised rewards that overcame his workers' homesickness, perhaps he hired those who had been banished from their homeworlds, offering them shares in the venture which would have let them live large in exile.

"In any case," the integrator continued, "his plans came amiss. Shortly after the mine began production, disaster struck: a tunnel collapsed, entombing all except Olabian himself, who happened to be at the surface expediting a shipment of gems to market. He quite reasonably abandoned the venture, coming back to Old Earth with only enough profit to purchase a small estate. To The Hutch he brought his son, and there they dwelt quietly until the boy was sent off to school."

I then examined Olabian's history since his return to Old Earth but found nothing of note. He had become a recluse, living alone in the manor. Torsten went earlier than most boys to a residential school, though that was not in itself an uncommon circumstance. I, myself, had gained most of my education in such places, my father having declared in my seventh year that I had become insufferable—I had corrected him once too often on some trifling matter.

I applied insight to the data and felt a faint tickle at the back of my mind, but nothing concrete emerged. I decided it would be best to take a closer look at the situation that had caused Torsten to worry. In the meantime, I tasked the Institute's integrator with amassing, from secondary and tertiary sources, all the information it could glean about the events in Orkham County.

"That may take some time," it said. "Several hours at least, perhaps even days. It will require an open inquiry on a number of worlds and there is no guarantee that persons who have the information—supposing they even exist—will be inclined to respond."

"Nevertheless," I said, and sent the integrator about its work.

At Torsten's urging I took a hiatus from my studies and returned with him to The Hutch. We traveled by balloon-tram to Binch then descended to hire an aircar that carried us to the estate. I inspected the grounds from the air as we spiraled down and saw that they were well tended, although I noticed that all work was being carried out by self-guiding devices. When we alighted at the front doors, no servant came to admit us; instead, the who's-there mounted on a pillar of the portico notified the house integrator and the doors automatically swung open.

"Where is my father?" Torsten asked as soon as we had entered, and a voice from the air informed us that Gresh Olabian was sequestered in his chambers.

"Is he unwell?" my friend asked.

"He does not say. He has asked not to be disturbed."

I was intrigued. "Can you not deduce his condition from observation?" I said.

The integrator replied, "My percepts were removed from the private chambers shortly after the master's return from the stars."

"Indeed?" I said. I could not recall encountering anyone who shut himself away from his own integrator. It was an unusual state of affairs, almost unnatural. "Did he give a reason?"

"My father is of an intensely private disposition," Torsten said. "I used to try to engage him in discussions appropriate between a son and a father, but he would soon run out of things to say and would retire to his suite."

I would have pursued the issue further but at that moment a door to an adjacent room opened and another person entered the foyer. From the way Torsten stiffened, I knew this to be Jabbi Gloond.

He was an unprepossessing fellow, past his middle years, with a chin that descended too far toward his chest and a wandering forehead that ranged almost to the crown of his skull. Between them was a nose the shape and texture of some root vegetable. His eyes were large and moist and I suspected that his lower lip only made contact with its upper neighbor when he was speaking, being left the rest of the time to hang as loose as an untucked shirttail.

He offered Torsten a tepid greeting without stopping, and proceeded on toward the kitchens where I could hear his honking nasal voice instructing the integrator to prepare a plate of pickled mushrooms stuffed with spiced eggs.

I would admit to myself, though not to Torsten, that I had expected something else: a swaggering bravo, a coldly imperious enforcer, a sly sidler. "He does not seem the type to intimidate a master miner," I said.

"You would think so," my friend answered, "but my father clearly lost his verve on Bain. He was never quite himself again."

I was shown to a large, airy chamber on the second floor, across from Torsten's favorite room when he was at home. The elder Olabian's suite occupied one end of another wing, down a wide aisle that led off from the corridor where our accommodations were. I asked where Jabbi Gloond slept and was told that he had a small space on the ground floor where he could reach the kitchens with the fewest steps.

"He has an unending appetite for delicacies," Torsten said.

I had read that the residents of Orkham County, faithful to the strictures of the Palmadyan Cult, subsisted on rude fare. I was sure it was wholesome, but no doubt some found it tiresome over a lifetime.

I asked if Gloond had made any other demands. Torsten knew of none. "The fellow seems to desire no more than to sleep late in a soft bed, consume copious quantities of dainties and have his intimate needs seen to by the personal apparatus in his room."

"Palmadyans are not renowned for sophistication," I said. "For Jabbi Gloond, such a regime as he now follows may approximate paradise. He has made no demands for funds? No suggestions about redrawing a will?"

"Not so far. Comfort and opportunities for indolence seem to be his desired goals, and here he has achieved them."

I was puzzled. Jabbi Gloond seemed to be no more trouble than any house guest who slips and ducks every hint that his optimum departure date has passed. Yet Gresh Olabian was reportedly ill at ease. I closed my eyes to seek insight but received only vague impressions.

"Anything?" said Torsten, who had seen me perform before.

"Premature," I said, "though I hope you will not be offended if I speculate that Gloond causes your father discomfort because he knows something that your father would rather no one knew."

"That is an obvious line of inquiry," my friend agreed. "But when I ask the old man if there is something he wishes to tell me, he retires to his rooms without a word."

We took luncheon in the great refectory. The Hutch's integrator was a superior model and provided a fine repast. Torsten, his father and I sat at one end of the long, grand table, while Jabbi Gloond occupied the farthest extreme, trenchering his way through mounds of roast vegetables and succulent meats. A strong odor of spice and pungent herbs emanated from the loaded salvers that appeared before him and he wielded his cutlery with a clattering brio that prevented his hearing our muted conversation.

"I think we must count Jabbi Gloond a lapsed Palmadyan," I said. "The cult requires its adherents to eat only what they have grown and prepared themselves, a stricture only slightly modified by the fact that all effort in Orkham County is communal."

"Not only communal but compulsory," said Torsten. "I think you have used too mild a term for the manner in which our guest has departed from the cult's teachings. He has not so much lapsed from Palmadyanism as leapt from it as far as humanly possible."

Torsten and I had agreed on this conversational gambit as a means to make a sideways approach to the question on the son's mind. We would lure the father into an exchange that we intended to shape toward a discussion of how he and Gloond came to be sharing a house.

"Indeed," I said, following Torsten's observation with a question to the older man. "You have seen Orkham County at first hand. Is Jabbi Gloond as atypical as he seems?"

But Gresh Olabian gave only a wooden shrug in reply and with pale, seemingly bloodless hands continued to pick without interest at a plate of herbs and softroot.

Undeterred, I bored in. "Although you used offworld labor to mine for blue-fires and shatterlights, you must have engaged local transportation and handlers to get them to the spaceport on Shoal Island. Only horse-drawn wagons can cross Orkham County and the drivers are all local folk. Was Gloond one of them?"

He made no reply, but this time Olabian looked at me. Although the waxy skin of his face did not register any emotion I thought I saw alarm in his otherwise expressionless eyes. My interest in Gloond appeared to disturb him.

It clearly emboldened Torsten. "If he is causing you difficulties, we'll soon tumble him out into the road," he said.

The elder Olabian said nothing and kept his eyes on his plate.

"Please, Father," said Torsten, "Henghis is very good at unraveling mysteries. I have urged him to become a professional discriminator. Whatever the problem, I'm sure he can help. We'll get to the bottom of Jabbi Gloond."

Again, though no expression animated the father's face I sensed a growing unease. But when I began to frame a new question, Gresh Olabian rose from the table without a word and departed the room.

Torsten watched his father go, his face a turmoil of frustration mingled with heartfelt concern.

At the other end of the table Jabbi Gloond paid no heed but continued to feed his apparently unrelenting appetite.

"Hmm," I said.

In the long summer afternoon, the old orange sun poured its tinted light through the trailing branches of a broad-boled dwindle that dominated the estate's south lawn. I had convinced Torsten that a round of pinking might take his mind off the situation. But when I came out with my stars in hand I found that my friend had prevailed, I don't know how, on Jabbi Gloond to operate the apparatus that flung the targets.

We spun our stars at the disks as they flew against the blameless sky, though my friend's mind was not upon the game. He clean missed an easy low-glide in the first frame and barely nicked a high tumbler in the second. As the fallen Palmadyan reloaded the catapult and reset its randomizer for the third interval, Torsten said, "Let us question him about his comings and doings. Perhaps he will let something slip."

I felt a stirring in the back of my mind, my other part stretching its intellectual tendons in anticipation of a pursuit. But some other region of my divided psyche made its influence felt and I said, "I am not sure there is anything to be gained by pushing into the thicket of secrets that your father and Jabbi Gloond share."

Torsten's brow darkened. "But obviously he is extorting favors from my father."

"Indeed," I said, "but they are trivial: some plates of spiced mushrooms and a narrow chamber that was intended for an undercook."

"Details! My father is victimized!"

"True, but he seems to have adjusted to the situation. He did not become disturbed until you spoke of my ability to penetrate an intrigue."

There was a sensation in my own back rooms, an inner grumble that told me that my inward companion was not pleased at the direction into which I was trying to move events. There was an even more forceful protest from the friend beside me.

"I must know what is going on," Torsten said. With that he made a peremptory gesture that caused Jabbi Gloond to slouch in our direction.

"Unpleasant knowledge is like an ugly but unreturnable gift," I quoted. "Once received it must be lived with."

Torsten struck a resolute pose. "Nevertheless."

"Very well," I said, "but allow me to put the questions."

At close quarters, the former Palmadyan was even less prepossessing.

The comprehensive traces of several meals adorning the front of his smock were as much an affront to the nose as to the eye. I examined his face and deportment for the known signs of a criminal disposition and found nothing remarkable. Nor were there indications of even moderate intelligence. Any illicit enterprise conceived by Jabbi Gloond, I decided, would be uncomplicated and its execution probably confined to a single stage. A two-step plan would be one too many.

"You are of Orkham County, I believe," I said.

"Yes."

"A remarkable place, Orkham," I said.

"Is it?" For a moment I thought to detect repartee, then I saw that the man was genuinely puzzled by my observation. While the sparse teeth of his mental gears were still grinding I threw him a direct question.

"Did you work for Gresh Olabian there?"

"No."

"Then for whom?"

"For Farmer Boher."

"What did you do for Farmer Boher?"

"Drove a wagon."

"It must have been a good and simple life, full of fresh air and healthful exercise."

He shook his elongated head so vigorously that the tip of his nose oscillated. "Food was bad, work was hard. Slept in the barn."

I understood that Jabbi Gloond had spent a lifetime doing what he was bidden to do. Asked a question, it was his reflex to answer it. Still, he was no running fount of conversation—more like a slowly dripping tap. But by patience and careful questioning I achieved an elementary view of his former situation. The Olabian diggings had been on Farmer Boher's land and Jabbi Gloond was the hand detailed to carry goods and persons to and from the mine site in the wagon. He had had only perfunctory contact with the mining party.

"Where you there when the accident happened?" I asked.

"Where?"

"At the mine?"

Now I saw craftiness mixed with apprehension blossom in his aspect, the sentiments as obvious as the open-pored tuber that was his facial centerpiece. "No," he said.

"You weren't there when the shaft collapsed?"

"No." Now there was patent relief in his face, telling me that I had asked the wrong question and that he was glad of it.

Insight came unbidden. "But you were there after?"

He looked away. "Don't remember."

"What did you see?"

"Nothing. Tunnel caved in. Was nothing to see."

I wanted to ask more but it now belatedly dawned on Jabbi Gloond that he was not obliged to satisfy my curiosity. He turned and sloped off toward the house.

"He was lying," Torsten said.

"Yes," I said, "but only a little."

"What do you deduce?"

I let the impression filter up from within. "Something to do with the accident. He knows something about your father's involvement. It cannot have been anything abstruse or Jabbi Gloond would have failed to notice it."

"Something as simple as my father's having caused the cave-in to rob the others of their shares?"

"Did the others have shares to be robbed?"

"I don't know."

Gresh Olabian was clearly not the warmest of men, but I did not sense in him the coldness of spirit that would be needed if he were to murder an entire mining crew. "And if he did," I said, "why would a troublesome Jabbi Gloond still have all his particles in place? He would make a small addition to the death roll. There are plenty of corners on the estate where his ashes might be tossed into the breeze."

"We need more information," Torsten said.

I reluctantly agreed, though again I counseled him to let the matter lie. "I sense no great evil here," I said. "Nor has your father asked for my help."

"But I have," was his reply, "and as my friend you are bound to provide it."

I could think of nothing to offer in response so I said, "Let us go see if the Institute's integrator has anything to report."

"Gresh Olabian's mining crew was a pastiche of exiles and banished criminals," the Institute's integrator reported when we used the communications nexus in The Hutch's study to make contact. It was an unimpressive room, containing only the commonest books and most of them were uncracked. The family connaissarium contained few relics or mementos, considering that Gresh Olabian had spent so many years off-world.

"The Gryulls," the integrator continued, "were from a minor sept of a warrior clan that had chosen the losing side in a voluntary prestige war involving several of the Umpteen Nations."

"I am not familiar with the Umpteen Nations," I said.

"'Umpteen' is the closest translation of the Gryull term. The next closest is 'More than anyone cares to count.' The species's numerical system only goes up to eight, that is, the equivalent of two four-fingered Gryull hands. After that come words for 'quite a few,' 'many,' and the term I translated as 'Umpteen.'"

"I take it that mathematical prowess is not prized in their culture."

"Indeed."

"Please go on," I said.

"The Gryulls were posted offworld for two cycles while they discharged their..."—again there was an untranslatable term that the integrator rendered as *second degree shame with liability for mild ridicule*—"...after which they could have returned home and resumed their careers."

"Were they close to a return?"

"They were, from a Gryull's perspective. They are far longer lived and thus generally more patient than humans."

"What about the Ek and their walking worms?" I said.

"Two of them were criminals of moderate notoriety according to their culture's norms. The other seems to have been some kind of cousin or a debt servant. Perhaps both. They fled offworld to avoid punishment."

"The Shishisha?" I asked.

The answer was vague, that species being notoriously unforthcoming about their laws and customs. "There are indirect allusions to its having assumed one of the Seven Proscribed Forms, thus making it ineligible for procreation. That's if I'm reading the term right; another interpretation is 'ineligible for cannibalization.' Or it could be that both translations are correct—little is known of the means by which Shishisha conduct their intimacies."

"And the Halebs?"

"They seem to have been motivated primarily by the shares that Gresh Olabian offered for their participation in the project."

"Ah," I said, "so he was dividing the proceeds."

"Yes," said the integrator, "though not until the mine's decommissioning, to keep the work force together. All stood to gain substantially, at least according to their own cultural definitions of 'gain' and 'substantial.'"

"So no one had a motive to destroy the enterprise before it produced great wealth?"

"None that I can ascertain. Solitary Eks sometimes go berserk from loneliness. However, the three in this case not only had each other but, even more important to their psychological health, they had their symbiotic partners. Unattached Shishisha can give way to despair. Or at least the state is conjectured to be despair. It is characterized by inertia but no one ever knows what a Shishisha thinks or feels, if the terms are even appropriate."

"And the cause of the shaft's collapse?"

"The region is volcanic and unstable," said the integrator, displaying a map of Orkham County marked with faults and magma chambers. "Since the disaster, there have been a number of serious upheavals in the same area."

"Are there images?" I asked but was not surprised to be told there were none. The integrator reproduced the texts of official reports on the incident and the results of a more recent geological survey of the area. A footnote mentioned the old mine cave-in.

I felt a stirring in the back of my mind. A picture appeared on my inner screen and after I had considered it for a few moments I told Torsten, "I believe that all this may soon take on a recognizable shape."

I have never been an aficionado of those tales where some fellow with more intellect than personality wields logic like a lancet to slice through layers of subterfuge and diversion to discover the pulsing truth. As a young man, however, I was familiar with the tropes. One of the standard ploys was for the discriminator to announce to the assembled suspects that the mystery had been solved and all would now be revealed. Invariably, this declaration led to the lights going out while the villain took flight or, more usually, attempted to murder the sleuth before his guilt could be uncovered.

My reading of the situation at The Hutch was that such a declaration would signal to Jabbi Gloond that his days of easy living were about to find their sunset. He would then depart—I judged him not to be the type that would opt for violent tactics—and life among the Olabians would return to its previous indifferent tranquility.

Accordingly, when we regathered in the refectory for dinner, between the soup and the ragout I flourished a copy of the printed information the Institute's integrator had provided me and said, "The puzzle is now solved. I have studied the reports from Orkham County and I know what happened."

I then turned a withering stare on Jabbi Gloond. Unfortunately, his attention had been consumed by his efforts to scrape the last drops of broth from his bowl and over the noise of his spoon he had not heard what I had said. I called his name and when his moist eyes rotated in my direction, I repeated my statement.

I watched his reaction carefully and saw a succession of moods flutter across the long dullness of his face: first came puzzlement, then cogitation as he worked at what I had said, followed by the dawn of realization as he grasped its import, and finally a mask of sad resignation, accompanied by a slump of his bony shoulders.

"There are just a few more facts to be added, details of legalisms and entitlements," I said, embroidering the fabric of my falsehood to heighten the effect on Jabbi Gloond. "I shall have them in the morning. Then we will settle matters once and for all."

Gloond's shoulders fell further. I looked across the table at Torsten's triumphant smile. The son turned to the unwanted guest and said, "Depart by any door you choose, or face the consequences."

Gresh Olabian, meanwhile, said nothing, nor did his expression change. His eyes remained on his plate and his pallid fingers rested immobile beside it. I examined him closely and confirmed my earlier intuition. I believed I knew what had happened on Bain.

The lights did not go out. Instead we were served five-flesh stew. Torsten ate his with more gusto than Jabbi Gloond. It was the happiest I ever saw my friend. His father sipped a few morsels from a spoon and when he thought I was not looking regarded me with a brief, expressionless stare.

I turned and offered him a reassuring smile. He would not meet my eyes but looked down again at his plate.

After dinner, Torsten and I played pick-and-ponder in the study while the two other inhabitants of The Hutch went to their chambers. Over a smoky liqueur Torsten asked me, "Do you really know all?"

"I believe so."

"Then tell me."

"It would be premature..." I began but he cut me off, demanding that I disclose what I knew.

I demurred. "I only suspect," I said. "And if in the morning, Jabbi Gloond is gone then you will have the result you sought. The Hutch will again become as you have always known it and you can let matters lie."

"I cannot believe that my father did anything discreditable."

"That is an appropriate attitude for a good son who has a good father. I believe the situation on Bain was unique and involved desperate circumstances. It need not be spoken of."

"But what about the secret?"

"Obviously it is something your father does not wish anyone to know. I believe that 'anyone' includes you, perhaps especially you."

"But *you* know it."

"Until it is confirmed, I merely suspect," I said again. "And if in the morning Jabbi Gloond is gone, I will rise and depart in his wake without speaking of it. Then all of this can be forgotten."

Late in the evening we retired. Although I still did not suspect the worst of Jabbi Gloond I locked my chamber door and set a chair against the opener. I left a small lumen aglow on a nightstand and got into bed. I turned the facts and my conclusions over in my head one last time, then turned myself over and fell asleep.

I came awake in complete darkness. I lay without moving, breathing as quietly as I could through my open mouth, listening. Something had awakened me but now the room was without noise. The silence extended, second after second, while I heard only my own pulse throbbing in my ears.

Then there came a whisper, nearby and off to my right, the faintest sound of a soft sole touching carpet. Silently I pushed back the covers, rolled across the bed to the night table on my left and reached through the blackness for the pinking stars I had left there after my game with Torsten. Applying insight, I spun a star as I would when blindfolded. I heard it strike home, a meaty thunk followed by a hiss. Then came sounds of motion receding.

I leapt from the bed and felt for the nightstand. When I activated the lumen its glow revealed that I was alone in the chamber, with furniture still set against the latch. I threw the chair aside, unlocked the door and stepped out into the corridor to find it empty. A moment later, a tousled Torsten appeared in sleeping attire from his quarters, rubbing his eyes and inquiring what was the matter.

I told him that there was nothing that need concern him. His eyes dropped to a spot just inside the door to my room. There lay a pinking star, one of its points glistening with dark liquid.

"Gloond!" Torsten said, and flung himself in the direction of the stairs.

"No!" I called after him but he paid no heed. I could only follow.

Gloond's cubby beside the kitchens was empty, the bed unslept in.

"Integrator," Torsten called. "Where is Jabbi Gloond?"

"Gone," came the answer. "He packed and caught the last jitney to Binch."

"No," said Torsten. "His departure is a ruse and he has returned to do us ill. Even now he may be entering my father's rooms with foul intent."

I put my hand on his arm and shook him gently. "How could Jabbi Gloond contrive to enter my locked room then, having sustained an injury, escape in seconds through the still barricaded door?"

Torsten tore himself away. "I do not know." He spoke to the integrator. Where is my father?"

"In his chambers, I believe."

"I must see that he is all right," Torsten said.

"No, leave him," I said. "All will be well."

But again he paid me no heed and reluctantly I followed him to the end of the corridor in the far wing. He touched the door control and when it would not open he ordered the integrator to override the mechanism.

The door slid aside and Torsten strode through the sitting room to his father's private bed chamber. He called for every lumen to be activated and the sudden flood of brightness chased all shadows from the room.

The great bed occupied the center of the space, and its center was occupied by a motionless, amorphous shape beneath the bedding. "Father!" Torsten cried, and before I could stop him he pulled back the covers.

Gresh Olabian's face was expressionless. His blank eyes looked up at us and then he slowly blinked. But our gazes were drawn first to the center of the pale forehead where, like a third eye, a deep puncture was slowly filling itself in, and then to what lay where his body should have been.

"I wish I had never brought you," Torsten said.

"I understand," I said. "I did try to keep you from discovering what I suspected had happened on Bain."

"You should have tried harder."

We were seated in the study. The geological survey notes were spread across a table. They told how less than a year ago another volcanic upheaval had rearranged the rocks into which the Olabian mine had burrowed. A deep crack now led down to where the mining party had been trapped. The footnote reported that someone had been sent down to place the ceremonial objects with which Palmadyans marked informal graves. I was certain that someone had been Jabbi Gloond.

He would have seen the unmistakable evidence of what had happened years before. Most of the miners had suffered death or near-fatal crushing injuries in the first moments of the cave-in. But a small space had remained, enough for the badly hurt Gresh Olabian and the only other member of his party left alive.

Jabbi Gloond's slow mind would have been longer coming to an understanding of what had happened after the cave-in than the instant leap accomplished the night before by that other Henghis Hapthorn who shared my mind. But eventually the Palmadyan would work it out. Then he would see in the secret that had been hidden below ground an opportunity to live the life he had come to crave once he had tasted—no doubt surreptitiously—the exotic foods that he hauled to Gresh Olabian's mining camp from the spaceport. He had worked his way back to Old Earth, scrubbing decks and latrines on a third-rate freighter, dreaming of an unending feast of spiced eggs and pickled mushrooms.

I looked at the geological survey notes and again I could envision Gresh Olabian and the other survivor making their agreement. Olabian was dying. He was desperate not to leave his infant son orphaned as he had been orphaned. So he transferred to the other all rights in the venture's earnings and the information needed to exercise them. In return, the surviving partner would see that Torsten would have a home and a father to give him a secure upbringing. The pact sealed, the other waited for Olabian to die, then it performed a necessary act upon the dead man's body before slipping through cracks and fissures, none of them thicker than a man's thumb, to reach the surface.

There the Shishisha assumed Gresh Olabian's likeness, wearing clothes from the mining man's tent as well as what it had brought up with it from the collapsed tunnel. When Jabbi Gloond came with the wagon, the facsimile of Gresh Olabian rode it to the spaceport and departed Bain.

Now the study door opened and the entity Torsten Olabian had called father for most of his life came into the room. The wound in Gresh Olabian's forehead was almost completely healed; the interaction between the Shishisha's fluid surface and the skin it had long ago flensed from Gresh Olabian's head and hands aided rapid recovery. I suspected that by now it had so integrated with the alien flesh that it could not remove them.

Torsten looked at the Shishisha and said, "No need to continue the pretense. You may resume your own shape."

"No," said the Shishisha, in its dry, whispery voice, "I am true to the agreement."

I said, "You need not have worried about me. I would never have revealed the secret. I only said what I did to make Jabbi Gloond flee, since his knowledge of your true identity was his only hold on you."

The Shishisha inclined Gresh Olabian's head. I took it as an apology and let it know that I harbored no ill will. I would not mention to the Bureau of Scrutiny that the creature's faithfulness to its pact with Gresh Olabian had led it to slither under the door of my chamber with the aim of silencing me forever.

"Still," Torsten said, "I think you had better go, Henghis."

I knew from the tone of his voice that our friendship would not survive the revelation I had been instrumental in bringing about. It mattered not that I had done so unwillingly and only at his urging. He had lost his father. The fact that it had happened many years ago on a far distant world signified nothing.

I gathered my belongings but left the pinking stars behind. I would not play again. I waited with Torsten at the gate for the hired aircar and when it arrived our leave taking was formal.

Not long after my return to the Institute I learned that my friend would not be rejoining its cloisters. He had gone offworld, leaving The Hutch to its solitary inhabitant's sad exile. I was surprised to note that the message that brought news of his departure was accompanied by a substantial sum.

I hope that you will not let the results of our unhappy association deter you from work for which you have an unsurpassed talent, it said, and that you will use these funds to set up as a discriminator. I believe the one with whom you share an intellect would enjoy that.

I cleared my mind so I could put the question to the inhabitant of its darker passages. I received an immediate and fierce affirmation. I fought down a resentment of the other's joy at a circumstance that had cost me a rare friendship.

Torsten's plan was as good as any other. I wound up my studies at the Institute. With Olabian's funds I secured a suitable workroom with adjacent living quarters and purchased the components of a high-functioning integrator that would serve as an appropriate research assistant to a freelance discriminator.

I hoped that this life would at least offer some interesting challenges, though I suspected that it would be a lonely affair. Friends would be few, most evenings would be spent with none but my integrator for company. As I dwelt poignantly on these prospects my other self gave the mental equivalent of an insouciant shrug.

For a moment I wondered whose life I was living. Then I put aside the incertitude as the product of vain regret and began to assemble my research assistant.

Guth Bandar

A Little Learning

Guth Bandar skirted the fighting around the temple of the war god, took a right turn off the processional way and descended the cramped, winding street that connected the acropolis with the cattle market. He ignored the shrieks around him and the whiff of acrid smoke stealing up from the lower town, where the invaders were firing houses they had already looted.

After a few paces he found the narrow alley and stepped into its dark confines. The passage led to the blank stone wall of a substantial house where a man in the robes of a prosperous merchant was scraping a hole beneath the masonry. Beside him was a leaden coffer. As Bandar squeezed past, the man finished digging. He opened the box long enough to strip rings from his hands and a chain from his neck and place them within. Polished gold and the glint of gems gleamed in the dim light then the lid snapped shut.

Bandar paid no heed. The merchant was always here at this point in the cycle. In a moment he would scuttle back to the street, there to be caught by a clutch of soldiers, iron swords out and bronze corselets crimson with blood and wine. They would torture the merchant with practiced skill until he led them, weeping and limping, back to the buried hoard. Then they would cut his throat and throw him on the rubbish heaped against the wall at the alley's end.

Now the man stood and turned to go. He passed Bandar as if he were not there, which from the merchant's point of view, he was not. Bandar continued to chant the nine descending tones, followed by three rising notes, which insulated him from the man's perceptions as it did from those of all the idiomatic entities intrinsic to this Event.

The chant was called a thran, one of several dozen specific combinations of sounds which enabled scholars of the Institute for Historical Inquiry,

119

where Bandar was apprenticed, to sojourn among the multitude of archetypal Events, Landscapes and Situations, which constituted the human noösphere—what the laity called the collective unconscious—of Old Earth.

Still chanting, Bandar climbed the stinking heap at the end of the alley. At its apex would lie a large amphora with a fractured handle. He would seize the amphora, prop it against the wall, then mount and scramble atop the barrier. There he would chant a new thran, opening the gate to the next-to-last stage of the test: a Landscape preserving an antique time when the world was mostly forest.

The apprentice had already made his way by rocket-tube and teeming public slideways across the world-girdling City of a hyperindustrialized global state that flourished and faded eons before, taken a short detour through an insidious alien invasion—it had failed—and traversed a rift valley where early human variants competed to determine whose gene pools would dry to dust in the evolutionary sun. Now a walk in the forest and a segue into one of the Blessed Isles would see his quest completed.

But when he reached the top of the refuse heap, instead of the great urn he found it smashed to fragments. That ought to have been impossible, Bandar knew; nothing changed in the noösphere. Events and Situations repeated themselves exactly and eternally.

There was only one possible explanation: Didrick Gabbris had already passed this way, climbed on the amphora and departed. But before doing so he had contrived to destroy the vital stepping stone.

Frantic, Bandar scoured the area, digging through the rubbish in hope of finding something of sufficient size and sturdiness to take his weight. But if there had been anything useful, Gabbris had removed it.

Bandar was left with three choices. His first option was to search the city and bring back something else to climb on. But his insulation from the idiomats' perceptions would not extend to a substantial object that was inherent to the Location. And the longer he interacted closely with the substance of the Location, the more risk that the thran's effect would weaken and he might be perceived.

Suppose some brutal soldier, startled as a chair was borne along by a vague, misty figure, thrust his spear into the mist. Bandar's corpse would thence forward be a permanent feature of the Sack of the City. His tutors had warned of the risks of "dying" in an Event. The sojourner's consciousness became bound to the Location, reforming as one of the idiomatic entities and forever "living" and "dying" as the cycle played out endlessly.

His corporeal body, seated cross-legged on a pad in the examinations room at the Institute, would remain comatose. It would be transferred to the infirmary, bedded and intubated, and consigned to a slow decline.

Bandar's second option was to find an out-of-the-way corner and remain there until the Event concluded and began anew. Then, when he came back to the rubbish heap, the amphora would be waiting for him. But that would take time—too much time, even though durations in the noösphere did not run at the same speed as in the phenomenal world.

Different sites had their own internal clocks. This Event ran far slower than reality; the few hours in which he waited out the cycle would be almost a day in the examination room. Bandar would be the last apprentice to complete the quest; he could abandon all hope of winning the Colquhoon Bursary and being admitted to the advanced collegia.

Which was exactly why Didrick Gabbris had smashed the urn. Gabbris would win the bursary. Gabbris would scale the academic heights, while Guth Bandar slunk back to his family's commerciant firm, to spend his life buying and selling and fretting over the margins between the two.

His third option was no help: He could intone a specific thran and a ripple would appear in the virtual air. He would step through the emergency exit and instantly plunge back into his own seated body. He might complain to the Institute's provost about Gabbris's perfidy, but by the time a board could be convened to investigate, the Event would have recycled and all evidence of the crime would have disappeared.

Glumly, Bandar weighed his options and decided to risk searching for a step-up. But as he started down the pile of refuse there was a commotion at the mouth of the alley and three soldiers appeared, pushing the merchant before them. They watched as he knelt and dug up the box, amid coarse jokes and pokes with a sword at the man's plump buttocks.

There was nothing Bandar could do. The way was too narrow for him to pass, even unseen. He must sit on the rubbish heap and sing the thran, waiting while the soldiers gloated over the treasure, argued over its division, then cut the merchant's throat and finally departed.

There would be no time to find something to step on. Sadly Bandar waited for the blood to spurt and the soldiers to leave. He would open a gate and return to the examination room. Perhaps his story would be believed and he would be given a make-up exam. But that was a faint hope; he could imagine the conversation.

Bandar would say, "I accuse Didrick Gabbris of malfeasance in the matter of the amphora."

Gabbris would not deign to sully a glance by directing it at Bandar. He would elevate his nose and say, "Words without substance fleetly fly but seldom stick. Bring forth your evidence."

"I have none but my character."

"Your character is a subjective quality. You perhaps measure it as large and splendorous, while others might call it mean and marred by envy."

"This is injustice!"

"Again, a subjective concept, while blunt facts resist manipulation. Failure must find no favor."

Senior Tutor Eldred would tug at his sparse side whiskers and make his disposition. He would be swayed by the force of Gabbris's views. Bandar's would seem the squeakings of some timorous creature.

The pathetic scene at the foot of the refuse heap was nearing its conclusion. The merchant said, as always, "There, you have taken all that I valued."

One of the soldiers drew a dirk. "Not quite all."

The merchant trembled. "My life is of no worth to you. Though you take it from me you cannot carry it away with you."

"Yet we are inclined to be thorough," said the invader.

Bandar waited. He thought of some of the Locations he had visited during his years at the Institute, the places he would miss. It was then, as he said goodbye to some of his favorites, that it occurred to him that he had a fourth option.

The Institute had issued the examination candidates a partial map of the noösphere, showing only the Locations they would need to navigate the test course. The full chart of humanity's collective unconscious was an intricately convoluted sphere, complexity upon complexity. It was the work of thousands of years of exploration by noönauts, many of whom had been absorbed by perils lurking in dark corners of the Commons.

Bandar did not have such a map. A noönaut could take on his journey only what he could hold in his memory, and to encompass the schematic representation of an organic realm that had been evolving for eons was itself a work of years.

But there was a physical representation of the full map in the communal study chamber and Bandar had spent many hours gazing into its labyrinthine depths. He could not reify it fully like a master, so that it would appear to hang in the air before him, twisting and rotating to display its maze of lines and spheres. But he could recall large parts of it, all of the major Landscapes, most of the First-Order Situations and more than a few of the significant Events.

The more he thought of it, the clearer grew his recollection of the map. He saw connections and linkages from this Event to a Landscape and from there to a Location from which he knew three paths radiated. In his mind's eye he could plot a route that would let him navigate to the test's final Location, a prototypical island paradise, where Eldred waited for the candidates to arrive.

It was just possible that Bandar could indeed find his way home. Better yet, he was fairly sure that some of the sites through which he would travel had advantageous temporal dimensions: the alternate route, though it required more steps, might actually be traversed in less objective time than the course the tutors had set.

The merchant had gurgled out his last bloody breath. The alley lay empty. Bandar made up his mind to try the long way home. Perhaps his resourcefulness would so impress the examiners that they would overlook his failure to follow the prescribed course. At the worst, if hopelessly stuck, he could exit through an emergency gate.

He risks nothing who has lost all, he told himself. Singing the thran, he returned to the processional way and followed it past the burning royal palace to the city's shattered gates. Dead defenders were piled high and he had to climb a rampart of bodies to reach the wooden bridge that spanned the canal.

A little beyond was a stand of date trees. A single attacker, pinned to a trunk by an arrow through his shoulder, weakly struggled to work the head free of the wood. His eyes widened when Bandar ceased intoning the insulating thran and suddenly appeared before him.

"Have you come to help me?" the soldier said, indicating the shaft through his flesh. "You do not resemble the god I prayed to."

"No," said Bandar. It was unwise to feel emotions, critical or supportive, in response to the idiomatic entities. They were not, after all, real people; they were more like characters in stories, no more than a collection of necessary attributes. The wounded soldier was probably a version of Unrequited Faith; to pull the arrow free would contradict his role in the Event and could cause the entity to act disharmoniously.

Bandar faced the space between two of the date palms and sang five notes. A wavering vertical fissure divided the air. He stepped through.

A gust of wind threw stinging sleet into his face. He was in a world of black and white and gray, standing on glacial scree that sloped down from a bare ridge above and behind him. The closest thing to color was the dark blue of mountains whose lower slopes were visible beyond the ridge until they rose to disappear above the leaden overcast from which the sleet was flying. If the wet clouds dispersed they would reveal no peaks; the tops of the mountains were buried in unbroken ice all the way to the pole.

Downslope, a cold, wet plain of lichen and coarse grass extended to a line of horizon that was largely invisible behind the showers of freezing rain. Far out he saw a mass of reindeer and the humped shapes of mammoths, identifiable by their peculiar bobbing gait. Closer, a ring of musk oxen turned curved horns toward a short-muzzled bear that circled the herd on long legs.

Good, thought Bandar. He recognized the scene. He had visited this Location before though not at these precise coordinates. Still, the connecting node that would admit him to the next site was near, in a narrow cave set back from a ledge that must be farther up the ridge. He strove to remember how the view before him had looked from that previous vantage. He had definitely been higher up and somewhere off to his right.

The experienced noönaut developed a feel for these things. Though he could not call himself experienced, Bandar could perform the exercise that enhanced his sense of direction. After a moment, he experienced a tiny inclination to go to his right. He let his will yield to it and the predilection grew stronger.

That's that, he told himself and turned in the direction. A motion from the corner of his eye caught his attention. The snub-faced bear was loping toward him across the flatland, broad paws flicking up spray from the wet lichen. It was almost to the bottom of the slope.

Bandar swiftly sang the thran of nine and three notes which had sequestered him in the sacked city. The bear's pace did not slacken and its small black eyes remained fixed upon him. Quickly, the noönaut intoned the seven-and-four, the second most common insulating thran.

The bear reached the base of the scree and began to climb. He could see its condensed breath smoking from its gaping mouth, its lolling tongue bright pink against its brown fur.

There were three other thrans Bandar could try. He suspected now that the oldest and simplest of them, the four-and-two, would insulate him from the idiomatic bear's perceptions. But if he was wrong, there would not be time to determine which of the other two would work. The bear had increased its speed, ears flattened against its broad head. It would be on him in seconds.

Bandar sang five tones and the air rippled behind him. He flung himself through the gap and tumbled to the ground in the date grove. The Event was still unwinding and the wounded soldier remained pinned to his tree. The man blinked at him but Bandar counted slowly to ten then sang the five tones once more. He stepped through the fissure.

As he had expected, much more time had passed in the ice world and it had recycled. The Landscape was as it had been the first time he had stood on the slope, the bear stalking the musk oxen out on the plain. Bandar saw it become aware of him, saw it turn toward him and take its first step. He sang the four-and-two; instantly the predator turned back to the herd.

Chanting the tones, the noönaut faced about and began to climb. The loose gravel rattled out from under each footstep, so that he slid back half a step for each one he took. The icy rain assaulted the weather side of his face and neck and his extremities were numb. Bandar paused and, continuing the thran, applied another of the adept's exercises: thick garments grew to replace the nondescript garb in which he had imagined himself when he entered the noösphere. Warm mittens and heavy boots covered his hands and feet and a fur-lined hood encased his head. For good measure, he imagined himself a staff. The climbing went better after that.

The top of the ridge was broad and only slightly curved. He made good time with the wind at his back and within a few minutes he saw the ledge jutting out of the scree. But when he scrabbled down from the ridgetop he was surprised to find several fissures and cracks in the rock.

He turned and looked out at the plain again. He was sure this was the spot his tutor had brought them to, but the class had been warned not to venture out of the recess, presumably because of the bear. They had only looked out through the narrow opening, to fix the scene in memory, then attended as the tutor had revealed the two nodes and sung the thran that activated both.

Bandar looked into the first fissure and rejected it as too scant in both width and height. The second was no better. The third looked promising, however. The opening was the right height and the darkness beyond promised that the cave was also deep enough. Throwing back his hood, he stepped within.

The gates would be to his right, and Bandar turned that way. Thus he did not at first notice the bulky shape squatting in the rear of the cavern holding her sausage-fingered hands to the tiny warmth of a grease lamp burning in the severed cranium of a cave bear's skull. He drew breath to sing the four-and-two but before a sound could emerge a noose of plaited rawhide dropped over his head and constricted his throat.

The Commons was the distillation of all human experience, everything that had ever been important to humankind, individually or collectively, since the dawntime. It was the composite memory of the species, the realm of the archetypes. Some were of great moment, battles and disasters; some were the small but vital elements of a full life, the loss of virginity, the birth of a child; some were simply landscapes—deserts, sea coasts, lush valleys, ice age barrens—against which generation upon generation of humans had measured their existence.

The elements of the noösphere were formed by aggregation. An event happened, and the person to whom it happened remembered it. That individual memory was the smallest particle of the noösphere, called by scholars an engrammatic cell. On its own, a single cell drifted away on the currents of the Commons and was lost.

But when the same event—or even closely similar events—happened to a multitude the individual cells were so alike that they cohered and joined, drawing vitality from each other, and forming a corpuscle. As a corpuscle grew it became more potent, more active, even to the extent of absorbing other similar corpuscles. Enough such adhesions and corpuscles aggregated into archetypal entities, permanent features of the collective unconscious. They took up specific Locations in the Commons.

Events, Situations and Landscapes were not precise nor accurate records. Rather they were composite impressions of what similar happenings had *meant* to those to whom they happened. They included every horrid crime and tragic defeat, every joy and triumph of the human experience, real or imagined, each distilled to its essence and compounded.

And all of those essential Events, Situations and Landscapes were peopled by appropriate idiomatic entities, like the mammoths on the sleet-swept plain, the tortured merchant in the burning city, and the immensely fat female cave dweller whose piglike eyes now regarded Guth Bandar from the rear of the cave, while whoever was behind him jerked the noose, leaving him dancing on tiptoe, struggling to breathe.

The fat one grunted something and another figure appeared from behind her bulk. This one was as lean and dried as the rawhide that constricted Bandar's throat, with a face that was collapsed in on itself and wrinkled up like dried fruit, framed by thin, white hair clotted together by rancid oils. She poked a wisp of wool into the grease lamp to make a second wick then lifted the skullcap and crossed the cave to hold it before Bandar's face.

She peered at him from rheumy eyes, toothless gums working and lips smacking loudly. Then the hand that was not encumbered by the lamp reached under his parka and worked its way into his leggings. She seized parts of Bandar that he would have rather she had left untouched, weighing them in her dry, hard palm. Then she made a noise in her throat that expressed disappointment coupled to resignation and spoke to the unseen strangler behind him.

"Ready him."

The noose about his throat loosened but before Bandar could gain enough breath to sing the thran a hood of grimy leather descended over his head. The noose was slipped up over the ill-smelling hide until it came level with his mouth. Then it was cinched tight again, gagging him. He tried to intone the thran but could not produce enough volume. Meanwhile, his hands were bound together behind him.

There were eye holes in the hood and a slit where his nose protruded, allowing him to breathe. He felt a weight on his head and realized that the headgear supported a pair of antlers.

The strong one who had held him from behind now stepped into view and he saw that she too was female, though young and muscular, with a mane of tawny hair and a face that mingled beauty with brute power.

She moved lithely to hitch a hide curtain to a wooden frame around the cave's mouth, closing out the light and the cold air that flowed in like liquid from the tundra. The old one was dipping more wicks of what was probably mammoth wool into the grease lamp, creating a yellowy glow on the walls while the fat one began to strip off her furs and leathers.

It was an ancient maxim at the Institute that a little learning made a perilous possession. Bandar realized that aphorism defined his predicament. He had been brought to this Location once before, but barely long enough to fix the place in his memory. He had misjudged its category.

When they had briefly visited an adjacent cave the tutor's sole concern had been to display the nodes that coincided there. He had not explained the Location's nature and when Bandar had looked out at the tundra he had thought that they were briefly passing through a mere Landscape; instead, it was now clear that this was a Situation.

In the dawntime, there had been an archetypal tale of three women— one young, one old, one in the prime of life—living in some remote spot. Questers came to them, seeking wisdom, and always paying an uncomfortable price. In later ages the Situation had evolved into bawdy jokes about farmers' daughters or poetic tropes about dancing graces. But here was the raw base, rooted deep in humankind's darkest earth. Bandar had no doubt that the final outcome of this Situation, as with so many others, was blood and death.

The grease fire was warming the cave as the crone and the girl efficiently rendered Bandar naked. The matron, now also uncovered, grunted and sprawled back on the pile of furs, giving Bandar more than an inkling of the first installment of the price he must pay.

The young one took a gobbet of the grease that fed the lamp and warmed it between her hands before applying it to the part of Bandar that the crone had weighed and found merely adequate. Despite Bandar's disinclination to participate, her ministrations began to have an effect.

Bandar realized that he was in danger of being pulled into this Situation, deeply and perhaps irrevocably. The longer one stayed in a particular place and interacted with its elements, the more its "reality" grew and the more integrated with it the sojourner could become. The speed of the effect was heightened if the noönaut abstained from intoning thrans or if he adopted a passive attitude.

The old hag was shaking a bone rattle and grunting a salacious chant about a stag and a doe. Meanwhile, the young one had finished greasing him and was surveying the result with a critical eye. Bandar looked down and saw that his virtual body was behaving as if it were real flesh. It was a worrisome sign.

Act, do not react was the rule in such a predicament. But outnumbered, bound and gagged, he had few options for setting the agenda. He mentally cast about for inspiration and found it in the expression on the face of the youngest of the three cave dwellers. She was regarding what was now Bandar's most prominent feature in a manner that more than hinted at disappointment.

Her look gave the noönaut a desperate idea: If it was possible to grow winter clothing and to create a staff from nothing, might he likewise be able to change the proportions of his own shape? His tutors had never spoken of such a thing, but necessity was a sharp spur. If it was possible for Bandar to increase the dimensions of his most intimate equipment, he might improve his position.

While the young one reapplied herself to his lubrication, Bandar employed the adept's exercises that had protected him against sleet and slippery footing, although now with a more personal focus. After a few moments he heard the rattle and chant stop. The crone was staring, open mouthed, and the tawny-haired one was blinking with surprise. Bandar looked down and saw that his efforts had been more successful than intended. What had before been merely presentable was now grown prodigious.

"That will need more grease," the old woman cackled. The young one agreed and scooped up a double handful.

When he was thoroughly lubricated, they manhandled him over to where the fat one lay in expectation. He was forced first to kneel between her enormous splayed thighs then to lie prone upon the mountainous belly. The crone took hold of his new-grown immensity and guided him until connections were established, which brought first a grunt of surprise from the matron then other noises as the young one placed a cold, calloused foot on Bandar's buttocks and rhythmically impelled him to his labors.

The woman beneath him began to thrash about, making sounds that put Bandar in mind of a large musical owl. For his part, he concentrated on mental exercises that placed a certain distance between his awareness and his virtual body, lest he become too involved in the activity and find himself on a slippery slope into full absorption.

Seize the process or be seized by it, he remembered a tutor saying. The Commons was an arena rife with conflict, where will was paramount. To control his place in a Location, the uninsulated noönaut must be the dominant actor, not one of the supporting cast. *How can I amplify my impact?* he asked himself, rejecting any further increase in size—he might damage the matron.

The idea, when it came, seemed unlikely to succeed. Still, he had heard that women could grow fond of certain devices used for intimate achievements. Bandar summoned his conviction and focused his attention on effecting the change. Within seconds a new sound rose above the matron's musical hoots: a deep thrumming and throbbing which he could clearly hear despite the fact that its source was buried in the mounds of flesh beneath him.

The matron now began to issue throaty moans with a counterpoint of high-pitched keening. She thrashed about with an energy that might have propelled Bandar from her if the young one hadn't continued to press down with her pumping foot. At last the heaves and flings culminated in a final paroxysm and Bandar heard a long and satiated sigh, followed almost at once by a rumbling snore.

Immediately, the other two hauled the noönaut from the matron's crevice and flung him down on his back, the vibrating immensity buzzing and humming above his belly. There was a brief tussle between youth and old age, quickly decided by the former's strength despite the latter's viciousness and guile.

The tawny-haired woman straddled Bandar and seized his conspicuous attribute. As she lowered herself onto it her eyes and mouth widened and tremors afflicted her belly and the long muscles of her thighs. Then she leaned forward, placed her palms on his shoulders and set to work.

Bandar saw the crone peering over the young one's shoulder with an expression that sent a chill of apprehension through him. Ritual slaughter might not be the worst fate he would suffer. He resolved to exert himself.

He reasoned that the same exercises that had enlarged some parts of him must make others shrink. While the young female lathered herself to a fine foaming frenzy above him, Bandar focused his attention on his still bound hands. In a moment he felt them dwindle until they were the size of a doll's. The rawhide thongs slipped off.

The young woman was quicker to reach the heights than her older cavemate but stayed there longer. Bandar bided his time. Finally, she emitted a long and thoughtful moan and collapsed onto the noönaut's chest. The old woman wasted no time but avidly seized the incumbent at hip and shoulder and rolled her free of Bandar. She stepped over him and prepared to impale herself.

Bandar bent himself at knee and hip to put his feet in the crone's belly, then launched her up and away. As she squawked in pain and outrage, he sprang to his feet and made straight for the hide that hid the exit.

His tiny hands gave him trouble, but when a glance behind showed his two conquests sitting up and the hag reaching for a long, black shard of razor-edged flint he put an arm between wood and leather and tore the covering away.

The sleet slashed at him. The bare ledge was slick with freezing rain. There was another cave a short dash along the ledge—it looked to be the right one—and he half-ran, half-slid toward it, the antler-topped mask bobbing on his head and his still enormous and buzzing bowsprit pointing the way.

As he went he tried to loosen the cord that pressed the mask into his mouth, but his puny hands hindered him. Yet he must free himself of the mask to chant the thran that opened the gate in the next cave or be caught by the pursuing women.

He decided to shrink his head. There was no time for refinement and he did not try to specify the degree to which his skull must diminish; he could put things to rights later.

As he ran he felt the mask loosen, then the cord dropped loose around his neck as the dimensions of his jaw diminished. He tossed his chin up and the antlered hood flew backward. From behind him he heard a grunt and a curse and a clatter. Someone had tripped over it and they had all fallen.

Bandar did not look back but threw himself into the new cave, which he was relieved to see was empty. He recognized it now, though he could not recall whether the gate he sought was to left or right.

If he had time, his memory or his noönaut's acquired sense of direction would tell him which to choose. But there was no time. He could not even intone the four-and-two thran and remove himself from his pursuers' purview: having spent so long uncloaked in this Situation and so closely involved with its idiomats, he could not hide himself completely.

The moment he entered the cave he chanted the opening thran. Nothing happened. Then the cave darkened as the doorway behind him filled with murderous females. Bandar had no time to work out why the thran had not succeeded. Fortunately, the answer came before full panic set in: he had sung the notes through vocal equipment that was markedly smaller than his regular issue; just as a miniature horn plays a higher note, his shrunken larynx and throat had thrust the thran into a higher register. Thrans had to be exactly the right pitch.

Bandar adjusted for scale and sang the notes again, and was rewarded with two ripples in the air. Arbitrarily he chose the one to his left and leapt through as the young cavewoman's nails sank into his shoulder.

He emerged into Heaven. All was perfection: verdant meadows with grass soft as velvet and dotted with flowers of exquisite filigree; groves of stately trees, each impeccable in composition and form; skies as clear and blue as an infant's gaze; and air as sweet as a goddess's breath.

The rift through which he had come closed behind him and Bandar stood a moment, a tiny hand to his breast as his fear ebbed away. At once he knew that he had taken the wrong gate—he should now be alone on a mountaintop from which he could have segued to the destination island.

He could retrace his route. The cavewomen's Situation would soon recycle. But first he should restore his body parts to their proper proportions and reclothe himself. He needed to make tones of the right pitch, and it would not do to encounter the Senior Tutor while stark naked and presenting the humming enormity that dominated his ventral view.

He looked carefully around. He was standing under some trees. There were no idiomatic entities in view and Heaven was usually a tranquil Location. But just to be safe he decided to move deeper into cover. He ducked to pass under the lower branches of a flawless flowering tree, the perfume of its blossoms at close range making his head swim. With each step the touch of the grass against his bare feet was a caress.

A very sensuous Heaven, he thought, and resolved to explore it more thoroughly when he was received into the Institute as a full fellow. Perhaps he would make a special study of such Locations; it would be pleasant work.

Secluded among the scent-laden trees, he concentrated on a mental image of his own head and performed the appropriate exercises for what he judged to be sufficient time. But when he raised his miniature hands to examine the results he discovered that his skull had remained tiny while his ears and nose had grown far beyond normal; indeed they were now as out of harmony with nature as the buzzing, vibrating tower that rose from his lower belly.

If I could see what I am doing, it would make the work much easier, Bandar reasoned. The setting seemed too Arcadian for an actual mirror, but the noönaut heard the gentle tinkling of water nearby. A *still pool would do*, he thought.

He followed the sound deeper into the grove and came to a clearing where a bubbling spring welled up to form a pool of limpid clarity. He knelt and gazed into the gently rippling water. The image of his shrunken face, albeit now centered by a trunklike proboscis and framed by a pair of sail-like ears, looked back at him with grave concern. He began the exercises anew.

"Bless you," said a mellow voice behind him. Bandar swung around to find a sprightly old man with the face of a cherub beaming down on him from under a high and ornate miter that was surrounded by a disk of golden light. The saint was dressed in ecclesiastical robes of brilliant white with arcane symbols woven in gold and silver thread. In his hand was a stout staff topped by a great faceted jewel.

"Thank you," said Bandar. "I'll be but a moment."

But as he spoke he saw the man's beatific expression mutate sharply to a look of horror succeeded by a mask of righteous outrage. Faster than Bandar would have credited, the jewel-topped staff rotated in the hierophant's hand so that it could be thrust against the noönaut's chest, and he was toppled into the crystal water.

"Glub," said Bandar as he passed below the surface. When he struggled back to the air he saw the old man looming over him, the staff set to do fresh mayhem. He had time to hear the idiomat cry out, "Enemy! An enemy is here!" before the gem struck Bandar solidly on his tiny cranium and drove him under again.

Bandar wondered if it was possible to drown in the Commons. He elected not to find out and kicked off toward the other side of the pool, swimming under the surface.

The throbbing queller of cavewomen was not diminished by the cold water. Indeed it tended to dig into the soft bottom of the pool so that he had to swim closer to the surface. But his action took him out of range of the staff and in moments he had hauled himself free of the water. The idiomatic saint was circling the pool, clearly intent on doing more damage, all the while bellowing alarms.

Bandar fled for the trees, but as he ran he heard the rush of very large wings. Casting a look over his shoulder, he saw a vast and shining figure passing through the air above the grove. The long bladed sword in its grasp was wreathed in flame and the look on its perfectly formed features bespoke holy violence.

Bandar fell to his knees and opened his mouth. The four-and-two would not work here, he was sure. And he doubted the nine-and-three would be efficacious. Given how his fortunes had fared today, it would be the three threes. This was the most difficult sequence of tones, even when the chanter was not possessed of mouse-sized vocal equipment absurdly coupled to an elephantine nasal amplification box, while distracted by vibrations from below and the threat of incineration from above.

His alternatives rapidly dwindling, the noönaut frantically adjusted his vocalizations to find the exact pitch. At least the giant ears assisted in letting him hear exactly how he sounded. The sight of the descending winged avenger lent urgency to his efforts and in moments he struck the right tones. He sang the three threes and saw the terrible beauty of the angel's face lose its intensity of focus. The wings spread wide to check its ascent; it wheeled and flew off, its flaming sword hissing.

The staff-wielding hierophant stood on the other side of the bubbling pool, scratching his head and wearing an expression like that of a man who has walked into a room and cannot remember what he came for. Then he turned and went back the way he had come.

The gate back to the ice-world was too close to where the saint was keeping his vigil. Bandar did not fancy hunting for it and standing exposed while seeking the right pitch for the opening thran, with hard-tipped staffs and flaming swords in the offing. He would find another gate and take his chances.

Chanting the three threes, he went out onto the luxurious lawn again but now its caressing touch mocked his dismay. He saw above the distant horizon a squadron of winged beings on combat patrol. In another direction was a walled citadel, giant figures watching from its ramparts, a glowing symbol hovering in the sky over the heads.

There could be no doubt: he had passed into one of those Heavens that offered no happy-ever-aftering; instead, here was an active Event—one of those paradises threatened by powers that piled mountains atop each other or crossed bridges formed of razors. In such a place an uninsulated sojourner would not long remain unnoticed. And neither side took prisoners.

If he stopped chanting the three threes, someone might launch a thunderbolt at him. Still, Bandar attempted the techniques that would restore his parts to their proper size. At the very least, he wished to be rid of the humming monstrosity connected to his groin; it slapped his chest when he walked and when he stood still it impinged upon his concentration.

But it was too difficult to maintain the complex chant through his distorted vocal equipment while attempting to rectify his parts. All Bandar could manage was to alter the color of the buzzing tower from its natural shade to a bright crimson. It did not seem a profitable change.

He abandoned the effort and concentrated instead on using his sense of direction to tell him where the next gate might be. In a moment an inkling came, but he was dismayed to recognize that the frailty of the signal meant that the node was a good way off.

Bandar set off in that direction, chanting the three threes, ears flapping from fore to aft and nose swaying from side to side, his chest slapped contrapuntally. After he had walked for some time he noticed that the signal was only marginally stronger; it would be some time before he reached its source.

While I was making alterations I should have doubled the length of my legs, he thought and scarcely had the idea struck him than he realized if he had had that inspiration in the sacked city he could have climbed onto the wall to open its gate and none of this would have been necessary.

The noönaut stopped and sat down. *I have been a fool,* he thought. *Didrick Gabbris deserves to win; he will fit this place far better than I ever could.* He felt his spirit deflate and resolved not to persist with the quest. He would open an emergency gate and leave the Commons.

But not here in the open, where someone might cast who knew what lethal missile in his direction. Without warning, in such a Location, an actual god might appear and unleash disasters that only an irate deity could conceive of.

Bandar rose and crossed quickly to the nearest copse of trees. Under their sheltering boughs he spied a troop of armored figures drawn up in a phalanx, the air above their head ablaze of gold from their commingled halos. Still chanting, he backed away.

He walked on, investigating one stand of trees after another, finding each under the eye of at least one brightly topped sentry. Several were peopled by whole battalions of holy warriors.

He would have to leave Heaven before he could find a safe place in which to call up an emergency exit. He wished he knew more about these Locations—his interests ran more toward the historical than the mythological—but he recalled that there was often a ladder or staircase connecting them to the world beneath. It was usually at the edge, sometimes wreathed in clouds.

He kept on until eventually he found himself descending a long, grassy slope which seemed to end in a precipice. Gingerly, he inched toward the edge. He would have crawled on hands and knees but his enormous red appendage hampered him.

Near the lip he looked out into empty air that was suffused with light from no discernible source. Far below, scattered clouds drifted idly, the gaps between them allowing glimpses of fields and forests beneath. Bandar shuffled closer to the edge to look almost directly down, hoping to see some means of descent but his view was hindered by the vibrating enormity. Finally he knelt and leaned forward.

There was something there, just beyond the last fringe of lush grass. He reached to move away the obscuring blades. Yes, that looked much like the top of a ladder.

"Ahah!" said Bandar, breaking off the thran to indulge in a moment of triumphant relief. Immediately, a scale-covered hand appeared from beyond the rim, seized his wrist with claw-tipped fingers and yanked him over the precipice.

Bandar's squawk was cut off by a hot, calloused palm pressed against his mouth. There was a reek of sulfur and he was clutched by rock-hard arms against an equally unyielding chest, then he heard a flap of leathery wings and felt his stomach lurch as the creature that held him dropped into empty space.

They spiraled downward, affording Bandar a panoramic view of what lay beneath Heaven. There was a ladder; indeed, there were many. But though their tops were set against the grassy lip from which he had been seized their bases were not grounded on the earth far below. Instead, they were footed on a vast expanse of stone paving that was the top of an impossibly colossal construction that rose, tier upon tier, to thrust up through the clouds and end just below the celestial realm.

The tower top was thronged by legions of blood-red creatures, some winged, some not, but all armored in shining black chitin and clutching jagged-edged swords and hooked spears as they swarmed up the ladders.

As Bandar spun downward he saw the topmost of the invaders being boosted onto the grass and heard the piercing sound of a horn. Then he and his captor descended into a cloud and for a time all was mist. They emerged to fly beneath an overcast, dropping ever lower toward a great rent in the earth from which foul clouds and odors emerged, as well as more marching legions of imps, demons and assorted fiends, all bound for the great tower.

The demon that held Bandar lifted its wings like a diving pigeon and plummeted into the reeking chasm. A choking darkness closed the noönaut's eyes and nose but he sensed that they fell a long, long way.

"In a moment, my servant will remove his hand from your mouth," said the occupant of the black iron throne. "If you attempt to say the name of You Know Whom"—one elongated finger directed its pointed tip at the roof of the vast underground cavern—"you will utter no more than the first syllable before your tongue is pulled out, sliced into manageable pieces and fed back to you. Are we clear?"

Bandar looked into the darkness of the speaker's eyes, which seemed to contain only impossibly distended pupils. He wished he could look away but he was by now too far acclimated to this Location, and the Adversary's powers gripped him the way a snake's unwavering gaze would hold a mouse.

He nodded and the palm went away. The other's upraised finger now reflectively stroked an aquiline jaw, its progress ending in a short triangular beard as black as the eyes above it. "What are you?" said the voice, as cool as silk.

Bandar wished he'd studied more about the Heavens and Hells, but he had always been more compelled by Authentics than by Allegoricals. He knew, however, that within their Locations deities and their equivalents had all the powers with which their real-world believers credited them. So, in this context, he faced an authentic Principal of evil—or at least of unbridled ambition—that had all the necessary resources, both intellectual and occult, to battle an omnipotent deity to at least a stalemate. Bandar, who could not out argue Didrick Gabbris, was not a contender.

The sulfur made him cough, Finally he managed to say, "A traveler, a mere visitor."

The triangular face nodded. "You must be. You're not one of mine and"—the fathomless eyes dropped to focus briefly on Bandar's vibrating wonderment—"you're certainly not one of His. But what else are you?"

Every Institute apprentice learned in First Week that the concept of thrans had originated in a dawntime myth about an ancient odist whose songs had kept him safe on a quest into the underworld. This knowledge gave Bandar hope as he said, "I am also a singer of songs. Would you care to hear one?"

The Adversary considered the question while Bandar attempted to control his expression. The distant gate he had sensed in Heaven was but a few paces across the cavern. He had only to voice the right notes, perhaps while strolling minstrel-like about the space before the throne, to call the rift into existence and escape through it.

"Why would you want to sing me a song?" said the Adversary.

"Oh, I don't know," said Bandar, and was horrified to see the words take solid form as they left his mouth. They tumbled to the smoldering floor to assemble themselves into a wriggling bundle of legs and segmented body parts that scuttled toward the figure on the throne, climbed his black robes and nestled into the diabolical lap. The Principal idly stroked it with one languid hand, as if it were a favored pet.

"All lies are mine, of course," the soft voice said, "and I gave you no leave to use what is mine." He nodded to the winged fiend that still stood behind Bandar and the noönaut felt an icy pain as the thing inserted a claw into a sensitive part and scratched at the virtual flesh.

"Now," said the Adversary, when Bandar had ceased bleating and hopping, "the truth. What are you, why did you come here and, most urgent of all, how did you contrive to enter His realm behind His defenses?"

"If I tell you, may I go on my way?"

"Perhaps. But you *will* tell me. Ordinarily, I would enjoy having it pulled out of you piece by dripping piece, but today there is a certain urgency."

"Very well," Bandar said, "though the truth may not please you." And he told all of it—thrans, Locations, examinations, Gabbris, the smashed amphora—wondering as he did so what the repercussions might be. It was no great matter if the odd idiomat saw a sojourner pass by; but Bandar had never heard of an instance where a Principal was brought face to face with the unreality of all that he took to be real.

At the very least, the Institute would be displeased with Apprentice Guth Bandar. Yet, whatever punishment Senior Tutor might levy, Bandar could not imagine that it would be a worse fate than being absorbed into a Hell. Chastising malefactors, after all, was what such Locations did best.

When the noönaut had finished, the listener on the throne was silent for a long moment, stroking his concave cheek with a triangular nail, the great dark eyes turned inward. Finally he laid a considering gaze on Bandar and said, "Is that all? You've left out no pertinent details that might construe a trap for a hapless idiomatic entity such as I?"

Bandar had thought about trying to do exactly that, but had not been able to conceive of a means. Besides, he had expected this question and knew that any lie he attempted would only scamper off to its master, leaving Bandar to reexperience the demon's intruding claw, if not something worse.

"It is all."

The Adversary stroked at his beard. "You can imagine that this news comes as a shock."

"Yes."

"Even a disappointment."

"I express sympathy." It wasn't a lie. Bandar could express the sentiment without actually feeling it.

"It repeats forever? And I never win," he indicated the cavern's ceiling again, "against You Know Whom?"

"Never."

"What would you advise?" the archfiend asked, then added, "Honestly."

Bandar thought it through but could come to no other conclusion. "You must be true to your nature."

The archfiend sighed. "That I already knew." He reflected for a moment then went on: "It ought to be comforting to know exactly why one exists. Instead I find it depressing."

A silence ensued. Bandar became uncomfortable. "I can offer one solace," he said.

The dark eyes looked at him. "It had better be exceptionally good. I usually need to see a great deal of suffering before I am comforted."

Bandar swallowed again and said, "When your Location's cycle ends and recommences, you will not know of this."

"Hmm," said the other. "Thin comfort indeed. Knowledgeability is my foremost pride. To know that I shall become ignorant is a poor consolation until ignorance at last descends. The battle up there may go on for eons. I must think about this."

Bandar said nothing and attempted to arrange his mismatched features into an expression of studied neutrality. He saw thoughts making their presence known on the Adversary's features, then he saw his captor's gaze harden and knew the archfiend had come to the inevitable conclusion.

The voice was not just cool now; it was chilled. "I see. If I keep you and make you part of this 'Location,' as you call it, then might I expect you to regularly reappear and remind me that I am not what I thought I was?"

"I do not know how much of my persona would survive the process, but there is a risk," said Bandar. "I would be happy to relieve you of it by moving on."

"Hmm," said the other. "But someone must suffer for my pain. If not you, then who?"

Bandar looked around the smoky cavern. All the demons and imps seemed to be regarding him without sympathy.

He thought quickly, then said, "I may have an idea."

Intoning the three threes, Bandar scaled the ladder that reached to the brink of Heaven. The first assault had failed and the invaders had pulled back, leaving mangled fiends and demons heaped on the tower's top and scattered about the narrow strip of celestial turf that marked the limit of their advance.

Angels of lower rank were now heaving the fallen over the edge and casting down the scaling ladders so that Bandar had to climb with scampering haste to avoid being toppled. He picked his way across the grass, stepping over bodies and dodging the cleanup. There was a sharp tang of ozone to the otherwise delicious air of Heaven; an inner voice told him it was the afterscent of thunderbolts.

No one paid him any notice as he made his way between regiments of angelic defenders, drawn up in precise blocks and wedges, their armor and weaponry dazzling and the space above their heads almost conflagrant with massed halos. But beyond the rearmost ranks he saw others laid upon the grass, their auras flickering and dim, shattered armor piled beside them.

As he neared the recumbent forms he heard again the whoosh of great wings. Huge figures gracefully alit and gathered up the fallen angels then took to the air and winged away. Urged by his inner voice, Bandar ran toward the evacuation and, seizing the robe of an archangel, climbed to the broad span between his wings. His tiny fists made it hard to hold on as the great pinions struck the air and they sprang aloft.

So far, so good, said the voice. Bandar was too busy clutching and intoning to frame a response. They climbed above the fields and woods of Heaven, until the great rivers were mere scratches of silver on green. For a long time, the archangel's wings dominated the air with metronomic strokes then the rhythm ceased and the great feathered sails held steady as they glided down toward a city of shining stone upon a conical hill, with serried roofs and pillars and windows that flashed like gems. The archangel alighted on a pristine pavement and carried the angel in his arms toward a vast edifice of marble and alabaster.

Down, said the inner voice, and Bandar descended, clutching handfuls of angelic fabric until his feet touched the polished flags. *Turn right and go up the hill. There's a staircase.*

Bandar wanted to say, "This is unwise," but he was afraid that to cease intoning the thran in this part of the Location would invite a blast from on high. He topped the staircase and came upon a broad plaza of more white stone accented by inlays of colored gems. On the other side of the square stood an enormous rotunda—yet more white stone, though this one was roofed with a golden dome. Its gigantic doors—still more gold, bedizened with mosaics of gems—gaped open, throwing out an effulgence of light and a glorious sound of massed voices.

Here we go, said the inner urging. Bandar advanced on trembling legs until he stood in the doorway. The interior was incandescent with magnificence. Rank upon rank of angels stood on wall-climbing terraces, singing unparalleled choruses to the great white-bearded figure who sat a diamond throne that grew from the middle of a diamond floor.

In, said the voice in Bandar's mind, *and keep chanting*. The noönaut's legs could not have felt looser if they had been made of boiled asparagus, but he did as he was told, crossing the brilliant floor until he stood directly before the throne. Its occupant's feet rested on a footstool that resembled a globe of the Earth, just at Bandar's eye level. He noticed that the bare toes bore delicate hairs of gold.

The sojourner stood, awaiting direction from within. It was hard to keep intoning the thran while the thousands of perfect voices sang in flawless harmony a song that thrilled the soul.

It's always the same song, you know, said his passenger. *He never tires of hearing it, and they know better than to tire of singing it.*

The music was climbing, crescendo upon crescendo, ravishing notes impossibly achieved and sustained, quavering tremolos that intoxicated the senses. It was all Bandar could do to keep intoning the three threes, especially with his distorted vocal equipment and the difficulty compounded by the sharpness of hearing that his elephantine ears provided.

Wait for it.

The thunderous chorus was now pealing out such a paean of praise that Bandar feared the golden dome might lift away.

Almost.

The voices soared to the brink of climax.

Now.

Bandar ceased intoning the thran. From the point of view of the idiomats, including the Principal on the throne, he suddenly appeared before them, with all his acquired anatomical peculiarities on full display.

The music stopped in mid-melisma. There was an instant silence so profound that Bandar wondered for a moment if he had been struck deaf. Then he heard the thrumming sound of the giant crimson monstrosity that still vibrated on his front.

Perfect, said the inner voice. *Open up, here I come.*

Bandar opened his mouth. He felt the same unpleasant sensation of stretching and an urge to gag that he had experienced when the Adversary had entered him down in the sulfurous cavern. A moment later the sinister figure was standing beside him, looking up at the divine face staring down at him from the throne of Heaven.

The archfiend raised his arms and cried, "Surprise!"

"It's always much easier to get out of Heaven than to get in," commented the Adversary, as they plummeted toward the lake of fire. When the heat grew uncomfortable for Bandar, the archfiend considerately sprouted wings—much like an archangel's though somber of feather—and swept the noönaut to safety in a subterranean passageway that led back to the cavern of the iron throne.

"Are you going to keep your promise?" said Bandar.

"Ordinarily, I wouldn't," said the Principal, "but I don't want you popping up in every cycle to remind me of my futility."

"Thank you," Bandar said.

"Although it goes against my nature to be fair, you do deserve any reward in my power to grant." The dark eyes unfocused for a moment as their owner looked inward to memory. "The expression on His face. The way His eyes popped. That was worth anything. I will keep the war going as long as possible just so I can retain that image."

"I will be happy to accept what we discussed," Bandar said.

"Very well." The Adversary looked at him. "It is done."

Bandar consulted his own memory and found there a complete chart of the noösphere, exactly like the great globe suspended in the Institute's communal study chamber. Or was it?

"Is it real?" he asked.

"I have no idea," said the archfiend. "Since your arrival my concept of reality has been severely edited. I used my powers to improve your memory. I can assure you, however, that it will lead you away from here, I hope forever. I do not want you back." His long fingers imitated the action of walking. "Off you go."

Bandar consulted the globe and saw that the gate in the cavern led to a selection of Locations, depending on which thran was used to activate it. He returned the map to his memory, chose the seven-and-one and stepped through the rift.

He was overjoyed to find himself in a shaded forest of giant conifers. He recognized a particular tree not more than a few paces distant, strode to it and sang a handful of notes. Again the air rippled and he departed the forest to emerge into hot sunlight on a white beach strung between laden coconut palms and gentle wavelets.

"I have overcome!" he cried.

"You have certainly achieved some sort of distinction," said the nasal voice of Didrick Gabbris. Bandar turned to meet his rival's sneer. Gabbris lounged in the shade of a palm. Beside him, Senior Tutor Eldred inspected Bandar in detail, from the tiny skull with its flapping ears and pendulous nose down to the minuscule hands and the crimson humming centerpiece. When he had finished the catalog, his face formed an expression that Bandar found uncannily like that which he had recently seen on a deity.

"I can explain," the apprentice said.

"Not well enough," predicted Eldred.

It was a prescient observation. The Institute decided that Guth Bandar was not what they were seeking in a new generation of noönauts. Nor was Didrick Gabbris, for Bandar's account of the shattered urn was believed and he had the compensatory satisfaction of seeing his enemy driven from the cloister while he was still being debriefed by a hastily convened inquiry.

Bandar learned that in the tens of thousands of years that noönauts had been visiting the Commons other sojourners had run afoul of Principals, though no one it seemed had ever shaken the confidence of both a god and his chief opponent. It was decided that the contaminated Locations would be declared out of bounds for a few centuries, to give them time to recycle.

Bandar returned to the family firm and took up buying and selling. But in his leisure hours he would sit cross-legged, and summon up his perfect map of the noösphere. He soon found an Allegorical Location entirely peopled by nubile young women. And with his ability to make useful modifications to his virtual anatomy, the idiomats were always delighted to receive him.

He decided that a little learning was only dangerous when spread too thin.

Inner Huff

By covering his ears tightly with his palms, Guth Bandar was able to listen to the songs of the Loreleis in various Situations without becoming entranced. That was good, because to be captivated by the heart-tearing beauty of the voices would mean being trapped forever in one of the myriad byways of the collective unconscious—the Commons, as it was called by the fellows of the Institute for Historical Inquiry, of which Bandar had become an adjunct scholar.

Today he was collecting his seventh siren song, this one from a little visited Location where the singers were concealed behind a prototypical waterfall. The water sprang from a crevice in a cliff that soared above a darkly silent forest of ancient hardwoods. It fell as a sun-sparkled curtain into a limpid pool where a rainbow perpetually shimmered over the splash of foam. The song of the unseen Loreleis interwove seamlessly with the sound of the water. The combination of natural and magic sounds was a unique iteration of the siren motif and Bandar was determined to capture and reproduce the effect.

He had entered the Location a short distance away, arriving through a node that delivered him to the foot of a spreading chestnut tree. Upon arrival he had immediately sung the appropriate sequence of tones that insulated him from the perceptions of any of the Location's inhabitants.

The most likely idiomatic entity inhabiting this corner of the Commons, apart from the Loreleis, would have been a tragic Hero drawn to his doom by the siren song, perhaps companioned by a hapless Helper or a Faithful Beast. Bandar had searched the immediate forest but found none such. Their absence argued for his having arrived at a point in the Situation's cycle where the song-ensorceled entities had already been drawn into the pool and romantically drowned.

He ceased intoning the insulating thran and immediately the mingled sounds of cataract and female singers came drifting through the trees. At this distance the song was indistinct but its appeal was strong; before he knew it, he had already taken an involuntary step toward its source and was even now taking a second.

Bandar clapped hands over ears and the sound was shut out. His uplifted foot, about to complete the next step, paused in midstride. He stood still. Slowly, in the tiniest of increments, he eased the pressure of his palms against his ears. The faintest sound came to him and he experienced only a slight inclination to move toward it.

He took a step, knowingly this time, then made sure to stop before further lightening the pressure of his hands. The sound of the waterfall was more clear-cut, the female voices woven through its splash and chuckle. Bandar took two steps sideways. Now a substantial beech stood between him and the deadly glade. He leaned his head against the cool, smooth bark and eased his palms away from his ears.

The song insinuated itself, like a delicious itch, into his mind. Using an Institute technique, he fragmented his consciousness, letting part of him absorb the sound while another element of his awareness recited a sequence of syllables. The effect was to distance himself from the part of him that was aching to lift his forehead from the tree and race ecstatically toward the deadly pool.

The song's cycle was no more than three minutes long. Then the voices paused for a few heartbeats and began anew. Rigorously concentrating on the syllabic chant, Bandar let the recording function of his mind gather and hold the melody. He was careful not to compare it to the other six Lorelei songs he had already collected. It would not do to contaminate the sample.

After the second hearing he believed he had it. He broke off the syllabic sequence and again intoned the thran. Chanting, he turned and went farther into the forest. At a safe distance he called into existence the great globular map of the Commons that was the prize and glory of his memory. He consulted its intricate web of colored lines and points of intersection, then went a certain distance to his left.

Now Bandar sang a new collection of notes, three short rising tones followed by a long descender. A ripple appeared in the air before him and resolved itself into a vertical slit. He stepped through and emerged onto a stony beach set between the waves of a wine-dark sea and a grove of ancient olive trees. Nearby was a clearing overgrown with wild grapes and berries.

He had scouted this Location a few days before and deduced that it was yet another version of the Desert Island. Remote and unpopulated earthly paradises were paradoxically popular in the Commons, bespeaking humankind's perennial desire to get away from one's fellows and the myriad demands of society.

A quiet place to sit and think was one of the island's attractions; the other was that it was but one node away from the eighth and final Lorelei Location, a rocky islet surrounded by crashing breakers. Again, drowning was the archetypical fate of those who fell beneath the singers' spell, but this one took its victims by the boatload.

Bandar went up the beach and into the grove, chanting a thran to hide himself from any idiomats; even a desert island might have an occupant, perhaps a visiting cannibal whose presence represented some archetypical fear of the Other. He poked about in the greenery but saw no traces of habitation, just a few goats and some pigs snuffling for fallen fruit beneath the olive trees.

He went back down the beach and sat on a flat rock, dabbling his feet in the cool water. He ceased chanting the thran and took up the exercise of the syllables again so that he could replay the waterfall song in his mind. Even with the prevention technique, there was a moment or two when he might have lost the necessary distance from the song's insistent beauty. But a fear of sitting enraptured in this spot, endlessly hearing the song until he was absorbed into the Location, helped him to remain unaffected.

He listened with critical attention and was pleased with what he heard. The seventh song in his collection was essentially the same as the other six, lending strong support to his thesis that the melody was itself an archetype: humanity's Song of songs from which all other airs and rhapsodies sprang.

If the eighth and final iteration of the Lorelei motif was the same as the other seven, Bandar would prepare a paper for presentation at the Institute's annual Grand Colloquium, to be held a few days hence. He would argue, he believed convincingly, for the Song being recognized as a new archetype, the first to have been identified in millennia.

There would be opposition, of course, and it would be led by Underfellow Didrick Gabbris, Bandar's lifelong academic rival. Gabbris would cite the unchallenged truism of Old Earth's penultimate age that everything that could ever have been discovered had by now been found, identified, discussed with full annotation and for the most part forgotten. But not the Song of songs, Bandar knew. He had researched the matter thoroughly. He believed he was about to add something new and—he relished the pun—*unheard of* to the annals of the Institute.

Gabbris would grind his teeth in helpless rage. Bandar took a moment to envision the event. He enjoyed the images so much that he let them appear on the screen of his consciousness a second time, with minor embellishments.

A tiny sound interrupted his reverie, the *click* of stone against stone. Bandar rose from the rock on which he was seated and turned. A naked woman, lithe and small breasted with raven hair and emerald eyes, had crept down the beach toward him. Her vulpine features were set in an expression of profound mischief and her hand held an olive wood staff. She was about to touch his shoulder with the carved head of a satyr that adorned the rod's tip.

Bandar could not step out of her reach; the flat rock pressed against the backs of his thighs. He opened his mouth to intone the four-and-two thran but before he could complete its opening tetrad the dark wood touched him.

His first impression was that she was somehow increasing in size, looming over him so that he found himself looking up at her from about the level of her thighs. He felt a growing strain in his neck. He was having to bend it back so that he might continue gazing at her face. That was, he realized, because he had sunk onto all fours. At the same time he noticed that the odors of which he had been only moderately aware—the faint smell of the sea, the stink of dried seaweed up the beach, the mustiness under the olive trees, the spice of the Nymph's flesh—had all grown both richer and sharper.

To ease the strain in his neck he lowered his head and regarded his hands. But they were no longer hands. Their digits had drawn together into two clumps, the nails expanding and darkening. *Hooves*, he thought, *and a pig's hooves at that.*

He heard a giggle from above him, the sound of a malicious girl relishing a prank. Then he felt a sharp pain in his buttocks. She had whacked him across the hams with her staff. He started forward, up toward the olive trees, and was encouraged to hurry when a second blow landed in the same region as the first.

"Hurry, pig," said a voice both melodious and cruel. "Funny, tasty pig."

A third swat followed. Bandar squealed and scuttled for the trees.

The noösphere, as the collective unconscious was more properly called by the Institute's scholars, lay hidden in the lower reaches of every human psyche. It was a labyrinth of interconnected Landscapes, Events and Situations, the cores of every myth, legend, fiction and joke. Its inhabitants were the archetypical figures that furnished the dreams of humanity— Wise Man and Fool, Hero and Destroyer, Maiden, Mother and Crone, Temptress and Comforter and a host of others.

An archetype commonly encountered was the Enchantress, realized in a multitude of motifs: the maleficent Wood Witch who magicked errant hunters into wolf-slaves; the Faery Princess who beguiled a lovestruck swain through an afternoon that became a decade; the teasing Coquette whose charms figuratively turned men into animals; and the island-bound Nymph whose spells went the whole hog.

A noönaut like Guth Bandar ought to have been sequestered from her powers by a thran, a specific series of notes—like the protective song of the Singer who visited Hell in the dawn time myth—that removed him from this Enchantress's purview. But thrans had to be sung continuously, not set aside while the noönaut relished an imagined triumph over a rival.

Now, as the Nymph drove him toward the rest of her herd of swine, Bandar endeavored to chant the four-and-two. His corporeal body, seated in his meditation chamber at the Institute, waiting for his consciousness to reanimate it, enjoyed perfect pitch; that ability transposed to his consciousness whenever it went sojourning through the Commons. When that consciousness was transformed into a pig, however, Bandar found that a porcine vocal apparatus could not strike the proper notes. His overlarge ears, flopping against his fatted cheeks, told him that he was producing unmusical skreeks and skrawks. These had no effect on his captor other than to provoke yet another blow from the staff and an admonition to "Keep silence, piggy, else I'll not wait for your fattening. I'll smoke your belly and boil your head tomorrow."

He was driven into the olive grove. To his new nose, the place was awash with the smells of mulch and overripe fruit crushed underfoot, overlaid by the rank reek of the goats and the now curiously appealing scent of the other swine. The Nymph drove him into their midst and they made way for him with squeals and grunts, regarding him with sad and knowing gazes. Their attention was soon diverted, however, when their owner struck the trees with her staff and shook the branches, causing a heavy rain of olives. The swine fell upon the fruit with snuffles of appetite.

One heavily larded specimen ignored the feed. A piebald boar, he showed not appetite but stark terror as the Nymph favored him with a weighing look. She poked a finger into the fat overlaying his ribs and gave a grunt that bespoke a decision reached. She goaded the hog with the foot of her staff and chased him toward a trail that led from the grove deeper into the island's center. The chosen one gave a shrill cry that, even though a pig's throat formed it, carried an unmistakably human note of fearful despair.

Bandar fought against panic. He also had to exert himself to overcome a growing interest in the ripe olives that littered the grove. He felt an urge to shoulder aside the other swine to get at the choicest morsels. These inclinations only deepened his fear.

A consciousness that stayed too long in any Commons Location was at risk of being absorbed. Even the insulating thrans could not keep the power of the place from overpowering the sojourner and fitting him into the matrix of an Event or Situation. The discovery and mapping of the noösphere over the course of millennia had seen countless numbers of explorers inextricably engrossed into Locations. Their consciousnesses had devolved into the semi-awareness of idiomatic entities, or died outright when their virtual flesh had been transfixed by a phalanx's spears or immolated by a dragon's breath.

Being transformed into a swine worked against Guth Bandar. It threatened to weaken the integrity of his sojourning self. He must leave this Location soon or risk losing his sense of identity. If he forgot who he was he would truly become a transmogrified pig, fattening on olives, until his turn came to encounter the knife and the rendering tub.

He tore his attention away from the delicious olives he had been munching while he contemplated his fate. He found he was even more drawn toward a young sow who was giving off an odor that grew more maddeningly compelling the closer she came. A big boar with well developed tusks was shadowing her. Bandar wondered how large his own tusks might be and felt a growing urge to paw the ground and voice a guttural challenge.

Concentrate, he told himself. *And get clear of that sow while you're still more man than pig.* He made a great effort and turned his head away from her delightful scent then deliberately followed his nose toward less freighted air. He found the path down which the Nymph had herded her victim and followed it. *No pig would willingly take this course,* he told himself, and felt better for it.

The path led him uphill through woods for a short while then leveled off in a long, broad meadow of short grass grazed by sheep. Bandar wondered if all the four-legged inhabitants of the island had been transformed from human idiomats and if the kind of animals they became were determined by the Enchantress's whims or by their own natures. He couldn't account for anything in his own make-up that would qualify him for pigdom, unless it was his penchant for rooting about in academic puzzles and turning up exquisite little truffles like the Lorelei song. These were decidedly unpiglike musings, a thought which encouraged him further.

He was finding that four limbs and strong hooves made for rapid locomotion. He was almost across the meadow now, following a path of beaten earth. Ahead was a stand of stately trees. Between the boles and branches he could make out an imposing building faced in marble, ornamented with columns and pilasters and set about with statuary. As he neared the trees he veered off the path and approached by a roundabout route. He came upon a garden with a pool and fountain beyond which a paved walkway sloped down to a grotto.

He followed it, his hooves clicking softly on the stones. It led him to a sunken lawn, shaded by a rocky outcrop beneath which a bower of fragrant grasses had been heaped up and covered with carpets of soft wool. On this reclined a stocky man of middle years, red of hair and beard, who idly contemplated the gold beaker in his hand before he raised it to his lips. A driblet of purple wine ran from the corner of his mouth to lose itself in his beard, but he paid it no heed, his bright blue eyes gazing at nothing.

A beguiled Hero, Guth Bandar thought. He regarded the idiomat closely, saw neither great thews nor features so striking as to indicate divine parentage, although there were scars on the man's arms and naked chest. *A very old type*, he concluded, *a swordster when necessary, yet more inclined to the craftiness of a trickster.*

Bandar was pressing his mind to remember what he'd learned of this variant of the Hero archetype. There might be some way to play upon its known characteristics to create a strategy that would lead to his being reconstituted as a human being. After which, he would forthwith intone a thran to shield him from the view of Hero and Nymph long enough to put some distance between him and them. A quick chant of a particular seven-tone sequence would open an emergency gate. He would leap through and return to his inert body in the meditation room.

In a crisis—if, for example, the Nymph came for him with the knife—he might try to conjure the gate while still in pig form. The risk would be that he might arrive back in his body to find that parts of his psyche were still more swine than human. There were already too many people like that on Old Earth—Didrick Gabbris merely the first that came to mind.

A voice broke into his thoughts and he realized that the figure on the bower was speaking to him. "I said, 'What are you looking at, pig?'" Now the idiomat shrugged and drank more wine. "Though even a pig might look at a king."

Bandar contrived as intelligent a face as his porcine features would allow. "Hmm?" he said, and though the arrangement of his huge nasal cavity gave the wordless sound a certain honk, he thought it sounded reasonably human for a pig.

"I have pigs of my own," the Hero said. "I'm king of an island, you know."

Bandar made the same sound, but altered the tone so that it sounded like, "Really?"

"Yes," said the idiomat, "but you know I'd be happy just to be a swineherd if I could see once more my wife and son."

"Hmm," said Bandar, with a nod and a note of sympathy.

"I really must do something about getting home," the Hero said. "Build another ship or something."

This time Bandar's "Hmm" offered encouragement, a spur to action.

There ensued a conversation, largely one-sided, in which the Hero King issued observations and Bandar replied with combinations of nods, wags and hums. The noönaut was surprised how much information could be exchanged even when one interlocutor's vocabulary could not rise above the barest minimum.

"You are decidedly insightful for a pig," said the Hero. "Indeed, I have known princes who could learn from you." He drank the lees of his cup and reached for a gold pitcher that stood on a nearby table. "If they weren't too busy sulking in their tents or stealing concubines."

The idiomat poured more wine and hefted the goblet, then paused with it halfway to his stained lips. "I like a good palaver," he said. "It seems to me I have not had a conversation of any depth since..." He appeared to be consulting a mental time line that would not hold its shape. "Since a long time," he finished.

"Hmm," said Bandar. Engaging in conversation, even under his present disadvantages, was helping to keep pigness at a distance. He was wondering how he could turn this encounter further to his profit. Perhaps the Hero could persuade the Nymph to undo the spell. Focusing on the matter with a pig's brain was not easy, however. He missed the Hero's next question.

Fortunately the idiomat seemed to be accustomed to repeating himself. "I said, 'It seems to me I arrived here with several companions.' You haven't seen any of them, have you?"

An agonized squeal from not far off claimed their attention. Moments later, the Nymph came tripping down the walkway, carrying a gold plate on which lay two fair-sized morsels of raw flesh. She went to where a brazier stood on a tripod and poked at its coals with a knife, blowing them into a glowing heat. Bandar backed into the undergrowth while she was laying the plate on the embers. His sharp ears heard a faint sizzle while his pig's nose caught a whiff of cooking meat. It smelled delicious.

"I've brought you a little treat, my dear," the Nymph said, over her shoulder. "Something to restore your vigor."

Bandar realized what the two frying objects were and where they had come from. Not far away must be a most despondent boar. He also had no doubt as to the fate of the king's erstwhile shipmates. He could not repress a gasp and a shudder.

Unfortunately, a gasping, shuddering pig could not fail to attract a Nymph's attention. She turned to regard him. The brows knitted above her sharp nose and the green eyes flashed then narrowed. Bandar was reminded that idiomats, even the Principals of Locations, tended toward simplicity. They were not real people, only rudimentary personas—much like the characters in myth and fiction to which they had given rise. Where people would pause and consider, idiomats invariably acted.

"Have you met this remarkable pig?" the king was saying, even as his consort crossed the lawn, knife in hand and unmistakable motivation in her face. Bandar turned and fled.

He had been a healthy young man in his virtual self, therefore he was a healthy young pig. He soon discovered how to go from a rapid trot to a fast gallop, although he wasn't entirely sure that pigs were built for the latter gait. He did not stop to ponder the question, however; he made his best speed with the sound of thudding Nymph footsteps closing on his tail. And on what flopped below them.

He ran up a slope, breaking through a shrubbery of artfully trimmed bushes, then onto another open meadow—this one with donkeys. They scattered as he burst through their midst, heading for a thick growth of trees that climbed toward what looked to be either a high hill or a low mountain at the island's center.

His pursuer's footsteps grew louder. He put on more speed but soon he heard her drawing near again. And now it became apparent that pig lungs and legs were designed more for the sprint than the marathon, whereas Nymphs were apparently tireless.

He could hear not only her footfalls but her breathing as he reached the trees and raced between the boles. Not far in he found thickets of thorn and bramble and into these he plunged without slowing. The sharp protrusions tore at his hide, but pigskin was thick and the scratches caused him far less discomfort than he would have experienced as a man. His long, low and relatively streamlined shape was also ideal for snaking through brush at good speed.

He soon left the Nymph behind. He could hear her cursing him, her voice receding as he went deeper into the woods. Fortunately, it seemed that her maledictions were not effective unless she was wielding the olive staff.

Bandar ran a little farther into the greenery then stopped in a small open space roofed over with prickly vines. He elevated his ear flaps and moved his head from side to side, but heard nothing to alarm him. He let his wide nostrils sample the air and scented no immediate danger.

He bent his forelimbs then let his hindquarters settle to the forest floor. He had to think. There was no point in seeking to enlist the Hero King's aid. The red-haired idiomat was the Enchantress's prize—her control of him was almost certainly what this Situation was all about. She would guard him closely.

Nor could Bandar hide out on the island and attempt to reshape his virtual flesh. For one thing, the technique required leisure to concentrate; he doubted the Nymph would afford him such. For another, the only time he had attempted the procedure he had distorted himself in freakish ways. Getting from swinehood to humanness was almost certainly beyond him.

Bandar's best recourse was to find a gate and pass through to somewhere less lethal. Then he might plot a course through to some Location where the Principal was a wielder of benign magic who would lift the Nymph's curse and restore the noönaut to his true proportions. There were relatively few such places and personas—the Commons dealt out more horror than happy fun times—but they were there to be found.

And Guth Bandar had the means to find them. He concentrated and summoned the map of the noösphere into virtual existence. He found it difficult to see deeply into the complex webwork of points and lines— his pig's eyes were not so placed as to enable stereoscopic vision of near objects. Finally, he cocked his head to bring one eye to bear and began to plot a route to salvation.

He found that there were two nodes on the island that connected the Nymph's Location to others. One was a single-direction gate that would take him into a nightmarish cityscape, an urban dystopia rife with crime and infamy where the only semblance of order was a brotherhood of bounty hunters. It was no place for an innocent pig; those that might not see him as food on the hoof would likely use him for target practice.

The other gate was a multi-destination node: depending on the sequence of tones employed by an approaching noönaut, it might open to any of five places. One was a mellow kingdom of strolling troubadours and itinerant tale-spinners. Better yet, a short jog across that Location would bring him to a gate into a children's Situation—luckily, not one of the many nasty ones, but a winter fantasia whose magical, merry Principal enjoyed bestowing gifts and bonbons on good little boys and girls. He would surely grant the wish of a good little pig.

The multifarious node waited in the meadow of the donkeys. That was a dangerously wide space to cross, especially if an angry Enchantress lurked nearby. It might take pig-Bandar more than one trial to find the right notes to activate the exit.

But he resolved to hazard the meadow, though he would wait for nightfall. In the meantime, he would practice producing tones from a pig's throat.

The moon rode full and high across a dark blue heaven, flooding the field with silvery light. Bandar stood beneath the last of the trees and surveyed the open space. Pig night vision was no better than the human version, but his ears and nose added a wealth of sensory impressions. The meadow's inhabitants stood clumped not far away, making donkey murmurs to each other. Of the Nymph there was no sign.

Bandar crept out onto the cropped grass, advanced a few steps and paused. He heard nothing. He felt the slight tingle in the back of his mind that told him he was near to a node and went in the direction that made the sensation increase. A few more steps and again he paused, again hearing and seeing nothing.

The gate was not too far now. He trotted forward, mentally rehearsing the sequence of tones he must sing to activate it.

Midway across the meadow, he heard a rustle of motion among the donkeys. He turned to look their way. A slim figure rose from amongst them. It was the Nymph and in her hand was the olive wood staff.

Swiftly she laid its leering tip to the backs of the donkeys. With each contact the touched beast changed shape, became longer and lower. Their excited braying became a baying, the deep bell of a hunting pack underlaid by slavering growls.

She touched the last of the herd then pointed with the staff. "After him!" she cried. "Rend him!"

Bandar had not waited for the transformations to be completed. He burst toward the place where the right combination of sounds would call up safety from empty air. But the pack moved faster than even a well-motivated pig. They swept across the meadow toward him.

He could feel the nearness of the node and he did not break stride before chanting the tones that should open it.

Nothing happened. He realized that running and chanting at the same time, especially with his less than expert control of porcine vocal equipment, were affecting his pitch and intonation.

He skidded to a halt before the spot where a ripple should be wavering in the moonlight. The air was undisturbed.

The pack came on. He could see them, long ears and dark muzzles, black lips drawn back from foam-flecked fangs. The collective sound they made, of appetite and blood lust, sent a shiver through Bandar's meat.

He took a short settling breath and sang the tones again. The beasts were almost on him. The lead hound gathered its hindquarters beneath it and sprang, stretching its lean body through an arc that would bring its jaws to Bandar's soft throat.

The ripple appeared. Bandar jumped. He heard the click of canine teeth closing on empty air. Then he was through.

The Commons was the original fount of all myth and legend. Explored over tens of thousands of years, all of its terrors and wonders were long since identified and cataloged. Yet among undergraduates of the Institute, the noösphere had paradoxically become the subject of a myth of its own. Though senior fellows and tenured scholars derided the notion, students whispered to each other that they sometimes felt that humanity's collective unconscious was somehow *aware* of their presence—and worse, that their traipsing through Events and Situations was resented.

How else to explain the ill luck that too frequently accompanied sojourns among the idiomatic entities? It was understandable that the early explorers, groping their way from one uncharted Location to another, might fall afoul of an anthropophagic giant or a murderous worm. But with the Commons now as well mapped as any place in the waking world of Old Earth, why should noönauts so often blunder into lethal traps and snares? Why must the noösphere be so unforgiving?

As a youth, Bandar had shivered at the speculations of his classmates. In his maturity, his views were aligned with the establishment's. Only the day before this exploration, overhearing a callow underclassman named Chundlemars regaling his friends with some apocryphal tale of a sentient Commons, Bandar had spoken sharply.

"The Commons is an aggregate of contending forces. Disunity is its most salient characteristic. Fool contends against Wise Man, Hero confronts Villain, Anima opposes Animus. How can these contentious fragments unite behind a single program?"

Chundlemars had had the temerity to dispute the issue. "Yet a mob, however disparate its members' views on a host of issues, can cooperate to attack an inimical outsider."

Bandar bridled. "The key word in 'collective unconscious' is 'unconscious,' not 'collective,'" he said. "To become aware of intruders, the unconscious must first become self-aware. Self-awareness is by definition consciousness. Therefore it is a logical impossibility for the unconscious to become conscious."

The student had bent before Bandar's tirade but had still shown fight. "Perhaps not impossible, but merely difficult," he had said, "hence its efforts to capture our attention are diffuse and seem inconclusive."

Bandar had disdained to continue the argument and with a brusque gesture had sent the youths hustling off to another corner of the Institute's grounds.

But now as Bandar gazed at the view that had appeared before him the moment he had come through the gate and onto this grassy hilly, a frisson of fear caused the skin of his back to twitch. If this Location was the sunny realm of bards and troubadours that he had sought, he ought to be able to see at least one towered and turreted castle, its conical roofs aflutter with gay pennants and gonfalons. There ought to be a fountain or two on verdant lawns and gentle woods with trees as round and symmetrical as a child's drawing.

Instead the noönaut saw a tangled forest broken only by a narrow, unpaved track that wound its way past scattered clearings in which rude dwellings stood next to vegetable gardens. Farther off stood a sturdier edifice of red brick with a slate roof and a chimney from which gray smoke idled.

But nowhere to be seen were shaded bowers or romantic ruins. Bandar listened but heard no lutes or dulcimers, only the cawing of two ragged birds. His pig's nose brought him not the scent of flowers and fruited trees but a faint odor of carrion.

Not good, he thought. He brought the map into existence again. He examined the symbolic representation of the node through which he had arrived and saw that it was even more multifarious than he had realized. The gate was identified by a yellow heptagon within a green circle, signifying that it led to seven destinations if sung to in one key, and yet another seven outcomes if the thran was dropped a full tone.

Yet Bandar had been sure the map had shown him a green pentagon in a yellow circle. He had carefully traced the outcomes. He should be in the land of song and story, on his way to the children's winter paradise. Instead, as he studied the map, he was not quite sure where he had landed. He tried to focus on the symbols identifying this present Location but the characters' lines kept wavering and blurring, as if seen through an intervening mist.

His impression, however, was that he was in one of the most obscure sites, a subsidiary of a tributary two steps removed from a minor whorl. That meant that there might be few gates out of this Location, perhaps even only one, and he would have no choice but to take it.

How had he misread the map? Accidents were always possible, but Bandar had planned his route with meticulous care. The adolescent fear of being surrounded by a malicious, resentful Commons crept out of the closet. Bandar resolutely thrust it back and mentally slammed the door. Perhaps his pig eyes did not resolve certain colors or shapes as well as his human orbs could. He would be more careful next time.

He raised the flaps of his ears and turned in a slow circle on the hilltop. Beyond the squawking of the birds he heard the sound of voices raised in argument. They were coming from a clearing some small way off.

The voices offered Bandar a means of discovering where he was. He would approach stealthily and observe and identify the idiomats, deducing from their characteristics the Situation or Event in which he had landed. Then he would find its precise position on the map and from there plot a route to safety.

The forest, when he entered it, was of the Sincere/Approximate classification: what the Institute called "forestlike" rather than a truly realistic mix of trees, underbrush and detritus. Its iconic characteristics told Bandar that he was almost certainly in a Class Four Situation: likely an archetypical joke or one of the lighter tales for children, possibly one so ancient that it had been superseded eons ago by new formulations. But nothing was ever lost in the Commons. Just as Bandar's essential gene plasm carried all the instructions necessary to build precursor species that had gone extinct a billion years before, so the collective unconscious preserved every Form and Type that the human brain had ever conceived.

Still, there were advantages to being stranded in a Class Four Situation: physical surroundings would count for little; the Situation's cycle would involve only indispensable interactions between the idiomatic inhabitants.

That would pose no difficulties if the situation revolved around, say, a sexual encounter between a lusty farmer's wife and a hired hand. The idiomats would be so intent upon each other that a pig would pass unnoticed. But if he was traversing a tale about a bridge-haunting troll that devoured talking livestock, Bandar might suddenly find himself added to the menu. He therefore made a light-hooved approach to the sound of voices.

He was hearing an argument; that much was clear from the tone even before he could make out the words. That it was a good-natured dispute, carried on without rancor, was a good sign: the disputants were unlikely to have weapons in their hands. Bandar stole closer, weaving stealthily through the generic underbrush. The arguers called each other "Brother," and seemed to be contradicting each other over the merits of construction methodologies—a pair of artisan monks was Bandar's first thought.

He eased his way through some cartoonishly rendered bushes, finding that his sharp hooves made no noise on the forest floor. The voices were quite clear now, the argument definitely about the strength of a wall. Apparently winds were a factor here, since one of the disputants was contending that the wall before them would collapse at the first breath. The other replied that its interwoven construction gave the barrier a resilient tensile strength, adding, "The willow bends where the oak falls."

Bandar moved closer. There were fewer leaves between him and the argument now. He could make out something blue. He pressed a little farther forward and saw that it was coarse cloth with yellow stitching, the leg of a utilitarian garment such as a workman or farmer might wear. He inched toward the leg and saw that it ended in a scuffed leather boot.

Not so bad, he thought. He was in some Wisdom Story, perhaps a minor variant of the Flexibility versus Rigidity dichotomy. Its idiomats would be exclusively focused on their debate and soon would come a great wind to test one theory over another. Bandar was not worried about the wind, by the time it came he would have traversed what must surely be a very small Location, found an exit gate and been on his way.

He backed away from the arguing idiomats. But as he did so he found that his pig's ears were better designed for pressing forward through underbrush, even of the generic sort, than for rearward motion. One of his flaps caught on a twig, which scraped over the protruding cartilage before snapping free. Above Bandar's head one branch snapped against another and the bush trembled, swishing its broad and simple leaves against each other.

"What was that?" said the champion of flexible walls.

"It came from down there," said the advocate for solid masonry.

The first voice dropped to a whisper. "Is it, You Know Who?"

The branches above Bandar's head were swept away by a stout walking stick and he heard the second voice take on a tone of horror and disgust as it said, "No, it's some kind of ugly monster!"

"Oh, it's hideous!" cried the other.

Now all Bandar wanted was to back out of the bush, turn and run. But he could not help looking up toward the voices. He saw above him, their features contorted in horror, the faces of two anthropomorphically rendered pigs.

"Kill it!" said Flexibility with an idiomat's typical decisiveness, and Rigidity raised his heavy cane to put his brother's advice into action. Bandar squealed and tore himself loose from the bushes, but now the two pig-men were crashing through the undergrowth after him and showing that in addition to their murderous impulses their humanly formed legs and feet could sustain a considerable speed.

Bandar deked and jinked, circling tree trunks and leaping over fallen logs. The brothers pounded after him and soon displayed a dismaying intelligence: they spread out, one seeking to cut Bandar off and drive him toward the other. Both, he saw, were armed with heavy sticks.

The noönaut dodged a blow that could have snapped his spine, ducked through the legs of its deliverer and burst out of the bushes into the sunlit clearing. A structure was in his way, its walls an interlacing of withes and flexible canes bound by fibrous cords, its roof a dense mat of woven reeds. Bandar raced around a corner and galloped across the open space, hearing the thudding bootsteps of his pursuers and the rasp of their breathing. They were gaining.

His short pig's legs were trembling and his pig's lungs were burning. He looked toward the trees on the other side of the clearing, hoping for a thicker bush, perhaps a bramble, through which he could insinuate himself while his pursuers were deterred. But he saw nothing that would suit and the stick-wielding pig-men were almost on him.

Then from the woods ahead burst a third pig-man, attired like the others, but with an expression of sheer terror disfiguring its already distorted features. This one paid no attention to Bandar but called to the two others, "He's right behind me! He destroyed my house with a single blast!"

The third pig-man sped across the clearing and into the woods. Bandar's pursuers immediately abandoned the chase and ran in the same direction, cries of panic fading in their wake.

Bandar had skidded to a halt, his legs limp as boiled celery, his breath coming in pants. He heard the clatter of the pig-men diminishing as they fled through the woods behind him on the far side of the clearing. Then he heard a new sound, an engine-like chuffing growing louder. It came from beyond the nearer trees.

He remembered the discussion of wind and the fleeing pig-man's mention of a house destroyed by a single blast. *An archetypical Storm elemental,* he thought, *an elemental with a yen to destroy weakly constructed buildings—therefore no danger to a bystander pig.* He stood to catch his breath as the huffing and puffing grew louder.

From the darkness under the trees, not far from where Bandar stood, a shape emerged. It was a running figure, knees high and elbows pumping, dressed in black overalls over a red shirt, with a bent and towering hat on its head. But it was the face that caught Bandar's attention—the long muzzle flecked with foam, the red, lolling tongue, the cruel, needle-sharp fangs.

Oh, my, he thought, *not just Storm, but Appetite too. An Eater.*

The great golden eyes turned Bandar's way and the idiomat scarcely broke its stride before swerving toward him. *Worse yet,* was Bandar's thought, *Indiscriminate Appetite, an Eat-'em-all-up.*

He flung himself back the way he had come, but the slavering pursuer was even faster than the pig-men had been and here in the clearing there were no obstacles to interpose between the Eater and the virtual Bandar flesh it craved.

He was headed for the stick house, specifically for a wall against which stood a pile of unused building materials. He leapt to the top of the heap, sticks flying from beneath his scrabbling hooves, one of them happily striking the Eater's bulbous nose and causing the pursuer to pull up sharply, though only for the time it took to shake its head and renew the chase.

The pause gave Bandar time to scramble atop the woven roof, cross the peak and slide down the other side. He heard the beast coming over the roof after him. The trees were too far away; the Appetite would run him down.

Beside Bandar, the door to the house of sticks stood open. He ducked inside and closed the portal after him, glad to see that it was made of thick timbers, closely fitted, and that it had a hinged bar that he could nose into place.

Scarcely had the barrier been sealed than the Eater struck it with force enough to make the door rattle in its mounts. A second blow followed but the timbers held firm.

Now it grew quiet. Bandar put an eye to a tiny gap in the woven wall and saw that the Eater had drawn some distance away. It sat on its haunches and studied the noönaut's refuge for a few moments, then exhibited the demeanor of one who has thought through a problem and come to a decision.

It began to draw in great gouts of air. Bandar saw its thorax expand and contract to unlikely dimensions, and now he knew what must come. Somehow, this idiomat combined the essentials of the Eater *and* a Storm elemental. He wondered for a moment what demented mythmaker had first welded the two together, then deferred speculation while he sought a way out of the refuge that had become a deadly trap.

The floor was packed dirt. Pigs' hooves ought to make good digging implements. He went to the wall opposite where the Storm-Eater worked to inflate himself and frantically scratched at the earth.

Fortunately, this was a Class Four Situation so the dirt was made of uniformly homogeneous particles, without rocks or boulders to block his passage. The soil flew, piling up behind Bandar's haunches as the hole deepened into a passage under the wall. Above the sound of his own labors he could hear the idiomat chanting, "Let me come in," in a singsong voice that carried the force of a gusty breeze.

There came a silence as the Eater waited for a response, then the walls shook and the door rattled as a blast of air struck the opposite wall. Bandar heard a snapping of sticks and a tearing of cords. He looked back between his legs and saw that the door and the posts that supported it were canted inward. The whole front wall was skewed out of true.

He heard another puffing and huffing. The Eater was refilling its body with a fresh storm. A second blast would surely blow the house in. Bandar dug faster, harder, deeper. Soon there was a pig-sized passage beneath the back wall. He wriggled into the hole, scraped more earth out of his way, the narrow hooves doing a gratifyingly fast and thorough job.

In a moment, he saw a chink of daylight above him. In another moment, the chink had become a swatch, then a fully realized hole. Bandar wriggled through just as the storm smashed the front wall to flinders. The strong door crashed to the floor, the outer walls blew out and the roof fell in. The wall beneath which Bandar squirmed was pulled inward.

But he was out in sunlight and across the clearing, keeping the wreckage of the house between him and the Eater. He could hear it thrashing through the debris, alternately cooing to him and smacking wet lips. Bandar ducked into the undergrowth and lay trembling beneath a bush.

The Eater kicked at the wreckage of the house, searching for him. Then Bandar saw it notice the tunnel he had dug beneath the back wall. The beast squatted and examined the gouge in the earth, sniffed at it with its elongated snout. Then it raised its head and peered about the clearing. Bandar resisted an instinctive urge to draw farther back into the bushes; should his movements shake his branches the Eater would be on him in seconds.

Its gaze passed over Bandar without seeing him. After a long moment, its head turned in the direction the anthropomorphic pigs had taken then it rose and set off after them. Bandar waited until it was out of sight then crept from cover. If this was the kind of tale he now thought it was, none of the idiomats would return to this part of the Location until the Situation had completed its cycle and begun anew.

He brought up the great globe of the Commons and examined it as best he could with one eye then the other. It was easier to see in the clearing's bright sunlight than deep in the Nymph's forest. He found the gate through which he had come from the Enchantress's island—it was still a yellow heptagon within a green circle—and saw where he must be: a small mauve spot in the shape of a diamond, with a white stripe running diagonally from one side to another. Squinting his pig's eye, he deduced that the exit gate was not far off, somewhere beyond the brick house, where no doubt the Eater was now laying siege to the three brothers.

Bandar collapsed the map and thought about the Situation. This was clearly an admonitory tale for children, not, as he had thought, about Flexibility versus Rigidity, but a very early version of the Three Wayfarers motif that constantly reappeared in endless variations throughout the collective unconscious. It would conclude with one or, more likely, all three of the pig-men turning the tables on the Eater. From the effects of the monster's wind on the house of sticks, Bandar could guess that the Eater would fail to blow in the brick house. Then, its elemental power literally blown out, it would somehow be captured and destroyed by the brothers.

Bandar's best course was to position himself where he could observe the Situation's end game. Then during the Pause that always preceded a renewal of the cycle he could pass through the egress node and move to the next Location: a Landscape of primeval prairie. He might have to dodge vast herds of ruminants and those who hunted them, but more likely he would be alone on a rolling plain of endless grass. The prairie connected to another Location—a mountain valley where no one ever grew old. From there, Bandar could loop back to the snowland where the good Principal granted favors.

He trotted down the forest trail and soon came to the clearing where the little brick house stood. He approached warily, staying within the cover of the undergrowth. He did not see the Eater, but he saw that a painted wooden sign that bore the legend "A. Pig" in cursive script had been blown off the door's lintel to land on a strip of bare earth from which the stalks of petalless flowers grew.

The Eater has blown himself out and is probably even now being dispatched by the pig-men, Bandar thought. He crept to one of the shuttered windows and peered between the slats. Within, he saw the trio gathered about an open fireplace in which a deep, black cauldron steamed. The bricklayer held the pot's lid in readiness and all three were regarding the chimney with evident expectation.

Of course, Bandar thought, *the frustrated Eater descends the chimney, is clapped into the pot to become the pig-men's dinner.* The Eater would be eaten by those he would eat: another example of the circular irony which abounded throughout the Commons.

He watched to see the final act of the tale. But moments later, he saw a portion of the floor behind the three pig-men suddenly subside. A dark, clawed paw emerged. The brothers did not notice. Another paw emerged, then the head of the Eater, then his torso followed. The monster made lip-smacking noises and now, too late, the pig-men turned and saw the horror emerging from their floor, which was of the same friable earth as at the house of sticks.

The Eater was between the pig-men and the door. The single room was small. The victims displayed fright and panic, the beast a terrible single-mindedness. The ensuing scenes were not pleasant to watch. Bandar tore his gaze away and ran as fast as his tired pig's legs would take him in the direction of the exit gate.

He did not fear pursuit by the Eater; the beast would be occupied in feasting for some time. But Bandar was sure the outcome he had just seen was not what was supposed to happen. By inadvertently showing the monster another way into the pig-man's house, he had interfered with the Situation, perverting the idiomats from their prescribed course.

Among noönauts, the term for such adulterated behavior was *disharmony*. To cause a single idiomat to behave in a disharmonious manner could cause ripples. To distort an entire Situation, even a minor one, from its proper conclusion was to ignite the fuse for an explosive manifestation of psychic energy. Bandar had no idea what was about to happen within this Location, but he was certain it would not be good for the errant pig who had triggered it. And he had no wish to experience it.

His noönaut's sense told him that the egress node was a short trot along the forest trail then across a meadow. He followed the tingling in his awareness and soon was running through generic grass. He pulled up short where the gate should be and chanted the appropriate opening thran. Nothing happened. Again his enhanced hearing told him that his pig's larynx and enlarged nasal chamber were distorting the pitch of the tones.

A sound from behind him made Bandar turn and look. A spiraling vortex had appeared in the air above the brick house. It grew darker as he watched, a miniature whirlwind descending toward the roof. When it touched, dark slates were wrenched loose and sent spinning. A cracking, grinding noise grew in volume as the vortex broke up the timbers of the roof. Beams flew, rafters shot out in all directions like missiles.

Now the tornado bored deeper into the structure and Bandar turned back to the gate. He chanted the thran again, but knew they were off key. Behind him came a rumbling, clattering noise. It sounded as if every brick in the pig-man's house was vibrating and bashing against its neighbors, and behind that the whirring roar of the whirlwind grew louder and louder. He could hear limbs cracking from trees and the ground beneath his hooves shook like a nervous beast.

The part of Bandar that was more pig than human—a part that grew larger, he now realized, whenever he was gripped by fear—wanted to do nothing but run away. He had to force himself to breathe calmly. He did not look behind him, and did his best to ignore the thunderous cacophony of destruction that battered at his sensitive ears.

He shaped his jowly cheeks *so*, and put his tongue *here* and tried once more. The thran was only three descending notes then an octave's jump. Even Chundlemars could have done it on first try. That realization angered the human side of Bandar. The anger seemed to help. He chanted the three and one and the air rippled obligingly.

Before he stepped toward the fissure, he took a look back. After all, no Commons sojourner in living memory had witnessed a full meltdown of a Situation, even a Class Four. He could never mention this episode—how Gabbris would gloat—but he owed himself a last glance.

Immediately, he wished he hadn't. The trees all around the house had been stripped of their leaves and blown flat. The structure itself was spinning like a square top, the individual bricks of which it was made holding their relation to each other though separated by wide gaps through which burst eye-searing flashes of intense violet and electric blue light.

The house spun faster and faster, the blasts of painful light coming in sharper paroxysms. Bandar saw the pig-men and the Eater thrown around in the heart of the whirlwind, like torn rags with flopping limbs, each burst of blinding illumination penetrating their flesh to show gaping wounds and fractured bones. Above the roaring of the wind Bandar heard a hum like an insane dynamo. The sound became a whine then a shriek, climbing through the frequency scale until it rose even above the pitch that pigs could hear.

Not good, Bandar said to himself. He scuttled toward the gate. But the last glance back had meant he had waited too long. He did not hear the explosion; it reached him as a shock wave, picking him off his hooves and hurling him through the fissure. He rolled and tumbled across a grassy prairie, the gate behind him still open, blasts of wind and beams of non-light streaming through the gap.

Bandar got his feet under him and struggled against the wind back toward the node. Objects struck him, none of them large enough to do harm though he heard something heavy thrum past his head.

The gate remained open. *That's not supposed to happen.* He chanted a closure thran, then had to repeat the notes before the node would seal completely and the light and wind died. That, too, was something he had never seen. Gates closed automatically. Closure thrans were only for the rare circumstance when a noönaut opened a gate then decided not to go through it.

With him and after him through the gate had come elements of the previous Location: some bricks, a hand-sized piece of slate, some fragments of wood and a few unrecognizable gobbets of flesh and splinters of bone. They lay strewn around him but as he watched, all of the debris melted into the long grass of the prairie, like water seeping into a sponge.

I've never heard of that, Bandar thought. Material from one Location, whether inert or "living," was not transferable to another. Experiments had been tried in the distant past and the principle of Locational inviolability was unquestioned. Now Bandar had witnessed a definite crossover. His report would make quite a stir, if he ever dared to tell what he had seen and, more culpably, what he had done. And if he ever made it back to human form and out of the Commons without being absorbed and lost forever.

He turned now and scanned the prairie, saw nothing to cause alarm. Far off above the eastern horizon a vast storm cloud towered into the otherwise open sky and he saw flickers of lightning from its base. In the same direction he could see tiny dots against the darkening skyline. *A herd of ruminants*, he thought, remembering the horned and shaggy beasts, herding in their millions, that formed an essential feature of this Landscape.

Neither storm nor herd concerned Bandar. He deployed and examined the globular map. There were several gates on the prairie, none of them far away, as if the Location had been designed as a transit zone for wayfarers. There were a number of such nodal gatherings in the Commons, and some scholars had advanced the notion that the convenience of their existence argued for the noösphere having been intelligently designed. Others held that random distribution could as readily account for the clumping of gates. Besides, the prospect of intelligent design raised the question: By whom? And that led back to the conundrum of a conscious unconscious—a knot that the scholastic community preferred to leave unpicked.

As did Guth Bandar at this moment. He determined that the gate to Happy Valley was about a quarter day's walk to the east. From there he would jump to the snow kingdom and beg a transformation from its Principal. Then he would summon an emergency gate and plop back into his body in the Institute's meditation room.

He set off toward the gate, his spirits bruised but resuscitated. He wondered if he could draft a monograph on the meltdown of the Class Four Situation without specifying the events which had triggered it. Perhaps he could profess ignorance of the cause while detailing the results. Anyone who visited the Location would find it back in its cycle; the idiomats would know nothing of what had happened to their previous incarnations and all evidence of Bandar's inadvertent tampering would have dissolved.

The more he thought about it, the more possible a paper became. He began to flesh out the essential elements of thesis, argument and recapitulation. The point to be made was that cross-Locational transfer was indeed possible. Perhaps such things happened often, though only at the end of a Location's cycle when any sensible noönaut would absent himself rather than risk absorption.

That's it, Bandar thought, *I'll say I bravely stayed to witness the cycle's renewal and thus saw the movement of material through the gate.* He would transform his own folly into courage and produce a commendable result. Didrick Gabbris would chew his cuff in envious gall.

Cheered, Bandar trotted on, composing the first lines of the projected essay as he went. Thus occupied, he did not notice what was before him until he felt the first gusts of wind on his pig's face and the first trembling of the ground beneath his hooves.

He was at the base of a small rise, its covering of long grass leaning toward him under the pressure of a growing east wind. He climbed the slope and looked beyond it.

As far as he could see, to left and to right in the rapidly failing light, the world was a sea of humping, bumping shapes. A million animals were on the move. And they were moving toward him.

Above the herd, the sky was almost black with lowering storm clouds, the narrow band between them and the earth whipped by rain and rattling sheets of hail. Lightning crackled and thunder rolled across the prairie. The herd moaned and blundered on.

Behind Bandar was nothing but open plain; no cover, no obstacle to break the onslaught of millions of hooves. He could not outrun them on his short, tired pig's legs. To left and right was only grass. But ahead, between him and the oncoming herd, the land sloped down to a small river, barely more than a stream, that wound its way like a contented snake across the prairie. In places, flash floods had cut deep into the thick sod and the clay beneath, leaving the stream to trickle between high banks. And one of those places was not far.

Bandar dug his hooves into the prairie sod and raced down the slope, the wind battering him now and the rumble of the herd's coming shaking the earth like a constant tectonic temblor. He did not look at the animals but fixed his eyes on where the river must be, for he had lost sight of it as soon as he had left the top of the low rise.

The thunder of massed hooves now equaled the voice of the storm. They would be on him in moments and still he had not found the river. He wondered if he had somehow veered from his course on the unmarked plain to run parallel to his only hope of salvation. But even as he conceived the thought the quaking ground suddenly disappeared from beneath his hooves and he plunged into a gully as deep as he was tall—or as tall as he would be were he still in human form.

He hit the shallow water with a shock to his forehooves and immediately scrambled to the far bank where the clay had been hollowed out by a past flood. He pressed himself sideways against the cold wall, feeling it cool his heaving flanks, unable to hear his own panting over the crescendo of hooves heading his way.

Something dark hurtled above him, the herd's first fleet outrunner leaping the gully. Then a second and another, then five more crossing the gap as fast as a drum roll. Now the body of the herd arrived, with the storm right behind it, and the light in the gully dimmed to a crepuscular shadow. But there was nothing Bandar wanted to see. He closed his eyes and hoped that the bank above him would not crumble and bury him beneath earth and thrashing hooves.

The stampede went on and on, but the soil above Bandar was woven through with the roots of tough prairie grass. It did not give way. In time, it seemed that the shaking of the ground lessened and that the thunder had rolled on across the plain. Bandar opened his eyes. Beasts were still hurtling over his head but there were gaps between them; the sky he glimpsed through those gaps was a sullen gray rather than an angry black.

A few more animals leapt the gully, then two more, then a single straggler and now, all at once, the herd had passed. Bandar edged out from under the overhang, wondering how he could scale the almost vertical clay wall and resume his journey. But the herd had left him a stepping stone: not far away lay the carcass of a beast that had plunged into the little canyon and snapped its neck against the west wall. It lay on its side. Bandar was sure he could climb onto its rib cage and from there jump to the eastern lip of the gully.

He trotted toward the dead ruminant, looking for the easiest point on the great corpse to begin his ascent. Thus he was almost upon it before he noticed that the tail, which should have been long and thick and tipped by a tassel of coarse hair was instead short, hairless and curled like a corkscrew. The animal's shoulders and chest, that should have been covered by a dense, woolly pelt were naked and hairless. And now, as Bandar circled the carcass, he saw the head: jowly and wrinkled, with sightless little eyes and a squared-off snout that he had last seen on the face of an enraged pig-man who had sought to crack his spine with a cudgel.

That's not right, Bandar said. Farther down the gully, another animal had fallen on rocks, breaking its back. It still lived and was making guttural grunts that Bandar recognized. He had heard the same sounds under the olive trees on the Nymph's island—pig sounds. *No, not right at all.*

Bandar went back to the dead beast and examined it closely. It was not quite a pig, though it was decidedly piglike. But it had horns and was easily four times the size of even the most prize-winning swine, and the color was wrong. It was someone's idea of how a pig and a herd beast would look if their gene plasms were mashed together.

Bandar had no doubt that this beast was a result of trans-Locational contamination. Which meant he would have an even more interesting paper to present, although the degree of his culpability had just taken a quantum leap. If his role in this event became known he would be branded a vandal and forbidden ever to enter the Commons except as all humankind did, in his dreams.

He climbed onto the dead animal and jumped to the east lip of the gully. The sky ahead was clearing, gray clouds scudding aside to reveal patches of blue. He called up the globe of the Commons again and determined that he was not more than an hour's trot from the egress node. He set off with mixed feelings: glad to be nearer to deliverance but uncomfortably aware that the fused idiomats he had left dead and dying in the gully were a reproach to him.

He had not gone far before the wind that had been beating at his face faded and died away. He lifted his head and smelled the rain-scoured air. He could not wait to be restored to human form but he would miss some of the pig's senses, especially the breadth and subtlety of the world of odors.

He trotted on, letting his mind wander, smelling the crushed grass and the various scents of small flowers that appeared here and there along his way. The wind changed direction but he did not take account of it when it freshened and gusted against his hams. Then a sudden squall brought the sting of hail.

He paused and looked over his shoulder. The sky was dark to the west where the storm had gone, but now he saw that the clouds had rebuilt themselves and were sweeping back toward him. *That's peculiar*, he thought.

He looked up at the roiling vapors, shot through with flashes of lightning. *That's peculiar, too,* he thought, seeing that the flashes seemed tinged with blue and even purple instead of bright actinic white light.

He watched for a moment longer then felt a shiver go through his body that had nothing to do with the chill wind. The sparse hairs on his neck rose and Bandar's pig's limbs began to tremble and his spine began to shake. His pig's lower jaw dropped open and he gaped at the vision that was forming in the cloud.

It was a vast shape, the most enormous face he had ever seen, but he recognized it: the long muzzle lined with teeth and ending in a twitching nose, the pointed ears turned his way, the suggestion of a crooked hat towering into the sky, and the huge eyes, lit from within by lightning, that were looking back at him.

More than pig-man stuff had been blown through the gate from the exploding Class Four Situation: the Storm-Eater had come too, and it remembered him.

The immense face of Appetite rushed toward him, carried on a sweep of wind and chill rain. Bandar ran.

The collective unconscious, through the personal unconscious of every human being, engages in a constant dialogue with each of us. So went the opening sura of Afrani's *Explaining and Exploring the Noösphere*, the first text encountered by students at the Institute for Historical Inquiry. *We may address our questions, our thoughts, our hopes and expectations to the noösphere in direct and pointed queries, but it will always and only reply through indirection and coincidence.*

Bandar knew his Afrani by heart. It was every neophyte's first assignment, undertaken not only for the knowledge of the book's contents but for the necessary taming and strengthening of memory.

The words *indirection* and *coincidence* now rang in his mind as he fled across the grasslands, the roaring, devouring Storm-Eater at his back. The Commons never spoke directly, he knew. Even when it spoke through those who had demolished the barriers between conscious and unconscious— the oracles and the irredeemably insane—its language was always one of riddle and allusion.

Bandar saw now that he had been enmeshed in a sequence of coincidences ever since he had left the forest of the Loreleis. The Nymph had turned him into a pig, then he had landed in a Situation where pig-men were the idiomats. The Nymph had turned her donkeys into pursuing hounds—why do that, when donkey hooves could be just as lethal to a small pig as canine fangs?—then he had been chased by an Eater with decidedly houndlike characteristics. And now he was being harried again by a similar manifestation of the idiomat, though now it sought to sizzle him with lightning bolts instead of clamping sharp teeth into his porcine flesh.

In the waking world, coincidences were often just the haphazards of chance—a coin could be tossed and come up heads ten times in a row—but in the Commons coincidences were never a mere coincidence. Concurrency was the language of the noösphere. There was meaning here, a message.

And what could the message be? The thought rattled in Bandar's pig's brain as he galloped on tiring legs across the gently rolling landscape, while bolts of fluorescent energy struck behind and all around him. *What question did I put?* he wondered.

He had wanted to know about the Song of songs, the Ur-melody wired into the human brain. But now, as he turned the question over in his mind, examining it from all angles, he could not discover even the most tangential relationship to his present predicament.

But if not the Lorelei's song, then what? A blast of lightning lit the storm-darkened landscape ahead of him and he swerved around the charred and smoking gouge it had made in the prairie sod. Of course, direct questions to the Commons never brought a clear answer. The key to receiving a message was to think about something else. Then the unconscious would steal through the back door, to leave its offering like the gifts of faery sprites who labor through the night while their beneficiary snores, all unawares, in his bed.

So as he ran Bandar turned his thoughts elsewhere, though it was a difficult task with lethal blasts striking all around him. But he took the attempts on his life as encouragement—what better way to get his attention?—and set his disciplined mind, even housed in a porcine brain, to the work. He rehearsed his activities before entering the Commons. He had dined with the vicedean of applied metaphysics; he had filled an order of offworld dyes and fixatives for a longstanding customer (Bandar ran an inherited family commerciant firm, hence his status at the Institute as only an adjunct scholar); he had reprimanded Chundlemars; he had sketched an outline of his Lorelei paper.

And now it came to him. His pig's tongue and lips could not put it into words, but he could make the appropriate sounds.

"Hmm," he said, in the tones of one who has seen the light, then, "Um hmm," again to indicate acceptance of the revelation.

Another flash lit up the landscape and by its light, just ahead, Bandar saw an unlikely sight: a hummock of prairie land was transforming itself into another shape. In moments, Bandar found himself rushing toward a small but sturdy brick house, its stout door invitingly open.

He crossed the threshold at a gallop, skidded on his hooves as he turned to get his nose behind the door and push it closed. The wind resisted his efforts but he found renewed strength and when the door met its jamb a lock clicked and the barrier stood proof against the storm.

The single room was bereft of furniture although there were three framed pictures on the back wall, each portraying an anthropomorphically rendered pig in a stiff-collared shirt and dark suit. Centered in the same wall was a wide and tall fireplace with a black cauldron simmering over a well-stoked blaze. Bandar crossed to the kettle and found that the handle of its lid had been designed to fit a pig's trotter, confirming his surmise of what must be done.

He balanced on his hind legs and slipped a forehoof into the handle and prized the lid from the cauldron. It came easily. No sooner was the cover free than the chimney rattled to a downdraft of cold air. Sparks flew and smoke billowed, setting Bandar's eyes to water and causing him to vent an explosive sneeze.

But even blind he could hear the *sploosh* of something solid arriving in the cauldron. He immediately clapped the lid back into place. The kettle rumbled and shook but Bandar leaned his weight onto the leaping, vibrating top until the commotion ceased.

Outside, the storm had ended. Beams of sunlight angled through the windows to illuminate the smoky air inside the house. *Now what?* Bandar wondered, and even as he did so his eye fell upon something he had not noticed before: a substantial ladle hanging beside the chimney.

Its handle, too, was shaped to fit a pig's hoof. He lifted it down then removed the cauldron's lid. A dark broth sent up steamy wisps of vapor. It smelled delicious. Bandar dipped the ladle and tasted the soup.

The broth tasted as rich as it smelled, but Bandar got no more than his first sip. As the stuff entered him, he saw the hoof that held the ladle become a hand once more, the foreleg become an arm. His back straightened and his legs set themselves under him again. He became a man standing in a little brick house, then the structure faded and he found himself atop a low rise.

The noönaut wasted no time in calling up an emergency gate. The air opened before him and he wanted to throw himself immediately forward. But he paused and said to the bright blue sky, "I will let them know."

A moment later he was looking through his own eyes at the worn furniture of the Institute's meditation room. He stretched the kinks out of his joints and muscles, rose and performed the usual exercises. When his body felt as if it fit him again, he crossed to the door that led out to the forum where students were wont to gather between classes.

He strode forcefully toward a group seated on the grass beneath a hanging wystol tree. Most of them looked up in curiosity; one showed alarm at being the focus of Bandar's gaze. The youth rose to his feet, a fearful apprehension seizing his features.

Bandar said, "Chundlemars, I wish you to come with me."

Chundlemars swallowed and said, "Master, I have thought better of my earlier observations about the noösphere's awareness. I withdraw them."

"Withdraw?" said Bandar. "To the contrary! You will expound them to me at length. You are henceforward my research assistant."

Chundlemars blinked. His chin fell toward his chest and remained there.

"Don't stand there gaping!" Bandar said, seizing the underclassman by one protruding ear and compelling him toward Bandar's study. "The Commons is awake and aware! It demands our attention!"

"What must we do?" said Chundlemars.

"What must we do?" said Bandar. "My boy, we are scholars and the Grand Colloquium is but a week away. We must quickly compose a thesis to grind Didrick Gabbris into a malodorous powder!"

Help Wonted

Guth Bandar had always liked the red-haired one best. Her figure was not as voluptuous as the blonde's nor was her face as perfect as the raven haired girl's, but there was an elfin quality to the way she looked back at him over her lightly freckled shoulder, a gamin's wry twist of the mouth and a glint of mischief to her sea-green eyes.

In a moment, he would rise from where he lay in the shade of the coconut palm. He would affect a comic growl and they would respond with giggles. Then the blonde would press fingertips to half-open lips and gasp, "Oh!" and the brunette would shriek while the redhead cocked one sun-dappled hip, before all three ran laughing into the surf.

The dream always unfolded this way, had done so for all the years since Bandar had found his way into this innocuous corner of the Commons, the great collective unconscious of humankind. There were more erotic Situations than this one, certainly there were more realistic representations of intergender relations, but it was to this Location that Guth Bandar often repaired when life became wearisome and his troubles outweighed his joys.

There was a sweet innocence to the place. As near as he could tell, the three girls were not even anatomically correct. Their breasts were well enough conceived, although the areolas were too perfectly round, but in the less obvious places things seemed only sketchily realized. It was the fantasy of a boy still approaching the cusp of manhood: the girls could be chased and finally caught, but after that it all grew a little vague.

Bandar wanted to prolong the moment before commencing the sequence that would inevitably end the Location's cycle. It was not the prepubescent frolic that lured him to this place, but its atmosphere: the aura of naiveté, of a world that had not yet encountered guile and cynicism.

For Guth Bandar had lately encountered both, and in too ample a measure. They had come in the unwelcome form of Didrick Gabbris, his longstanding rival at the Institute for Historical Inquiry, where gathered those who spent their lives exploring the Commons—the noösphere was the technical term—and among whose number Bandar had been glad to count himself.

But now his tenure as an adjunct scholar had been abruptly terminated. He had been required to return his gown and pin and to vacate the little office in the basement of the Institute's connaissarium where he had conducted his researches. The fellows and scholars had ceremoniously turned their backs on him, looking anywhere but at Guth Bandar while he trudged to the great doors of Magisters Hall and departed.

The day should have ended in a triumph, the once-and-forever scotching of the odious Gabbris. But when Bandar had presented his revolutionary thesis—that the collective unconscious had paradoxically achieved consciousness, that the noösphere had become self-aware—the assembled noönauts of the Institute had turned on him. Snorts of disbelief and hoots of derision had battered at Bandar's ears, and the ranks of scholars assembled for the Grand Colloquium had become a sea of outraged faces and shaken fists.

The blonde idiomat came up the beach and offered Bandar a theatrical wink, pursed her full lips in an unwitting parody of eroticism, then turned to flee in anticipation of pursuit. But Bandar smiled wanly and flourished a weak hand. When he remained recumbent beneath the tree, she reformed her lips into a moue of dismissal and went away with what would have been a swish and flounce of fabric had she been wearing any.

Bandar knew he would soon have to get up and play out the sequence or see the dream dissolve. He had not come to this Location through the noönaut's techniques—a series of recondite mental exercises accompanied by the intoning of specific patterns of notes, called thrans—but by the more mundane expedient of falling asleep and allowing his own personal unconscious to connect him to the Commons. Even so, he was no ordinary dreamer; he could lucidly focus his awareness within a dream so that its figures and events became almost as real as if he walked through his waking life.

Still, there were limits. If he did not get up now and respond to the idomatic entities' importunings, he would overstress the fabric of this Situation and it would pop like a bubble. He essayed a small growl and put one elbow under him. The three girls tittered and coquetted a few steps away.

"Guth Bandar," said a soft voice beside his ear.

The noönaut felt a shock and a shiver as if an icy finger had trailed up his spine. The girls could not speak—prepubescent boys do not look to their fantasy objects for conversation—and there should have been no other entity within this Location.

In the Commons, when things went wrong they tended to go disastrously, dangerously—and all too frequently—lethally wrong. Bandar did not hesitate but mentally reached for the procedure that would propel him posthaste from the dream into full consciousness. But his cognitive grasp closed on emptiness; something was blocking his technique.

"Stay," said the voice, and now Bandar had to turn to face whatever was there, because one rule every apprentice noönaut learned was always to confront the unconscious. *To run is to be run,* went the old maxim. *To stand is to withstand.*

But when he stood and looked behind him, there was nothing to face down. The voice had come from the jungle beyond the coconut palm, an indifferently realized pastiche of leaves, vines and creeper that was only slightly more convincing than if it had been painted on stage cloth.

"Who speaks?" he said.

The answer came not in words but as a ripple in the air: the familiar sign that a gate had opened between this Location and some other corner of the Commons. The exit's presence deepened Bandar's worry: he knew every inch of this palmy beach and knew that the only way in and out, whether he came as a dreamer or as a conscious chanter of thrans, was eighteen paces to the left of the tree, a spot just past an ornate conch shell washed up above the limit of the surf.

He took stock of his situation. *I am stranded in a dream, bespoke by an unknown entity and beckoned to enter a gate that ought not exist. My day proceeds from defeat to who knows what further drama!*

A terrible thought occurred to him. *Have I become a natural?* he wondered. It was an accusation that Didrick Gabbris had hurled at him in the Grand Colloquium, and Bandar had shrugged it off as merely another dart of abuse chosen from his rival's copious quiver of epithets and slanders.

Now, standing in the warmth of this generic beach, Bandar felt a shiver and an unaccustomed chill. Could Gabbris have been right?

All humans could visit the collective unconscious and did so nightly; the Commons was where the engrammatic stuff of dreams cohered in nodes and corpuscles called Locations, cyclical and eternal. A minority of humankind could consciously enter the wondrous and dreadful realm in which the composite experience of humanity was gathered and distilled to its essences. That minority was further divided into two classes: one was composed of Institute scholars trained in the techniques of orphic thrans that kept them from being perceived by the noösphere's archetypal inhabitants; the other category comprised the irredeemably insane—psychotics whose shattered personas had merged utterly with one of the primal entities loose in the shared basement of the human mind.

The significant difference between noönauts and the deranged was that the scholars retained an awareness of themselves as distinct from their putative surroundings—Bandar knew the people and things of the Commons were not "really real," though the dangers they posed might be—while loons and ravers could not reliably distinguish between a ravenous vampire and a hapless neighbor, which was why a chance encounter on the sidewalk could move in unexpected directions.

Guth Bandar reminded himself of this crucial distinction as he heard again the whispered summons from the darkness beneath the palms, where the rift in the air still quivered. *Can I be mad* he asked himself, *if I am willing to consider the real possibility that I am indeed mad?* He realized that the question led only to a conundrum: the judgment of the insane must always be suspect; only a sane man's verdict could be relied upon, but a sane man would never pronounce himself mad.

"Guth Bandar," said the soft voice. Bandar thought about fleeing the summons. If he couldn't wake himself up, there was another way out: noönauts who sang their way into the Commons could chant a specific thran that would open an emergency exit. Quite likely the same thran would pluck Bandar from this dream and in a second he would wake up in his bed, doubtless drenched in sweat, his limbs atremble.

But he left the seven notes unsung. Gabbris's victory in the Grand Colloquium had stung Bandar's pride. He was no natural. He was a true noönaut and he knew that the Commons had indeed communicated with him, as if it were a conscious entity. He had not been able to convince his peers and betters at the Institute, might never be able to do so. But a true scholar does not turn aside when confronted by the inexplicable. He penetrates the mystery.

Bandar squared his narrow shoulders and advanced to the rippling slit in the air. Without hesitation, he stepped through.

Beyond the beach was a luminous fog, a mist so dense that Bandar's hand, held at arm's length, became a doubtful object. Bandar knew that there were three fog-bound Locations in the collective unconscious: one was a Landscape (or more properly, a Seascape), that featured a ship enshrouded on an archetypal ocean; another had the same combination of elements but was classified as an Event, because the ship ran aground and broke up on unseen rocks, casting passengers and crew into the cold sea; the third was an urban Landscape where the idiomats stumbled on cobblestoned streets, feeling their way along walls of brick and fences of black iron on which the mist condensed and chilled their fingers.

This was none of those three, Bandar was sure, but to be certain he used the noönaut technique that summoned up his detailed globular map of the Commons. He rotated the sphere until he found the Location with the beach and its winsome idiomats, then identified each of the befogged Locations. As he had expected, there was no direct connection from the beach to any of the three; he would have had to pass through a Garden, a Class Two Massacre and a Class One Natural Disaster just to reach the nearest.

Now Bandar refocused his awareness on the sphere and employed another aspect of his noönaut training. The result of his effort should have been to create a small pulsation in the symbol that represented whatever Location he now occupied. But though he applied the method again and then still once more, with increased intensity, not one of the emblems in the sphere responded.

That is impossible, Bandar thought. It meant that he must be in some corner of the Commons that was not on the map. But the noösphere had been fully explored and charted tens of millennia ago. The Great Delineation had been the work of thousands of generations and it had cost the lives of untold numbers of members of the Institute for Historical Inquiry, men and women who had bravely ventured into Locations and been absorbed into their spurious realities before they could ascertain which combinations of tones would screen them from their idiomatic inhabitants' perceptions, or find the way out before the Situation or Event reached the end of its cycle and reformed to begin anew.

Perhaps Gabbris is right, Bandar thought. *Perhaps I have taken leave of my senses and become a natural.* He imagined the uproar that would ensue if he returned to the Grand Colloquium and declared that not only was the Commons aware of its own existence, but that it contained at least one Location that had remained undetected during the vast span of time since the first noönaut, the Beatified Arous, found his way through the Golden Door. *Madness,* he thought, *yet here I am.*

"Not madness," said the soft voice. "Merely something new."

In the fog, the sound seemed to come from all directions and from none. Bandar collapsed the sphere then turned and peered about him, but there was only the ubiquitous vapor. He looked up to see if he could identify a direction from which the light came, and thus orient himself, but no part of the unseeable sky was brighter than any other.

Now he became aware of a shape a little to his right. He turned to face it, at the same time beginning to chant the four-and-six thran, the sequence of tones that was most commonly effective.

"It will do you no good," said the voice.

Bandar switched to the seven-and-three.

"Neither will that." The shape was becoming clearer. It was human in size and outline.

He tried the four-four-and-two.

"Nor that." It was moving closer, though Bandar saw no motion that suggested walking. It seemed to float toward him through the mist.

"Who are you?" he said. "What do you want of me?"

"You know who we are," said the voice.

The figure had come close enough for Bandar to see that it was definitely human, but that was its only definite characteristic. Its progress stopped when it was near enough for him to have touched its face, and he stared, trying to bring form and features into focus.

But he could not. The face and figure before him constantly shifted, a set of features appearing and disappearing every second in a constant series of slow dissolves. He saw an old man, a young girl, a scarred warrior, an evil king, a sad-eyed clown, a were-beast, a matron, a shining god. The form beneath the face shifted in harmony, showing him lush robes succeeded by battered armor, replaced by rough-sewn animal skins, which gave way to roseate nakedness supplanted by samite threaded through by gold.

"I know who you are," Bandar said. "You are the Multifacet." He used the term every loblolly apprentice learned in his first week at the Institute. It denoted the crowd of archetypal personas that made up the human psyche and from which every individual assembled a personality, some taking more of this one and less of that one, and everyone's individual mix evolving over a lifetime, as nature and circumstances dictated. But here they were assembled in one vessel.

"Yes." The answer came when the figure was that of a young stripling, the voice breaking to make two syllables out of one.

Bandar let anger infuse his reply. "You are the one who has ruined my career."

A wicked witch-king answered, "But to a purpose."

"No purpose of mine."

"We could give you an argument on that. We contain all that combines to form you, after all."

Bandar folded his arms across his chest. "But we have not arrived at 'after all,'" he said. "Instead, I am in the springtime of my life, which you have just diverted from the only course along which I ever sought to shape my years."

The shifting faces regarded him through a succession of eyes—sharp, mild, innocent, cunning—then the voice of an aged queen said, "We require you to perform a service. We will reward you, as best we may."

"Reward me? Very well, return me to the Institute's good graces and I am yours."

"We cannot," said a portly toper. "A life at the Institute will not shape you to do what you must do."

"Then how will you repay me for the loss of my heart's desire?"

A bearded prophet answered, "With useful qualities that are ours to bestow: the power to persuade, the knack of winning trust and affection, luck in small things." By the time the speech was finished, the speaker was a sly-eyed rogue.

"None of these came to my aid in the Grand Colloquium."

"Your path does not lead through the Institute."

"My path?" Bandar said. "If it is not mine to choose, by what definition does it remain *my* path?"

"We cannot debate with you," said a slack-mouthed idiot that became a proud hierophant. "You are chosen. You must accept."

"And if I will not?"

"You must."

"What is the service you require?"

"We cannot tell you that."

"When would I have performed it and be free of you?"

"Not for many years."

"Then why disrupt my life now?"

"You must have time to grow into the kind of man who can do what must be done."

"What kind of man is that?"

There was no answer. Bandar had had enough. "You abort my career then offer me trinkets for some service you will not define. I decline your offer. Instead I will awaken now and let you seek out a more credulous implement for your obscure purposes. I recommend Didrick Gabbris."

He opened his mouth to sound the seven notes that would pluck him from this nebulous place and let him wake in his bed. But the protean figure before him raised a hand, smooth and full fleshed as it came up, transforming into a black gauntlet as it mimed squeezing with thumb and forefinger. Bandar's throat closed. He could make no sound, not even a moan around the obstacle that his tongue had suddenly become.

A rift opened in the pearly mist. Bandar's eyes narrowed against a burst of raw sunlight, then he felt himself propelled through the node. He fell to his knees and pitched forward. Burning sand stung his palms. Heat swaddled him and the air was thick with the rank odor of stale sweat.

"Up!" said a harsh voice. A line of fire cut across the noönaut's shoulders. He would have screamed if he could have, but his voice was still imprisoned within his chest. The lash came back, this time striking the same flesh and creating a pain that compounded the first to evoke an astonishing effect. Bandar leapt to his feet and looked about him.

The desert stretched in every direction but to his rear, where trees sheltered a substantial town beside a broad river, with grain fields beyond the farther shore. Ahead was a massive pile of masonry, each sand-colored, oblong block as long as Bandar was tall and half his height in cross-section. He could measure their size accurately because just such a block was immediately before him, snared in a net of fibrous ropes and with peeled logs beneath to roll on. The ropes went forward to rest upon the shoulders of a gang of straining, half-naked men. Two others were busy pulling logs from behind the back of the stone and running to position them just ahead of its inching progress. A few more were at the rear of the procession pushing the block forward and it was here that Guth Bandar found himself. They all wore long kilts of linen and not much else, although some had sandals and a few wore skullcaps. Bandar looked down at himself and found that he was similarly attired.

But the hands and arms he saw, the pot belly and spindly shanks leading to splayed flat feet, were not those of Guth Bandar. It was an unheard of circumstance. A noönaut entered the Commons in his own virtual image. But Bandar here was clearly not Bandar in appearance. Somehow he had been thrust into the "flesh" of an idiomat. It was but the latest impossibility that Bandar had had to swallow, but it was the one that worried him most.

"Push!" said the voice that had accompanied the whip. The noönaut hastened to place his palms against the sandstone and shove before the braided leather could revisit the welt made by its previous landings and bring about an as yet hypothetical but entirely likely third degree of agony whose existence Bandar did not wish to confirm. The stone was cool against his sweating palms and the effort needed to move it across the rollers—aided by all the other straining muscles in the work gang—was not as taxing as he would have expected. Indeed, the men pulling and repositioning the rollers seemed to be working harder than the haulers.

The labor required no mental effort, however, other than to remember to step over the rearmost log as it was pulled from beneath the block. Bandar was thus able to give his full attention to his predicament. The more he considered it, the worse it became. The amount of activity around him, the scope and scale of the site, told him that this was not just a Landscape, nor was it a mere Situation: this was an Event, and a Class One Event at that.

The scholars of the Institute categorized the myriad Locations of the noösphere into three types. The simplest were Landscapes, which were recollections of the archetypal settings against which the long story of human existence had been carried out. They ranged from the painted caves that sheltered humankind's infancy, through jungle and farmed plain, to cityscapes of all ages, including the most decadent of Old Earth's penultimate age.

More complex were the Situations, which preserved all the recurrent circumstances and rites of passage that were the landmarks of human life, from birth through the first kiss, to the meeting of soulmates and on to the gathering of kin around the deathbed. Situations also covered all the darker milestones to be encountered between cradle and grave: the stillborn child, the lover's betrayal, the breaking of friendship's bonds and the lonely death in the wilderness.

Most detailed of all were the Events, the turning points great and small on which history had pivoted: from the fire-hunt that chased mammoths over cliffs to the first planting of crops, through the founding and sack of cities, to the taming of frontiers and the building of topless towers.

Landscapes were classified according to their size, from a back street to a trackless ocean. All of them recycled quickly. Situations were ranked according to their complexity: some might involve no more than one person's hand enfolding another's; others might require a cast of thousands. But the duration of most Situations was brief, from a moment to at most a few hours, then the elements reformed and the process began anew.

Events, however, might range in duration from under a minute (for a Class Six occurrence like a sprinters' foot race), to a span of many years, even of more than a lifetime, as in such Class One Events as The Opening of the Territory or The Invasion of the Barbarians.

As Bandar shoved against the block of stone and gazed about him at the scores of other work gangs playing their parts he became more and more fearful that he was trapped in a Location that might endure for as long as a slave—for surely that was what he was in this place—could expect to live.

Unable to speak, he could not sing the tones that would hide him from the perceptions of the idiomatic entities around him. Nor could he activate an exit node and escape back to the waking world. Until his voice returned—and he refused to believe it would not—he was stuck in what was obviously an early version of a Class One Event: The Building of the Grand Monument.

Bandar continued to push, the cycle of the rollers continued, and time wore on as he looked about him and waited for his throat to heal. He was hoping that the cause of his muteness was induced hysterical paralysis, which might fade with time, rather than a magic spell. In the Commons, magic worked effectively and permanently. He grunted and achieved a chesty sound. But when he sought to generate different tones he could not convince himself that he was meeting with success.

His efforts attracted the attention of the idiomat next to him, a heavy-featured man whose back and chest were slabs of muscle and whose arms were corded with hard flesh. The entity turned his small, close-set eyes on Bandar and regarded him without favor, then said, "Shut up, dummy," and laughed at his own wit. In case there was any doubt that the injunction should not be interpreted as friendly banter from an amiable workmate, he accompanied it with a slap of his plate-sized hand that left Bandar's virtual head ringing.

Bandar subsided. He would wait until he was alone to try again. He had only to manage the seven tones and his consciousness would be freed from this imprisoning false flesh. He would wake at home in his bed.

The passage of the sun told him that he had arrived in the Event at about midmorning. By the time the men's shadows were pooled about their feet, they had brought the block more than halfway to its destination. At that point, a two-wheeled cart caught up with them, pulled by a leather-skinned old man wearing only a kind of diaper. The overseer with the whip, a skinny fellow with a squint in one eye, called a halt. The slaves immediately stopped their labors and began what looked to Bandar to be a practiced routine: some pulled from the cart a few poles and a wide bolt of cloth and quickly created an awning whose back wall was the stone block. Others extracted baskets of round, flat loaves and terracotta jars that sloshed with liquid confined by wooden stoppers. The men gathered to sit in the shade of the cloth while the food and drink was passed around.

Bandar lowered his buttocks to the hot sand and accepted a chunk torn from a loaf and a wooden cup from the man next to him, a young-looking idiomat who offered him a shy smile and a friendly word. The old man in the loincloth stooped to pour from one of the jars and Bandar smelled the yeasty odor of beer. He drank half a cupful in one gulp, finding it sour but refreshing, then bit off a mouthful of bread and chewed. It was tough though flavorful, despite occasional iotas of grit that scored the enamel of his teeth.

He swallowed and regarded the idiomats with circumspect glances, sorting them into types. Travelers in the noösphere had to remember that its inhabitants were only facsimiles of human persons. Principals of Class One Events and Situations might be somewhat internally varied and nuanced. One such had been the satanic Adversary from whom Bandar had received the permanent gift of memory that enabled him to reify the map of the Commons as a color-coded globe. But none approached the complexity of even the simplest human being. The average idiomatic entity was no more than a bundle of basic motivations and responses, enough for it to play its role in the Location's action. It most resembled a character out of fiction.

So the youth with the shy smile was almost certainly a variant of Doomed Innocence. The big man who had slapped Bandar, and who now hulked with two Henchmen where the awning's shade was deepest, was a classic Bully—and perhaps a lethal one if provoked. The noönaut glanced about and saw other instantly recognizable types: a blank Despair mechanically chewing his crust, a self-possessed Loner off to one side, a bluff Salt-of-the-Earth with chin up and eyes clear, and now here came a smarmy Toady to bring the Bully a refill of beer. The squinting overseer appeared to be a variation on the universal Functionary, specifically an Unambitious version, which was a relief to Bandar, who might have found himself under the rein of a Sadist or Martinet. There was no Hero or Unrecognized King in the mix, so Bandar came to the preliminary conclusion that this gang was no more than a background element in whatever main stories were woven through the Event.

That was a small mercy, since it meant he was unlikely to find himself as a Spear Carrier in a revolt with a life expectancy of hours at best. He would probably have enough time to work out a means of extracting himself from this Location, although time was an enemy as well as a friend: eventually, he would become absorbed into the Event, his consciousness abraded away until only some rudimentary functions remained. His real body would lapse into a coma and dwindle to lifelessness while what was left of Bandar repetitively pushed a stone block across a desert, until the extinction of the human species.

One of the fastest routes to absorption was to interact with the elements of the Location. Bandar had to eat and drink and breathe the hot dry air—here his virtual flesh had all the needs and limitations of his real body lying asleep in his room at the Institute—but forming relationships with idiomats was the greatest danger. So when the Doomed Innocence asked if he was all right, Bandar turned his shoulder and stared into the heat haze that filled the middle distance. The idiomat turned away and was drawn into a conversation among the other men concerning appropriate tactics in some form of team sport.

After they ate, the gang was allowed a siesta. Bandar copied the others, scooping out holes for hip and shoulder then reposing himself on the sand, but though he closed his eyes his mind remained active while stereotypical snores erupted around him. He sorted through his options: the restriction of his voice might wear off, but that was nothing to count on; he might find a magician who was willing to help; he might somehow train an idiomat to sound the seven-note emergency than for him, though how he might do that while mute was hard to imagine and besides, it would require encouraging an idiomat to act contrary to its nature—the technical term for such behavior was *disharmony*—which could lead to sudden and even contagious violence; or, best of all, he could find or make a musical instrument that could be tuned to produce the right tones in the right sequence for the right duration.

There was nothing within eyeshot that offered any promise. Bandar would have to wait until they moved to a richer environment: the encampment wherever this crew overnighted. With that issue settled, he turned his mind to the question of what had brought him here. It was not a happy series of thoughts. The collective unconscious was apparently, paradoxically, conscious. It was aware of itself. Worse, it had an agenda, a will of its own. Worse yet, it had no qualms about interfering with the consciousness of an individual—or even several; Bandar now realized that the harsh reception he had received at the Grand Colloquium might well have been stimulated by the Commons. Worst of all, the individual consciousness that had been selected for the most aggravated interference was Guth Bandar's.

He could content himself with one realization, however: He had not been dumped into this specific Location by random chance. Nor had he been sent here to be eliminated; there were many Locations in the Commons where life expectancy was to be measured in seconds. Instead of being popped into a lightless steerage cabin far below the deck of a sinking ocean liner or into the path of a superheated pyroclastic cloud rushing down the slope of an erupting volcano at almost the speed of sound, he had been eased into a slowly evolving Event.

Bandar knew enough about the noösphere to be certain that the self-aware Commons had placed him here so that he could receive the collective unconscious's most routine product, that which was dispensed through myth, fable, joke and every other kind of story from classic literature to popular entertainment: a lesson.

He couldn't learn his lesson if he were dead, and it would do him no good if he was to be absorbed into this Event. So the wisest course was to go along with the Commons's scheme, until he could contrive an escape.

Bandar lay awake and mulled. The obvious lesson to be drawn from being enslaved and forced to push massive blocks under punishing sun and lash was obedience. Although, he reminded himself, the noösphere was not always obvious. Sometimes it delivered its messages through side doors or by the sudden emergence from the background of some overlooked but telling detail. He resolved to remain vigilant.

After what seemed a long while, the overseer crawled out of the shade beneath the cart where he had slept in relative isolation and began kicking feet and poking buttocks with the butt of his whip. The slaves arose, stretching and yawning theatrically, and drained the last of the beer from the jug. Several of them went off behind an outcrop of rust-colored rock to relieve themselves then straggled back to strike the awning and load it, along with the empty baskets and beer jugs, into the old man's cart.

The cart trundled back toward town while Bandar and the others resumed their labors. As the afternoon wore on, the block inched toward the monument. Bandar scanned the huge structure, trying to determine what its ultimate form and dimensions might be, but it was early in the construction process and all he could know for sure was that the final creation would rest upon a colossal foundation of stone.

As the sun touched the horizon, they delivered the block to a staging area where a man wearing a linen wrap and a headdress chased with colored threads used a stick of charcoal to draw symbols on its upper surface. The stone was apparently no longer the concern of Bandar's gang, because the overseer efficiently chivvied them into a double column and directed them to march back the way they had come. The return journey was remarkably quick after their laborious day-long progress.

Bandar found himself walking in the middle of the formation, Doomed Innocence on his left and the Toady literally on his heels. But he paid no attention to either the former's renewed attempts at conversation nor to the latter's treading on his tendons. His placement in relation to the others would not be coincidence—in the Commons, coincidence was never a random event, but rather a sign that the noösphere's operating system was functioning at optimum efficiency. The less Bandar responded to idiomats' overtures, the more slowly he would be absorbed.

Near the end of their march they passed a substantial encampment of linen tents set in neatly ordered rows around a playing field where idiomat soldiers drilled in formation with spear and shield or sparred in pairs with wooden swords and war hatchets. The slave quarters lay on the edge of town, an unwalled cluster of large huts made from plaited reeds and thatched with matted straw. Cooking fires burned in mud-brick ovens, tended by typical female idiomats: a few Crones, some Maidens (both the Demure and Saucy variants) and at least a couple of Sturdy Matrons, all dressed in lengths of coarse cloth wound about their bodies and pinned at the shoulder. They were stirring communal pots full of the evening meal, a bubbling concoction of generic grains and meat scraps with a pungent odor.

Bandar found that the food was eaten communally as well, with everyone seated on woven reed mats surrounding a bonfire in the open space at the center of the slave quarters. First he must get in line and take a shallow wooden plate from a stack on a table. Then he shuffled along to where a Demure Maiden ladled out a thick concoction of grain, vegetables and chunks of gray meat. Bandar saw a complex exchange of looks between the Maiden and Doomed Innocence and wondered if this was the situation in which he was supposed to involve himself. He did not meet the young female idiomat's gaze as she ladled out his share. He looked about for utensils but saw none; then he noted the man in front of him taking some thin flat bread from a stack on a nearby table where he also collected a cup of the weak beer.

Bandar did likewise then followed the fellow over to some empty spots on the mats, several feet from where Doomed Innocence was clearly saving a space for his friend the mute. Bandar paid no heed to the increasingly puzzled idiomat's attempts to attract his attention. Instead he watched as the man beside him put the bowl before him on the ground and tore off a swatch of bread half the size of his palm; then, holding the scrap between thumb and fingers, he used it to pinch up a mouthful of the bowl's contents. Bandar copied the action and was rewarded with a taste so spicy that he reached at once for the beer.

The heat of the day faded rapidly as full dark came on. Bandar shivered and wondered where he was to spend the night. Probably one of the big huts, with everyone squeezed together for warmth, he decided. Though not quite everyone, as the squinting overseer led the Maiden who had served Bandar his food toward a smaller hut at the edge of the open space, while Doomed Innocence regarded them glumly.

Bandar knew that the archetypal Mute usually manifested in one of two main sub-archetypes: Sinister or Sympathetic. He seemed to be of the latter species. He had no idea how the collective unconscious had contrived to replace an existing figure; it would be well worth a paper for the Institute, if he survived to write it, and if the scholars would ever deign to listen to him again, now that their minds had been subtly poisoned against him from within.

He was not yet sure what his role was supposed to be, but his speculations became moot when a steaming dab of pottage unexpectedly struck Bandar's bare chest, the stuff hot enough to sting. He brushed it away with the backs of his fingers, then looked up to see the Toady sneering at him from the other side of the communal fire, a short lath of wood cocked in his hands, ready to flick a second scalding missile Bandar's way. Behind him, the Bully and the Henchmen stood laughing.

Bandar reacted without thinking, a flash of anger causing him to hurl his empty beer cup at his tormentor so that it struck the man square in the forehead. The Toady fell back, howling, his feet kicking in the air. A general laugh went up from the crowd but quickly subsided when the Bully leapt to his feet, glared at Bandar and pointed a thick, calloused finger. "You!" he said.

Bandar had regretted the flinging of the cup even as it left his hand. In the Commons, it was best to act only upon conscious reflection. An automatic response could be a sign that the Location's rules of procedure had begun to seep into the noönaut's virtual being, a precursor to absorption. Now he had scarcely the span of two breaths to reflect on how to respond to the Bully, because the big idiomat and his thugs were coming around the bonfire and the expression on their faces left no doubt as to what they intended to do.

Bandar knew a number of techniques for self defense—it was a necessary skill for anyone venturing into the noösphere. But a Sympathetic Mute would not stand and fight a Bully and his gang. For him to do so could introduce a sharply disharmonious element to the Location, triggering potentially dangerous chaos. Serious disruptions could even cause an Event to reinitiate itself prematurely; if that were to happen, Bandar's consciousness would not survive the changeover. He thought these things as he sprang to his feet and ran into the darkness, the bellowing idiomats pounding after him.

No walls confined the slaves. Once out of town, they had nowhere to go but the desert and the river that probably teemed with crocodiles. Bandar took his chances with the town. It was laid out haphazardly, and first he ran through narrow streets curling among huts and rough corrals that penned baaing goats and sheep. Then he came into broader streets, though still paved only with dirt, of more substantial habitations, mud brick with wooden shutters over glassless windows; some were even walled compounds with gates of squared timbers. All of these details Bandar acquired on the run, finding his way by the light of a half-moon, augmented by occasional oil lamps flickering in windows or by burning torches affixed over gates.

The Bully and his gang stayed with him through every twist and turning. The big idiomat was probably too simple to do other than follow his nature, Bandar thought, and too strong to tire easily. The noönaut did not look back but he could hear his pursuers' heavy footfalls and panting breaths coming ever nearer. The Mute was not built for a long chase.

He was racing down a wider street than most, the way lined with walls and stout fences. Here might be Officials in whose presence the Bully would have to prostrate himself and forego his violent intentions. Bandar saw an open gate flanked by burning brands, a lit courtyard beyond. He took the risk of slowing, felt the angry idiomat's fingers graze his shoulder as he turned and dodged through the gate.

He had hoped to find a person of rank at ease in his yard, perhaps with guards or stout servants who would cow the bully. Instead, Bandar pulled up short in the dust-floored open space, seeing only a moderately ample mud-brick house with an open front. Here, under a thatched awning, an idiomat man and boy were doing something the noönaut did not have time to identify, because the pursuing Bully immediately struck him from behind and knocked him sprawling.

Bandar tumbled to the ground and tried to roll away, but a foot caught him under the ribs and the pain and impact drove the air out of his virtual lungs. The Bully and his gang stood over him, mouthing imprecations Bandar couldn't quite catch over the roaring in his ears, then a second kick grazed his head and the night erupted in colored lights.

He hugged his head between his forearms and curled up, waiting for the next strike. But it didn't come. He heard another voice, then the sound of flesh smacking flesh followed by grunts and a moan. Bandar inched apart his arms just far enough to peek out.

He saw the Bully getting to his hands and knees, blood pouring from a nose that had acquired a new angle. A brawny man wearing a scarred leather kilt was bringing one sandaled foot to connect with a Henchman's buttocks, causing him to stumble quickly through the gate and into the street. The other thug, along with the Toady, stood beyond the gateway wearing looks of wide-eyed consternation.

In a few seconds the yard was cleared, Bandar's former pursuers issuing dire threats but putting distance between themselves and the brawny idiomat who laughed as he slammed the gate shut then turned to regard Bandar. "What did you do to set that lumbering mutton thumper after you?" he said.

Bandar got to his knees and strove to reorder his breathing. He indicated to his rescuer that he had no voice, and saw the man nod. The idiomat approached and put a thickly calloused hand under Bandar's arm, lifting him to his feet as if he weighed no more than the skinny youth who was watching them from the open space before the house.

Bandar recognized the setting: the front of the house was an open-air smithy—with anvil, forge, hammers and tongs, tub of water—and the older idiomat was a Smith while the younger was clearly a version of the Shiftless Apprentice. The noönaut now experienced a shiver of alarm as he noted that the Smith was a more than averagely realized idiomat. His intervention to save Bandar argued that he was at least partially formed of Hero-stuff, and therefore potentially a more significant figure in this Event, perhaps even one of its Principals or Subprincipals.

I should get away from here, he thought as he bowed and gestured to disavow any need for the Smith's further care and solicitude. The pain in his abdomen was fading.

"If you say so," said the idiomat, returning to the anvil where he had been working before Bandar erupted into his yard, "but your friends might be waiting for you down the street. They didn't seem the kind to forgive and forget."

Bandar shrugged. Interaction with a Principal would accelerate his absorption. He needed to put distance between himself and this element of the Location. He bowed again, managed a grateful smile, and turned toward the gate.

"Good luck," he heard the Smith say. Then he heard something else: a *clink* of metal on metal, a *clink* that was precisely the tone of the second note in the seven-note emergency escape thran. Bandar turned back.

The work was not hard. Bandar took the place of the lazy idiomat boy who operated the bellows. This was a sewn-up goat-skin with two wooden handles that Bandar pulled aside and pushed together, filling and emptying the trapped air which rushed through the skin's neck to feed the glowing charcoal in the forge.

The overseer had come in the morning, Bully and Toady eager in his wake, to demand the runaway's return. The Smith had stood up to him, speaking in tones of genial reason.

"The Subgovernor constantly demands that the work proceed more quickly. He needs more tools, sharper tools. I need strong arms at the bellows. Why don't we go and ask His Excellency?"

Bandar saw alarm flicker in the Functionary's eyes. "We need not trouble the Subgovernor," the idiomat said.

"Then it is settled."

"My tally will be short."

The Smith gestured to the boy. "Take back this boy you gave me the last time I said I needed help. He's better at running errands than squatting at the bellows. Let him bring your cup and carry messages."

Faced with a combination of unyielding will and an avenue of lateral evasion, the overseer acceded. The boy went, Bandar stayed, and the Bully left with thunder in his face, cuffing the Toady out of his way at the gate.

Bandar easily settled into the rhythm of the Smith's days. In the early morning and evening he attended at the forge. When the heat grew oppressive, they worked in the relative cool of the mud-brick house, sharpening iron chisels and wedges with file and whetstone and shaping the molds of damp sand in which bronze and copper castings were made. The Smith seemed pleased with his efforts and they worked well together. For his part, Bandar felt comfortable in the role of helper. At least he was not involved in the inevitable strife that would pit Doomed Innocence's infatuation against the overseer's appetites. Nothing hastened a noönaut's absorption into a Location faster than joining in a conflict.

At midday, along with the rest of the town, they took their siesta, Bandar curling up on a rough mattress of coarse cloth stuffed with grass against the back wall of the smithy. He had never slept in the Commons before; sensible noönauts rarely stayed long enough to feel the need and when they did, they sang open a gate and left. He noted that he experienced no dreams, though this made sense to him when he thought about it: a conscious unconscious was enough of a contradiction in terms; the dreams of dreams were not to be thought of.

Every other day, in the evening, a wagon arrived, driven by an overseer drawn by a donkey and surrounded by a squad of guards armed with sword, spear and shield. When the entourage halted in the smithy's yard the gates were closed and the guards took up positions to secure the area. Bandar came out with the Smith and together they took from the overseer—this one the type classified as Exacting Functionary— three baskets of iron and bronze tools to be sharpened or repaired. They carried them into the smithy where, under the watchful eye of the overseer and the captain of the guards, each item was counted out and checked against a tally.

When the procedure was completed, the Smith brought out a second load of tools that had been refurbished over the preceding two days. Again, each tool was meticulously checked against a list written in charcoal on a roll of papyrus. When every piece had been accounted for, the wagon was loaded and reversed, and the guards alertly checked the street before allowing it to roll through the gate.

Once the days had settled into a routine, Bandar took action to change his situation. While the rest of the household napped in the heat of the day, he rose from his straw tick and went to the forge. To anyone who might chance to observe him, he was a smith's helper arranging tools and materials in better order on the workbench. But his true purpose was to strike each metal object with a small scrap of iron, listening to the note that rang in response.

The medium-sized tongs were what had made the note he had first heard, the second in the series of seven. A strip of iron banding, used to strengthen tubs and barrels, sounded with the frequency of the fourth note. That left five to be discovered. Bandar worked his way along the bench, found a punch that rang with the tone of the third.

He allowed himself a moment of happy anticipation. He had worked out the situation. The Multifacet had sent him here for some purpose. He was sure it had to do with Doomed Innocence, since he had been plunked down in the virtual body of a Sympathetic Mute who would have been the youthful idiomat's natural companion in the work gang. Bandar was supposed to learn a lesson of altruism, perhaps even of self-sacrifice, which would suit him for whatever task the Commons wished him to perform in the future.

But the noönaut had been too canny. He had broken out of the context in which he had been placed, found a new setting in which all that was required of him were his functioning arms. And now he was putting together the means to open a gate and leave this Location. After that, he would never again come unawares into the Commons; he knew techniques that would keep him safe once he was free of the stricture at his throat. The noösphere would have to find another patsy.

He turned his attention to some hoe blades heaped in the corner and after a few tries found one that rang with the frequency of note seven. *Three to go*, he thought, then he noticed a wooden plank beneath the hoes, set flush with the dirt floor and so discolored by ash and soot that it blended in with the packed earth around it.

Curious, Bandar brushed aside the Smith's tools and examined the wood. It seemed to be a small trapdoor. He used the edge of a hoe to pry it up and peered within, finding a layer of sacking. This he pulled up, disturbing what was underneath. He heard a *clonk* that, to his pitch-perfect noönaut's ear, was the exact sound of note number one in the seven-tone thran. *Another down and only two to go*, he thought, and reached into the hole.

His fingers closed around cold iron and he brought up what he had found. It was a broad-bladed spear point, needle sharp at the tip and razor edged down both sides. He tapped it with the little bar of iron and it rang true. He set it down and reached deeper into the darkness, careful of cutting himself, and found more spear heads then a long bundle wrapped in sackcloth that contained three rudimentary short swords. He struck one with his rod but the sound it produced was off-key and useless.

A horn-skinned hand closed about the back of Bandar's neck and he was pulled up and to his feet, then still higher so that his toes barely brushed the ground. He felt himself rotated until his eyes met those of an angry idiomat. The Smith shook the noönaut so that his virtual bones rattled within him.

"What are you doing?" was the Smith's first question. The second was, "Who sent you?"

Bandar opened his mouth, but no sound emerged. He tried to convey by facial expression alone that he was innocent of any ill intent, but he knew that his grimace of pain kept creeping in to overshadow the message. With a grunt of disgust, the Smith flung him toward a corner and Bandar landed hard on his back and one elbow. The pain felt very real.

He struggled to rise. He saw another face peeking into the smithy from the yard: the old man in a loincloth who had brought lunch to the work gang. But Bandar's attention was soon reclaimed by the Smith. The big idiomat had gone to the forge and was now turned toward him. In his hand was a heavy maul and behind the anger in his honest face was an underlying expression of reluctant determination.

The little iron rod Bandar had used to test for tones had rolled free. He reached for it and struggled to his knees. If he had read the situation correctly, his appealingness as a Sympathetic Mute, coupled with the Smith's beneficent nature, could deliver him from the latter's anger—provided Bandar performed the right action. He stood up and went to the workbench where he struck the tongs, then the punch, ringing two pure notes from the metal. He struck the strengthening band, then from the three he played a simple tune.

The Smith now regarded him with a mixed countenance. Bandar tried for his most appealing expression as he crossed to the hoe blades and spear points and brought one of each back to the bench. He arranged them in a simple scale then played another tune for the idiomat, wishing as he did so that he had all seven tones needed to open a gate. But the song and the innocence of Bandar's borrowed face were having the desired effect.

"You just wanted to make music," the Smith said.

Bandar enthusiastically signaled an affirmative and the idiomat put down the maul, his face showing almost as much relief as Bandar felt. The old man came into the smithy and said, "We should have known. He's too simple to be a spy for the Subgovernor. Come, let's get these things stowed before somebody sees them as shouldn't."

The noönaut enthusiastically helped transfer the weapons to baskets and hide them in the cart, and when the Smith unthinkingly counseled him to say nothing, he tapped his lips and smiled. They all laughed together, the Smith with a hearty boom and Bandar in heartfelt mime. The idiomats left him there and went into the house, doubtless to conspire further, Bandar thought. For his part, the noönaut assiduously fell to seeking the other two notes of the escape thran. He found tone number six in a copper ladle used to drip water on cooling metal, but the fifth and last note remained elusive.

Bandar struck his way about the forge with an energy that was increasingly desperate. This Location was not what he had thought it was: the Event was not a variant of The Building of the Grand Monument; it was an iteration of another great trope of the Commons—The Rising of the Oppressed. But, once again, Bandar's situation had started bad and become worse: the idiomat to whom he had attached himself was a Principal of this bloody Event. Worst of all, although Bandar was not particularly well-versed in Revolts, he was enough of an Institute scholar to know that they almost always culminated in a massacre of the rebels.

The clandestine weapon-making was a sophisticated operation. Every piece of iron that entered the smithy was accounted for, from the raw ingots sent down from the City under guard by troops of the Governor's own household to the tools and implements distributed and collected each day by the Subgovernor's men at the slave camp. Even the pots and pans in which the communal meals were prepared were kept under guard.

But midway along the route between the Monument and the town someone with a knowledgeable eye had noted an outcrop of iron ore. The area soon became a place where slaves would relieve themselves, an activity they were allowed to do without being closely watched, the guards being almost as likely to go unsandaled as most of the workers. Unobserved, the slaves would break off handfuls of the friable rock and deposit it in the baskets from which the old man distributed bread at lunchtime, and which found their way to the smithy where the Smith would smelt the ore into iron and fashion weapons from it.

The old man who brought the ore also took away the weapons, carrying them back to the communal huts where the women hid them in the thatch and beneath the dirt floors. Bandar deduced that the arming of the slaves had been going on for quite some time and, judging by the ancient courier's excitement, the Rising was imminent.

It was an inspired plan. Not for the first time in his career as an aficionado of the kaleidoscope of human experiences exemplified in the Commons,

Bandar marveled at the ingenuity with which the simple contrived to counter oppression by the mighty. But he also knew that a talent for brilliant improvisation was rarely a match for phalanxes of trained and well-led soldiery. He definitely needed to find the missing fifth note and complete the thran.

Still, nothing rang with the right frequency, although the noönaut *tinked* and *tonked* on every possible object in the smithy and the attached household. His ability to search during his spare time grew limited, however, because the Smith required him to assemble various metallic items on the workbench and to reproduce tunes that the idiomat liked to hum while working at the forge.

It would not have been an intolerable existence but for the imminent threat of annihilation. Even so, Bandar found himself slipping into the routine of the days, taking pleasure in small things. The Smith was an agreeable sort, almost always of a pleasant disposition, being an idiomat idealist who lacked the full array of subtler sensibilities that would complexify the personality of even the most simple real human being. Bandar kept finding in himself an urge to be of help to the fellow, even to the point of wondering if there was some way he could prevent the cycle of the Event from fulfilling itself, which must surely end with the Smith heroically dead.

He resisted the urge, which was not ultimately put to the test. No options presented themselves for altering the inevitable flow of the Event toward its sad conclusion, and Bandar was resolved not to try to create one. If he were truly a misplaced idiomat—although he would have to be an Iconoclastic Genius rather than merely a Sympathetic Mute—Bandar might fortuitously discover an elementary explosive or craft a primitive aircraft that would give the slaves some advantage over the authorities.

But he was quite sure this was not an archetypal rendition of the Traveler Displaced in Time. So the moment he introduced disharmonious material, the Location would begin to accumulate stress on an exponential scale. Bandar had already been inside a Class Four Situation while it was coming apart because of his inadvertent interference; the thought of what it might be like to experience the dissolution of a Class One Event did not bear thinking of.

So he continued his search for the fifth note. It had the highest frequency of the seven, more than a full octave above the lowest. Bandar was starting to think that no object of iron, bronze or copper that he was likely to find around the smithy would produce it. A plate of very thin iron might do.

He wondered if he could convince the idiomat to fashion a xylophone. But between his open and surreptitious labors the Smith was already so occupied that the likelihood was scant, even if Bandar could somehow communicate the idea.

Then one evening, as he helped the Smith fashion a mold in which to cast a set of bronze weights, Bandar heard the elusive note. It came from beyond the outer wall, from the cross street that the Smith had told him ran to where the Subgovernor's mansion sat on a slight rise overlooking town and river.

Bandar rose and took up the jug that held the water they used to dampen the sand of the mold. He went toward the well at one side of the yard, but instead of stopping continued on to the gate and looked out in time to see the source of the sound: four slaves were carrying a curtained litter, escorted by a squad of spearmen. Ahead of them all stepped an idiomat whose attire and bearing identified him as a variant of Pomposity in Office—a major-domo of some sort—who carried a staff that curled into a loop at one end. Hung within the loop, gleaming in the day's dwindling light, was a small silver bell. As the party approached the next intersection, the servant shook the staff so that the bell sounded again—it was indeed precisely the right note—and every other idiomat on the street stopped, turned toward the litter and bowed.

The Smith had come to see what had caught his helper's attention. "The Subgovernor's First Wife," he said, following it with an eloquent twist of his mouth. "Come, we must finish."

Bandar went back to their work, but as he crossed the yard he heard again, fading into the distance, the sound that could offer him deliverance.

The calendar was built around the phases of the moon, with observances performed at its maximum wax and wane. Twice each month of twenty-eight days, all work ceased and all the town, high and low, slave and free, gathered at the white stone temple at the river's edge. Priests clad in fine robes hemmed and cuffed with metallic thread carried a great disk of beaten silver down to the water, where they ritually bathed the pale orb then bore it in a mass procession back up the broad stairs to the sanctuary. At the culmination of the ceremony, the high priest would bless the assembly then all would return to their dwellings for a celebratory meal, a siesta and, in the late afternoon, rowdy team sports and dancing.

The Rising was set for the moment of the benediction. The shuffling throng on the steps was always a heterogeneous mingling of slaves, townsfolk and soldiers. Traditionally, when the hierophant spoke the concluding words of the rite—"It is done. Go now."—the mix would separate into its component streams, with the slaves walking back to their compound under loose guard, everyone glad of the feast and leisure to come.

The Subgovernor and his family sat on a platform to one side at the top of the steps, attended by their senior servants and a squad of bodyguards. Behind them a broad ramp descended to a paved road that led up the rise to the mansion. They were no more than a few paces from the front of the throng on the upper steps, and today that portion of the crowd was unusually thick with strong male slaves.

The underpriests carried the moon disk into the temple. There came an expectant pause then the high priest spoke the ritual words. As usual, the crowd sighed and a hubbub of murmurs broke out as people turned and began to descend the steps. Then the day became unusual.

Instead of turning and leaving, some thirty slaves at the fore of the crowd stood still, so that the intermixed townsfolk and soldiers drew away from them. From beneath their long kilts some of the men brought out short swords. Others produced lengths of turned wood to which they quickly fitted broad bladed spear points. As one, and without a word, they charged the Subgovernor's party.

The guards, lulled by the familiarity of routine had already turned away. The rapid scuffle of feet on stone alerted them, however, and they swung back, attempting to establish a line, shields locked and spears coming down to form a bristle of points.

But the slaves had practiced their tactics too many times on the trampled ground where they were allowed to play muscular games with a ball of cloth wrapped in horsehide. They hit the guards before the line could form, and once broken, the guards were no match for thrice their numbers. While the priests and townsfolk looked on in horror, the slaves slaughtered the bodyguards and seized the Subgovernor and his entourage at spear point.

The townspeople scattered to their homes amid cries of horror. The soldiers shouldered their way free of the mob of fleeing civilians and, under the barked orders of their officers, assembled halfway up the steps, forming two lines angled toward the rebels on the platform above. They set their spears and shields and waited for the order to advance.

Bandar had watched all of this from near the bottom of the steps where, in the company of the Smith, he had stood through the ceremony. Now, as the townsfolk fled, he saw the great mass of slaves, men as well as women, stand gaping in horror and consternation at the armed confrontation until a double squad of soldiers was directed by their commander to surround them and march them back to camp.

With kicks and blows from their spear butts, the soldiers rapidly shaped the hundreds of slaves into a column and began to march them away. But they had gone no more than a few paces before a great shout and clashing of weapons came from the top of the steps. Many of the soldiers marching with the column could not resist turning to look toward the source of the racket. They saw the rebels around the Subgovernor bellowing and smashing their iron weapons together, and that was the last thing they saw because their momentary distraction was the signal for scores of those they guarded to draw concealed knives and stab them.

"Now!" cried the Smith, and pulled from beneath his kilt the heavy maul with which he had once threatened Bandar. He threw himself against a maniple of soldiers who had had the presence of mind to close together and were spearing the knife wielding rebels from behind their shields. The Smith attacked from their rear, crushing skulls and spines with his great hammer and in seconds the guards were dead, their corpses plundered for their weapons.

"Make a line!" the Smith shouted. "Those without arms pry up the paving stones!"

A few of the slaves hung back, frightened and uncertain. But Bandar saw even Crones and Maidens digging their fingers into the cracks between the flags, upending them then lifting the squares to dash them down. The impact shattered the stones and hard, eager hands reached for the jagged fragments.

The Smith's voice boomed out—"All right, at them!"—and the slaves charged up the steps toward the double line of soldiers, even as the officers were frantically screaming at the rear rank to about face. A hail of sharp-edged stones came arcing over the heads of the upsurging armed rebels and the soldiers who had reversed to meet them threw up their shields to ward off the barrage. But these soldiers were not the stones' intended targets. Instead the jagged chunks of rock flew over their upraised shields to smash into the unprotected skulls and spines of the spearmen still facing the thirty who had seized the Subgovernor.

As men fell moaning or unconscious out of the upper rank, leaving gaps and causing those not hit to glance worriedly over their shoulders, the majority of the thirty rebels above left the Subgovernor and his entourage in the custody of a few men with swords. Screaming just as they had practiced so many times on the ball field, they formed a bristling wedge and threw themselves at the wavering line of soldiers at the same moment as their friends from below struck the lower rank of spearmen.

It was a brutal business. Though Bandar had seen it in other Locations, with men who wore different garments and wielded more sophisticated weapons, it was always the same. Metal pierced flesh, blood spattered from slashing wounds or fountained from severed arteries, to a chorus of high pitched screams and bestial grunts. He watched with an expert eye and decided that this might well be one of those Risings of the Oppressed in which a gifted Hero—for so the Smith undoubtedly was—carried the day. But then he saw Doomed Innocence roaring in the front rank of the rebels, stabbing with his spear, his Demure Maiden at his side wielding a long knife with the skill of a butcher. And Bandar remembered that even the successful revolts usually lasted no longer than it took for fresh troops to arrive in overwhelming numbers.

He skirted around the edge of the melee, careful to maintain a safe distance. He kept experiencing an urge to go toward the Smith, to help him in some indefinable way. Suddenly it all became clear. *I am becoming embedded in the Mute's dynamic. He is a Hero's Helper. That is the role that the Commons wants to press me into.*

But Bandar resisted the pull. He had to avoid danger because if he died in this Location, his consciousness would be irrevocably meshed with its elements. He would be the Mute forever, unless the Commons had a means of extracting him at the point of death, a possibility in which he was not willing to trust his existence. Besides, Bandar was still Bandar and he had his own agenda, the crowning piece of which awaited him at the top of the steps.

The slaves had surrounded the remaining soldiers, pressing them into a tight cluster, jammed so closely together that most of them could not bring their weapons to bear. More chunks of masonry were now flying from all sides, smashing into the trapped remnant. Wherever an impact rocked a spearman a rebel was waiting to slip sharp iron through the gap. The action would not last much longer. Bandar dodged around the rear of the fighters and climbed toward the Subgovernor's party.

He put on his most appealing face, smiling and gesturing happily to the men who held the dignitaries, clapping them on their shoulders as he slipped among them. At the rear of the group the First Wife's major-domo stood ashen faced, his brow glistening with a chill sweat, the hooked staff of office quivering in his grasp so that its little silver bell tinkled too softly to be heard over the sounds of murder.

Bandar stepped up to the terrified idiomat, put the thumb and finger of one hand to the ringing metal, then brought up a knife in the other. The major-domo flinched but Bandar offered him a harmless smile and sliced through the thread that held the bell. Then he turned and sped across the top of the temple steps, seeing from the corner of his vision the priests clustered within its entry, all white of eye and open-mouthed.

In a few moments the noönaut was down the steps, past the heaped corpses of the column guards and into the empty streets of the town. With the fifth note clasped in his hand, he made his way at a fast trot past closed gates and shuttered windows, to arrive at the smithy hardly out of breath.

He set the silver bell on workbench then began assembling his seven-toned instrument around it, reaching for the tongs and the other pieces then bringing from under his kilt the spear point he had been issued but had not used. When the seven items were arranged in proper order he allowed himself a brief smile and a small sigh of satisfaction, then he turned to look for the small rod that was his striker.

A dark figure came between him and the bright world outside the smithy. It took him a moment to make out the habitual sneer of the Toady. Then he saw the hulking form of the Bully and the Henchmen. Bandar realized that he could not recall having seen any of them in the fighting. But he saw that they carried weapons, swords of gray iron whose edges gleamed with the brightness of fresh sharpening, still unblooded.

He grasped it all in a moment. The Bully cared nothing for the slaves' cause. Instead he would help suppress it, seeking to be granted the only life such an idiomat could aspire to: as an overseer given a whip and plenty of unnecessary encouragement to use it.

And so he would lurk here until the Smith came home—as he surely would, humble in his moment of triumph. Then, while the victorious slaves celebrated in the streets, the Bully and his gang would wait in the house and treacherously stab the Hero to death. When the night grew quiet, they would steal away, carrying the butchered idiomat's head in a basket, aiming to meet the army that the Governor would soon send down river to put the town back to rights.

All of that Bandar knew in the time it took him to blink in surprise. It was an old story, of course; that was why it had been preserved forever in the collective memory of humankind. What surprised him was the strength of the desire that now filled him, the powerful urge to run from here at all speed, to find the Hero and warn him. Even as he marveled at the power of the impulse, he saw that one of his hands was reaching back for the spear point while his mind was seeing a picture of the Mute breaking through the four men, slashing as he ran.

Then the whole situation became academic. The Toady was shouldered aside by the Bully. The last Bandar saw was the smirk on the thick lips and the smug satisfaction in the close-set, beer-colored eyes as the big man drove his sword through the noönaut's belly and up into his heart. The pain was like ice and fire together, and then it was gone. And so was Bandar.

The thugs, the smithy, the town instantly ceased to be. Bandar was back once more in the luminous mist. The Multifacet regarded him placidly from the eyes of a cartoon lion.

"You have failed," Bandar said.

"Have we?"

"You wanted me to be Helper to the doomed Hero, but I would not."

A tusked demon smiled in return. "Yet you wished to."

"I fought the urge, and prevailed."

The demon became a saucy tomboy. "Because you knew whence it came. What will you do when its source is less obvious?"

Bandar set his jaw. "Be as subtle as you like. I will be on guard."

A kind-eyed saint smiled and said, "Not if you don't remember."

As these last words were spoken, the figure dwindled rapidly, as if it rushed away from Bandar at great speed, pulling the mist twisting and roiling in its wake. The noönaut blinked and found himself reposing in the shade of the palm tree, the generic ocean rippling and whispering up the gently sloping beach and the three gamins beckoning him to pursue them. The blonde gave him her unintentional parody of a come-hither look while the red-haired one cocked one hip.

Bandar smiled and sat up. A shadow of a thought crossed his mind. Hadn't he been thinking of something just now? He reached for the memory, but whatever it had been, it had now ebbed away. He got to his feet and chased the three giggling idiomats out into the waves where, as always, the sequence faded and a new dream took its place.

In the morning, Bandar formally resigned from the Institute for Historical Inquiry and caught the noon jitney to the balloon tram station at Binch. He would return to Olkney and take up a position with his

Uncle Fley, who operated a housewares business in which there had long been a standing offer of a junior executive post for Bandar, Fley having no heirs of his own.

It was with a mix of feelings that Bandar watched the ground fall away as the tram car ascended high above the tracks. He saw, far off, the Institute's grounds, the neat cloisters and formal gardens, the grand old halls and the students' cottages, and a tear came to his eye. But then he turned his mind resolutely toward the future: Uncle Fley, though only a commerciant, was a man of integrity and quiet accomplishment. He struggled against the vicissitudes of existence with courage and without complaint.

There was a nobility in the simple life, even a kind of heroism, Bandar told himself. He experienced a gentle urge to stand by his uncle, to be of help.

Other Tales

Shadow Man

For as long as he could remember, Damien Bonnespine knew somebody was there, watching him.

Not all the time. There were long spells between the moments when he would feel the shiver across his shoulders that made his neck hairs stand up. But eventually it would happen again and he'd know they were back. Then for the next few minutes he'd feel them watching him.

He couldn't see them, and he always thought of them as a crowd of shadow men—no faces, no details, just vague silhouettes with shaded eyes turned his way. When he was little it had creeped him out, but nothing bad ever came of it. He didn't feel threatened, just watched.

When he was nine he told the mom. She gave him the same scared but careful look he already recognized, even back then, as a signal that some of the thoughts that slowly bubbled up to break at the surface of his mind were best kept unsaid. Thoughts about pain and how animals squirmed and yelped when things happened to them. How interesting it would be to know if people squirmed and yelped like that.

When Damien was fifteen, the mom found the cat trap and the stuff he kept in a box way back in the crawl space under the house. She took him to a doctor. There were machines and needles and stupid pictures he had to look at and talk about, but some of the doctor's other pictures were way cool—dead people, and some who were not dead yet, but were opened up like the cats, showing slick red meat and yellowy bones.

One time, while he was looking at the pictures and talking about them, he felt the familiar chill across his shoulders and the tickle of hairs lifting. The doctor must have seen something in Damien's face because he said, "What are you thinking now?"

Damien told him. The man made notes on his pad and asked a lot more questions. "Were there voices? Do the voices want you to do things?"

Damien said there were no voices but he didn't think the doctor believed him. They made him take pills that filled his head with cold, silent noise. He couldn't think and sometimes when he tried to talk the words got lost for a while. He stopped going to school but the mom got him lessons from the school board to do at home and a computer that connected to a tutor. But one day he was so interested in a picture he had found on the Internet that he didn't hear her come in until she was looking over his shoulder. She took the machine away.

Now, at eighteen, Damien Bonnespine used the public library's computers to look at pictures. His interest had broadened and he read about interesting people: Jeffrey Dahmer, John Wayne Gacy, Richard Ramirez, Frank Spisak. He was living in an abandoned butcher's shop near the cement plant. Some other kids slept in the rooms upstairs but they let Damien have the downstairs all to himself. He had stopped taking the pills and now his head was hot and busy again.

It was morning and Damien was thinking about the new girl who had come back to the squat with the others yesterday. She was only thirteen and her button nose and slanted, almond-shaped eyes reminded him of a cat. He was sitting on the old counter top, the wood scarred with cuts and scratches, letting his thoughts circle the girl when he felt the familiar shivery prickle.

He paid no attention, concentrated on the pictures in his head. Then he caught a flutter of motion to one side. He didn't turn toward it, just let his head drift a little in that direction until, from the corner of his eye, he saw the shadow man.

It was like seeing something on tv when thunderstorms screwed up the reception: a man shape, dark but without detail of features or clothing, speckled with dots that flickered and flashed. Damien turned his head an inch more and saw that the staticky man was not watching him now. He was bent over, poking at something where his waist would be.

The years of catching cats had made Damien very fast. He set himself, inhaled a long, deep breath—then, as he let it out, he threw himself from the counter top and crossed the room with one long stride and a flying leap.

His outstretched hands sank into the dots and sparks and met cloth-covered flesh beneath. The man squawked and tried to pull free but Damien yanked the shadow man toward him while shooting his head forward like a striking snake so that his forehead connected hard where the watcher's face should be. He felt bone snap and heard a gargly yelp.

The man was not big but Damien was. He lifted the watcher off his feet and slammed him against the door of the long-gone butcher's walk-in cooler, did it again and again until the body flopped loose in his grip.

He let it slide to the floor. It was still flickering and winking but that was the only movement. Damien reached into the static and felt around the waist where the man had been poking. He found a belt with a row of studs on it, traced his fingers along its length to a clasp. He undid the fastener and pulled the belt free.

Now his hand was encased in a blur of light and dark. Damien felt for the studs, pressed them singly and in combinations, but the effect didn't change. Then the belt gave a hiss that became a hum that grew louder before it abruptly stopped. The sparks and shadows disappeared and Damien could see his hand again. It was holding a strip of metallic fabric set with a panel of buttons. From the panel came a smell of fire and ozone.

Damien poked at the controls some more but the thing was dead. He turned his attention back to its owner and saw a small man with a sharp-featured face that put Damien in mind of a ferret. He had been pretty bald for someone so young but Damien could tell from the interesting angle of his neck that he wouldn't have to worry about getting any older.

The body was wearing a one-piece jumpsuit with a peculiar fastening system down the front. There were pockets but nothing interesting in them. Tied to one wrist by a looped cord was a small, flat oblong of metal about half the size of a cigarette pack.

Damien freed the object and examined it. He identified what looked to be a lens and next to it a pinpoint microphone. There were controls etched into the side and the upper surface. He touched them. At first nothing happened, then suddenly a screen appeared in the air, crowded with symbols and icons. There was writing, too, but Damien couldn't read it. It looked vaguely Chinese.

Damien reached out a finger to one of the icons. Dozens of thumbnail images flooded the scene, and when he touched one of the miniatures it expanded to fill the viewing space and the figures in it began to move.

Damien recognized the scene: the attic in Gacy's house. He'd seen a tv movie about it but they hadn't shown anything interesting. But now, as he watched, he understood. This wasn't a movie. This was real.

He found how to minimize the image and touched another of the main screen's icons. He watched, fascinated, for a few moments. That was Dahmer's kitchen. There he was at the stove, humming. Another selection and Damien was watching Bundy creeping into a darkened bedroom. Then a man he didn't recognize, in a city where the cars flew, and another in some place where the sky was red.

He ran through the entire menu, sampling, mentally marking the ones he wanted to come back to first. Until an image brought a sharp intake of breath: the cramped space beneath his mother's house, a figure lit by a flashlight kneeling in the back corner, putting on his heavy gloves to lift a spitting, struggling tabby out of the trap.

He watched his juvenile self, reliving the memory. Then he canceled the image and chose another: looking at the pictures in the doctor's office; then the time with the stray mongrel and the propane torch.

But there were pictures he didn't remember, couldn't have remembered. They showed a Damien grown into his twenties, into his thirties, showed him in places he'd never been, with people he hadn't met yet.

He turned his eyes from the screen and regarded the body slumped against the grimy wall. Damien had never known what people meant when they said they regretted things they'd done. Now he almost understood.

He wished he could talk to the man. They had had a lot in common. As he dragged him into the cooler, Damien felt that it had been—he sought for the right word, then found it—an *unfortunate* way to treat his first fan.

He turned back to the images of the future Damien, watched the way he did things, how he controlled the situations. He thought again about the girl with the cat's eyes and began to make some mental notes.

The Devil You Don't

The frantic sparks fly up into the November night like lost souls seeking safe harbor who, finding none, extinguish themselves against the unheeding darkness. Or so I might write it if ever I should put pen to paper to tell this tale. But I shall not.

The fire itself is confined by the blackened steel barrel. I poke again with the gardener's fork and another flurry of sparks shoots up, and with them scraps of burning paper. By the flickering light of the flames I can sometimes see a printed word or two before they are consumed: *Alamein, Rommel, Singapore, Yalta.*

The books are thick. They will take time to burn but I have learned patience. I have always taken the longer view. Perhaps it is a sense of history. Perhaps it is just how I am formed. But, in the arena of public life, he who takes the longer view must win out in the end.

The gardener has left in heaps his cullings from the bygone summer's flower beds. I gather another armful of dried stalks and withered blossoms and throw them onto the flames. The flare of light illuminates the disturbed earth that the gardener turned over this afternoon and the pile of red bricks that have lain here much longer—more than a year since I abandoned building a wall to take Mr. Chamberlain's reluctant call.

First Lord of the Admiralty, then. Prime Minister now. It was what I had always wanted, I will admit, though I would have preferred its arrival under less perilous circumstances.

The books are burning well. I leave them and kneel beside the wall. The cement with which to mix the mortar is just where I left it and there is water at hand. I lay a red, fired brick atop the black soil, trowel its side with mortar then place a second beside it.

Another pass with the trowel, then another brick. The work proceeds as it always did, a step at a time. That is how walls are built. As are lives. And futures.

The man appeared from thin air. I wanted to think he had stepped out of the darkness but the space behind him was well lit by the lights of Chartwell's great house, my house. I had not been here since the start of the war.

"Please don't be alarmed," he said.

"I am alarmed," I said. "My visitors usually make less startling entrances, and then only when invited."

"I mean you no harm."

"I am relieved to hear it."

"I've come from the future."

"Now I am alarmed anew," I said.

There was a policeman in the house, a Special Branch man with a pistol. But I did not call out. My visitor begged me to allow him to demonstrate his bona fides.

I did so and was soon convinced. He had a watch that displayed time through ingenious means and a device no larger than a calling card that could extract a square root in the blink of an eye. He showed me coins and paper money bearing the likeness of the young Princess Elizabeth, grown grandmotherly beneath the Crown of State.

"I am glad to know that the royal family endures," I said. "You bring me a heartening sign when one is sorely needed."

"I have brought you more than signs," he said. "I have brought you wonders."

He produced a package of books, small paperbound editions such as I had not seen before. I took them in my hands. The titles had a ring to them: *The Gathering Storm; Their Finest Hour; Blood, Sweat and Tears.*

Then I saw the name of the author. It was mine own.

"What are these?" I said.

"Your memoirs," he said. "The war years, at least."

"Then I survive," I said.

"More than that. You win."

"I am glad to hear it."

"It was touch and go for a while," he said. "But that was not the worst of it."

"Oh? Then what was the worst of it?"

I have not often seen a man look so forlorn. "The cost," he said. "The sheer waste. The horror."

I did not know how to comfort him. I set the books down on a heap of bricks then brought out cigars and offered him one. He seemed delighted to take it. His face shed its melancholy and he exhibited an exhilaration I have seen only in the shining eyes of schoolboys encountering their idols on the sidelines of a cricket pitch.

"I knew you would be here tonight, alone," he said, when he had puffed his cigar alight. He had studied my life, he said, choosing a night when I had come to the old place, away from memoranda and telephones and committees, to wrestle with my old black dog of a mood that had gripped me since the terrible raid on Coventry two nights ago.

He savored the rich Cuban leaf, blew out a long stream of blue smoke, then said, "But now you can stop all of it before it happens—the Blitz, the Battle of the Atlantic." He looked wistful for a moment then continued. "My mother's younger brother drowned when his ship was torpedoed off Newfoundland in 1942. Fifty years later, she still cried for him."

"I am very sorry," I said.

"But you see, now he doesn't have to die," he said, gesturing to the books with the hand that held the cigar so that a scattering of ash fell upon the cover of the one entitled *The Hinge of Fate*. "It's all in there. Hitler's plans, his blunders. His invasion of Russia, D-Day, all of it."

I looked at the books atop the bricks but did not touch them.

"Now you can strike where he is weakest, shorten the war, save tens of millions of lives."

"Are there others like you?" I asked. "Other travelers through time?"

He told me that the channels by which he had come back to me were abstruse, unknown to any other. He had hit upon time travel by the most outrageous twist of odds. "But once I knew I could come here, I had to," he said. "The war was the most terrible thing that ever happened. But with these books you can prevent the worst of it."

"Hmm," I said. "Show me."

He bent to retrieve one of the volumes. I reached for a brick.

I mortar a second layer of bricks over the first, tapping each carefully into line with its brothers. The man from the future lies with his wonders beneath the fire-hardened oblongs. His books are ashes now.

I wonder if he understood, as the light was going out of his eyes, that I must accept all the horrors to come. That is the price to be paid for the knowledge he had brought me, the knowledge that we will be able to endure and that then will come brighter days.

But would they still come if I had looked into those books? If I could see the present as the past through my own future eyes, would I not surely wander from the path that I now tread in darkness, though with a good hope that it will lead us eventually to those broad sunny uplands?

I must choose the devil I know, though I know him now to be even more horrid than I feared, because the devil I don't know may well be even worse.

Yet the man from the future has not striven in vain. He has done much good. Because of him, my black dog is once more whipped back to his dark kennel.

I finish the second layer of bricks, stand and brush the dirt from the knees of my trousers. I lay the trowel on the unyielding surface.

I shall carry on. We shall see it through.

Go Tell the Phoenicians

The K'fondi were driving Livesey and his BOOT team three stops past crazy, but that was not why the station chief hated me at first sight.

Mainly it was my record, which was laying itself out as Livesey tapped the panel of his desk display. I held myself at something like attention, set my lumpy features on bland, and looked over the chief's regulation haircut to where the window framed the unknown hills of K'fond.

"If Sector Administrator Stavrogin wasn't biting my backside, you'd never have set down on my planet," Livesey said, "but I promise you, Kandler, while you're attached to this establishment, you'll go *by the book*. Or I'll chase you all the way back to Earth and bury you in whatever stinking kelp farm you oozed out of."

There was more, but I had heard the like from the ranking Bureau of Offworld Trade field agent at just about every assignment I could remember. I was a foreign body in the Bureau's innards, a maverick among a tamer breed, tolerated only because I was also BOOT's best exo-sociologist. But wherever I was sent in, it was a sign that the field agent in charge was out of his depth. If I turned out to be the reason a mission was successful, a corresponding black mark went into the file of the BOOT bureaucrat who had screwed up.

They sent me in because I got results. But the day I stopped getting results, the uneasy symbiosis between me and the Bureau would fall apart. With luck, I might land at a Bureau training depot, lecturing batches of budding Liveseys on the intricacies of the ancient alien cultures they'd be rehearsing how to loot.

Without luck, I'd be back on Argentina's Valdés Peninsula, stacking slimy bales of wet kelp, just as my father had done until he wore out and died. So I kept my mouth shut through the chief's opening rant, and watched a gaggle of K'fondi boost each other over the station's perimeter fence. They frolicked across the clipped lawn like teenagers at the beach.

Livesey turned to follow the direction of my gaze, swore bitterly, and punched his desk com.

"Security," he said, "they're back! Get them herded off station! Move!"

The aliens wandered over and gawked through Livesey's window, giving me my first look at K'fondi. They were the most humanoid race Earth had ever found. On the outside, a K'fond could pass for any fair-sized, bald human who happened to be thin-lipped, large-nosed and shaded from pink to deep purple.

Closer examination revealed subtle differences in joints and musculature, but the K'fondi were a delight to those exobiologists who argued that parallel evolution would produce intelligent species that roughly resembled each other. We could breathe what the K'fondi breathed, drink what they drank, eat what they ate.

No one knew what K'fondi were like on the inside, but there would be some major differences. For one thing, they were thought to lay eggs.

Security heavies arrived to coax the natives off the station. None of them seemed to mind. One departing visitor—even without breasts, she was slinkily female in an almost sheer gown slit on both sides from shoulder to knee—paused for a parting wave and a broad wink through the window.

Livesey leaned his forehead against the window's plastic and swore with conviction. "Tell me how I'm supposed to negotiate a trade agreement when they treat this station like some kind of holiday camp?"

"Is it just the local kids come to look around?" I said.

Livesey turned with a glare of bewildered outrage. "As far as I can tell, that was their negotiating team. Go get briefed."

Outside, the K'fond air was rich and unfiltered, the slightly less than Earth-normal gravity added a spring to my step, and I headed for my quarters in a tingle of excitement. I loved the beginning of every new assignment, ahead of me a whole alien culture to explore. It was almost enough to let me forget that the Bureau of Offworld Trade would use my work to help pick the K'fondi clean.

I hated BOOT, but the Bureau was the only path to field experience for an exosociologist. It was an arm of the Earth Corporate State, the final amalgamation of the Permanent Managerial Class of multinational corporations and authoritarian regimes that had coalesced just as humankind took its first steps toward the stars.

For a bright boy who ached to escape from Permanent Under Class status, who thirsted to meet and encompass the strange logics of alien cultures, BOOT was the only game in the galaxy—and I'd played it my whole career.

Brains and a willingness to outwork the competition had taken me from my parents' shack through scholarships and graduate school, then out into the immensity on Bureau ships. Now, with a score of alien cultural topographies mapped to my credit, every new assignment was more precious than the last.

Soon, I would be ordered out of the field, sent back to a plain but secure retirement on Earth. I could settle into a university chair, write a textbook and train the next generation of bright boys and girls who would assist the Bureau in its beads-and-trinkets trade.

Beads and trinkets were Livesey's vocation, and it was an ancient calling. The Phoenicians started it off, tricking Neolithic Britons into accepting a few baskets of brightly colored ceramics for a boatload of precious tin ore. Later, the Portuguese traded cloth for gold, the French and English gave copper pots for bales of furs, or worn-out muskets for manloads of ivory.

Every planet had something worth taking: a rare element, a natural organic that would cost millions to synthesize on Earth, a precious novelty to delight the wealthy and powerful. And on each world, the natives wanted something Earth could supply.

If the aliens could have haggled in Earth's markets, they would have gotten fair value. But only Earth had lucked into the ridiculously unlikely physics behind the Dhaliwal Drive. As in the days of the Phoenicians, he who has the ships sets the price.

Earth's corporate rulers would have had no moral objections to conquest, but systematic swindling was far cheaper and the PMC was leery about arming and training the PUC. There was no Space Navy to eat up the profits from the beads-and-trinkets trade. For the aliens, and for me, it was just too bad.

My job now was to get a handle on K'fond culture, particularly its economics, and tell Livesey what technological baubles the locals would jump at. In my spare time before rotation back to the Bureau sector base, I might be able to work up a paper for the journals.

But the trade agreement came first. That was in the book, and the Bureau went by the book.

My quarters were in a row of standard-issue station huts. I threw my gear onto the cot and turned to the stack of data nodes on the compcom desk that was the only other furniture. I plugged in the first one and the screen lit up.

There was nothing remarkable about the report of the seed ship that had discovered K'fond. I speeded up the readout and skimmed the highlights. Unmanned craft passes by, drops robot orbiter, moves on. Orbiter maps surface and analyzes features until its programs deduce the presence of cities. Orbiter opens subspace channel to Office of Explorations sector base and tells OffEx about K'fond.

Then OffEx reports to headquarters on Earth, which commissions a K'fond file and copies it to BOOT. BOOT puts together Livesey's team and sends them from the nearest sector base to establish contact. Every step neatly marked by its own cross-referenced memo. By the book.

But the pages started falling out when Livesey's team tried contact procedures. I plugged in the project diary, saw Livesey bring his ship into orbit over K'fond. I checked the time code: given the slowness of bureaucratic response and the temporal dilation effect of the Dhaliwal Drive, about three standard years had elapsed since first discovery. And in those three years, BOOT's robot orbiter had somehow gone missing.

Things only got worse for Livesey. He ran out the ship's ears to eavesdrop on surface communications; all were intricately scrambled. He dropped clouds of small surveillance units; each stopped broadcasting shortly after entering the atmosphere. The book said his next option was a manned descent, and Livesey had already chosen volunteers when the ship's com received a signal from the surface.

In clear, unaccented Earth Basic, someone said, "Welcome to K'fond. You are invited to land at the site indicated on your screen. Please do not divert from the entry path we have plotted for you."

The com screen showed a map of the smallest of K'fond's three continents; a series of concentric circles flashed around the spot where Livesey was to put down.

I laughed. The terse prose of the official diary did not record Livesey's outrage when the cherished contact procedures were brushed aside. But I could imagine the chief's fear at making planetfall without a bulging file of information garnered from the ship's spy gear and the missing orbiter's surveys.

Livesey and three others had dropped down to a field several kilometers west of a K'fond town. The video showed a small crowd of aliens clustered around the shuttle. Then the scene shifted to visuals taken by the contact team as they emerged from the craft. I slowed the image speed and looked closely.

A dozen K'fondi of both sexes were coming toward me. No two were dressed alike, their garments ranging from flowing robes to close-fitting coveralls. One female wore nothing but a metal bracelet. I magnified her image; egg-layer or not, except for the absent navel, she looked scarcely less mammalian than many fashion models. I tracked to an almost nude male, and saw the pronounced sexual differentiation.

I thumbed the flow speed back to normal and saw what Livesey had seen. The K'fondi flocked toward the contact team like kids let out of school. The BOOT men were jostled and seized, and the camera showed one agent tentatively reaching for his needle sprayer. But the aliens were patently friendly and curious. They fingered the Earthmen's clothing, plucked at hair, chattering nonstop amid what looked much like human smiles and laughter.

It was like seeing a first contact between Europeans and the peoples of the South Pacific five hundred years ago. But that reminded me of what had been done to those long-gone dwellers in paradise by the "civilized" visitors they had rushed out to welcome.

I looked at the glad K'fondi faces. "Hey, have we got a deal for you," I said to the screen.

The tapes of later contacts chronicled Livesey's descent into frustration. The K'fondi really did act like rambunctious teenagers on a holiday. And yet many of them showed what I thought were signs of aging. I flipped forward to one of the "negotiating" sessions.

A chaos of K'fondi chattered around an outdoor table somewhere on the station. None of them spoke Basic, and Livesey was struggling through sign language and the few words of local speech the lingolab had identified. The K'fondi were not listening. Some were passing around a flask. One couple left off nuzzling each other to slide beneath the table, and began demonstrating the similarities of K'fond and human love-making. Livesey put his forehead to the table and groaned.

I speed-ran the other tapes, witnessing several more encounters between BOOT and the K'fondi. I didn't bother with the file of correspondence between Livesey and sector base; I could imagine the SectAd's memos advancing from neutral to querulous to plain nasty. If the chief didn't get results here fast, BOOT would demote him so far down the hierarchy he'd need a miner's helmet to find his desk.

Which meant he'd be leaning hard on me to get those results for him.

The problem was simple: the K'fondi didn't make any sense. They had a high-tech culture, and somebody on the planet could beam a message to an orbiting Bureau ship in a language no K'fond should have known. Yet the K'fondi who came on station acted like eighteenth-century Trobriand Islanders on their day off.

The language puzzle intrigued me. I buzzed the station switchboard and was connected with the lingolab. The call was answered by a harassed man of middle years who introduced himself as Senior Linguist Walter Mtese. He gave me directions to his lab.

I stepped from my hut into a warm midafternoon. This part of K'fond seemed a mellow, balanced place. Temperature, humidity, even the light breeze were perfectly matched. An occasional cloud threw interesting shapes on the distant slopes, and the air was soft and good on my face. *A place to settle down in*, I thought. But that kind of thinking led nowhere. Earth law prohibited residence anywhere but where the state could keep an eye on you, and that meant Earth.

I cut between two storage huts and came suddenly face to face with the K'fondi that Livesey had had thrown off the station a couple of hours before. I observed that they liked close physical contact on first encounter; in fact, it couldn't get much closer than the way the pink female snaked her arms around my neck. Her skin was smooth and hot—K'fond body temperature was equivalent to a human's raging fever. She smelled indefinably of fruit.

"*Jiao doh vuh?*" she inquired.

I tried to gently shrug off the weight of her arms. Physical contact between human and alien on first encounter can represent anything from a polite greeting to an indiscriminate appetite. The correct response was to try to imitate the gesture offered, according to the Bureau book. But as she pressed her chest against me and followed with her hips, I realized that going by the book this time would involve seriously violating several BOOT regulations.

With smiles and soft-voiced disclaimers, I disentangled myself and stepped back. The pink woman shrugged very humanly and said something to her companions, then they all wandered around the corner of the building without a backward glance. Seconds later, I heard a human voice shout "*Hey!*" followed by a burst of K'fond giggles. Then the group came pelting back around the corner, pursued by two puffing guards. I flattened myself against the supply hut and let the chase roll by. The K'fondi were enjoying the game.

Walter Mtese wasn't enjoying the K'fondi, I found when I entered his lingolab. Mtese was pure Bureau. A pattern of commendations and certificates decorated his walls, testaments to the linguist's integration into the BOOT view of the universe. But for a successful bureaucrat, Mtese looked a harried man.

"I think someone's playing an elaborate practical joke on us," he complained, as he hooked me up to the snore-couch. "These people get by with a vocabulary of under a thousand words, most of which have to do with sex, booze and bodily functions. Tell me how that's compatible with a technological civilization."

"How are they at learning Basic?" My voice sounded strange in the confines of the headpiece he was fitting over my ears.

"They don't learn anything," Mtese answered. "I spent a whole morning—that's six standard hours—trying to teach two of them ten words. I'd have had more luck training snakes to tap-dance. Give me your arm, please."

I felt the hypo's aerosol coolness. Subjective time slowed as the drugs depressed selected regions of my nervous system while goosing others into hyperawareness. Around a tongue now grown larger than the head that contained it, I managed to speak.

"What does '*jiao doh vuh*' mean?"

Mtese snorted as he punched codes into the snore-couch controls. "It's the standard greeting between males and females, usually answered in the affirmative, and followed by immediate direct action. It's a wonder they've got the energy to walk."

The snore-couch's headset began murmuring in my ears, the drugs took hold, and Mtese and the lingolab evaporated into golden warmth as the machine flooded my neurons with incoming freight.

Back at my hut, I found that knowing K'fondish was no big help. As the last wisps of Mtese's chemicals effervesced out of my brain, I reran Livesey's encounter tapes. The linguist was right: K'fondish conversation was at the level of the street corner banter of good-natured juvenile delinquents— simple, direct and highly scatological. If the alien who had spoken in Basic over the ship's com was one of the "negotiating team," he was keeping his mouth shut.

Livesey's records and the lingolab had taught me all they could. The next step, by the book, was firsthand field contact. According to procedures, that meant encountering the natives under controlled conditions, on station ground, and guided by a welter of Bureau regulations devised by bureaucrats who had never left Earth. I saw no reason to repeat Livesey's failure. Besides, it was always more instructive to meet aliens on their own turf.

The transport-pool guard refused me a ground car without an authorized requisition. He was still refusing as I wheeled a two-seater out of its stall and waved my way past gate security. The highway was wide, flat and empty. I urged the car up to cruising speed, took the center of the road and headed east. Five minutes from the station, I reached under the instrument panel and pulled loose a connection. Now the car's location transmitter couldn't tell tales on me. I nudged my speed a little higher, and went looking for K'fondi.

The quality of this planet's technology was obvious in the agricultural zone on the town's outskirts. A house-sized harvester trundled through a field, collecting a nutlike fruit that emerged packed in transparent containers from the harvester's rear port. A flatbed truck with a grapple followed along, stacking the containers on itself in precise rows. Neither machine had an operator. In the distance, herd animals grazed near the shores of a lake that swept across the horizon to lap against the geometry of the town's central core.

The highway connected with a grid of local and arterial roads, and I met up with other traffic. Self-directed trucks and driverless transports neatly avoided my passage, or maintained pace with me at exact, unvarying distances. Then the traffic dropped away down side roads as the highway took me into the residential suburbs.

Neat houses of painted wood or colored stone were intermixed with towers faced in metal or glass. The town looked lived-in—I saw lawns that needed a trim, a fence that was giving in to gravity, and one cracked window mended with tape. It was only after a few minutes that I realized I wasn't seeing any K'fondi. The streets were deserted.

The emptiness began to play on my nerves. Field work can be dicey. Trampling on a society's direst taboos is so easy when you have no idea what they are.

Maybe this part of the town was forbidden, or this time of day had to be spent indoors. Maybe it was death to approach this place from the west. Maybe... anything. At the university, we'd all heard the story of the technician who'd casually swatted a buzzing insect. He had protested that he had not known that that particular species was "sacred for the day," as the alien priests had apologetically proceeded to dismember him.

I finally found the K'fondi, lots of them, as I nosed the car out of a side street onto the lake drive. I was suddenly in a town square, beachfront and park all rolled into one, and it was the site of a carnival that made Rio's Carneval look like a Baptist church social. Knots of K'fondi surged in a cheerful frenzy through a crowd so dense it flowed like fleshy liquid. Some kind of music thumped and screeched loud enough for me to experience it as repeated *tumpa-tumpas* on my chest. K'fondi in a grab bag of costumes bobbed to the rhythm or gyrated with flailing elbows along the edge of the mob. As I stopped the car, an eddy of the crowd swirled around me. One dervish began beating out a tattoo on the engine compartment, while a large female jumped onto the hood and began a dance that had various parts of her moving in several different directions at once.

More K'fondi joined her, making the car sag and groan on its suspension. I mentally ran through all the time-tested phrases recommended for first encounters, but with this crowd I realized that I might as well declaim Homer in the original Greek.

The car was rocking steadily faster, and common sense said it was time to bail out. The crowd swallowed me the way an amoeba takes in a drifting speck. Aliens pressed me from all sides, but none paid me any attention. My head seemed to shrink and swell with the sound of the music.

Way back in school, in an attempt to make us grateful that the ECS had rescued our world from self-destructive hedonism, they'd shown us images of rock concerts from the Decadent Period. What I was experiencing among the K'fondi must have been the kind of sheer fun those old DP mass gatherings had looked to be.

The music wound down to a last subsonic rumble and crashed in an auditory rain of metal. As the sound dwindled, I could hear voices again, even pick out words I now recognized. The crowd began to thin around the knoll. Some went splashing into the lake. Others drifted back toward town or into the trees farther up the shore. And some couples entwined arms and legs, sliding down each other to the ground.

I scanned the departing remnants of the crowd. A few meters away, I thought I saw the pink female from the station among a handful of K'fondi skirting the knoll. Or it may have been a complete stranger—learning to tell aliens apart can take practice. I hurried to catch up, fell in beside her and touched her wrist. She turned without slowing, and regarded me with scant interest.

"*Jiao doh vuh?*" she asked, and my lingolab-educated brain translated the phrase as "Do you want to?"

"Do I want to what?"

She looked puzzled for a moment. "It's just what people say."

I said, "My name is Kandler. I'd like to talk to you."

"Why talk?"

"Talking is what I do."

Her shrug was almost human, and I took it as an acquiescence. "I want a drink," she said, heading toward a row of low-rises bordering the park.

The K'fond bar could have blended into most Earth streetscapes, if you ignored the unusual colors of the patrons. When we had found seats at a table in the back that was crowded with her friends, I learned that the pink woman's name was Chenna—no surname or honorific, I noted—and that the town was called Maness. Chenna's friends remained anonymous. I could just barely hold her attention long enough to ask a question and receive an indifferent reply. Everyone else in the bar was enjoying the outpourings of a couple on a small stage, who were tootling some kind of flute that had two mouthpieces. I was thankful it was purely an acoustic instrument; my eardrums still hurt from the pummeling they had taken in the park.

A robot server brought us a round of drinks without being summoned. I sniffed the tall frosty tumbler, and recognized the same fruity aroma that had lingered around Chenna at the station. The concoction tasted sweet and dry. I waited a few moments to learn if I would be racked by intense pains or stop breathing. When nothing much happened, I judged the drink safe and took another sip.

By saying her name a couple of times, I got Chenna's attention again, and posed a few more questions. No, she didn't work, although it seemed to her that she might have once had some kind of job. She thought she hadn't been in Maness very long, but it was hard to tell.

If Chenna was hazy on her own personal history, the rest of K'fond society was nonexistent to her. I couldn't find a word in my new vocabulary for "government," but I tried to phrase a question about who got things done on K'fond.

"Machines," she replied airily, waving to the robot for another round. I drained my glass and reached for a second.

"But who tells the machines what to do?"

Chenna actually looked as if she was rummaging through her mind for an answer. But then she laid her cheek on an upturned palm and said, "Who cares?"

I put away my exo-soc question kit and opted for passive observation.

The bar was filling up. The flute players had given way to an *a cappella* group that seemed to know only four notes, but the K'fondi happily sang along with them.

A male at another booth took some kind of cigar from a box on the table, and tried to light it with what looked like an elementary flint and steel lighter. When he couldn't get a spark, he persisted in thumbing the device with increasing frustration. Finally, he slammed the lighter to the floor and followed it with the cigar.

I rose and retrieved the battered object. A quick examination showed that the screw holding the steel ratchet to its mount was loose. With a twist of my thumbnail, I tightened the screw, and flicked the action. A flame wavered on the wick. I doused the flame and put the lighter back on the owner's table. The K'fond picked it up, flicked it alight, and pulled another cigar from the box. I received not even a glance as the alien blew smoke toward the stage.

Back at Chenna's table a third round had arrived. I sipped and watched, and listened to the surrounding conversations. It was like Livesey's contact sessions: a lot of laughs, and half the words spoken were the K'fondish equivalents of "hey" and "wow" and the details of amorous adventures.

The fruit drink tasted good, felt good inside. But I noticed that the room had now begun to expand and contract in rhythm with my own heartbeat. That made me laugh, which made me wonder why I was laughing so loud. Chenna was looking at me now; they all were. I found it odd when their faces were abruptly replaced by the bar's ceiling, and I tried to figure out what the hard flat something was that was pressing itself against my back. Then the world turned black and gently fell on me.

"I've been reading your job description," Livesey said. "It doesn't say that an exo-soc steals ground cars, leaves the station without permission, and is found at the gate giggling and smelling like a fruit basket. At least you had sense enough to program your car to bring you back."

I didn't think now was the time to correct the chief. Time enough later to wonder how a K'fond could figure out which end of the ground car was the front—never mind how to program an offworld computer.

I had expected Livesey to chew me out, but the chief seemed to have passed through rage and frustration while I was still in sick bay. He was now settling into acid despair. He spun his chair away from me and gazed with helpless hate at K'fond's hills.

"Actually," he told the window, "you were more useful in a drugged stupor than you've been conscious. The bio-chem techs pumped some interesting stuff out of your stomach. It might make a decent anesthetic or a recreational lifter for the PMC youth market back home.

"Either way, it won't be enough to save us." Livesey swung back to face me. "As a purely formal question, I don't suppose you learned anything worth knowing from your little jaunt?"

I had been asking myself the same thing since I had woken up, sore-throated from the stomach pump. The drug in the fruit drink left me feeling reasonably fine, and the part of my brain that lived to puzzle out alien social patterns had gone right to work.

"Yes," I said. "Item one, that's a real city over there, not a backdrop whipped up to fool us.

"Item two: the K'fondi who live there really live there. They're not actors putting on a show for our benefit.

"Item three: their technology is at least equal to our best.

"Item four: the K'fondi we've seen couldn't possibly have created that technology; they can't even repair a simple machine.

"Item five: something funny is going on. There's a piece missing from this puzzle, and if we can find it, or even figure out its basic shape, the rest of the pattern will fall into place."

Livesey grunted. "You're as stumped as I am. We've been looking for that missing piece of information since we landed. You want to hear our working hypotheses?"

He didn't wait for an answer but ticked off the options on his fingers: "Maybe the K'fondi we see are the mentally deficient. Maybe they're just the pets of the real dominant species. Or the whole place is run by supercomputers their great-great-granddaddies built while their descendants have declined into idiocy. For all we know, they're just a planetful of practical jokers having a good laugh on us."

The station chief smacked the desk. "But, dammit, somebody gave me landing coordinates in Basic. Somebody is scrambling all microwave communications. Somebody knocked out the survey orbiter. And, having done that, our mysterious somebody has apparently lost all interest in us."

"You're wrong," I said. "Our mysterious somebody is very interested. He's hanging back and watching. And if he won't come to us, we'll have to go find him. And by 'we' I mean me."

"Go ahead," Livesey snorted. "Take all the time you want, so long as you're finished in the next week."

"A week? This could take months. I've got to—"

"You'll be finished in a week," Livesey interrupted, "because *I'll* be finished in week. That's when SectAd Stavrogin arrives. Here's the signal." He waved a flimsy at me. "I'm being demoted and shipped back to Earth, as soon as Stavrogin settles in. And, Kandler, I'm taking you with me. Under arrest."

"What, for appropriating a ground car?"

"No, I'm sure I'll think of something better. And, between my remaining authority and your record, I'll make it stick."

"But why?"

"Because I don't like you." Livesey spun back to the window. The interview was over.

I couldn't just lie on my bunk and wait for Stavrogin. I reran the diaries, looking for some clue, some insignificant piece of data to ring the alarm bells in my unconscious. I had a nagging sense that I was missing something that would make it all fit together.

But I saw nothing that helped, just more frolicking K'fondi, more remote scans of distant cities too far away for any detail. Livesey's orbiting ship was not equipped for close-in scan; the exploration orbiter was supposed to be there to handle that chore, with ultrascopes that could count the blades of grass in a square meter of the planet's nightside from fifty kilometers up. But the orbiter was gone, and since—according to the Bureau's book—it was impossible for an orbiter to be gone, there was no provision for getting another one. Maybe Stavrogin would have the clout to get a new high-orbit probe. And maybe I would read all about the solution to the K'fond puzzle back on Earth—if a newspaper ever blew over the fence of the punishment farm.

I paced and considered the situation. The K'fondi had put the station where they wanted it. All attempts to surveil other parts of the planet had been stopped. So, whatever they were hiding must be somewhere down the road from Maness.

Which meant taking a trip down that road and looking around. A ground car or flyer would probably bring me into hard contact with whatever had knocked out the spy drones. And if the K'fondi preferred to shoot first and sift the wreckage later, I would end up in some alien coroner's in-basket. But there was another way: risky, but I thought it just might work.

Then I paced out my own situation. If Livesey meant to sweeten the bitter taste of his failure by kicking me into prison, why should I spend my last days of freedom helping the Bureau?

If I solved the K'fond mystery, Livesey would still probably go under; even last-minute success couldn't divert BOOT discipline once it was wound up and set loose. Livesey, falling, would use me as something soft to land on. Livesey, saved, would ruin me out of sheer spite.

But I wouldn't be doing it for the Bureau or the chief. This was for *me*. I had always had to know what made alien societies tick, and if making the pickings easier for ECS's interstellar swindlers was the price of that knowledge, then it was a price I was at least used to paying.

Before I was dragged off K'fond and chained to a bulkhead, I wanted to know what the hell was going on.

Five minutes later, I walked into the supply hut and began pulling things off the shelves. The quartermaster clerk decided he had better things to do than to ask questions of an eco-soc with a reputation for lunatic behavior. In the medical stores I found an antiseptic wash that dyed the skin. A jumpsuit stripped of its Bureau insignia would pass at medium range for a K'fond coverall. I scooped up a belt and pouch, which I filled with rations, depilatory creams, and some other useful items. Finally, I took a geologist's hammer to the arms locker and selected a small pulser that tucked into the palm of my hand.

The motor-pool guard was prepared this time to stand his ground when a purple Kandler climbed into a surface car. But the pulser's output end convinced him to decamp quickly enough to avoid being run down.

On the open road, the wind of the car's passage chilled my newly bald head. Where I began to meet Maness's automated local traffic, I turned at the first major intersection and drove on for a couple of kilometers. I parked the car on the side road's grass border, pulled out the connections on the com panel to stop its annoying chirping, and settled down to watch the robot trucks go by.

Before the long K'fond day drifted into evening, I spotted the kind of transport I had been looking for. But, fully loaded, it was outward bound. I marked its size and characteristics, and was able to identify the same kind of vehicle heading empty in the direction of Maness. I put the car back on the road and followed.

The empty truck wove through an increasingly dense grid of industrial streets. Here there were no houses, and apparently no K'fondi were needed to run the automatic factories. The truck pulled into a side street leading to a low-rise, open-sided building. By the sound and smell of the place, I knew it was what I was looking for.

I slowed the car to a crawl as it bypassed the street the truck had turned onto. Pushing a few buttons on the car's console told it to go home and it whirred away, leaving me alone on the empty street.

It was now full dark, and the K'fondi hadn't bothered with many streetlights in this part of town. Keeping to the abundant shadows, I crept around the rear of the building where the truck had gone. The vehicle was nudged up against a loading ramp, behind which was a corral full of tapirlike creatures with curly horns and sad, muted voices. By the ringing in my ears, I judged they were being induced into the trucks by some kind of general sonic prod. No herders, either live or robot, were in sight.

That made it easier. I hopped the corral fence and stooped to hide among the cattle. Gritting my vibrating teeth against the sonics, I bulled my way up a ramp and into a slat-sided transport. The animals stamped and brayed at my smell; for me, the feeling was mutual. Inside the truck, the sonics were damped. I crouched in a rear corner.

The truck soon filled. Its rear gate swung closed, and the engine murmured through the floorboards. The vehicle jerked forward, sending a set of horns scraping across my back. It turned to exit the stockyard, and then it stopped.

I held my breath. Were sensors in the truck reacting to my shape or size or the smell of my sweat? Would alarms suddenly ring, floodlights sweep toward me, robot cops come to hustle me off to the interrogation rooms? But then the engine coughed and, with another lurch, we were mobile again. A few minutes later, I was rolling out of Maness. My compass told me we were heading north.

The chill bars of first light through the truck's slats brought me awake. I had spent the night in a hay-filled corner, pressed by warm bodies, and dozing despite the cattle's tendency to snore. I got up, stretched, and peered out at the suburbs of a city. It could have been Maness, except that it was bigger, lacked a lake, and was built halfway up a mountain range that rivaled the Andes. By my rough reckoning, I was five hundred kilometers from the station. I should be out of any K'fond quarantine zone.

The truck was now well into the city's industrial district. Time to move— my fellow passengers might be heading directly for the whirring blades of an automated slaughterhouse. I climbed the truck's side and sliced through its fabric top with a knife from my belt pouch. I boosted myself up and out, clinging now to the outside of the vehicle. I lowered myself until my feet dangled over the pavement blurring along below. When the truck slowed for a curve, I hit the street running.

Seconds later, I was your average K'fond, purple and bald, taking an early morning constitutional through the city's empty streets. A broad avenue led down toward the heart of the city, and a half-hour's walk brought me into a grid of residential streets. In a postage-sized park near a high-rise complex I found enough undergrowth to keep me out of sight. I'd lie low until the K'fondi came out of their homes, then blend in with all the other purple and pink inhabitants.

I ate some rations behind a screen of fernlike plants and watched for pedestrians. About the time the morning chill began to fade, a naked K'fond child—the first I'd ever seen—came out of a high-rise and walked down the footpath to stand by a striped post. Another approached from up the street, then several more. *Bus stop*, I thought. And the long passenger vehicle that soon came to pick the children up must be a school bus. As it left, more children arrived to wait for the next one.

So far, I had seen no adults, but with the K'fond commitment to partying, sleeping late would be normal.

As the third busload of children rolled away, there was a noise behind me. I turned to see three kids entering the park from the opposite side. Naked as all the others, these wore belts and holsters carrying lightweight toy weapons. *Playing cops and robbers*, I told myself, and hunkered lower behind the ferns. I didn't want to be taken for a K'fond child molester.

I could hear them approaching, talking rapid-fire K'fondish too fast for me to catch the meaning. They seemed to be passing my hiding place without noticing me. I held my breath. Then the ferns parted right in front of me, and I was crouching eye to eye with one of the kids.

"Uh, *jiao doh vuh?*" I tried.

"Oh, I really don't think so, Mr. Kandler," the child replied. "No adult would say that to a child, even if they weren't all biologically set to keep their distance from us." It took me a few moments to realize that I was being spoken to in clipped Earth Basic, and that the weapon leveled at my face was no plaything.

The child gestured with the gun. "This is a device we use on adults who pose a danger to themselves or others. It's harmless to them, but we're not sure how effective it would be on your nervous system, so it's set at maximum. I advise you not to do anything unreasonable."

As the child spoke, his two companions came through the undergrowth to triple the number of weapons now surrounding me at a discreet distance.

Moments later, face down in the K'fond soil, I was efficiently stripped of everything but my jumpsuit. Then the children herded me out of the park and into a no-nonsense vehicle that had pulled up at the curb. I had the last of the three rows of seats to myself. The kids sat forward, facing me with weapons aimed.

"I suppose my disguise was pretty obvious," I said.

One of them replied, "The disguise was fine. At first we thought an adult had wandered into that meat transport. Then we took a closer look when you were on the road. But you could never have blended in here."

"Why not?"

For an answer, the child waved at the cityscape unrolling beyond the car's windows. What I saw told me that, of course, they had to have spotted me immediately, disguise or not. To blend into this city's population, I would have had to make myself over as a small, pink, sexless doll with big eyes. The streets were full now, and not one of the K'fondi was an adult. It was a city of children.

"Where are you taking me?" I asked.

"To a place where some of us will talk to you."

I couldn't read the inscription on the building we arrived at, but it had government written all over it. The council chamber I was ushered into could have passed for the ECS seat of power in Belem—if everything hadn't been half-sized. But there was nothing diminutive about the authority of the K'fond children gathered around the gleaming, crescent-shaped table. I knew power when I met it.

They gave me a large enough chair and sat me down in the middle of the space enclosed by the crescent. For a few seconds, the K'fond world council looked me over in silence. Then the child at the center of the table's arc leaned across the glossy expanse. The voice was thin, but I didn't doubt the note of command it carried.

"Welcome to K'fond, Mr. Kandler. We've been looking forward to meeting you. Your personnel record told us more about the Earth Corporate State than a month's subspace communications."

"You've read my record? But how?"—then I got it—"You've been using the survey orbiter's com link to listen in."

"True, Mr. Kandler. We went up and got your probe shortly after it alerted your sector base. We don't mind telling you, its technology fascinated our scientists. And of course we were overjoyed to learn that interstellar travel is in fact possible.

"Which brings us to the point of our meeting. Mr. Kandler, what can you tell us about the Dhaliwal Drive?"

Three days later, the station com center received and recorded a signal from the project's missing exo-soc. I reported that I had penetrated to the core of K'fond society and was "making progress." Then I signed off without waiting for a reply. It was my last direct communication with the station.

Two days after that, Sector Administrator Stavrogin arrived to take charge.

If Livesey was everything a by-the-book Bureau chief should be, then Yuroslav Stavrogin was a sector administrator to delight the book's authors to the lowest flake of their flinty hearts. Pinch-faced and slim, with the eyes of a bored shark and the delicate hands of a Renaissance poisoner, he perched primly on the edge of a K'fond chair and waited. Beside him, Livesey looked nervously around the alien reception room and sweated. Through the open window came the sounds of Maness at play.

I watched through a concealed aperture as the brass cooled their heels. I remembered Stavrogin. Back at sector base, he had once made me rewrite a lengthy field report from scratch—a week's pointless work imposed on me for no discernible reason. When I was bold enough to ask why, he had coolly replied, "Because you need to be reminded of who I am, and of what you are not."

I closed the spy hole, picked up my new briefcase, and stepped through the door. Livesey's face opened in surprise, but Stavrogin knew better than to show his. Still, I was not what he had expected.

Yesterday, with the station in an uproar over the sector boss's arrival, a signal had come in. In clear Basic, a K'fond voice had specified that Livesey and Stavrogin, identified by name and rank, were instructed to present themselves at the Maness district office of the planet's government. Once again, detailed directions followed, and these had led the two Bureau officers to the building. A robot major-domo had shown them to the reception room and left them to stew a while. And then in walked their missing exo-soc.

"Kandler, where the hell have you—" Livesey spluttered, but was cut off by a mere lifting of Stavrogin's finger.

"Specialist Kandler," rustled the dry voice, "we can plot your recent itinerary later, but we are shortly to meet the K'fond trade negotiator. You will therefore advise us forthwith of the results of your fieldwork."

There was a desk and chair. I walked over and sat down. From my briefcase, I pulled a sheaf of paper and tossed it onto the desk. "My report," I said. "I won't give you the full details now; you can read it at your leisure. I'll just summarize.

"The K'fondi are a highly sophisticated culture, with a well advanced technology. They have been a unified planetary state for some centuries, long enough for the administrative apparatus to evolve into a kind of cooperative anarchy."

Stavrogin sniffed, but I elected not to notice.

"They are very interested in trade," I continued, "a great deal of trade, but only on rational terms."

Livesey burst in. "They're as rational as a bunch of spacers on Cinderella liberty. Drunken, fornicating..."

"Oh, those are just the adults," I laughed. "I'm talking about the kids."

Stavrogin's voice could have cut glass. "Tell it."

I leaned back in my chair, and put my feet on the desk.

"Well, it's that missing piece of information we were looking for. K'fond adults really are just about as useless as Livesey says. All they want to do is enjoy their retirement and make more little K'fondi. The eggs are almost a by-product, since they don't even tend their offspring after they're weaned.

"But the kids do all right," I continued. "Childhood is long here, very long. K'fondi reach intellectual maturity quite early, but puberty doesn't come along until thirty or forty years after. And they have drugs to hold their glands in check for another decade if they want to keep putting off sexual maturity.

"That gives them a whole working lifetime without distractions. They don't waste their youth in adolescent turmoil and fruitless rebellion, because adolescence comes at the end of life, not the beginning. They aren't bothered by sex or any of its complications, like jealousy or getting up to change diapers. The infants are cooperatively raised by older children.

"And when their glands finally get to them, and the hormones reduce their mental acuity to the level of alley cats, they settle into a place like Maness: a retirement community out in the country, with plenty of beds and bars. A few children stick around to patch up cuts and bruises, and protect the newborns until they can be shipped off to the nurseries."

Livesey snapped his fingers. "They're like those extinct fish, the ones that didn't mate until they were ready to die. What were they called?"

"Salmon," I said. "We didn't figure it out because the K'fondi made sure we didn't see their cities full of children or the few kids around Maness. So we kept looking at it from our own perspective, from the chicken's point of view."

"Chicken?" asked Livesey.

"Sure," I said. "To a chicken, an egg is just a means of getting a new chicken. But to an egg—or to a K'fond child—an adult chicken is just something you need to get a new egg."

"Fascinating in its place," Stavrogin cut in, "but we are about to negotiate a trade deal. You will advise."

I smiled. "Sorry, Mr. Sector Administrator. Appended to my report is my resignation from the Bureau, and appended to that is my surrender of citizenship in the Earth Corporate State. And these," I produced a document covered in cursive K'fondish script, "are my credentials as adviser to K'fond's economic committee. Shall we open negotiations?"

"You can't do that," Livesey said.

"He has done it," Stavrogin said, "though little good it will do him. Very well, 'Mr. Adviser' Kandler, you may rot among your alien friends in this backwater. But trade—if there is even to be any trade—will be on Bureau terms; only Earth has the Dhaliwal Drive."

I smiled. "Not for long, Stavrogin. These people—*my* people, now—have had near-space travel for generations, but until now they've had nowhere to go but up and down. They've always dreamed of reaching to the stars, but didn't know how or even if it could be done. The survey ship's passage answered the second question; and I had enough of a layman's grasp of the Dhaliwal Drive to sketch an answer to the first."

I put my hands behind my head and stretched back in my chair. "They're smart and they have no distractions—they'll roll out a prototype starship within a year."

Stavrogin's face went paler, while Livesey's grew dangerously red. I held up a hand to forestall an outburst.

"We may decide not to deal with the ECS," I said. "After all, there's a whole galaxy of civilized races that the Bureau has been robbing. I'm sure they'll be interested in what we have to offer."

Livesey looked to be on the verge of detonation. But Stavrogin was struggling to recover. "I'm sure we can come to some mutually satisfactory understanding," he said. "As you say, there's a whole galaxy dependent on the trade made possible by the Drive. There's still plenty for both of us."

"You don't understand." I took my feet off the desk, leaned over its polished surface, and said, "Go tell the Phoenicians: beads and trinkets won't cut it anymore.

"K'fond's main export will be starships."

Bearing Up

He would kick and yell his way out of dreams where the bear was after him, his chest cold and sweat-slick, breath bellowing. When he was little, the noise brought Mom or Dad to check on him, tuck him back in, kiss the bad stuff away.

At fifteen, he didn't want his parents coming to his rescue—well, maybe he wanted it a little, but it would have bent his self-image. So it was enough if Mom called out, "Are you okay, Mike?" from across the hall, and he would call back, "Yeah, I'm okay."

He would hear them mumbling about him, but in the morning nobody made a big deal about it.

He'd been having the bear dream for as long as he could recall, although it didn't start out as a bear. Back when he was a kid, it had been dinosaurs: dagger-toothed tyrannosaurs hopping through the patio doors, hunting him across the family room at the old house in Ottawa.

Another time, a golden-eyed tiger glided after him into the garage, and once, when he was really little, the Cookie Monster had shadowed him around the day care, all goggle-eyed and blue-shaggy, peering at him from behind the activity centre.

But, by the time he was into his teens, it was the bear. It would come for him every five or six months; not that he could count on it to keep to a schedule, so sometimes it could be twice in the same week. The settings would vary, but never the sequence of events.

He'd be doing something ordinary—getting off a bus, walking up his front steps—when he would catch a flicker of movement from the corner of his eye. He'd turn, and there'd be a glimpse of something dark sliding around a corner or dipping down behind a wall.

The glimpse always shot him through with a bolt of white terror. He would back up, turn around, edge off in another direction. But if he fled the house, it would be lurking in the yard. Get back on the bus, and it would come snuffling at the automatic door. Try to outrun it, and he would feel its breath bursting hot on the back of his neck.

At the end he would be trapped, hedged in, the bear stalking closer and closer. That was the worst part: it seemed to *enlarge* itself towards him, like a dark balloon swelling across his field of vision, or as if he were a lost spacewalker falling into a vast black planet.

And then, the instant before it touched him, when he was sprung tight as a musical saw, there'd come a high-pitched whine, loud enough to make his teeth buzz, and he would burst out of the dream, sweating and gasping, his muscles weak as blue milk.

He'd once asked the school counsellor if she knew anything about dreams.

"Well, of course, I'm influenced by Jung," said Mrs. Skinner, interrupting her perpetual search for order in the jumble on her desk, which was crammed into a former supplies closet beside the washrooms. Mike stood, because the visitor's chair was buried in books in which an adult explained exactly what you had to do to be a successful teenager.

"Okay," Mike said.

She located a form printed on blue paper, lifted her eyeglasses to squint at it, then tucked it into a yellow file folder. "That means I view the psyche as being fundamentally fragmented," she continued.

"Okay," he said again, edging toward the door.

She closed the yellow file, then reopened it. She took out the blue paper, peered at it again, then slipped into a red folder, and looked up at Mike.

"How do I put this? Jung's idea was that each of us is a collection of different people inside our heads—like your personality is made up of different pieces that mesh together, well, more or less. When they don't mesh properly, that's trouble."

"Trouble like scary dreams, like where something's chasing you?"

"Uh huh," she said, picking up a green form, and frowning at it as if willing it to change color. "A monster in a dream might be some part of you that frightens you, some fear that your unconscious wants you to deal with, maybe, and so one part of you is trying to get in touch, to get you to look at the problem. But you don't want to, so you run from it, but you can't get away."

"So what do I do?" Mike asked.

"Stop running. After all, anything or anybody you meet in a dream is only another part of you, so what's to be afraid of?" She peered up at him through filmed lenses. "Is there something you want to talk about?"

He had a feeling that if he started talking about the bear with Mrs. Skinner, he'd find himself wandering into parts of the forest he wasn't ready to deal with yet. Things would come up. Things like having to move *here* from Ottawa, like leaving all his friends behind, like being lonely, like not fitting in. Like being scared but not knowing why.

Here was the small town of Comox, at the end of a little stub of land that hung off the east coast of Vancouver Island into Georgia Strait. It was home to a few thousand people, many of them attached to the air force base at the landward end of the peninsula.

Three squadrons operated out of CFB Comox. One flew the big, gray submarine-hunting Auroras that wheeled over town on four throbbing turboprops, their fuselages so jam-packed with electronic detection gear that the crew could spot a Coke can half-submerged in the Pacific from a mile high. Or so he'd heard kids at school saying.

Another squadron flew forty-year-old T-33 jet trainers, the same machines that every serving pilot in the Canadian Forces learned to fly in, the fast-movers that zoomed up from the base and out over the harbor, with torpedo-shaped pods at the tips of their stubby wings that made each one look like a flying X.

Whatever he might be doing, Mike stopped and looked up when the planes flew over. Especially when the air force aerobatics team appeared over Comox one bright, spring morning, for two weeks of practice. He couldn't believe how the local folks just kept puttering around in their gardens, not looking up as ten red and white Snowbirds hurtled over their roofs, practising how to spiral up and loop down in tight turns, wing-tip to wing-tip, so fast and so just right.

Mike's father was neither a jet-jockey nor a sub-hunter. He had been posted in March to the third group operating out of CFB Comox, the historic 442 Search and Rescue Squadron. He was an air force SARtech—a specialist, he liked to say, "in getting people out of situations where if they had any sense they wouldn't have got themselves into them in the first place."

SARtechs went out in the slow-flying de Havilland Buffalo—big brother to the tough little Twin Otters that the bush pilots used to open the Canadian north—or in the lumbering, two-rotor Labrador helicopters. If a fisherman abandoned a burning boat, the Lab would hover in the air so that Dad could jump into the cold sea, put a harness around the man before hypothermia killed him, and wait in the water while the victim was winched to safety, and they lowered the cable again to retrieve the SARtech.

It was dangerous work. Once, a Lab was picking stranded rock-climbers off a mountain. The shivering civilians had been lifted aboard, and the last rescuer was coming up the cable, when an engine suddenly shuddered and died. With the Labrador at maximum payload, one rotor couldn't hold the helicopter in the air. It fell, crushing the life from the SARtech dangling beneath it.

Mike's father said there was no point thinking about it. Somebody had to go when people needed help; if it was risky, then it was risky, but somebody still had to go.

"It's not being a hero," Dad said. "It's just a job that's got to be done. It's *my* job."

"You didn't have to be a SARtech, though," Mike said. "You volunteered. You used to be a cook."

Dad shrugged. "Don't worry about it. Nothing's going to happen."

"But don't you get scared sometimes?"

"You don't let that get in the way." His father hunted around in his mind for a moment; he wasn't good with words. "You have to walk through the being scared part. 'Cause on the other side of scared is this other place where everything opens up, you feel really great, and... and you're just *there*."

Mike didn't tell his father about the bear. He told Jonah Hennenfent, the only kid he'd gotten to know at Highland, Comox's senior high school. Jonah was smallish and rounded, with hair that stood up straight and a tendency to practise new facial expressions even if other people could see them. His parents were ground crew at the base; they'd transferred in from the fighter base at Cold Lake at about the same time Mike's family had arrived from the east.

The two newcomers had met in the principal's office in mid-March when they'd both arrived to start school. They'd hung out together from time to time over the summer, and were still an exclusive group of two now that September was almost over.

Mike told Jonah about the bear over sandwiches and drink boxes in the lunch room—no details, just the core of the dream.

Jonah waived his arms and experimented with a mouth-open, full gawp. "That's your totem, G!" he said, having dipped deeply into aboriginal culture over the summer, starting when his parents took him to a performance by the Komoux Band's storytellers and dancers at the native Big House down by the shores of the estuary.

"As if," said Mike.

"For sure, G," said Jonah. "This is your spirit guide trying to get in touch with you. It goes, 'Hey, man, let me get a little closer.' And you're all, 'No way, bear, I'm outta here!' But it's gotta keep coming back 'cause it's gotta make contact. You should, like, do a vision quest. Go off in the bush and don't eat."

Mike moved Jonah off the subject and into more comfortable areas. He told him about the time he'd been carsick, and had thrown up out of the window before Dad could find a place to pull over.

"I splattered these people waiting for a bus. It was just their shoes, but it totally grossed them out."

"Yow!" said Jonah. "A drive-by hurling! Awesome!"—and forgot about the bear.

At dinner, Mom said, "You don't seem to be making a lot of friends since we moved here. Just Jonah."

"I'm okay," Mike said.

Dad said, "There's a good Air Cadets squadron at the base. You guys could join. You already put in two years with the Ottawa group."

Mike concentrated on his mixed vegetables, separating the peas from the carrots.

"They'd teach you how to fly," Dad said. "That's what you always wanted to do when you were a little guy. Get up there and slip around."

"Guess I'm not a little guy anymore."

Mike's chore was the after-dinner dishes. He was methodically scrubbing fried rice off a teflon-coated skillet whose powers of non-stickiness had long since been scratched away, and not thinking about anything much when he said, "Mom, do you worry when Dad goes out on a mission?"

His mother put three plates on the counter by the sink and looked through the archway into the living room, where Dad was watching the sports report on tv.

"I used to," she admitted. "But your father's very good at what he does." Then she sighed. "Besides, there's no point worrying. He loves it. He's not going to stop doing it. It's a big part of who he is."

"Pretty dangerous, though."

"Doesn't matter. It's what he does. What you and I have to do is live with it." She put a hand on Mike's arm. "Are you afraid he might get hurt... or something?"

"Nah," Mike said. "I was just wondering how you felt."

On an afternoon late in September, a wind blew up—not a big wind, but big enough to whittle white points onto the gray-green chop of Georgia Strait. And that was too big for the comfort of four couples who had crowded into an undersized skiff to go hand-trolling for coho salmon three miles out from the boat launch at Point Holmes.

The boat owner, a welder who worked at Field's sawmill, decided it would be wise to head for shore. But when he pulled the lanyard on the outboard, it started, sputtered and died. He did all the things he knew to do: checked the spark plug, checked the fuel line, checked the gas tank—and found it empty. He'd forgotten to fill up before launching.

By the time the skipper had identified the problem, the wind was brisking up, causing the overloaded skiff to wallow in steepening waves, shipping water over the gunwales.

He looked at the white faces of the three men and four women who had come out with him, without life jackets or even warm clothing, and said, "We're gonna row in. Break out the oars."

The oars were pulled from beneath the thwarts and run through the oarlocks, and the two strongest men tried to haul the boat shoreward. But the wind was offshore, and growing stronger as each long minute passed. Even with two men to an oar, the overloaded skiff barely made headway.

"We're in trouble," said the welder, watching the light fade behind thickening clouds, and reached for the emergency radio in the locker below his seat. Fortunately, he was more conscientious about the strength of the radio's batteries than the contents of his gas tank. When he tuned to the emergency channel, depressed the talk switch and said, "Mayday, mayday," CFB Comox came right back.

"I won't be home for supper," Dad said over the telephone. "There's some boaters in trouble." Five minutes later, they heard the Labrador racketing up from the base and heading out to sea.

An hour crawled by. Mike and his mother sat in the darkening kitchen, drinking coffee and trying not to look out the window. The clouds were low, eight shades of gray raggedly streaming on the wind that bent the tops of the fir trees out back. Cold rain tittered on the glass.

They turned on the lights and drank more coffee, talking about nothing. Mom started dinner, and Mike set the table, then they realized that neither of them was hungry, so they brewed more coffee.

Near eight o'clock, they heard the helicopter coming back, and started dinner again. But a few minutes later, the Labrador passed overhead again, heading back out.

By nine, with the sky black and the wind stage-whispering around the eaves, the Lab was still up. Mom called the dispatcher at the base. Mike saw her knuckles whiten on the handset, heard her brief question, watched her face go quiet. She hung up.

"There were eight of them in a little boat, out of gas," she said. "The Lab couldn't carry all of them and the crew too. Your father volunteered to stay in the boat until they came back for him. When they got there, no boat. Probably swamped by a wave and sunk. They're looking."

At eleven o'clock, Comox's missing SARtech was the second story on the CBC late news. The tv showed file footage of Labradors taking off, and a colored map of where the search was concentrating.

Mike watched the images and heard the reporter's accompanying voice-over: "Georgia Strait fills a deep and narrow trench between Vancouver Island and the rest of North America. Strong tidal currents sweep the bone-chilling water southeast, down past the Gulf Islands and on into the Strait of Juan de Fuca, then around the southern tip of the big island.

"Anything floating on the surface gets flushed out into the north Pacific and lost forever. Unprotected from the cold, in seas tossed high by stiff winds, a human being in the water can die in a few hours. Add a survival suit and expert knowledge, and life expectancy—and hope—increase. The search continues."

The camera cut back to the news reader, who began talking about a freeway pile-up in Coquitlam. Mike switched off the set.

"They'll find him, and he'll be all right," Mom said. Some of her friends had come over to help them wait. They talked cheerfully, in low voices. Mike nodded and said, "Yeah, sure," a lot, but he didn't hear most of it.

By midnight the sky was clearing, stars making holes in the clouds and poking through in twos and threes. CFB Comox had everything up—Labs, a Buffalo, an Aurora—and a Coast Guard ship was quartering the strait below where Dad had last been seen.

Mike couldn't stay inside anymore. He put on his jacket and slipped out the back door.

They lived on two cleared acres that backed up against a stand of second-growth timber in Comox's northeast corner. The valley's big spruce and cedar were long gone, cleared to make farmland and lumber back before the twentieth century was a toddler. The yard was unfenced, the lawn ending in a thicket of blackberry bushes that grew over a ditch between their property and the woods.

Mike sat on the back steps for a minute, but he could still hear the encouraging voices from the living room. The wind was dying, making a stillness under the trees, and he got up and crossed the lawn to where he could cut through a gap in the blackberry bushes. A few meters into the woods lay a waist-high, half-buried boulder forgotten by some careless glacier. It was a good, solid place to be.

Mike walked around the rock then leaned his forearms on the old granite so that he was looking back toward the house. The stone was cold and the wetness left by the rain seeped into his jacket sleeves. He listened: far to the east, a search plane's engines murmured at the edge of his hearing.

The last clouds tattered and moved off, letting the full moon silver the floor of the woods. The kitchen light shone yellow between the stark bars of the trunks. Then the plane's engines faded into the distance, and the only sound was a drop of rainwater working its way down through the branches.

In the perfect quiet, Mike caught a flicker of movement from the corner of his eye. He turned to look, but the best night vision is peripheral vision, and all he could see straight on was a darkness in the gap between the berry bushes.

And then the darkness shifted. He froze. He heard a heavy body rustling among the thorny blackberry runners, wet smacking noises, and a whuffling exhalation of breath.

People had told him about bears coming into town to gorge on blackberries. Naturally, he'd imagined meeting one. But somehow, his imagination had always supplied daylight.

Back slowly away, they'd said. But the moment he moved to ease his weight off the boulder, the berry-eating noises stopped. He distinctly heard the animal *sniff* twice, followed by a deep-throated *huff!* Then it came toward him.

Now it was just like the dream, a black mass growing steadily larger, looming between Mike and the lights of the house. And, as in the dream, he couldn't move.

The bear eased forward, slowly but without hesitation, until only the width of the boulder separated them. It rose up and leaned its forelegs against the stone; Mike heard the scrape of claws on granite. Then the animal stopped still, as if posing for a picture of two friends leaning toward each other over a small table.

Mike's skin moved of its own accord; his neck hairs prickled his collar. He was so completely filled by fear, it felt as if thunderless sheet lightning played across the muscles of his back and down into his thighs.

Then the lightning died and all he could sense was the unavoidable *reality* of the bear: the sight of its rough head silhouetted against the house lights; the oily-musty smell of its fur; the snuffle of its breathing; the wet warmth of its breath on his face.

It's so real, he thought. *So completely real. But it feels just like a dream.*

It was silly. He knew it was silly, but he also knew he had to speak to the bear. He whispered, "Do you want to... tell me something?"

The bear cocked its head sideways, and eased back a little, as if it were deciding how to answer this unusual question.

But Mike already had the answer. As if a tap had been opened, all of the fear suddenly drained out of him, and he was filled instead with a peculiar sensation of lightness—as if he might now just float away, up through the forest canopy, off between the stars, to someplace where he was somebody else altogether, somebody who was so much *more.*

It could have been only seconds, or it could have been forever, that he and the bear faced each other across the boulder. Then the back door opened and his mother's voice called, "Mike! They found him! He's all right!"

And then, like magic, the bear was *gone.* He heard it scuttling through the trees. Mike laughed, because the feeling of lightness did not disappear with the bear. The feeling stayed with him, even after his father came home, enfolded Mike and Mom in one giant hug, then ate a big stack of buttermilk pancakes, and slept for sixteen hours straight.

The bear never came back, not to the woods, not to Mike's dreams. And that summer, he and Jonah learned to fly a glider.